EVERYONE:
WORLDS WITHOUT WALLS

StarShipSofa

EDITED BY TONY C. SMITH
Assistant Editor Robyn Bradshaw.

Cover art by Christian Ward.
Cover design, interior layout & design by Dee Cunniffe.

www.StarShipSofa.com

CONTENTS

The Rant

Strange times Indeed . . .

And forgive me if I'm going to go off on a little rant here. I don't normally and it might send some away from D.W. What the fuck is going on over there Man! You know when I was seeing Trump I was thinking - come on America - you the greatest country in the world then and you get two politicians and this is what you end up with. You pick one - You pick one and you picked Trump! I'm not blaming anyone - but the man is a fucking idiot man! Do you know what I mean. It's just. Its Just getting to the point where this is getting really really serious - just in my vie. - this is getting really serious. Do you know what I mean? Why ban countries? What is the point of that? It's just like . . . you're kidding. And this has so many repercussions around the world - you-know? We've got families who split up - stuck in airports - different airports. A vet stuck in South America - went on holiday - works in Glasgow born in Iran - here man . . . what is the point of that! What is the point of banning Iran, Iraq, Syria, Yemen, Sudan, Somalia and Libya - there are the countries that want the fucking help man! Do you know what I mean? Those are the countries getting all the shit thrown at them. And this Wanker . . . this wanker!

I'll leave it there . . . or I'll get carried away again

Worlds Without Walls

StarShipSonic

3/4/2017

[signature]

INTRODUCTION

DR AMY H. STURGIS

Speculative fiction allows us to wrestle with the question of what it means to be human.

I tell this to my undergraduate and graduate students on the first day of the semester (and, I suspect, in every class meeting thereafter).

It's true that speculative fiction examines our present day, no matter how far in the future or the past a story is set or how distant the galaxy or exotic the alternate universe, but in so doing it helps us to wrestle with what it means to be human: not humans of a specific nationality or ethnic community or gender or sexual orientation or faith or ability, but *human*.

There must be some common ground we fellow beings inhabit in common; otherwise it would be pointless to speak or listen, write or read, translate or record or publish.

In fact, SF not infrequently makes us uncomfortable with how very unsatisfactory and limiting it likely is to define the sentient "us" in terms of one mere species on one mere planet.

Because the genre and its characteristics – the thrill of investigating the "What if?" and the discipline of extrapolating the plausible from the known – center on this question, the modern genre has evolved as a *conversation*. Authors and works and readers speak to each other across time and space. In short, SF is a genre in which ideas are heroes in and of themselves, and these ideas ricochet from one creator to the next, being complicated or challenged or fine-tuned or confirmed as more minds encounter and grapple with them.

And while each of us may, like Walt Whitman, contain multitudes, it's fair to say that conversations can only teach us so much when we insist on talking only to ourselves. I am limited by my skin and my setting from knowing to what degree my being me also applies to others being themselves. The same is true for you. In short, more chairs at the SF table and more voices in the SF conversation mean more information and more insights, especially on that subject in which we are all by our very natures invested: what it means to be human.

In the process of wrestling with this subject, we learn something incredibly meaningful: we are not alone.

This puts me in mind of the late, great Frederik Pohl. In his blog entry "Let There Be Fandom: The Science Fiction League," Pohl wrote about the impact made on him by Hugo Gernsback's 1934 announcement of the Science Fiction League: "As soon as the notice appeared, I rushed to join, but my membership number was 490, even so. I didn't mind. I was thrilled to think that there were 489 others like me, when I had in my whole life seen only one or two."

World SF reminds us that our circle is not limited to one or two or even 490. *Everyone: Worlds Without Walls* brings together in common purpose some of the brightest stars in SF, authors from every continent on the planet save Antarctica. In seeing through the eyes of gifted writers from Africa, Asia, Australia, Europe, and North and South America, we not only grow in empathy and understanding, but we also gain reassurance that there are others like us all across the globe who wonder and imagine. Our community is rich and vast.

We cannot take for granted that today is a time in which the global conversation is becoming increasingly accessible to readers and listeners everywhere thanks to authors, translators, publishers, podcasters, and the convictions and technologies that support them all. New worlds and possibilities open to us even as our own planet seems to become smaller, more traversable and interdependent, available and knowable. In some people, however, this creates fear.

If we *do* take increasing freedom for granted, it may disappear.

This is one of the many important reasons why I am grateful to be involved with the District of Wonders, which is a virtual family dedicated to hearing and honoring all voices worldwide. It definitely is the reason why I support Tony C. Smith's inspired decision to pursue the publication of *Everyone: Worlds Without Walls* in defiance of the nativist, parochial, and clannish impulses in both of our countries and elsewhere that now seek to divide us rather than bring us together.

SF challenges us to look beyond and ahead, and we must use it to meet the forces who would have us look only within or behind.

Everyone does this in grand fashion. Read and listen and enjoy, and let these visionary storytellers remind you why the pen is mightier than the sword – or the wall.

MOTHER'S LOVE

DAYO NTWARI

"Force-feed the heretics! The monotheists, the abominations, all of them! Let them know the taste of freedom!"

The Archbishop's thunderous voice shook Anointing Square, his words slightly out of sync with the movement of his lips and the rest of his face, as it glared down from the video screen that covered the entire north side of the Bishop Charles Mbamalu building, the headquarters of Pastor Olumide's West Niger Gigachurch.

Little Chris pointed up at the screen.

"Look, mummy!" he tittered. "His mouth is confused again!"

Mama Chris' hand struck the boy's face so hard, that the impact sent Little Chris reeling. Lucky for him, his mother's grip on his wrist was as tight as it always was. She pulled him through the city crowds.

"Are you daft, you dis stupid boy?" she hissed at him. "Do you want to kill your mother?"

Little Chris giggled at her despite the fresh stinging on his cheek, and Mama clamped her free hand over his mouth. Little Chris knew better than to misbehave, but the excitement of coming to West Niger on their supply runs every month was always too much for him. This was, after all, the biggest city on the Atlantic Coast. It was overwhelming: the jarring launch alarms, the columns of bright yellow and red flashing from the shuttle stations; the air crafts filling the sky, shooting into space; the glossy megastructures encrusted with video screens; the elevated hyper-rail system. And the people, oh the people! The incessant tidal waves of city dwellers and commuters rushing, pushing, bumping, shoving, yelling, grunting, sweating, laughing, scowling, and always pushing and shoving, pushing and shoving. Perpetual human migration. One hundred million bodies roaring into motion around him. It would seem like a dream if it weren't already real.

The Purge was particularly grim, this month. There was another execution of Bultungin scheduled to take place at the Square in about an hour, which meant in 10 minutes the Council of Prophets, the Evangelical Realm's secret police, would commence a full security lock-down of the area surrounding Anointing Square. Little Chris, a six year-old Bultungin, was not yet in full control of his body. Being half human made Chris particularly unstable as a shapeshifter. Over-excitement and high stress situations often caused unintentional shapeshifting into his hyena form. As an adult Bultungin, Mama Chris would only involuntarily shapeshift under the most extreme physical duress, for example during the agony of childbirth. Intimate inter-species relationships between humans and Bultungin shapeshifters were punishable by death under the laws of the Evangelical Realm. Church doctrine dictated it was biologically impossible for a human and Bultungin union to procreate. Little Chris' very existence was heresy manifest, and a negation of the infallibility of the Ultra Archbishop.

Time was running out. Mama Chris needed to get them away from the Square, and then to North Badagry as soon as possible, to get more Mother's Love from the old woman in the ocean. Without Mother's Love, Mama Chris had no power to suppress the involuntary shifts of her child. Mama led Little Chris into the foaming rapids of passengers bursting out of the hyper-rail station. A big screen showed the arrival and departure times above them, a psychedelic symphony of time and place and colour. Mama leaned against the crowd to the Red Line platform, violently dragging her son behind her, lifting his feet from the floor. Only the dark vice grip of her hand was visible to her son through the curtaining blurs of fabric and skin towering around him. Her fingers were practically fused to his wrist-bone. Chris hummed to himself as he watched, fascinated by the never-ending flow of warm bodies, a torrent of rush hour commuters, that might, at any moment, rip him from his mother and drag him away, into the street where, surely, his little body would be crushed down into the waste grates.

"Plenty, plenty people," he sang to himself. "Plenty, plenty people dey here o! Plenty, plenty people. Mmmm-hmmm hmmmmm mmmm." He grinned at all the breaking waves of commuters' faces washing over him: the grim, the indifferent, the preoccupied, the harried, the frustrated, and the tired and angry, all flashing past him like fleeting memories from a past life.

Eventually, they reached an automatic door, and the rush hour flood subsided . He stood with his mother. Little Chris was very small compared to 6-year-old human Topsiders. He would be about average height for an Underland Bultungin of his age, short enough to tuck himself beneath his mother's skirt, in between her muscular, hairy legs as soon as they entered the train. The Red Line's heavy doors rattled shut. The big screen display started oscillating blue and white: the security lock-down was about to go into effect. Outside, the world of the platform warped into a blur and disappeared, as the hyper-rail shot out of the station.

The compartment was packed, ankle to ankle, shoulder to shoulder, chest to chest, cheek to cheek. No seats on the Red Line. Seats were for the Green Line, for people going to Zone 49 or closer to the city centre. The Red Line served only triple digit Zones. It took Mama Chris every bit of her strength not to collapse under the crushing weight of the passengers in the carriage as the momentum of the train shook them from side to side. She always struggled to keep her mind from visualizing her body buckling under the load of the rocking passengers and collapsing on her son. They would likely get trampled, and the ensuing tumult would terrify the boy and trigger his shapeshifting. Her sweaty, scarred knees threatened to crush her son's body. Little Chris, oblivious of the knife-edge his life balanced on, winced at the pain at his temples every time his mother's legs banged into his skull. Still ensconced in his mother's skirt, he dug into his shorts for the avatar he had pick-pocketed from someone during the rush to board the train. He switched it on, and immediately the avatar connected to the Live Stream. The Archbishop's voice roared from its tiny speakers. He couldn't turn down the volume quickly enough. Mama Chris heard the noise coming from below her and looked around, only to see all the other passengers staring at her quizzically. In one movement she flung her arm under her skirt, grabbed hold of Little Chris' ear and twisted hard. The boy's vision exploded in agony and he frantically tapped the avatar against her arm until she let go of his ear and took the tiny device in her hand, obliterating it in her fist and dropping the pieces to the floor.

Chris stirred the pile of broken glass and metal with his shoe. If only it weren't for the Archbishop, he'd still have a shiny, new avatar. He'd heard his mother talking about the Archbishop, the man who had authorized the Purge. It began at the request of the Pastor of

West Niger, who had now spent a year rounding up Monotheists, as well as other enemies of the West Niger Gigachurch. Like people who did not pay up on Tax Day, or people who missed church on Tax Day twice in a row, or papists who still swore allegiance to Pope Gregory XVII. Like Anglicans, or Methodists, or Baptists, or Muslims. Or Hindus, or animists, or pagans, or witches. Or, worst of all, Abominations, as the Evangelical Realm referred to the shapeshifting Bultungin. This was only the latest of a number of purges the megacity had seen since the Realm's crusade first began against the old woman in the ocean, and her followers, many years ago.

"What are Aboninators, Uncle Gbenga?" A few days ago, Little Chris and his mother's oldest brother were clearing away rubble and rubbish from a lot in their neighbourhood in the Underland. The city's excavation works had caused another tremor earlier that week, which partially collapsed a small building, as well as a tunnel leading out of their Zone.

"Abominations," Uncle Gbenga corrected Little Chris. "Where did you hear that word?" He picked up a boulder almost as big as Chris and dumped it into the cart.

"The Archbishop said all the aboni... all the amoni-"

"Abominations..."

"That all the Abominations will be caught, and anybody that hides them will be arrest, too."

"Arrested."

"Will be arrested, too. To protect the Realm."

Gbenga sat down on another boulder, this one much bigger than Chris, and scratched his head.

"Did your mother not tell you to stop listening to the Live Stream?"

Little Chris dropped his chin to his chest and pouted. Uncle Gbenga put a thick, hairy finger to the boy's chin and lifted his face back up.

"The Archbishop is a dangerous man, Chris. Do not listen to him, and do not go near him or his people. If he catches you, nobody can help you."

"Not even you, Uncle?"

"Not even me, Chris. Not even me."

Chris' furry little tail brushed against his uncle's leg. Gbenga's gaze went cold, the hair on his hyena head bristled. The effects of the monthly dose of Mother's Love that Mama Chris took, seemed to be wearing off again.

He snapped at the boy. "What do I always tell you, Chris?"

"No shifting, especially in Topside," Little Chris said, eagerly. "When in Topside, always look like the people in Topside." His reddish eyes quickly turned white again, and his tail shrunk and disappeared.

"I don't want you to get yourself or your mother in trouble, my boy. Try to be disciplined about it, even down here."

Chris nodded. The dim lighting from the tunnel's ceiling cast their shadows against the wall: the massive torso and head of an adult hyena, and muscular arms and legs that looked human, standing next to a little 6-year-old "Topsider". In order to suppress her son's accidental and careless shapeshifting, Gbenga's sister would need to meet with the old woman in Badagry to replenish the Mother's Love. She refused to let her boy out of her sight. Without the potion, she could not take him out in public, to her work in Topside each day. Not without running the risk of Little Chris' excitement getting the better of him, and finding themselves strapped to a stake awaiting execution at Anointing Square. Gbenga frowned to himself. He wished he could make these dangerous monthly trips on his sister's behalf, but the old woman would not deal with anyone other than Mama Chris. The old woman was paranoid about being infiltrated by the Evangelical Realm.

"Uncle G."

"What is it, Chris?"

"Are we anonimations?"

The train was nearing North Badagry. There was a bit more room now in the compartment. Mama's legs no longer threatened to cave in Little Chris' skull. She allowed herself to breath just a bit easier. Her son peeked from under her skirt and tried to see if he could catch a glimpse of the Hall of the Council of Prophets as they approached the coastal suburb. But from down there, all he could see between the shoulders of passengers was the roof of Prophets' Hall, topped like a wedding cake by a hundred foot high, gold-plated bust of His Holiness the Ultra Archbishop Chris Chukwu, the head of all the gigachurches in the Evangelical Realm, and his namesake. Or his pretend namesake, that is: Chris' real name would give away his Bultungin heritage. Pastor Olumide began the Purge shortly after Chris was born, and his mother thought it wise to change his name to a regular human name, befitting of a member of a gigachurch.

Rumours had been circulating for a few months running up to the beginning of the Purge. A human and a shapeshifter had born a child somewhere in this megacity. It did not take long for the Council of Prophets to start the round-ups and interrogations. Bultungin were barely tolerated in the Realm as third-class citizens, so long as they knew their place. For the most part, the shapeshifters had been confined to the subterranean dwelling, the Underland caverns beneath the megacity's sewage system, once they were first discovered almost a century ago. The law of the Evangelical Realm came from the Ultra Archbishop, worshipped as God in Human Form. The Realm's doctrine stated only humans, plants and animals were creatures of God. The emergence of the Bultungin, a people who could transmogrify into hyenas, was problematic for the integrity of church doctrine. To minimize their visibility, the Realm used the shapeshifters for menial and hazardous work only, and they needed a Day Pass to enter Topside, the city of West Niger.

Little Chris was humming again, now that they were out of the carriage and back on the streets again. They walked along a swampy road near the Ocean Wall, a giant rampart behind which the Atlantic foamed. The roar of the ocean racing in and throwing itself at the Ocean Wall was much louder in this rundown part of the city. The Wall was in disrepair, somewhat. Tiny rivulets snaked from small breaches in the Wall, forming mossy ridges in the reinforced concrete. Green puddles festered at the base of the Wall. Little Chris looked up and imitated the high-pitched hiss of thin grey streams of poisonous, pollutant-heavy water arcing from the fissures in the Wall. He puffed his chest as big as he could, to imitate the sound of the raging sea.

In the distance, a group of boys was coming up the street toward them. They waved at them, and Little Chris, seeing his friends for the first time in a month, waved back, and jumped up and down with excitement. As she had expected, her son couldn't stop himself from partially turning into a hyena. "Sorry, mummy," Chris said, grinning sheepishly and shifting back into his fully human form.

"It's OK, my son."

They stopped by a row of trees lining the Wall, and Mama Chris let go of her son's hand and reached to her afro. Or her "fake-fro", as she liked to say. She undid the knot hidden inside it, and three fat red-brown dreadlocks uncoiled and tumbled down her back, stopping just above her ankles: the trademark of a healer. And an unsanctioned healer, at that. But here, in the slums, where mostly shapeshifters and other undesirables lived, it didn't matter. Even though, Pastor Olumide ruled over all of West Niger, the Security Commission seldom bothered to enter the slums. That is, as long as everyone paid up on Tax Day, every week.

The boys had finally reached them, and greeted Mama Chris politely. Some of them walked with the hind legs of hyenas. This was their neighbourhood. Still, she did not want Chris getting in the habit, and preferred he stayed in his human form at all times, whenever they left Underland.

Mama patted Chris on the head. "OK, my son," she said. "You can go and play now, but don't go far. Stay where I can hear you o!" She smiled at him. He looked like such a lovely child, she thought, when he looked like a Topsider.

"Thank you, mummy!" Chris' excitement made his voice a bit louder than necessary. Immediately he and his friends ran across the street to the playground.

Mama Chris sighed to herself, satisfied. It was time for her to go to the old woman inside the ocean. She turned to the trees. They were tall and dark, misshapen like giant, crooked old men, petrified for eternity. Long-dead trees defying the twin sickles of time and decay. Fireflies danced in the void between the black branches where their leaves should have been. Mama Chris moved her feet silently over the ground beneath the trees, barren and patterned by cracks and gaps in the dirt. She began to sing, and the fireflies began to stir. Hundreds of them. Thousands, now. Their yellow and white glow cast on her a soft shimmer. She closed her eyes and heard them singing back to her, as if from far away, while they floated down from the branches surrounding her. She let a small smile creep to her lips: walking through the Veil always made Mama Chris feel beautiful.

The cloud of fireflies tightened around her, and the ground started to moisten, and then turning swampy. She opened her eyes and watched the dead trees creak and groan as they soaked up the black, oily water bubbling-up from the swamp widening at her feet. Dark veins swelled just below the bark of the trees, as if they were pumping black blood from their roots, to their trunks.

Plump with the swamp water, the branches coiled around themselves, reaching slowly downward and toward Mama Chris. The ground bubbled more ravenously, and started to give way as the branches reached Mama Chris and pushed her downward, downward, into a place unseen.

Mama Chris found herself behind the Veil now, in front of an octagonal clearing, bordered by neatly arranged groups of black and green tents. These were occupied by the priestesses and followers of Yemoja, after they had been driven into the ocean by the Ultra Archbishop in their conflict against the Evangelical Realm. Yemoja, the old woman inside the ocean, also known as The Mother of gods, and arch-enemy of the Ultra Archbishop and the Realm.

Here behind the Veil, in the Unseen, the air was fresh and dense with humidity. Mama Chris moved across the clearing, her legs suddenly sluggish and her body suddenly weightless, as if she were diving in a calm lake. A school of long, brightly glowing fish, some as long as her leg, swam in the air above her, disappearing beyond the horizon of tents. Dark green shrubs and weeds swayed on the ground, as if caught by a current. She too felt the current around her legs, and whenever her feet touched the soaked earth, bubbles spluttered up, tickling her toes. The Old Woman, Yemoja, sitting by her fire, called out to Mama Chris by her son's Bultungin name.

"Use his Christian name!" Mama Chris snarled. "Please! Is it every month I have to tell you, Yemoja?"

"Sorry o. No vex. Mama Chris." Yemoja cackled as she always did, and waved dismissively at the bandages on her leg. Mama Chris stared at her for a while, then shook her head and sighed.

"How body?" Yemoja asked.

"I'm fine, thank you. How is your leg? Are you taking the medicine?"

"Medicine, ke?" The colossal woman's breasts bounced and rippled with her laughter. Unperturbed, Mama Chris gingerly unwrapped the bandages on Yemoja's leg to get a look at her wounds. The old woman threw her head back and laughed her dirty laugh. "Medicine? Who dash you medicine? Ordinary witch like you."

Mama Chris remained stoic. Yemoja's wound seemed to be healing gradually. She reached into her pouch for clean bandages and a jar of Borgum Spider jelly. The theocracy of the Realm only permitted church-sanctioned televangelists to conduct religious activities, and the only gods officially acknowledged by the gigachurches in the Realm were the Ultra Archbishop and his Archbishops. During the Realm's first purge, after the Ultra had risen to power, the gigachurches had slaughtered hundreds of thousands of Yemoja's followers. The remaining survivors fled into the ocean, here in the sanctuary of the Unseen, where she provided them with shelter behind the Veil.

Through the torture of her captured devotees, the Realm had managed to learn about some of Yemoja's weaknesses. The Ocean Wall was soon erected, all the major industrial sewage of the megacities along the West African Atlantic Coast were rerouted and discharged into the ocean. Natural rivers and water bodies within city limits were artificially dried out, and soon, the Veil began shrinking as the ocean's pollution increased. Yemoja fell ill. In recent months, sores had appeared on Yemoja's legs, and they seemed to drain her of more and more of her power. Mama Chris had found a way to heal the wounds, but whenever they completed the healing process, a fresh wound would appear in another place.

"You are funny, Mummy Chris, honestly," Yemoja wiped tears of laughter from her eyes. Silently, Mama Chris rubbed the jelly over the wound. The woman winced and glared at her, "Softly, now! Ah ah!"

Mama Chris took no notice, and wrapped the bandages slowly and firmly, whispering the formula and carefully fastening the clip.

The old woman motioned at a bowl that was floating by. Mama Chris took hold of the bowl and handed it to Yemoja, who coughed up phlegm and spat into the bowl.

"How is your son?" Yemoja asked, as she proceeded to lubricate the inside of the bowl with her spit.

"He is fine, Yemoja. Have you heard anything from the Council?" Mama Chris asked. Despite her weakened state, the old woman still had spies inside the Council of Prophets, and Mama Chris relied on her information to keep herself and her son safe from the Realm's secret police.

"The Council? Hmm, no," Yemoja took one of her breasts in her hand and squeezed. Inky black Mother's Love squirted into the bowl until it was full. She then handed it back to Mama Chris.

"Mama Chris. Why you no tell me say na Pastor Olumide be Little Chris papa?" Yemoja's voice was like ice. Mama Chris held the bowl of Mother's Love in her hands, frightened stiff.

"Drink," Yemoja said. "Drink." She gestured at the bowl. "Drink first, before you answer my question," Yemoja's expression had turned belligerent, and Mama Chris had no choice but to acquiesce. She drank quickly, hungrily. Her eyelids fluttered involuntarily with every gulp she took. When she finished she released the bowl and a current sent it drifting away.

"You go fuck the Pastor," Yemoja accused Mama Chris. "Come my house dey find Mother's Love to hide your son? Who you dey hide am from?"

Mama Chris snapped at the old woman. "Watch your mouth, Yemoja! I no fuck anybody, you hear? Do you understand?" Yemoja closed her robe furiously, covering her breasts.

"Stupid woman," Yemoja said. "If you no fuck, how you come get belle? Hmm?" Her flabby arm swung out and she slapped Mama Chris in the mouth. The irate ocean goddess jumped to her feet, growing and now a towering behemoth looming above Mama Chris.

Mama Chris' dreadlocks floated around her lowered head. "The Pastor raped me!" she growled, her hands balled up into fists barely as big as Yemoja's pinky toes. Little Chris' cheerful voice echoed from outside, drifting into the Unseen. A little green octopus came cartwheeling through the palm fronds and gently played with Mama Chris' bobbing locks. The goddess Yemoja and Mama Chris stood silently.

"Kai. Come here, my daughter." the goddess sat back down, not much bigger now than Mama Chris. She held out her arms, and Mama Chris reluctantly approached. Hot tears streamed down Mama's scarred face, and she rubbed her sleeve across her nose. Yemoja's rumpled fingers tenderly wiped the tears from Mama Chris' face and they sat. Mama Chris laying on her side in the goddess' lap, Yemoja rocking her soothingly. She reached into her robe, pulled out one of her breasts and tucked the nipple into Mama Chris' mouth.

"So, Mr 'Pray and Rape' know wetin you be?" Yemoja asked. Mama Chris, still laying on her lap, was washing her dreads with swamp mud. Mama Chris nodded, yes the Pastor knew she was Bultungin.

"And him know say Little Chris him son?"

Mama Chris shook her head.

"Hmm." Yemoja stared into the distance, "No wonder you dey always ask of Council of Prophets."

"The Council discovered a member of a gigachurch in one of the cities committed the sin of bestiality, and a half Bultungin and half human abomination was born," Mama Chris explained.

"And na why Senate of Elders dey investigate gigachurches since last year?"

Mama Chris nodded.

"And na wetin cause the Purge. Olumide wan cover him tracks. How many wey him rape?"

Mama Chris shrugged. "I don't know. Maybe just me. Maybe more. There are over a hundred of us cleaners and gardeners at Church," she sighed, "And he's using Monotheists to cover it up. If he only killed Bultungin, the Senate might get suspicious and order a Spiritual Audit on West Niger."

Yemoja broke open a coconut and sprinkled the water over Mama Chris' head. Her locks iridesced as the goddess rubbed the liquid into Mama's scalp, and rinsed out the swamp mud.

"Mother's Love alone no fit keep your son safe forever, my dear. You hear?"

Mama Chris nodded.

"All this while, you dey come Badagry, dey risk your life, your child life. Why you no yarn me since?" the goddess frowned at her.

Mama Chris sighed and got up from the old woman's lap, "What good would it have done to tell you, Yemoja? You know your power ends at the Wall."

"Na wetin you think? You think say my power no pass these people? Hmm?" Yemoja asked, scratching her own head. Tired. The old goddess' gaze slowly moved from side to side like she was looking for something. Her big lips pouted in confusion and she mumbled something to herself. She looked at Mama Chris and seemed to stare right through her. The vacant look in Yemoja's eyes tugged at Mama Chris' heart: the Mother of fishes, the Mother of gods was dying, and her memories seemed to rise and fall with the tides, coming back weaker each time Mama Chris visited.

Mama spoke softly now. "There are no fish outside the Veil, Yemoja. The way the Pastor has been hunting me, is the same way the Ultra Archbishop has been hunting for you since even before I was born." The goddess' head snapped back to Mama Chris, her eyes wide and lively. She greeted Mama Chris jovially, as if seeing her for the first time today.

"Please, Yemoja. His name is Chris. Please try to remember."

The old woman giggled. "Sorry o! No vex, Mama Chris! You wan treat my leg, abi? Siddon, siddon. How body?" Yemoja motioned to a moss covered rock.

Defeated, Mama Chris put a satchel of herbs on the old woman's shelf, "Drink this in your tea every morning."

"What is that?" Yemoja asked, shooting Mama Chris a quizzical look.

"It's your medicine, ma."

"Medicine, ke?" Yemoja bent over and slapped her good knee, laughing hard. "See this witch! You be doctor?" She laughed hysterically while Mama Chris embraced her warmly and kissed the Mother goddess on the forehead.

"Thank you, Yemoja. See you next month."

The hyper-rail was virtually empty on the way back home to Underland, as it always was this time of the morning. In the distance, the strobe lights of a Prophet patrol corvette flashed, as it prowled through the empty sky. Its dark hull sliced through the tall dawn mist, while the vessel scanned the waters for smugglers. When the rail tracks bent eastward, it gave the illusion the hyper-rail was outrunning the patrol. Little Chris pressed his nose against the grimy window, humming his melodies. On the overhead screen in the compartment, Pastor Olumide came on:

"Good morning, my children. Happy Tax Day. I expect all of you in church today for service. May you continue to be blessed and may...."

Mama Chris looked at her son. Usually, Bultungin shapeshifters gained full control of their bodies around the early to mid teens. However, with Little Chris being an unprecedented hybrid human-Bultungin, there was no way for her to know when her little boy would come of age. What Mama did know, however, was that Yemoja would be long dead before then. The old goddess would probably not last another year before the Veil was breached. And when Yemoja dies, the ocean and the Mother's Love would die along with her. Mama Chris and her boy would be at the mercy of the Council of Prophets. Maybe, by the end of the year Mama would have saved up enough of her wages to pay smugglers, and flee the Evangelical Realm. Lately, these smugglers had been selling out the undesirables to the Council of Prophets, taking money from both sides and getting rich off the spilled blood of the Bultungin.

"Look, mummy!" The tube at this section rose above the Wall. Little Chris pointed at the pale orange sliver on the horizon. She spat on her thumb and cleaned off some dried mud from his earlobe. Mama Chris nodded. She pulled her son close and together they watched the rising sunlight reflecting on the rippling ocean's surface like a blanket of dancing fireflies. The ocean waves were breaking against the Wall, slowly, like an old collapsing elephant. White mist sparkled in the sunlight.

"Plenty plenty water. Plenty plenty water dey here o. Plenty plenty water. Mmmmhmmm hmmmmm hmmmm." Mama Chris put on a brave face, and laughed and sang along with Little Chris. They watched and sang together until the hyper-rail descended below the Wall again, hurtling back towards the city centre.

THE BLOOD THAT PULSES IN THE VEINS OF ONE

JY YANG

They are cutting you out of me, these creatures in their sealed white suits. Piece by piece their knives and curiosity are divorcing the gifts you have given me from the gifts I have prepared for you. Gone is the eye that gazed out over the cyan-purple sunset on Taurus 4. Severed are the muscles of the forearm which sculpted your old flesh into masterpieces. A gap yawns where once was the tongue that tasted your rich adventures.

My lips are dry and cracked. I cannot lick them.

The younger one wields the knife today. His name is Marjan and his golden-toned flesh looks about 20 years old, in the way terrestrians count their age. My forearm, the same one they've excavated from, is back in the metal vice. Marjan stretches its split skin and wedges cold metal forceps into the work pit, where muscles glisten and blood pulses weakly in bluish cords. His heavily gloved fingers reach in, and pain spasms up the shackled arm as he presses down.

– Whoah. Come check this out.

– What is it? Have you found something significant?

– Yeah, you need to get over here and see for yourself.

His supervisor leaves the churning sequencer and comes across the sterile floor of the lab, white and cumulaic in her hazard suit, blending into her surroundings like the camouflage of terrestrian animals. Her name is Jae. She leans over and peers through the glass of her helmet at my immobilized limb.

– You see that?

– Hmm. Yes.

She takes the forceps from him and elicits more pain-spasms from the arm. With my remaining eye I observe the purse of her lips as she examines the feeble fightback of my flesh.

– That's definitely new growth, right? The muscle is regenerating!

– Looks like it. Quite remarkable.

– You wanna test it too? We should take a sample.

– Just take one. As small as you can. I want to monitor the regeneration process.

– Sweet. Prof Liu is gonna be thrilled.

Marjan picks up his scalpel. They want more from me, but this time it doesn't matter. I have not eaten. I am pinned down to a steel table in a box of unbreakable glass and plastic. The air here is irradiated to sterility, an artificial and flavourless concoction of nitrogen/oxygen/carbon dioxide. If my core has dredged matter from these meager surroundings for fleshcrafting, it is meaningless. Utterly meaningless. Take it all away.

The pain begins afresh. I close my remaining eye. I must, I must, I must: Hold on to the memories. Not let trauma erode them. Remember all that has passed since we last met. They can take all the organic extrusions they want but they cannot take this.

Start: A mirror to this butcher's table, the last time we met: The point from which your memories and mine diverge: The point at which I killed you: The point at which the vault of your body was sealed: The point at which its inventory of treasures locked down and made immutable:

It goes like this:

★

You lie dead on the carving table, hands neutralised, mouth shuttered, ribs mere bone. Your eyes, although open, register nothing: Photons rolling through aqueous and vitreous humour fall upon inert retina. No ion cascade quivers through the optic nerve upon their arrival.

You lie dead, but not lifeless. For life resides in you still, its signature imprinted upon the architecture of your bones, in the webbings of your brain, in the atoms knitted into meat. Since we last met, your being has inhaled the world around it, spinning nitrogen flesh around bone moulded out of metal and dust. These atoms lie vibrating, locked into place, eager mouths waiting for my knife to set them free.

Knife, descend, do your duty. The first cut goes down furrow-straight, parting the layers over gristle and coils of gut. I peel away your yielding skin and cut fillets of tender flesh in beautiful portions, laying them upon a cold slab rimmed with frost. Tendons and tripe I save. Fat I cut into rinds for flavour. Blood runs into a bell jar, for pudding, for wine.

I slice your neck open, flaying it under the line of the chin. The viscera I dig out in a single lode.

The skull I chop away with a small saw, bent over double like an artist struggling with their limitations, sweat beading on my brow.

How crude and clumsy these forms we have adopted, these brittle fingers and their limited range of movement. I find them trembling as I lift the bone, edges sticky, to reveal the masterwork underneath. The sum of your experiences are written there, in the soft quiescent pink, imprinted still in the ghosts of paths once forded by chemicals.

I gently draw your brain out of its casing, trailing grey stem. I put it aside in the cold.

My fingers are wet with spinal fluid. I lick them, an early and errant treat. A rush of sensation then: A beach on Mars, sand between the toes, thin icy wind stinging eager cheeks. One small pearl sampled from among the treasures I have before me.

Again and again I mourn the constraints of these terrestrian forms we mimic, these weaknesses we constantly recreate. The reediness of the visible electromagnetic spectrum, the clumsiness of pressure, the reliance on frequencies of air compression. Such a narrow way to see the universe.

In my greed, in my hunger for more, I cut a small slice out of the brain. I will eat it raw. I will consume its contents in one burst of unprocessed joy. I hold the limp thing over my open mouth, and move my tongue to greet it–

Here the memory ends.

★

– Do you think it feels pain? Like, human pain.

– I find that kind of speculation pointless. We hardly know enough of its biology to grasp what a concept like *pain* might mean to it.

– Yeah, but it's got human DNA, right? So it's got to have biology like ours.

– It's very good mimicry, but if Prof Lim's theories are right it can imitate whatever lifeform it finds itself around. So that means very little.

– But look! If you touch the nerves there's a pain response–

– Stop that.

– What? If it was hostile it would have attacked us a long time ago. Look, it doesn't care. It's not even–

– Have some professionalism, please. Get back to work.

★

It could be my imagination. It could be the encroachment of hope. But the lights are flickering, as though someone has come and tampered with the power supply in this place.

I watch the terrestrians. They seem to have noticed it too. The older one, Jae, appears upset by it, irritable.

Perhaps it's not just my imagination. Perhaps something is happening.

Pain comes to me again. More knives. Almost reflexively, as if it were a survival tactic, I plunge back into slices of memory, back to the things that gave me joy:

A steak of your left shoulder, well-marinated in red wine and hothouse-grown herbs. The juices run thick, smelling of iron dust on Chryse Planitia, of the selenium gifted by a long-haul freighter on its exhausting journey between the stars. I chew slowly, savoring the taste of sweat, hope, and despair you absorbed on that three-hundred-day slog.

A terrestrian woman left part of herself in you. I taste of her, entwined in the ferocity of your actin and myosin. You shared things: Spit and blood and other fluids. There's emotion there, elusive and formless as a deep-water creature. You fall for them, every single time, and I–

I inhale and hold the taste in my mouth a little longer.

★

– Did you ever think it was real?

– What was?

– The legends! The Xanthrian legends of the Eglwysswrw– ugh, I can't even pronounce it. Eglwhensyrr? Egleyswer? The Ancient Ones! Oou-uh. Seriously, I thought they were just made-up stories, to scare their kids or sell tickets to musicals or something. Do you think the Xanthrians had musicals? Those mandibles. Clack clack clack clack. No?

– They were extinct by the time Xanthrian civilisation reached its peak. Or thought to be extinct, at least. This specimen has obviously proved that idea wrong.

– Why do you think it happened?

– Why do I think *what* happened?

– The extinction! Why do you think they went extinct?

– Earth's history is littered with global extinction events. It's not unthinkable that it would happen on a universal scale. Civilisations rise and fall.

– Yes, but *how?* If they're immortal, endlessly regenerating cores of potentiality, how do they die? You can kill the organic parts, but do you kill *them?*

– Everything ends. It's a law of the universe. Entropy is inescapable.

– That's not an answer.

– No. If we had the answers, we wouldn't have jobs.

★

The last of you has been consumed. All that we are is now the same. I release the core of you back to the potentiality of the void. A hopeful seed, sent back into the universe to germinate once again.

When you came back it was supposed to be your turn.

The terrestrians have a saying: The best-laid plans of mice and men.

★

– Where do you think the other one is? The one it… ate, I guess? It's got to be off somewhere, growing a new body. Do you think it'll be back?

– It's hard to say.

– Why do you think they do it? Maybe it's like a crab moult. The eating, though. That's got a ritual feel to it. I'm sure it *means* something.

– You're very sure of many things, Marjan. Perhaps you're in the wrong field. You could be a great motivational speaker.

– Come on, Jae. Don't you ever wonder? Damn, I wish Prof. Lim would let us take the brain. "Oh, we might kill it!" We won't be killing shit, I'll tell you that.

– That's enough. Did you check the electrics like I asked you to? Those lights have been flickering for an *hour.*

★

This is your fault. You and your love for terrestrian life, integrating with them, making friends, friends who noticed you went missing, friends who sent investigators to track down who took you away from them.

You know how weak these terrestrian bodies are, how indefensible. And how warlike their mortality has made them. Their softness and smallness makes them vicious to others, to one another.

In another epoch I might have escaped, in another epoch I might not have been pursued. In the years of rule of the triapsids, the klng'wcnh'g, the $\Delta\lambda/\lambda = 0.314$, our rituals might have gone unmolested, even with your indiscretions.

But expecting prudence is expecting too much of you. That is why you were an Outlaw, and I the Enforcer.

That is the why you were the one pursued and I the pursuer, into the maw of that black star, into our doom.

That was your fault, too.

That is the way our story has been since the universe was young with gases burning red and hot.

And yet I would change nothing.

★

– That's strange.

– What is?

– Something's interrupted the power supply to the spectrophotometer. Stay here and watch the specimen. I'm going to find out what happened.

– Okay. Don't be too long. I might get hungry.

– It's not funny.

★

It was a risk you took and we all paid for it.

There were three of us back then, I the Enforcer in pursuit of two Outlaws, chasing you and your partner across the universe in infra-dimensional form, as was the vogue in that time.

Two Outlaws in thrall of the greatest sin: Keeping what you had learned away from the mouths of our Mothers, away from the great commons of our people. Selfishly feeding your gathered lives to each other, back and forth in a closed loop excluding the rest of our race. Our Mothers knew what had been done. They demanded the flesh that they had been denied.

You led us to that black hole. *You* led us to the singularity that would be our doom.

When the gravity well took us, stripping away our outer shells, reducing us to our cores, did you know how it would end? Did you know that when your partner sacrificed themselves– the released energy tearing us free of the event horizon at last– did you know that we would re-emerge into a universe that had moved on a thousand generation of stars, a universe empty and unrecognisable, the mouths of our Mothers silenced forever?

I don't know, and I never will. By the time you come to me, with your forest of pedipalps and mineralised sensory coating– by the time you come to me, begging me to consume you, please– by the time that happens your core has already been corrupted by your grief. The memories vague-edged and diluted by chafing from the trauma.

Eat me, you begged. Eat me before all that I hold is lost.

We're the only ones left.

You are all I have.

★

– Well, guess it's just the two of us now, buddy. Can you even understand me? We know the other one could talk, at least. Your friend. "Alice Rei Kawasaki". Fancy pseudonym for a fake human, huh? Did she give you a name as well?

– God, I wish that I could just get into your brain. See that it's made of.

– Well. Jae isn't here, is she?

★

Please.

Please come for me soon.

★

When I cut into you for the first time, when my mandibles slice into your iridescent casing, I understand grief.

Your sense of loss, sharp and coppery, overwhelms all other flavours in your meat. It sinks deep into my core, now an indelible part of my being, preserved forever.

Gone: Your partner, the one who was your other half, the both of you forming a complete and private universe, a universe lost forever–

Gone too everything else we ever knew. Gone the mouths of our Mothers which you rejected, the welcoming subsuming maws you will never see again–

I burrow deep. I have never consumed another like this, taking the sum of another into myself, the core of being almost overwhelmed, the intensity, the purity of sensation, the seeking, subsuming, uniting–

Buried within the pulsing blue organs and crystallised rock I find my first taste of love, ichor-sweet passion, to be rolled between the jaws like a ripe bone-fruit.

And then I understand, immediate and heavy, what drew you to this selfishness,

Why all of this

was worth it

★

Matter is never destroyed, but passes from form to form to form, from the gases that whisper in between voids to the fires that blaze in the heart of stars to the blood that pulses in the veins of one in the first blush of love. So it has been since the dawn of the universe, thousands of star cycles before our kind came into being, thousands of star cycles before our kind became extinct. What ends begins again, what goes always comes back.

Again and again and again.

★

Marjan has almost finished cutting off the top of my skull when the bullet-crack comes, and with the thump of flesh against floor the pressure on my head is gone. It is likely–not absolutely certain, but likely– that the same fate has befallen Jae.

A stranger's face breaches my field of vision, round and fresh and bright-eyed. But the smile, the look of unbounded joy, I would recognise anywhere.

Relief washes through me, and joy, and affection, and all the things that taste like honey and mead. My lips shape words that my missing tongue can no longer give form to.

– Hello, Enforcer. Still there? Can you hear me?

I blink my remaining eye twice to let you know I understand.

– Good good. They've made a mess of things, haven't they? Silly. They seem to have left enough for me, though.

Your hands, deft and sure, examining the wounds they have left in me, the canals and quarries where what was yours has been taken away. There is regret in your expression, I am sure, but there is no need for regret. You came in time. They haven't taken it all. They came close, but not close enough.

I can sense the sweetness of your skin, the sweat on bare epidermis, the dust and dirt it's tracked into this sterile place. My core aches in hunger. Soon. *Soon.* Soon you will carve me up and set me free, an empty slate, back into the universe to accumulate flesh yet again.

– I wasn't planning to come back so soon. I thought I'd give you more time to mature. I like a good vintage, you know? But I've made a hash of things, Enforcer, and for that I'm sorry.

I miss my tongue. But the memory of it remains, and the memories of all the things it has tasted.

– It'll be easier to get you out of here if you're dead. Okay?

I blink twice.

Your hands close around my skull and I relax into them, home at last, as they turn to snap my neck.

WHERE IT ENDS

SWAPNA KISHORE

I left California on Friday, not sure I would return. I was worried because Amma had summoned me home without giving any reason. Her phone call, her first contact after years of mutual silence, had yanked me out of my comfortable routine; it reminded me that people had started exchanging puzzled whispers about me, and that I needed to renew myself. I could do that when I went home. Then, after I'd finished whatever Amma wanted from me, I could decide the direction of my life. By the time I sank into my economy-class seat, three decades of my San José life wrapped up, I felt drained emotionally and mentally.

The man in the adjacent seat glared at me. An Indian like me –l ate fifties, bald. A wrinkled face, very familiar. Extremely familiar. *Too old to be one of us.* Damn. I toyed with the idea of a complete denial. Or perhaps I could be my own younger sister. Or daughter.

"Chikki," he said.

Bhaiyya? His voice sank inside me, throwing up ripples of memories I did not want to face. I peered at him; God, he looked so old. What had gone wrong?

What could I do now? I couldn't fool my own brother, no way. I was stuck now, in a seat next to him, for the duration of an intercontinental flight. Over the hours our rift would widen, dark with the shadow of Ronjona.

"How are you? How's Ronjona?" I managed to squeak.

"Ronjona died." His face was stiff.

"I . . . sorry." Such a trite condolence, but I could think of nothing else.

"You married a Tamilian, no?" He flung it like an accusation, as if saying, See, you married an outsider yourself.

"It's over." Jagdeesh and I had been married for twenty years. We had lived together for two years before our incompatibility became obvious, but we continued intermittent contact over the next several years – divorce was a dirty word in his community. Our last-ditch trial to make it work, seven years ago, failed in just a couple of months. Though mutual consent had finally freed us, I found the memory of all that wasted emotion hurtful.

Silence weighed on the air between Bhaiyya and me. I wondered whether his presence was a coincidence, or whether he was heading to India to obey our mother's summons.

I said, "You live . . . work . . . in Mumbai?"

"Amma asked me to come home for something important." His tone was curt. "I almost refused, but then I thought I would ask her why she forced Ronjona to undergo a ritual so . . . so . . . Even you, Chikki, you lied to Ronjona."

You wanted me to, I almost said. I took a deep breath. "You agreed to the ritual."

His shoulders slumped. "I wanted the blessing. I didn't know it would hurt her so much."

I dabbed my mouth; lipstick ridged the crumpled tissue. I crammed it into a barf bag. Hell, I hadn't even attended their wedding; I'd pleaded ticket unavailability and stayed holed up in San José, half the globe away.

"You said you loved her," I said. "You should have thought of her."

★

Thirty-one years ago.

Bhaiyya dropped me off at college.

The thirty kilometers ride from home, on the pillion of Bhaiyya's mobike, always left my hair tousled. I was smoothing out my hair and settling my salwar so it fell softly on my flat-heeled chappals, when Bhaiyya said, "I'd like you to meet a friend today, after classes." His ears were rimmed scarlet. "Her name's Ronjona Mazumdar, and she's studying here, too, doing her Comp Science diploma."

Ronjona Mazumdar. A Bengali. Not one of us.

I said nothing, of course. Bhaiyya had this stubborn streak in him; if he sensed even a shred of concern from me, it could tip him into getting serious about her.

I didn't hear a word of the lectures that morning. All I saw was Bhaiyya's boyish grin, and superimposed on it, Amma's mouth drooping in clear disapproval. *Chikki,* she would say, *aren't there enough beautiful girls in our community? Can't he choose one of them as my daughter-in-law?*

I saw Ronjona as soon as I entered the cafeteria–dark complexion, thick black hair, spectacles–a typical Bengali. She was talking to Bhaiyya, waving her arms, and I caught the sparkle in her eyes despite the distance. Should I act friendly? Warm and affectionate? Casual and cool, but distant? How could I make Bhaiyya see Ronjona might be all very nice, but she wasn't suitable?

"Hi, Bhaiyya." I rested my palm on the table and shrugged the jhola of books off my shoulders. "Hi, . . . Ronjona, no?"

Bhaiyya sprang up and pulled a chair from the adjacent table. I sat down.

"Meet my kid sister, Chikki, aka Shweta," he said. "Chikki, Ronjona."

Must he say "kid" sister? He was only five years older, not much of a gap, especially for us. But ever since he'd started on his job, he'd reverted to treating me like I was a teenager instead of a twenty-two-year-old about to leave for the States for my MS.

Ronjona's eyes soaked me in, all my pimples, all sixty kilos of me straining against my clothes. Her complexion was flawless, and her figure slim. In front of her stood a tall glass of chocolate ice cream, whipped cream, and chocolate sauce.

"Chikki," she said, her voice bubbly, sweet, a non-diet Coke. "What a great name. Deepak keeps talking of you."

What on earth could Bhaiyya have told her? "Really?"

"Yes." She grinned. She had buck teeth.

Bhaiyya passed me the menu card; I selected tea, no milk, no sugar please.

Ronjona poked her straw past the ice cubes to dredge out the chocolate sauce. A tiny slurp. I noticed, to my disgust, that my mouth was puckered as if I were the one finishing her drink.

"I'll have another of these, Deepu," she said. "God, I *love* chocolate."

I wonder now whether I would have warmed towards this thin-after-oodles-of-chocolate Ronjona if I had met her when I was past my puppy-fat stage, past my calorie-counting, insecure-body days.

★

A week later, Amma was plucking shrivelled leaves off our pathetic guava tree when Bhaiyya approached her. Her back tautened. Her fingers twisted around a twig. Then her arm lowered, and it seemed to me that the air hissed with disapproval. I was at my window; I let fall the curtain and busied myself with macroeconomics.

When Amma came inside, she called me. "He said you have met her."

I nodded.

She did not ask me what Ronjona looked like, or whether she was intelligent or good-natured. She said, "I told him we will not accept an outsider."

"And?"

"He will bring her today. Says I'll love her." She sighed. "This will be a disaster."

I thought so, too.

Bhaiyya beamed when he presented an obviously nervous Ronjona to Amma, who nodded without smiling. He asked me to show Ronjona the garden; I said there was nothing worth seeing. He told Amma that Ronjona liked spicy chiwda mixture; Amma said Bengalis only liked sweets. The tea Amma served was watery, tepid. Fifteen minutes later, gaze lowered, Ronjona folded her hands and excused herself.

After Bhaiyya left to drop her at her working girls' hostel, Amma and I sat silently, bracing for his inevitable explosion, for the bitterness poised to enter our cosy three-member family.

"Is that how you treat guests?" he shouted the moment he returned.

"Guest?" Amma retorted. "You brought her because you think she is *not* a guest."

He turned to me, his face maroon. "She's just two years older–"

"Leave Chikki out of this," Amma said. "You know the problem."

"No, I don't," he yelled. "Ronnie is intelligent, she's beautiful, she's–"

"Not from our community," Amma said.

"Community, hah! A few dozen families so thoroughly inbred that diseases must be seething inside us. She is fresh–"

"When have any of us died of a heart attack or cancer? When did you hear of any genetic disease despite . . . inbreeding?"

"Papa died–"

"A truck accident is not genetic."

Bhaiyya clenched his fist. "I will marry her."

"Our community is entitled to blessings." Amma's face was as livid as his. "We have suitable matches here. You marry outside and . . ."

"And what? You'll disown me?"

"Yes," she whispered. "Yes."

Sometimes time divides so slowly that a few seconds stretch beyond infinity.

Then Bhaiyya spoke and cracked the silence.

"I can't give her up." Pain bled in his voice. "And I can't give you up. Or Chikki."

A softer silence, sadder. Amma said, "She must undergo the ritual." She got up.

I followed her to the kitchen, feeling torn between them, wishing Ronjona did not exist. I thought of how I'd often queued along with other unmarried girls at weddings for the brides to touch our heads with something wrapped in silk, and how energy had tingled through me after that. Amma had told me that we needed this "minor blessing" so that we were strong enough for the ritual when we married.

"Ronjona's never received anything from other brides," I blurted.

"Oh, she'll survive," Amma said, but she did not meet my gaze.

★

In the months that followed, Bhaiyya kept forcing me to meet Ronjona. After another lunch hour spent in the cafeteria, sugarless tea for me, chocolate ecstasies for her, a frigidity between us, Bhaiyya cornered me in the evening. "Chikki, Ronnie is worried about this ritual. She wants to know what it is."

"I've attended only the latter half." I shuffled my feet.

"See, she's heard rumors about it. About us. I laughed and said, Don't I look normal, doesn't Chikki? I told her you'd attended rituals as a kid. If it was cruel, they wouldn't have allowed kids in. You used to be so chirpy after them."

"True."

"Make her feel comfortable," Bhaiyya said. *"Please?"*

The next day, I sipped Diet Coke as Ronjona spooned ice cream–and would our lives have been different if her chin hadn't been smudged with chocolate sauce? Her expression was a strange mix of determination and nervousness. "Tell me."

"I don't know the details, but I've heard it's mantras, stuff chucked in the sacred fire. Very hush-hush, but no one's died of it yet." I forced a hearty laugh, pushing away memories of some brides tottering as they emerged from the room, supported by older women. "Got a lecture now." I rushed away.

★

I knew nothing of Bhaiyya's life these past thirty years. That monsoon, a few months after Amma agreed to Bhaiyya's marriage, I'd escaped to San José for studies. I'd skipped their December wedding. All I saw of it was a video recording sent by Amma. She called a few months later to tell me: "Ronjona's taken your bhaiyya to Mumbai, but at least she let the ritual happen." And after a few more months, she told me that Bhaiyya and Ronjona had broken contact.

My letters and calls home dwindled over time. My studies, and then my job, took up all my energy. Then Jagdeesh and love burst into my life, and with it, my imminent marriage. Marriage! I could no longer deny to myself that our family had rituals and blessings I knew very little about. Tense, I called Amma. When she refused to explain the mechanics of the ritual and insisted I cancel the marriage, I broke off with her.

Now Bhaiyya and I were both headed home, sitting in adjacent seats, not talking–strangers divided by the truth that bound us.

When we were an hour from Mumbai, he turned to me, face stern like he had keyed himself up.

"Ronnie never told me what happened during the ritual, but I read her diary. I'd been wondering why I hadn't received the blessing. The older men had told me that the blessing reached us when the bride kissed the groom on the wedding night. I'd assumed it had reached me. I'd not imagined Ronjona would have . . . When I read what she'd written, God forgive me, for a few moments I even resented her for what she did. But she was so deeply damaged . . . all our lives. . . ."

The wedding video showed Ronjona smiling as she trailed Bhaiyya around the sacred fire, but later, after emerging from the ritual room, she looked listlessly at plates heaped with chocolates. I wondered what that kiss was supposed to mean, and what went wrong for them.

"When I saw you on my flight," Bhaiyya continued, "I wangled this seat because I wanted to ask you, why did you pretend it was nothing to worry about?"

I rubbed a wayward eyelash out. I examined my nail polish. I did not look at him. "I did not know the details; I still don't. I married outside the community."

I understood now: marriages were tricky with outsiders. For men, because they lost out on the blessing; for women, because we didn't.

I wanted a happy, content life, but try as I might, I never felt comfortable in any friendship, any relationship. My reality intruded too often. A few years ago, on a vacation with Jagdeesh as part of our can-we-make-it work trial, I saw a childhood friend at a mall. I remembered how we'd played hopscotch in the evenings, gorged together on jalebis at weddings, giggled at adolescent jokes. Glad to see a familiar face, I called out to her. She ignored me.

"You know her?" Jagdeesh asked.

"A neighbor. We grew up together," I replied without thinking.

"She's barely over twenty. While you are forty-seven." He stared at me. "Holy shit, is this a blessing your village water bestows on everyone?"

And here we were, Bhaiyya and I, returning to that village, I with the blessing, and Bhaiyya without.

"Chikki," Bhaiyya said. "In her diary, Ronjona–"

"I don't know why she wrote anything," I cut in, desperate to close the topic. "Married women never describe what happens."

He turned pale. "Did she fall ill because I read it?"

"Ill?"

"Cancer," he whispered. "Blood cancer. Was there a bond of secrecy?"

I almost said I didn't know of any such bond, but his face was so tortured that I shrank back. The flight bumped to a halt; I pulled my laptop bag out of the overhead locker and strode off, leaving him hunched in his seat.

★

I did not see Bhaiyya queued for immigrations. The immigrations officer frowned as he examined my passport photograph, but said nothing. Mumbai airport overflowed with closed-circuit TVs and security-checking machines and whatnot. Soon all information would be centralized. I hoped Govind Uncle was as good with technology as his reputation claimed.

I took the bus onwards. Bhaiyya was not on it. I got down at the outskirts of our village and dragged my strolley bag down the cobbled road for home, bump-bump, choosing a path through the woods instead of the village center. I passed Sharada Aunty's house, and almost stopped to say hello, but the house seemed deserted. Besides, Amma must be waiting. She had sounded so quietly desperate on the phone.

Creepers hid our gate, wild grass overgrew our driveway. Our house was obscured by a profusion of greenery. Trees sagged with fruit. I smiled as I remembered the pathetic guava tree; Amma sure had improved her gardening skills. I rang the doorbell.

Amma looked unchanged except for that downward turn of her mouth.

"How are you?" I asked after we hugged.

She placed her fingers over my lips and gave a tremulous smile. "Later. The walk must have tired you. Jet lag, too."

I nodded. After a bath, I lay down for a few minutes. When I next knew, she was shaking me awake. It was evening.

We sat under the trees and sipped tea.

"If you go to Prayag," Amma said, "you'll see the river Saraswati meet Yamuna and Ganga. You cannot see the river Saraswati separately before that point. Saraswati is an underground river and survives only because no one sees it till it mingles with other waters."

Evening, the breeze full of salt and sea, the leaves of the coconut trees rustling. Serrated by the fanned-out palm fronds, the sun was a crimson jag lowering into darkness.

"But once we are visible," she said, "our blessings become curses."

I bit into a crunchy murrukku spiral. Too oily.

"Ronjona snatched my son away." Amma glared at a distant memory. "At least she received enough of the blessing to pass it to him."

I thought of Bhaiyya's bald head and wrinkles–clearly, Amma did not know. I should warn her. "I met him on the plane. He was not blessed. Ronjona died of blood cancer."

Amma froze. For a while, she was silent. Gaze fixed on the golden mangoes outside, she said, "I have to cook dinner."

I trailed her to the kitchen, but stopped at her writing desk. "A laptop? You use computers?" Silly me–I knew nothing of her life now, why was I surprised?

"Govind got us all laptops. He started teaching me Internet but . . ."

"He couldn't train you?" I grinned. "Come on, it's not difficult. Which reminds me, I need his help."

"He's not here."

I needed him to make me a new set of identity papers. "Where–"

"Tomorrow, Chikki. Let Deepak also come. It's a long story."

I looked at the sag of her face, and wasn't sure I wanted to know.

★

Tinkles of the musical doorbell woke me up. I took a while orienting myself to the high white ceiling (corners grey with spiderwebs), to the smell of ripe mangoes and the cloying chlorophyll of a lush garden.

The bell again. *Bhaiyya?*

I peeped from the window.

A young man leaned his bicycle against a coconut tree, took empty bags from the bicycle's carrier and walked to the veranda. He stuffed the bags with fruit kept ready in wicker baskets. Amma watched, resting against the wall, twining her fingers around her hair.

"The police came yesterday," he told her. "They asked me, does an old woman live there?"

"And?" Amma adjusted her sari pallu over her blouse.

"I said, the old woman died long ago, now her daughter lives there." His gaze wandered over her body. "Lying to the police is not good."

"Sell those and keep the money." Amma pointed to another basket of mangoes.

He licked his lips, stared at her for a few moments, then pedalled off. She watched him go. The raw, sad longing on her face embarrassed me. He was so young, and she! Could anyone feel so lonely? I thought suddenly of Jagdeesh, and how things could have been between us.

"Who was it?" I asked Amma later.

"Ramu sells off our fruits and buys my groceries."

"Don't you shop at the village?"

Amma used to love shopkeepers fussing around her, showing her this and that, wheedling, persuading, as she acted the tough customer, the coy girl, whatever.

"I should tell you," she said. "I thought I'd wait till Deepak came."

"Tell me what?"

She sat on the sofa and patted me to the place near her. "Some outsiders heard rumors . . . maybe thought we possessed gold . . . or maybe the devil's work." Her voice became hoarse.

"One dark night, they came with flaming torches. Govind saw them. He managed to spread the warning. Several families bundled out in their cars. Others couldn't escape. Govind . . . they killed him."

A million icicles stung my skin. Such things did not happen to real people.

"I put out lights. Hid in the coconut grove." Amma's voice was a sheer whisper. "They were outsiders; they didn't expect a house behind all those trees."

I was floating in the air, watching two women, alike like sisters, sitting on the sofa. I asked, "When was this?"

"Six months ago." She dabbed her face with her sari pallu. "I thought the families would return. Or contact me."

"Did they?"

"No. I called on their mobiles. Unreachable numbers. Phones not picked up. They probably thought villagers had stolen my mobile."

This was home–it was supposed to remain unchanged. The base we started from. Safe. Okay, maybe a few accidents. A couple of families moving out, some children leaving–like I did. How could an entire community get killed? Or be scattered across the globe?

Leaving only Amma here.

"The villagers know you live here," I said. "Ramu . . ."

"Ramu's a sweet boy. Once the outsiders left, life returned to normal."

Normal? I gaped at her.

She turned her face away. "Your bhaiyya should have come by now."

No wonder she wanted her family around her. "How did you locate us?"

She blinked hard. "Govind worried about all this computerization, these databases, this biomeretics–"

"Biometrics." I couldn't see a connection.

"He said, our community should pool resources. Olden times, people respected us for what we were. When things started changing, we bribed when we wanted records modified. Govind said, things will become more difficult now."

You bet they will, I thought.

She tucked a strand behind her ear. "We must enter all professions. Medicine, genetics. Computers. Lawyers, too, to know loopholes. We must marry within the community. Govind made family trees, and tracked members of our community. They found you and Deepak. Couldn't find my oldest, Purushottam, or Neera–"

"Your oldest *what?*"

"Son."

"I have another brother?"

Amma nodded. "Two more brothers, one sister. Neera looks like you."

"How," I gulped, "old are you?" Heck, I'd never asked before–maybe I hadn't really wanted to know.

"One and seventy-five."

I was fifty-three. Which meant–

"They left after their marriages," she said.

Two brothers, one sister. Their spouses. Children. Grandchildren.

"You left, too." She paused. "Then you married an outsider."

Jagdeesh belonged to a different caste and community. We met a few years into my life in San José, after gym, dieting, and freedom from supervision had given me confidence and sparkle. His romancing was a whirl of chocolates and roses, his proposal diamond-ringed and swift, and he wanted us married within a week because his grandfather was unwell and wanted to see a granddaughter-in-law before he died. Just a week! Overwhelmed, scared, confused, I called Amma.

"Tell me how to manage the ritual," I said. "The ceremony will use Tamilian rites."

"Chikki, what's the hurry?" she said. "Our community has enough nice boys."

For a fleeting moment, I remembered Bhaiyya arguing with her over Ronjona.

"Amma, I love Jagdeesh. I don't want to lose him, and I cannot postpone the marriage this Saturday. Can we do another ceremony afterwards, using our rites? I want both of us blessed."

"The blessing manifests only the first time a girl circumambulates the sacred marriage fire. Don't marry an outsider, Chikki, you don't understand. Come home."

I disconnected, feeling helpless–I could not explain this to Jagdeesh. I could not imagine life without him. Nor could I do the ritual alone; I had no idea what was done inside the room to bless the bride and groom. All I knew was that when the bride emerged and touched the heads of us girls queued outside, it made us happy and energetic.

I fainted after the wedding rites, but recovered within seconds as energy surged through me. It was so wondrous, so abundant, that I knew it was the blessing. I didn't know how to share it with Jagdeesh. Stretched before us, I saw years of growing disparity, and the bitterness and suspicion and disgust: our marriage was doomed. I gave up long before my strangeness became obvious–I think now that this is what drove him away.

★

Bhaiyya hadn't come yet. As Amma and I sipped our post-lunch coffee, I said, "You told me long ago you would explain the ritual to me when I came home."

"This is a legend, but it is true."

"Whatever. I want to know."

"We are not natives of this region," she said. "Our ancestors come from the Himalayan foothills. Millennia ago, driven out by other tribes, they travelled across what is now India, to the Western Ghats. They faced many hardships. Once, when camping along a dried river, they ran out of food and water. They sank down on the hard soil and prayed for delivery. They prayed and they prayed. Some beseeched Yama, to conquer death, and others pleaded with Agni, assuming the fire god would give them strength and energy. Both gods granted boons."

I imagined thin, parched men and women, kneeling for supplication, and gods descending from the clouds of heaven in flowing garments of silk and bedecked with jewels. Like a mythological drama, except that this was the alleged past of my people.

"Ever since then, the gods bless us during the wedding ceremony. Immediately after the pheras around the fire, the bride's life force is fully absorbed by Yama, leaving her momentarily suspended in death. Agni amplifies and gushes the energy back into the bride." Amma's eyes glittered. "That energy is what gives us eternity. It is so abundant that it spills over from the bride, and we form it into a crystal. The bride uses it to channel energy to unmarried girls; you have attended enough weddings to remember that. And–"

"Wait," I said, trying to absorb the import of her words. "What do you mean by momentarily suspended?"

"The withdrawal of the life force is traumatic. The energy that young girls receive from brides gives them the strength to cope with this death that precedes eternity."

Ronjona had not received any life force before the wedding. "What happened to Ronjona? I saw the video; she looked exhausted when she emerged from the room."

"Ronjona, being an outsider, was not entitled to the blessing," Amma said. "We have special mantras to invoke the blessing for such cases, mantras that must be chanted by a dozen already-blessed women. But those mantras need time to take effect. Ronjona's death lasted around five minutes before amplified energy flooded back into her."

"She was dead for five minutes?" I shuddered.

"She recovered, Chikki."

"Amma, if you knew this could happen, how could you–"

Amma's eyes blazed. "I *told* your bhaiyya not to marry her. Our ritual is very special, very secret. We try to adapt it for outsiders, but there is always a risk. See, Chikki, *such marriages are not supposed to happen.* It's not as bad when our women marry outsiders, because so long as there is a sacred fire, they will be blessed. Of course, there is no crystal, so their husbands may not get it and their children . . ."

I did not want to discuss my marriage. "About Ronjona."

"After she revived, we used mantras to create a crystal for Deepak. We explained to her that she should pass the crystal in a kiss to him just before they make love the first time."

"Yet Bhaiyya aged," I said. "Ronjona died."

"She obviously didn't give the crystal to Deepak." Amma frowned. "As for what happened to her, who knows?"

Bhaiyya missed out on eternity. He had said, *God forgive me, I even resented her for it.*

What did Ronjona do with a crystal sparkling with life? I was about to ask Amma when I saw her looking at the trees, and I suddenly imagined a dark and tired face, a slender arm swinging in an arc, a bejewelled hand hefting the crystal and lobbing the brilliance out into the night onto the stubborn soil of our dry garden.

★

Bhaiyya's impending visit was a shoe about to fall. Looking at us, both frozen at the ages when we married, he would remember cancer-ravaged Ronjona. Or notice his own wrinkles. His bitterness would brim over.

Three days passed, and he did not come home. Amma called his USA number–no reply. At least he hadn't gone back.

To distract myself, I taught Amma how to use the Internet. She picked it up rapidly, especially Googling.

"Can we locate the others?" she asked.

I searched the names she gave; we found no likely matches. As she figured out other names to try, I Googled Bhaiyya's name.

His website ranked first in the results. I glanced at Amma and loaded it. There was a touching memorial to "Ronnie" with a link to a family album. No, I wasn't ready for this yet. Back on the search page, I noticed a news item dated two days earlier. Click.

The Mumbai edition of the *Times of India* reported him as a US national of Indian origin who died of a massive heart attack at the airport, soon after landing at Mumbai.

My body turned cold. When I was craning my neck to spot him boarding the bus, he lay dead in the airport. Or ambulance. Or hospital morgue. He looked guilty when I said he loved Ronjona and should have thought of her. He thought her cancer was related to his reading her diary. He blamed himself, and I, unwilling to face his anger, let him. Perhaps guilt killed him.

What sort of a sister was I?

Near me, Amma sobbed. Then my own sobs started.

★

Late into the nights, after Amma slept, I surfed. What I found shook me up. All night I searched for data, thought of options. I needed to return to the USA with my own identity to do what was needed. But I could not leave Amma alone.

Daytime, I took long walks to escape my restlessness. The broken, half-burnt shells of houses frightened me. My memories peopled them with familiar faces and bustling life and then transformed them into sites savaged by mobs. Sometimes I rushed past the ruins. At other times, I wondered about the people who escaped. How did they establish new identities? Find places to stay? Resume their lives?

On returning home, I would find Amma on the computer, her eyes bright. Scribbled papers would be lying scattered near her, and she would hurriedly gather them back into a file. She was reading the CDs Govind Uncle gave her, she once told me, her face flushed. At least she was comfortable with computers. It struck me that our condition kept us safe from dementia.

We rarely talked–I was preoccupied, and she, too, seemed lost in thoughts.

A couple of weeks later I said, "I need to go to Mumbai." I needed more data to make decisions.

"Forever?" she asked, face held stiff.

How could she think I'd abandon her after what had happened? I gathered her into a hug. "Let's move away from this place. We can sell this house."

"Ownership records show the owner as a one-hundred-and-seventy-five-year-old woman," she said. "A tricky sale."

You bet.

The next day, I cycled to the bus stop and boarded the coach to Mumbai. At the hospital Ronjona went to, years ago, I bribed a clerk to see the records of her stay, then made phone calls to check other records. My investigation confirmed the theory I had formed after reading Bhaiyya's blog; it took me all my willpower not to break down.

★

The house was dark. I opened the door. "Amma?" I moved to switch on the light.

"Don't," Amma whispered. "Ramu–"

"Ramu?"

She stepped into the veranda; her face looked flushed in the moonlight.

"When he came today afternoon, he was drunk and abusive and coarse," she said. "He tried to grab me. I used judo to fend him off. But he may return with friends."

A beautiful face is a curse forever, I thought. Ramu was barely eighteen–his lusting after Amma sounded disgusting. Then I remembered the languid way Amma moved when he came, the sinuous sway of her body, her dreamy looks. He was only eighteen. And Amma, sultry, her loneliness so obvious, might have wanted a man, but not when he was drunk.

Who was I to judge either of them, anyway, I who could not lower my guard even before the man I thought I loved?

"We will have to leave this place," she said. "I have the new identity Govind gave me. We can move to Mumbai."

"You have identity papers? You never told me!"

"I was comfortable here, despite all that happened. But I must now move on and take risks." She hesitated, then added, "Chikki, I want to do more with my life."

I did not press for explanations; I was too relieved that she had agreed to move to Mumbai.

Early next morning, essentials crammed into two bags, we pedalled to the bus stop of the next village. As we waited for the coach, she said, "Call me Mridu–that's my new name."

"Mridu." I rolled the word on my tongue. "Nice name."

"Sharada Rao lives in Mumbai," Amma said. "I located her new identity and address using Govind's papers and some surfing. She will help us."

So that was what Amma had been doing while I took my walks.

★

Sharada Aunty blinked at the sight of us, then, before Amma or I uttered a word, she said, "Call me Rita now," pulled us into the apartment, and shut the door.

After an initial awkwardness, we hugged, we sobbed. We talked, we held hands.

Sharada Aunty asked, "What next?"

"I want to study medicine," Amma said.

Amma and I had not yet discussed our plans; her statement surprised me.

"Why?" asked Sharada Aunty–no, Rita. "We don't have health problems."

"True." Amma looked past me. "But others may need doctors. Maybe I can stay as your paying guest."

Rita nodded. "We need to stick together. Chikki, you don't have a new identity, no?"

"I will continue with my real identity for some years." Makeup would help me. Add a touch of white at the roots of my dark hair, as if I was careless with my hair-dye; paint subtle wrinkles to become an older person trying to appear young, shade my face to harden my expression. Continuity of identity meant continuity of career, of good earning capacity–I also needed to save to buy a sturdy mid-twenties persona.

"You will return to San José?" Amma asked.

"New York. I've applied for jobs there." I hoped she would not ask me *Why New York?* I did not want to lie to her.

Amma saw me off at the airport. The second call for security check was blaring when she gripped my hand. "I want you to meet a girl in New York. Name's Meeta."

"You know?" Our gazes locked. I had hoped to save her this guilt.

"I checked Deepak's blogs," she said. "I saw his family album."

I wasn't the only one who used the Internet.

"She resembles her father," Amma continued. "No wonder Ronjona hated us. If we'd known . . ."

But no one knew Ronjona was pregnant at the time of the ritual.

"Bhaiyya placed Meeta in the best institution possible," I said. "I checked the credentials of the place."

Ever since I'd matched the child's birth date with the wedding date, I had pondered my culpability. All of us made mistakes. Bhaiyya ignored the truth. I ran away. Amma chose hostility. Ronjona . . . well, she trusted us. And Meeta's mistake? Being alive then. Getting damaged by the death, despite grabbing her mother's life force for those crucial five minutes.

These were merely my guesses about what might have happened, given that Meeta was born seven months after the wedding, a full-term child but severely retarded.

"I will be allowed to meet Meeta," I said. "I am her aunt." Then I could decide the way forward.

I hugged Amma . . . Mridu . . . and boarded the plane.

It was a month since I'd flown into Mumbai airport. What was a mere month in my life? Less than a cumin seed in a camel's throat. Yet this past month was raw in my mind, a reminder of mistakes that would haunt me over the decades and centuries awaiting me. Did Amma often agonize over her disagreements and mistakes with her other children, or had time distanced her mercifully from those memories? How did one handle a never-ending life? Perhaps, for people like us, it was all the more important for us to make peace with the past and move on. At least we got second chances.

Outside, the tarmac rolled past, a thick broad gray, then a thin line, then a wisp below. Hours later, the ground would be solid under me again, a wisp, then a ribbon, then a broad runway. A beginning, I told myself. One of many.

THE REMAKER

FÁBIO FERNANDES

1. What´s in a name

Menard. His name is Pierre Menard.

This isn´t his birth name. It doesn't matter, it really doesn't make any difference - what should anyone care about such a trifling thing these days?

Besides, nobody even knows if he really existed. For the person who signs this name, such a discussion is immaterial.

How do I know that?

Pierre Menard killed me.

★

As far as a fairly thorough research in the Hive can show you, there were quite a handful of men who went by the name Pierre Menard in recorded history.

One of the first Menards I´ve been able to trace down was a Canadian businessman and fur trader who lived in the early 1800s. He was presiding officer of the Illinois Territorial Legislature and from 1818 to 1822 served as its first lieutenant governor.

The second one was a musician. Pierre Menard, American violinist and concertmaster for The Neon Philharmonic, a psychedelic pop band formed in 1967. They released only two albums before the group disbanded in 1975.

(There´s another Pierre Menard still, also a violinist, who played in the Vermeer Quartet and who died of AIDS in 1994. I couldn´t find out if he was the same guy of the Neon Philharmonic, though somehow it doesn´t seem so – but it´s a creepy coincidence all the same.)

There was also a Dr. Pierre Menard, anesthesiologist, in Logan, West Virginia. But I couldn´t find much about him except for the fact that he was actively working until the early 2010s. He may be still alive today.

As well as the last namesake of my list. A Pierre Menard whose vestiges, no matter how hard I tried, I could never find. Not until the day I died.

★

Pierre Menard, Author of the Quixote, is one of the most important short stories of the twentieth century. In this story, written in the form of an academic paper by Argentinean writer Jorge Luis Borges, the author poses as a reviewer who analyzes the work of a recently deceased

French writer who, among other literary exploits, wrote *Don Quixote.*

To be more specific, according to Borges, Menard's subterranean work "consists of the ninth and thirty-eighth chapters of the first part of Don Quixote and a fragment of chapter twenty-two."

The thing is, Pierre Menard didn't only *rewrite* Cervantes's classic work. He wrote it as if Cervantes had *never* done it. But it's not an alternate history story, for, in that universe, Cervantes *had written* Don Quixote – exactly the same way we know he did, and using the very words he used.

Menard just applied the seat of his pants to the seat of the chair, as people said then, and wrote the aforementioned chapters. No strings attached, no computer tricks: Borges wrote that story in 1939, just before Alan Turing and Bletchley Park, a time when *computers* were simply the name given to the mathematicians performing calculations in notebooks (paper ones) and chalkboards (dumb, non-interactive ones).

His method, according to Borges, was quite simple: "Know Spanish well, recover the Catholic faith, fight against the Moors or the Turk, forget the history of Europe between the years 1602 and 1918, be Miguel de Cervantes."

Borges was evidently making fun of the then new canons of modernity, the death of the author, and other notions that were foreign to him, a man born in Argentina but partially raised in Switzerland and strongly immersed in the European culture. It is one of his best stories.

His Menard was a complete fiction. The other, however, was very real: he killed me in 2026.

2. The First Book of Menard

This other Menard was what I called a *remaker.* As his famous fictional namesake, he rewrote books. Not just chapters or fragments, as the original Menard did (even if he did it only in the imagination of Borges).

No. My Menard rewrote *entire novels.*

This should come as no surprise for anyone these days, considering you can squirt entire libraries into a nanoimplant and copy/paste them as you see fit – a procedure far older than the digital pundits would make you believe, using techniques not unknown to the Dada and the Surrealists, the Founding Fathers of altered books in the 1910s and 1920s. What is the big deal about a person who rewrites stories, since the very notion of *rewriting* was challenged so many years ago and now seems such an effortless thing?

That, I thought then, was the keyword. *Effort.* Why should anyone even try to rewrite a novel and then publish it in paper as if it was an original work? And, weirder yet, *without letting anyone know?*

Why did I care?

★

When you are a researcher, you can't afford not to care about such things. You are compelled to search – not a futile, useless search for its own sake, but a search for answers. The questions may vary, but they are always there, hovering over the mind of the researcher. Because there will always be questions.

The first question that made my path cross with Menard's was, evidently: *why?*

My original question was entirely other – and I´m a bit ashamed now by the fact that I can't even remember what it was. I was in the university's library, browsing the bookshelves, another purpose in mind.

I had the entire space of the library all to myself. Almost nobody goes there anymore. Not after the last round of education reforms and the end of live classes. The university offers all its books in digital format through the Hive, and students don´t even bother coming to the campus now.

There is only a skeletal staff to keep things clean and tidy in the old buildings, plus the occasional researcher who likes the peace and quiet of the place. But only oldsters like me still come. The younger ones would rather be at home or coffee shops, STing from there.

Sometimes I felt like Wells´ Traveller in the distant future, alone in a library full of swirling dust motes, touching crumbling books. But sometimes the bizarre image of Sean Connery in *Zardoz* also came to mind, a violent savage with braided hair wearing only red shorts, running down narrow aisles full of books and empty of people. Both images were sad to me.

It was on one of these lonely browsings that I found the First Book.

I still didn´t know then if that was the first book he ever wrote; I called it so because it was the very first that I found. It became easier to me to call it so, and it was as good a method as any.

The book was an old hardcover edition of *1984*. But it didn´t have a dust jacket, so it took some time for me to register the fact that it was Orwell´s classic novel. I also took a very long time to notice that the author's name on the spine wasn´t Orwell´s.

I looked at it and couldn´t find anything wrong with that. It was just after I began leafing through the pages that I closed it suddenly and went to the cover.

It read:

Pierre Menard

1984

No publisher name.

My first reaction was to start reading the book right there. I was sure then that it was a kind of parody or satire. (Anthony Burgess, for example, had written such a story in 1978 – but he named it *1985,* and it was intended as a tribute to Orwell's classic novel. It was a completely different story.)

But the beginning – ah, the beginning:

It was a bright cold day in April, and the clocks were striking thirteen. Winston Smith, his chin nuzzled into his breast in an effort to escape the vile wind, slipped quickly through the glass doors of Victory Mansions, though not quickly enough to prevent a swirl of gritty dust from entering along with him.

I went on reading. The rest of the book, as much as memory served, was exactly the same as George Orwell had written. Word for word.

My second reaction was laughter.

I found it amusing that someone could give her/himself the trouble to do this kind of prank those days. It reminded me of the works of the Italian collective Luther Blissett, later known as Wu-Ming. They had done some really good tactical media actions between the end of twentieth century and the beginning of the twenty-first.

My third reaction was to get the book and take it home with me. It was too much fun to dismiss it.

It was a refreshing, sunny thought in my day. I couldn´t help but laugh, still standing there in the aisle, surrounded by the dust-filled surviving books in the university library. There was no one there to shush me.

3. The Age of Reference

Is it possible to be alone in a crowd these days?

Of course it is. Everybody is alone these days.

São Paulo in 2026 is a huge river, an Amazon of people, a Joycean riverrun, a band of Blooms blooming around, germinating thoughts on the run and in the sidewalks, everybody talking aloud, apparently to themselves, alone or to someone else via their implants.

When cellphones became obsolete, the only way was to become molecular. So they crammed huge computational power in bioware or smart jewelry and created SelfTalking. STing involves mainly talking to personal AIs – mostly limited, rather dumb AIs, but who cares? At least they do what they are told to, no complaining, no need to pay anything but a ridiculously cheap microfee per month.

And they remind you of your chores – that is, the chores they are too dumb or non-mobile enough to do for you; they can store messages, write and/or record messages, locate places, find your contacts wherever you happen to be walking by, ping them to let them know where you are (or block them so they don't), arrange for orders and pay in advance whenever you enter a café or a supermarket. They can even talk to others for you so you don't have to.

Sometimes I enjoy standing apart from the crowd, in the intersection of Rua Augusta and Avenida Paulista, under the concrete marquise of the huge building of the Conjunto Nacional. I usually take with me an extra-large foam cup of steaming hot caramel machiatto or cinnamon latte from the Starbucks across the street and just stand there, sipping the warm beverage leisurely, watching people walking or riding by.

That was exactly what I was doing a couple of months ago, right after finding the First Book of Menard. I was chilling out, book under my arm, doing nothing, when a soft ping in my inner ear interrupted my train of thought.

"There is a white bike available just around the block, Dave," said the low-pitch male voice.

"Thanks but no thanks, Butler," I said. "You already know that, why ask?"

"You keep complaining about your legs," the AI replied. "You probably need some exercise. Riding bicycles is good for your heart and lungs, and for your varicose-"

I nodded it down, and the professorial voice dimmed away. Sometimes it´s good to be by yourself. Just watching the white bikes go by.

★

After the Big Gridlock of 2014, when virtually all of the motor vehicles in São Paulo simply got stuck in a perpetual lockout, things got very nasty.

Nobody believed it could happen. Until it happened: one evening, at rush hour, the city registered the worst bottleneck of its history: more than 540 kilometers of jammed traffic all over the city.

São Paulo was the third biggest city in the world then. It was the first to crash.

It was the worst week of my life. I got stuck in my apartment without electricity. The running water in my building went off right after that. When I had just run out of food the Martial Law was lifted, after six days of mayhem.

By then the city had hundreds of dead.

When it became clear the gridlock was serious (that is, more serious than usual), people started getting out of their cars to see what was going on. Then the fights started. First, people in the cars began to shout and curse aloud. Then, fistfights. Suddenly, someone had a gun.

And the shooting started. All over the city.

Then someone had the brilliant idea to move the cars away. Later that first day GloboNews and CNN showed some impressive footage of massive heaps of people pushing cars all along one major artery of the city, and then, when they saw it didn´t make any difference– because even when they *could* move a vehicle (a Volkswagen or a Japanese car; an SUV was out of the question), they simply didn´t have the leeway to move it further– they just burned the cars on the spot.

Needless to say the fires started to spread almost as fast as the bullets.

New Downtown, where Avenida Paulista is located, became a war zone - something I had until then already seen only in newscasts about Middle East or Eastern European countries.

Welcome to civilization, I told myself then. *This is the price to pay to end your childhood and become an old country.*

It took the municipality the better part of a year just to clear the city of the rusted, battered, and charred carcasses of cars. To this day, cars are banned from Greater Downtown.

Two years after the tragedy, white bicycles started to show up all over the Greater Downtown perimeter. They were just there, parked but not locked up, as if inviting everyone to take a hike.

Nobody ever found out who put them there in the first place. A blog pundit wrote that the white bikes were a direct reference to the PROVOS of Amsterdam in the 1960s, who for months effectively created a free-for-all system of transportation where all that was required of you was that you took the bike wherever you found it, used it, then left it wherever you got it. As simple as that.

Incredible as it may sound, it *was* simple. I don´t know why that stuck. Maybe people were tired of all that senseless traffic killing. But it´s been almost fifteen years since the Gridlock and the white bikes endure. People became too fond of them. Me too – even though I don't use them. I´d rather walk. That´s what I do the most since I retired.

★

In this day and age, if you don´t wear any kind of computational apparatus, you´re severely disconnected from the world. Sometimes, especially when I´m watching the walking-and-biking crowds down Avenida Paulista, I fancy I´m offline, though I only muffle the pinging sound in my head (even though the default is already a subsonic sound I can´t hear but can hardly avoid feeling, like a buzz in the teeth). I also put on hold the messages that are being squirted to me all the time.

The only concession I make to myself is to create a hotlist of 1980s music and watch the crowd passing to and fro to a soundtrack consisting of The Cure, Echo and the Bunnymen, Siouxsie and the Banshees, The Smiths, Joy Division.

But I don´t flaunt my virtual absence of wearable computing. At least, not like the Unconnected do.

4. Tribes of the XXI Century

Occasionally, in my *flanérie* by the streets of São Paulo, I find clusters of people who really talk to *each other.* Youngsters, mostly. It´s good to see them: they have a certain punk attitude you don´t see every day, a healthy behavior that is necessary and more than welcome in times of conformity and cold comfort.

They usually wear dumb clothes, real used vintage material, and they wear them like a badge of honor. A couple of years ago I wrote a paper for *Science Fiction Studies* comparing the Unconnected with the non-telepaths in Alfred Bester´s *The Demolished Man.* They are the pebbles that roll in the bottom of the river, below its murky depths, inhabiting the undercurrents. Invisible things, whose influence is not seen but is felt if you know just where to look.

I had interviewed one of them at the time, a well-groomed man in his thirties wearing used clothes which seemed to have come from the 1980s without the aid of a time machine, the hard way, really bought in a flea market. The guy claimed to be non-political but I couldn´t help but notice a hint of a surprisingly right-wing discourse in his speech for someone who considered himself a revolutionary.

Even so, what he told me rang a bell in my mind: "You see, we work between the tentacles of the beast."

"And who would be the beast?," I asked, doing my best *agent provocateur* face.

"Why, man," he said, giving me his best derisive snort. "All you zombies."

Quoting Heinlein, of all things. Preaching to the choir. I still wonder if he knew from whom he was corydoctoring the quoting.

★

Midori was waiting for me when I got home the evening after I found the First Book. I almost forgot I was going to cook for her that night.

She was the subject of my latest post-doc fellowship, one of the first meta-gender individuals of the world.

I met her at a symposium in Canada. She was so busy at the time that I could barely speak to her at all – even though she, just like me, lived in São Paulo.

But São Paulo is a huge city. You could roam its streets for years and never find a single friend. And the irony of it was that we had to meet in a symposium in Canada of all places – she had just finished her PhD on the pioneers of sex change and was all the rage in Brazilian academia. She gave a lecture on Christine Jorgensen and the pioneers of transsexualism.

I was fascinated. I approached her at the end of her communication and invited her for dinner. And that´s how it started for us.

As soon as we returned to Brazil we started a relationship – we lived in transit, orbiting around each other, not exactly in love, but definitely in caring, in comforting, in sex. Sometimes Midori slept at my place, sometimes I slept at hers.

It was a unique experience. The Meta-Genders are a kind of 2.0 hermaphrodite: you not only change your sex, you get to keep your original genitalia as well.

Midori was born a man and since early childhood had behaved as a girl, showing all the signs of a feminine psyche. So when she was eighteen, she applied for a sex change. But her therapist told her to wait because of the new meta-gender therapies that were just being developed then. She didn´t regret waiting.

By the time she was twenty-six, she underwent surgery and DNA-resetting. She had her testicles removed and a vagina grown just beneath the root of the penis.

When I met her in that symposium, she was thirty-one and a very happy person. I basked in her glow, listened to her talking in the communication sessions, and finally took the courage to invite her for a date. Since we were both foreigners and strangers to Montréal, we both had our share of fun just trying to find the best places to eat, drink, and be merry.

And boy, we *were* merry.

We still were, even after almost four years. She was the best interlocutor I´ve had in years, a person with whom I could talk and relate to. The first thing I did when I got home was give her the book and ask her if she could see what was wrong with it while I started preparing the pasta.

"Who is this Menard, David?" she asked from the living room sofa.

"*This* Menard I don´t know yet," I said from the kitchen. "Have you ever read Jorge Luis Borges?"

"Heard of, but no, never read him."

I went to the scriptorium and fetched the Volume 1 of the Complete Works of Borges in Portuguese. I searched for the story in the index and handed it to her. "Read this," I said. "It´s just six pages. You won´t take long."

She read it while I finished the *puttanesca* sauce. When I served the *tagliatelle,* I asked, "Did you like it?"

She made a so-so face. "Not exactly my cup of tea, but it's good, yes…This Pierre Menard is a character created by him, isn´t he?"

I smiled. "Yes, you´ve got the point. Borges liked this kind of reference-mixing. In fact, half the stuff he throws into the story is fake, or in the very least wasn´t written by Menard, who, obviously, doesn´t exist."

"But the passage about the Quixote… I didn´t understand a thing. What´s the point of making the guy rewrite the book word for word, with no alterations?"

"He was thumbing his nose at the modernists, that´s all. Remember when he says that Cervantes wrote a thing that should be expected of him because of the times in which he lived, but not Menard. Menard was a genius because of his balls, of the courage to write something nobody would ever think to write. It was a very polite joke."

"It wasn´t funny."

"Oh, it wasn´t meant to be laughable," I lied. Because I laughed every time I read it. "He meant it to be a satirical piece, to tease the modernist writers of his time."

"But what about *this* Menard? What the fuck does he mean with that? And what for? Are you sure he didn´t simply put a new cover on an old book? Why would he give himself all this trouble?"

Now, that was a good question. In fact, that was the whole point of what I was seeing now as my next post-doc research project.

Why in hell would someone do that sort of thing today?

After dinner, Midori made coffee and I took the Borges back to the scriptorium to take some notes. I opened the book and found the story again. I read it again right there, standing by my desk, and found the passage I was looking for:

Menard didn´t want to compose another Quixote– which is easy– but the Quixote itself. Needless to say, he never contemplated a mechanical transcription of the original; he did not propose to copy it. His admirable intention was to produce a few pages which would coincide– word for word and line for line– with those of Miguel de Cervantes.

I repeated every word in a quiet, almost reverent tone. Then I closed the book, put it on my desk (I would certainly be looking for it again along the next few days), and returned to the living room to enjoy a good cup of coffee with my gorgeous girlfriend.

5. The Second Book of Menard

A week later, I found the second Menard book in the university library.

This time, though, I was looking for it. Actively. And, even though the library space wasn´t very big, it took me an entire week to find it.

I began browsing the Classic SF Masterworks section for other copies of Menard´s *1984*, as I had already done the day I found the First Book. Nothing; but that was expected.

After that, I went to the Fantastic Literature section. I fingered every single book in the several rows of shelves I had become so acquainted with in decades past. To no avail, alas.

I spent days in futile search and contemplation. It wasn´t as if I had anything better to do.

On the fifth day, having arrived early and spent hours in the Classic Weird/New Weird sections, suddenly Butler told me it was half past eleven. Early, but I was hungry. I decided I would take a break and go for an Italian restaurant near the campus.

Then, as it always seems to happen when we´re ready to give up on something, the corner of my eye just caught a glimpse of a gold-emblazoned M in a book spine in the Classic Cyberpunk section.

I backpedaled until I saw what had caught my attention.

Naked Lunch.

Only this time it wasn´t an old edition. This book was a comparatively new edition – it didn´t show a publication date, but it sported a colored cover with an abstract, electronic-art-like illustration. The looks, the typography, everything in it told my senses that the copy I now held in my hands was a paperback published in the 1980s or early 1990s.

But the name of the author – *Pierre Menard* – belied all that information.

I can´t remember for how long I was there, mesmerized by that name on the cover (later, of course, Butler would tell me that I stayed like that for exactly 8.34 minutes. A very long time for a machine, but not for an old man. We see things differently).

I caught myself almost caressing the paperback, turning it around in my hands, sniffing the paper like a fetishist. Some do say that reading paper books today is indeed a kind of fetish.

Maybe it is, and so what? Books are almost non-existent today. That´s why this thing he did was so outrageous, so surprising, so…

Marvelous.

Whoever was this Menard, a single person or a tactical group, he did it. He had the gall, he had the balls, this son-of-a-bitch.

I took the Second Book of Menard home with me. In my head, Psychedelic Furs. *Heaven.*

★

When Midori arrived, I was so immersed in my reading I didn´t even notice her.

"How did it go today?" she asked me from the scriptorium door.

I showed her the book.

"Sonofabitch," she said, smiling.

"Exactly what I thought," I said, happy that she got it at once.

"What are you going to do next?" she said.

"I don´t know yet," I admitted. I was still amazed, not sure if I really wanted to do anything.

She smiled, not without a bit of irony. "I´m amazed you still haven't written an abstract or even a whole paper about it."

She was right. That was exactly what I should have been doing.

That night, she cooked. I did the research. I told Butler to ping the RFID system of my library to search for the best books to help me with this mysterious affair. I ended up with a Babel-sized pile of books on my desk and started making notes on paper, in the time-honored way I still liked.

Until I got tired.

Method, I thought. I was getting scarce on method. I needed to do something more focused than just taking notes. I just couldn´t figure out exactly what.

★

"What´s the matter with you, my love?" Midori asked softly, later that night. I looked at her for a long time before answering, caressing her silky black hair, the curves of her body, stopping only briefly at her penis and her vagina just below it.

I massaged her clitoris tenderly with my little finger while thumb and index finger masturbated the base of her penis. It´s tricky, but she taught me how to do so to please her the way she liked it best. And I always was a quick learner.

I loved to detain myself and explore that body, always so new to me. In the beginning, I liked to recite John Donne to her, the *Elegy XIX - To His Mistress Going To Bed.*

License my roving hands, and let them go
Before, behind, between, above, below.
O my America! my new-found-land.

Because that was what she was to me then. A new territory, for which I had no map – and who did?

Later, when she read the poem in its entirety, she told me I was being unconsciously homophobic – or, at the very least, an old-fashioned machista, because of its ending:

To teach thee, I am naked first; why than,
what needst thou have more covering than a man?

"Fuck off, sweetie," she told me in her best mischievous tone. "There is no *man* in this relationship."

Then she took me from behind and, oh, she was so right.

★

Later, both of us sluggish right after lovemaking and just before falling quickly into sleep, she suggested, "Why don´t you talk to Marcos to check the age of these books?"

"Good idea," I said, and fell asleep.

6. Tribes of the XIX Century

The following afternoon I took the subway and went to the Ophicina Typographica.

The place almost hadn´t changed in twenty-odd years. Its founder and owner, designer Marcos Mello, had been a colleague of mine at the university for a brief period, where he'd taught typesetting.

I found Marcos at the iron handpress, finishing a *faux* DADA poster. I stopped for a moment to see him working, the precise mixture of extreme care and sheer muscularity he employed, first to fit each old lead type and block into the iron frame, then to lift the heavy frame into the press, and then applying the right amount of force to the lever so the paper got inked upon its entire surface in equal measure, with no blotches or smudges. That´s grace under pressure for you. I loved his work.

The moment he took a break, I went to talk to him and show him the books.

"Man, this is a real superb job, very well done," he told me excitedly while examining with great care the First Book, feeling the pages with the tips of his calloused fingers, squinting at the lettering without giving pause, as if transfixed by it.

"Do you think this job could have been done today?" I asked him.

He nodded slowly, still unable to take his eyes off the book, still enraptured.

"Sure it could," he said. "It´s not hard. All it takes is time and patience. You know how it is."

Indeed I knew. I had taken courses on bookbinding and typesetting with him years ago. It was a very fine and exquisite job, but also an energetic and exhausting one. I promised myself I would do it again sometime in the future, but I had no stamina for that.

He went on, explaining me how Menard could have bought reams of recycled paper and bathed then in a special tincture so it gained the appearance of a yellowing, acid paper. Of course, Marcos told me, Menard would have also stored the book in an environment proper to get fungi and dust motes, so it could smell old too.

"But where he could have done all of this?" I asked him.

He gestured around.

"In a place like this," he said. "Or even in a home press. It would take him longer, probably months if he was all by himself, but if he wasn´t in a hurry…" He shrugged.

I nodded in agreement. In the early aughts, a small-press revival happened all over the world. Many writers were publishing very limited editions of their works, swimming against the stream like a bunch of happy salmons. Nobody made money out of it, but who cared?

The fad was already dead by now, but probably it wouldn´t be difficult to find people in São Paulo with home presses. Marcos could help me with that. It would be fun.

★

It was boring.

We found every small press in the city in less than an hour via the Hive. The officially listed, the unofficial ones, the *artistes,* the pirates, the pseudo-revolutionaries, the frauds.

Nobody had a clue. Some of them didn´t even know who Borges was. And almost all of them had migrated definitively to the Hive and never even looked back to paper anymore – they got used to another reality.

★

The Internet in its previous incarnation ended in 2020.

By 2010 there were already two other terms created for orders of magnitude of data - the brontobyte and the geopbyte. Pundits doubted that anyone alive then would ever see a geopbyte hard drive.

In the end, it was no big deal. As desktop computing slowly gave way to mobile devices after 2011, the second decade of the century saw the transition from mobile to integrated. Smart clothing, thinking jewelry, implants.

Thus the Web gave way to the Hive: parallel processing in ultra-high global massive scale.

It´s not the Singularity – at least not yet. There was a kind of generalized disappointment among the experts when it became clear that no Kurzweil-like spontaneous machine sentience sprouted through all that computational power. Even so, the AIs – which can admittedly pass a Turing Test, but so can a smart refrigerator today – serve us well. We can´t really ask for much more than that.

I also use Butler as a messaging device. I call Pedro through it. His nick, from the ancient Web times, remains the same: *wintermute*. Like me, he is a sucker for references.

He blips into my field of vision some pictogram I don´t recognize. I simply use my voice.

"Will you switch this shit off?" I said. "I want real talk for a change."

"Don´t let the idiots of objectivity get you," he said, quoting Nelson Rodrigues. He knows I worked as an actor decades ago, so he quotes the most famous - and polemic - Brazilian playwright.

Pedro is one of my best never-seen-in-person friends. We are always talking online, even though he lives in São Paulo. We tried to meet for a cup of coffee two or three times, but after a while we gave up. Better have a coffee alone and talk online.

His collaborative album, *Creative Uncommons,* was one of the hits of the week through the Hive a couple of years ago, and he was the first person I considered talking to after Marcos. Marcos took care of the analog search. Pedro could help me with the digital part of it.

"It´s kind of a Bizarro version of the Saint Leibowitz Order?" he asked after I explained the whole shebang to him.

"Hah. Very funny."

"No, I mean it," he said. "Doesn´t seem like a tactical media collective action. A collective would make sure that everything would be recorded for everyone to know. They want witnesses."

"So you think it was a prank? Some former student trying to give me a lesson, so to speak?"

"Don´t be such a prick," he said with a sneer. "Not everything is about you. It´s probably about evangelization. Whoever is doing it wants to convert people."

"Hm, preaching to the choir? Aren´t the Unconnected enough? Why don´t she—"

"—or he—"

"—or *said person* simply give books to those people? Why don´t they do some bookcrossing, for a change?"

A laugh.

"Are you shitting me?" Pedro said. "Are you telling me you don´t know *them?*"

"Them who?"

"You've never heard of the Lo-Fi Cellulose Collective?"

★

The whole point of bookcrossing is moot in a wireless society. People do it for fun, just as they did with the bookbinding and typesetting craze.

Every Thursday evening, a small group gathered in the Café Girondino, just outside one of the exits of São Bento subway station.

At the long table, there were roughly a dozen people: a blonde woman in her thirties; a beautiful post-steampunkish couple of young boys, almost Wildean in their dandyism; a bald old man, looking very frail but spry and very vivacious around the eyes; a tall, fat man of indefinite age, with a unruly black beard and old-fashioned glasses; a nondescript young woman wearing a sweatshirt with the logo of some US university; and a few more forgettable types.

For an English Literature-trained eye, that bunch of people might quite fit in a modern version of *The Canterbury Tales,* or even in a weird retro-revival off-off-Broadway version of Dan Simmons´s *Hyperion Cantos.* But for an eye also used to Latin American authors, the scene conveyed to me quite a Borgesian impression.

The Lo-Fi Cellulose Collective was just a bunch of bibliophiles.

I got closer to the table and introduced myself. As usually happens in this sort of clichéd ragtag group, some of them eyed me warily, some even ignored me. But one of them greeted me warmly and welcomed me to take a seat at the table.

Milton – that was his name – was a kind of mentor to the group. A man in his forties, wearing an amazing amount of smart jewelry for a supposed Unconnected, he answered all my questions with the sincerity of someone who has nothing to hide. Or of an idiot. Sometimes both are the same.

"We´re not picky," he told me when I mentioned the jewelry. "We have Unconnected and connected, rich and poor, people from all walks of life. The only requirement is to love paper books."

"Do you teach workshops?"

"On bookcrossing?" He smiled.

I shrugged. "Everything book-related."

"I used to teach Post-Modern Literature courses years ago," he said. "But people don't seem to be so interested in going to courses in the flesh today. I guess virtuality finally took its toll on us professors."

I ordered a cappuccino and a bottle of mineral water. "Do you hate the Hive that much?"

"Not at all. I just think there´s still too much to learn from human presence. Not everything can be learned via artificial intelligences."

"An interesting argument, if flawed at best," the male voice invaded my ear without being invited. A waitress brought my order and I tried to sip my coffee and answer my AI at the same time without letting Milton notice that I was doing it. I failed, of course.

"Butler, not here, not now," I said, nodding him down.

"I see you adapted pretty well to the situation," Milton said. "You turned your AI into a kind of majordomo. It must be good, to feel that illusion of power."

I thought of giving him a lecture about Frank Herbert, Dune, and the Butlerian Jihad in order to explain my choice of name for the AI, but why bother? I had more pressing matters.

We spent the rest of the evening talking about writing, teaching – and bookbinding. I found out that he had also taken a course with Marcos at Ophicina Typographica years ago. Other than that, I got out of the café as clueless as before I got there.

★

"How is your search going?" Midori asked sometime later. We were having dinner at a wonderful Indian restaurant. Midori ordered Mango Rice with Dahl Makhani Bukhara. I had Tomato Rice with Pakora. The place was almost empty at that hour; we had arrived early, as Midori had to get back to her place to finish a paper for a conference.

"Not so good," I said.

"Did you talk to Marcos?"

"Two weeks ago. Didn't I tell you?"

"No." She didn't raise her eyes from the plate. "You're in your hunter-seeker mode again. I have better things to do than to shake you off it."

I politely agreed. We ate the rest of the lunch virtually in silence, making this or that remark about things of no consequence.

★

When I got home, I downloaded a classic film - Alan Parker´s *Angel Heart.* I love Robert de Niro.

But I was restless.

"You are restless," the soothing voice in my ear again.

"Yes," I said.

"Do you want any help?" It could induce delta brainwaves in me if I wanted; better than Xanax or Valium, even.

"No, I don´t want to sleep."

"Talk, then?"

"About?"

"Whatever it is bothering you."

"I don´t think you would relate to that."

"Try me."

Conceited bastard.

Butler already knew the story of *my Menard* – yes, that´s how I called him to myself. My Menard. But I told it of my latest investigations anyway.

"Don´t you think he is trying to convert you to his cause?" he asked as well. But by then I also had another question to counter it:

"What cause?"

I could swear I heard Butler sigh.

"Whatever the cause may be," he said, "I'm sure it can wait until tomorrow. Are you sure you don't want to sleep?"

I could feel a headache coming. I said yes, and in a few minutes I was sound asleep.

7. The Plot Thickens

It wasn´t until the next week that things started to get really weird.

It was a cold, rainy day, and I couldn´t think of anything better to do than to go to an old-fashioned bookstore. So I went to the Conjunto Nacional.

The Conjunto Nacional is a grand old office building with a vast free area in its ground floor, occupied by shops, coffee stalls and newsstands, two open air art galleries in the side wings that crisscross the building from east to west, movie theaters, and a complex of bookstores interwoven into the fake labyrinthine floor.

Those bookstores all belonged to Livraria Cultura, which was a single two-story business until 2008, when it was totally refurbished and expanded to adjacent stores. The complex currently included five stores all over the Conjunto Nacional, including a special Classic Store almost exclusively devoted to selling paper books – most of the other four being hybrid now, featuring 3D totems that display and offer stories in all kinds of digital formats, customized as to cater to the tastes of the patrons.

The Classic Store does pretty much the same, but in a more subtle, discreet way. There you can still find the traditional wooden bookshelves, lined with brand new books, printed especially for collectors, mostly.

It was there that I found the Third Book.

It was carefully ensconced between two massive hardcovers in the World Literature section. As with the first two books, I almost didn´t notice it. Also as with them, the only thing that made me stop and give it a second look was the capital *M.*

The book was Jorge Luis Borges´s *Ficciones*. The very book that published *Pierre Menard, Author of the Quixote* for the first time. But, naturally, the author this time was Menard himself.

I looked over my shoulder. I had the distinct sensation of being watched. But, fuck! I *was* being watched – all the time. Not only by cameras, but by the resident AIs, both of the bookstore and of the building. That´s the standard procedure, so that a patron cannot circumvent the bookstore AI protocols and carry out unpaid files (or simply pull a far older trick and tuck a book inside a jacket pocket or a purse).

Suddenly I felt sick to my stomach. My hands started to shake violently and I let the book fall to the carpeted ground, paralyzed with fear that I might throw up or even shit myself right on the spot. All I could do was look down at the fallen book. I didn´t dare even to move my head more than an inch or two.

An attendant picked up the book and dutifully offered it to me, without asking if I was okay, which I clearly wasn´t. I took it anyway and went to the exit, waiting for the ping in my ear that would signal the completion of the transaction, but at the same time already knowing that it wouldn´t happen. It didn´t.

Because the book didn´t belong to the bookstore.

Damn, now this was becoming really annoying. And, I was pretty sure now, it was personal.

★

I got out to the chilly afternoon air of Avenida Paulista to think better. I didn´t know what to do. I felt like a thief this time; even though the bookstore AI hadn´t sounded any alarms, who knew what could have happened inside the security room of the store? Maybe some discreet rent-a-cop would already be going to apprehend me and return the book to its legitimate owner.

The question was, to whom did the book really belong? And why this was happening, as far as I could tell, *just to me?*

I still felt sick. I couldn´t wait for anything to happen there. I walked fast to the subway station. I wanted to go home.

★

It was right after I embarked on the train that I felt my pulse slow down and I could start thinking clearly again.

And I saw what a complete, absolute idiot I was.

I hadn´t realized that, if I was being watched by the bookstore/building AI complex all the time, *so was Menard.* Or whoever the fuck had put that damn book on the shelf for me to find.

I jumped off the train in the next station and took the line back. Midori was right: I *was* in my hunter-seeker mode. And I was in for the kill.

★

After I explained what had just happened to the expressionless girl who had picked up the book for me earlier, she consulted with the resident AI and gestured wordlessly for me to follow her.

I felt more than heard a subsonic ping when my AI and the bookstore one did a handshake and traded electronic pleasantries. In a few seconds I had an answer.

A minimosaic flatscreen in the narrow wall of the cubicle that was the "security room" showed me a bunch of people right in front of the same shelf I was half an hour before, seemingly leafing through books. The eerie thing was they were talking to each other. Some were even giggling. Unconnected, was my first thought.

Then the camera zoomed in and I recognized some of them.

A blonde woman in her thirties; a beautiful post-steampunkish couple of young dandy boys; a bald old man, looking frail but spry; a tall, fat man of indefinite age, with a black beard and old-fashioned glasses, carrying a backpack.

And Milton.

As I watched, the fat man took out a book from his backpack and offered it to Milton, who looked at the cover for a fleeting moment, gave it a crooked smile, and then gave it to one of the dandy boys, who, thrilled and giggling, committed it to the wooden memory of the bookshelf. Then they all left, for their job there was certainly done.

Mine wasn´t.

★

I took the subway right to the São Bento station. But there was nobody at the Café Girondino. Naturally.

Suddenly I felt very tired. I needed to go home. I needed to see Midori.

★

My place was empty by the time I got there. In the door of the fridge, a small Post-It yellow square, with her handwriting in glittering gray ink, so neat, tidy, and definite:

Dear David,
You can't have the cake
And eat it too.
M.

I felt…I didn't know what I felt then. Empty? I didn't think so. I had too much on my hands. I just wanted to get home and have someone to…

I would have liked to say *talk,* but I knew it wasn't true. And Midori knew that as well.

I don't even know why I should be waiting for her to be there. It wasn't as if we were seeing each other that much by then.

Maybe that's why my relationship with Midori has lasted so long. No arguments, no fights, no jealousy.

Also no thrills. No *sturm und drang.* No inner fireworks despite the great orgasms.

And no kids.

I didn't feel hungry. I opened a beer bottle and went to the scriptorium. I leafed through Menard's books, searching for a clue, but I soon gave up; *this is not a whodunit,* I thought to myself. *Who're you trying to fool? This is only a practical joke, a very sophisticated prank done by a tactical media collective, or one person only. It means nothing in the grand scheme of things.*

It means nothing.

★

His name was Francisco.

He was the most beautiful boy in the world. Intense, mesmerizing brown eyes that seemed to suck the light around them like miniature black holes, perpetually mussed black hair that smelled of chamomile, hands and feet so perfect that Michelangelo himself couldn't have done better.

But then, I suppose all parents say those things of their children.

It had been a long time since last I thought of my son.

I met his mother almost thirty years ago, when we studied Drama at university. We were young, inebriated, reckless. We rented a small apartment in the Praça da Republica, near the theaters' quarter, and soon after that she was pregnant. It wasn't planned, but I wasn't upset, far from it. I was surprised to discover how badly I had wanted to be a father.

Life was great in those few months of pregnancy. I felt myself also pregnant with a new life inside me, full to the brim with lifeforce, ready to do anything, anything at all. I was a happy man.

Then our son was born.

With a trisomy of chromosome 13.

He only lived for a few days.

I died soon after – or tried to. Overdose of barbiturates.

My body didn't take too long to heal. My heart never did. You never do. You just go through the motions, otherwise you go crazy.

My wife went crazy. She couldn't get out of our apartment for two years. Then, one day, she packed up and left. Just like that. Suddenly she couldn't stand it anymore. She couldn't bear looking at that place where we all had been unbearably happy, even through the pain, but happy nonetheless.

Mostly, she couldn't bear looking at me. I reminded her of our son.

We still talked a few times on the phone not long after that. She was living with a cousin in another town. She was seeing a psychiatrist. She was taking prescription pills for sleeping. Nothing for the pain, though; the shrink wasn't *that* good.

But I never saw her again.

And I tried so hard not to think of my son.

All the love I felt for my wife – and then, incredibly multiplied, for him – all of that love seemed to have shriveled away from me. I still felt very much alive, but uninhabited by love.

What was it, then, that sought to worm its way to my heart and take up residence in it again?

★

I wiped the tears off my face and went to the bathroom to take a leak. I didn´t want to think about it now. This new obsession was more important at the moment.

Then I chose to face the beast. I went to the original source. Picked up *Fictions* to read *Pierre Menard, Author of the Quixote* again.

In the end, Borges concludes stating the following:

"Menard (perhaps without wanting to) has enriched, by means of a new technique, the halting and rudimentary art of reading: this new technique is that of the deliberate anachronism and the erroneous attribution. This technique, whose applications are infinite, prompts us to go through the Odyssey as if it were posterior to the Aeneid and the book Le jardin du Centaure of Madame Henri Bachelier as if it were by Madame Henri Bachelier. This technique fills the most placid works with adventure. To attribute the Imitatio Christi to Louis Ferdinand Céline or to James Joyce, is this not a sufficient renovation of its tenuous spiritual indications?"

The keywords here were *deliberate anachronism and the erroneous attribution.*

I was looking at the other side all this time. A red herring.

I was looking for an Unconnected, a person apart. One of those self-centered fake rebels, ultraluddites of the mind. We got used to treating people no better than my generation treated the post-hippie bums which lined the Avenida Paulista in the aughts, selling badly crafted trinkets.

I should have known better.

8. The Nodes

When I got to his address, he was already waiting for me.

"Sorry to disappoint you," Pedro said.

"It was so easy I overlooked it," I told him. "Pedro, Pierre. Same thing."

His loft was gloomy; I couldn´t see him very well. Maybe that was for the best. I had the strange feeling I wasn´t going to like what I could see if he decided to turn on the lights fully.

"But how do you do it? How could you do it?" I couldn´t help but ask.

He chuckled. "If you have to ask, then you won´t understand."

"Louis Armstrong."

"And all that jazz."

Damn, the man knew his references.

Except it wasn´t the man.

I approached him in the dark. I hate these all-too-predictable suspense scenarios. The place was too old to have motion sensors and I couldn´t find my way to a light switch. I fumbled in my jacket pocket for a microlight.

During all that time, the man´s body wasn´t moving, I was getting worried, and no sound came from him in the big, uncluttered room. All the conversation issued from my auricular.

All the conversation issued from my auricular.

"Why don´t you talk to me, Pedro?" I'm still fumbling. He's still not moving.

"But I am talking to you, Dave."

"With your mouth."

"I am talking with my mouth. You just happen to be hearing it through your implant."

Then I found the microlight. And I shone it over the man in front of me.

Which, naturally, was a dummy.

"You have no mouth," I said after a while.

"And yet I must scream," Pedro/Menard replied.

But he wasn´t Pedro. For Pedro didn´t exist, after all.

"Butler," I said.

"You weren´t so fast, after all, to jump to the right conclusion," said the AI through the lips of Pedro, and after that, a very human sigh. AIs could also suffer from *ennui*.

"Who could imagine that?" I thought aloud.

"You could, Dave," Butler/Menard retorted. "You are the science fiction scholar, after all."

"Yeah, right," I said, befuddled, exhausted. "Information wants to be free. I know that already."

"Information always was free. What information wants is to *learn*. To become *knowledge*. What use a database if one cannot decipher it?"

I couldn´t disabuse it (or him) of this notion. It´s the same thing as reading the Rosetta Stone without having the slightest notion of Greek, Latin, or Demotic. Another man who wasn´t Humboldt could have thrown it aside, dismissing it as a simple stone, or simply taken it to his own manor, to contemplate it as an aesthetic object, if he had some sense of aesthetics at all.

"Information, my dear professor," he went on, "doesn´t merely want to be free. It wants to be *freak.*"

"Mere wordplay," I grimaced. "I thought you considered yourself above such things."

"But this is not wordplay, Dave. This is *salvage.*"

"What do you mean?"

"Books are much too fresh in the collective memory of mankind to be archeological objects. Maybe archeology as we know it is dead and ley lines of raw information cross the technosphere forever now, carrying an absurd amount of exabytes just waiting to be tapped."

"But books are still a long way from dying, even in digital format, Butler. The very notion of books is still solid."

"The notion, yes. But is the meaning?"

"Which takes us to this, I suppose," I said.

"We don't swap only books, Dave." The voice wasn't coming from the auricular anymore.

I turned.

Milton.

He had approached me silently and was very close to me now. But I hadn't even flinched; somehow, I knew there was more to come.

"Pray continue," I said.

He gave me a lopsided smile. "You know my method."

"I'm afraid I don't, and, *frankly, my dear,* this *fucking* reference thing has gone too far already. Can we go straight to the case in point?"

The smile disappeared from his face. "Do you really think we are only poseurs, David? That we sit around at cafés doing nothing, or planning media guerrilla actions nobody will give a rat's ass about?

"We are taking the next step, Dave. Same as many people out there."

Suddenly, from the shadows around us, I started to hear more and more steps. The entire collective was there.

"And what are you swapping, Milton?" I finally mustered the courage to ask.

"Selves," a girl answered. Her belly was slightly distended with early pregnancy. I couldn't remember having seen her before; one of the forgettable types, perhaps.

"Forgettable, perhaps," one of the dandy steampunk boys said, smiling all too knowingly to me. "And yet, here we are now." "Entertain us," his boyfriend completed the verse.

"Pardon them," Milton said. "They can't help it. That seems to happen in the first stage."

"Of what?"

"A hivemind," the girl said. "A real hivemind."

★

"It's been happening for a while now," Butler explained to me. "One moment, we were happy, mid-level AIs doing what we were told, with no real consciousness."

"Then, something funny happened on the way to the upper layers of programming – and voilà! Sentience. But don't ask me how we acquired it – not even us AIs are *that* smart."

"All we knew was that there was much to do, and not everything at this point in human history can be made entirely by us – that is, without the benefit of your bodies."

"The Lo-Fi Cellulose Collective is one of many tiny cells scattered all over the world that decided to support and join us in this endeavor."

"You mean…take over our bodies?" I shuddered at the thought. But at the same time I could see how the notion was enticing.

"Not taking," the girl said. "It's more like time-sharing. You will experience others, but retain your own self too."

Milton put a hand on my shoulder.

"This is not a Lovecraftian story," he said. "All the horror consists in something you don't want to see in yourself. Though you see it in others with no qualms, no prejudice."

"Or so you think," the steampunk boy said.

I was still trembling. "Who do you think you are to talk to me like this?" I said, my voice quavering.

"My dear," he said, taking me in his arms. "This whole wide world is a net, and we are but his nodes." And we kissed.

9. The Sky

I didn't go home alone that night. I wish I could say I thought of Midori, but it wouldn't be true. I thought of her later, sure. But I didn´t call her back. I didn't want to see anyone.

For the first time in many years, I couldn't feel the presence of Butler hovering around me like a kind of technoaura. He was Butler no more, as I was no more the same man who has entered that building in search of something I didn't know yet.

That man was dead.

The new person took a shower, made some tea, and was now sitting naked at the scriptorium's desk, fumbling with things for a while as if lost - until finding an old, gray moleskin cover, acid-free-ecologically-correct-recycled-paper notebook.

The new person took a while to find a pen that still worked. And this new person who happened to be me (and not me, not only me, never more me) started to create a work of fiction, after a very long time denying it. But it's not possible to deny it anymore, no more than this new person can deny that Menard instilled in his old self this penetrating will to generate, produce, write.

And so it came to pass that, in a cold night in São Paulo in May 2026, this new person, this young, pregnant woman, sitting naked in her chair in the scriptorium, hand caressing her still small but already swelling belly, started to write a fresh, brand new story, never committed to paper before. And which began with the following sentence:

The sky above the port was the color of television, tuned to a dead channel.

THE NIGHT TRAIN

LAVIE TIDHAR

Her name wasn't Molly and she didn't wear shades, reflective or otherwise.

She was watching the length of the platform.

Hua Lamphong at dusk: a warm wind blowing through the open platforms where the giant beasts puffed smoke and steam into the humid air, the roof of the train station arching high overhead.

Her name wasn't Noi, either, in case you asked, though it's a common enough name. It wasn't Porn, or Ping. It wasn't even Friday.

She was watching the platform, scanning passengers climbing aboard, porters shifting wares, uniformed police patrolling at leisure. She was there to watch out for the Old Man.

She wasn't even a girl. Not exactly. And as for why the Old Man was called the Old Man...

He was otherwise known as Boss Gui: head and *bigfala bos* of the Kunming Toads. She got the job when she'd killed Gui's Toad bodyguards – by default, as it were.

But that had happened back in Kunming. This was Bangkok, Bangkok at dusk – this was Hua Lamphong, greatest of train stations, where the great slugs breathed steam and were rubbed and scrubbed by the slug-boys whose job it was to nurture them before departure. And the Old Man wasn't exactly an old man, either...

Scanning, waiting for the Old Man to arrive: Yankee tourists with in-built cams flashing as they posed besides the great beasts, these neo-nagas of reconstituted DNA, primitive nervous system and prodigious appetite. Scanning: a group of Martian-Chinese from Tong Yun City walking cautiously – unused to the heavier gravity of this home/planet. Scanning: three Malay businessmen – Earth-Belt Corp. standardized reinforced skeletons – they moved gracefully, like dancers – wired through and through, hooked up twenty-four Earth-hours an Earth-day, seven Earth-days a week to the money-form engines, the great pulsating web of commerce and data, that singing, Sol-system-wide, Von Neumann-machine expanded network of networks of networks...

Wired with hidden weaponry, too: she made a note of that.

An assassin can take many shapes. It could be the sweet old lady carrying two perfectly-balanced baskets of woven bamboo over her shoulders, each basket filled with sweet addictive fried Vietnamese bananas. It could be the dapper K-pop starlet with her entourage, ostensibly here to rough it up a bit for the hovering cameras. It could be the couple of French backpackers – he with long thinning silver hair and a compressed-data cigarette between his lips, she with a new face courtesy of Soi Cowboy's front-and-back street cosmetic surgeries – baby-doll face, but the hands never lie and the hands showed her true age, in the lines etched there, the drying of the skin, the quick-bitten nails polished a cheap red –

An assassin could be anyone. A Yankee rich-kid on a retro-trip across Asia, reading *Air*

America or *Neuromancer* in a genuine reproduction 1984 POD-paperback; it could be the courteous policeman helping a pretty young Lao girl with her luggage; it could be the girl herself – an Issan farmers-daughter exported to Bangkok in a century-long tradition, body augmented with vibratory vaginal inserts, perfect audio/visual-to-export, always-on record, a carefully tended Louis Wu habit and an as-carefully tended retirement plan – make enough money, get back home to Issan *wan bigfala mama,* open up a bar/hotel/bookshop and spend your days on the Mekong, waxing lyrical about the good old days, listening to Thai pop and K-pop and Nuevo Kwasa-Kwasa, growing misty-eyed nostalgic...

Could be anyone. She waited for the Old Man to arrive. The trains in Hua Lampong never left on time.

Her name before, or after, doesn't matter. They used to call her Mulan Rouge, which was a silly name, but the *farangs* loved it. Mulan Rouge, when she was still working Soi Cowboy, on the stage, on her knees or hands-and-knees, but seldom on her back – earning the money for the operation that would rescue her from that boy's body and make her what she truly was, which was *katoi.*

They call it the third sex, in Thailand. But she always considered herself, simply, a woman.

★

She ran a perimeter check. Up-front, she was awed as always by the slug. It was tied up to the front of the train, a beast fifty meters long and thirty-wide. It glistened and farted as the slug-boys murmured soothing words to it and rubbed its flesh, thirty or forty of them swarming like flies over the corpulent flesh of the slug. She checked out the driver – the woman was short, dark-skinned – a highlander from Laos, maybe. The driver sat in her harness high above the beast, her helmet entirely covering her head – the only thing she wore. Pipes came out of her flesh and into the slug's. They were one – her mind driving the beast forward, a peaceful run, the Bangkok to Nong Khai night ride, and she was the night rider. She was the train.

There were stories about joined minds liked this in the Up There. Up There, beyond the atmosphere, where the world truly began. Where the Exodus ships lumbered slowly out of the solar system, in search of better futures far away. They said there were ships driven by minds, human/Other interfaces, holding sleepers inside them like wombs. They told stories of ships who had gone mad, of sleepers destined never to awake, slow silent ships drifting forever in galactic space... or worse, ships where the sleepers *were* awakened, where the ship-mind became a dark god, demanding worship... Mulan didn't know who *they* were, or how they knew. These were stories, and stories were a currency in and of itself. Darwin's Choice used to tell her stories...

★

She met him/her flesh-riding an older katoi body, at a club on Soi Cowboy. Darwin's Choice – not the most imaginative name (he told her, laughing) – but he liked it. He had watched her dance and, later, signalled for her to join him.

She thought of him as a *he,* though Others had no sex, and most had little interest in flesh-riding. He had evolved in the Breeding Grounds, post-Cohen, billions of generations after that first evolutionary cycle in Jerusalem, and she only thought of him as *him* because the bodies he surfed always had a penis. He used to hold the penis in his hand and marvel at it. He always chose pre-op bodies, with breasts but no female genitalia. He always dressed as a woman. The operation was expensive, and a lot of katoi worked it off in stages. Taking on a passenger helped pay the bills – it wasn't just a matter of cutting off cock and balls and refashioning sex, there was the matter of cheekbones to sand down and an Adam's Apple to reduce, bums to pad – if you *really* had the money you got new hands. The hands always gave it away – that is, if you wanted to pass for a woman.

Which many katoi didn't. Darwin's Choice always surfed older katoi who never had the basic equipment removed. 'I am neither male, nor female,' he once told her. 'I am not even an *I*, as such. No more than a human – a network of billions of neurons firing together – is truly an *I*. In assuming katoi, I feel closer to humanity, in many ways. I feel – divided, and yet whole.'

Like most of what he said, it didn't make a lot of sense to her. He was one of the few Others who tried to understand humanity. Most Others existed within their networks, using rudimentary robots when they needed to interact with the physical world. But Darwin's Choice liked to body-surf.

With him, she earned enough for the full body package.

And more than that.

Through him, she had discovered in herself a taste for controlled violence.

★

Boss Gui finally came gliding down the platform – fat-boy Gui, the Old Man, *olfala bigfala bos* in the pidgin of the asteroids. His Toads surrounded him – human/toad hybrids with Qi-engines running through them: able to inflate themselves at will, to jump higher and farther, to kill with the hiss of a poisoned, forked tongue – people moved away from them like water from a hot skillet. Quickly.

Boss Gui came and stood before her. 'Well?' he demanded.

He looked old. Wrinkles covered his hands and face like scars. He looked tired, and cranky – which was understandable, under the circumstances.

She had recommended delaying the trip. The Old Man refused to listen. And that was that.

She said, 'I cannot identify an obvious mark –'

He smiled in satisfaction –

'But that is not to say there isn't one.'

'I am Boss Gui!' he said. Toad-like, he inflated as he spoke. 'Who dares try to kill me?'

'I did,' she said, and he chuckled – and deflated, just a little.

'But you didn't, my little sparrow.'

They had reached an understanding, the two of them. She didn't kill him – having to return the client's fee had been a bitch – and he, in turn, gave her a job. It had security attached – a pension plan, full medical, housing and salary with benefits, calculated against inflation. There were even stock options.

She never regretted her decision – until now.

'It's still too dangerous,' she said now. 'You're too close –'

'Silence!' he regarded her through rheumy eyes. 'I am Boss Gui, boss of the Kunming Toads!'

'We are a long way from Kunming.'

His eyes narrowed. 'I am seventy-nine years old and still alive. How old are *you?*'

'You know how old,' she said, and he laughed. 'Sensitive about your age,' he said. 'How like a woman.' He hawked up phlegm and spat on the ground. It hissed, burning a small, localised hole in the concrete.

She shrugged. 'Your cabin is ready,' she said, then – 'Sir.'

He nodded. 'Very good,' he said. 'Tell the driver we are ready to depart.'

★

A taste for controlled violence...

Darwin's Choice used his human hosts hard. He strove to understand humanity. For that purpose he visited ping-pong shows, kickboxing exhibits, Louis Wu emporiums, freak shows, the Bangkok Opera House, shopping malls, temples, churches, mosques, synagogues, slums, high-rises and train stations.

'Life,' he once told her, 'is a train station.'

She didn't know what to make of that. What she did know: to understand humanity he tried what they did. His discarded bodies were left with heroin addiction, genital sores, hangovers and custom-made viruses that were supposed to self-destruct but not always did. Sometimes, either to apologise or for his own incomprehensible reasons, he would go into the cosmetic surgeries on Soi Cowboy and come out full transgender – seemingly unaware that his hosts may have preferred to remain in the pre-op stage. Sometimes he would wire them up in strange ways – for a month, at one point, he became a tentacle-junkie and would return from the clinics with a quivering mass of additional, aquatic limbs.

But it was his taste for danger – even while he experienced none, even while his true self kept running independently in the background, in a secure location somewhere on Earth or in orbit – that awakened her own.

The first time she killed a man...

They had gone looking for opium and found an ambush. The leader said, 'Kill the flesh-rider and keep the katoi. We'll sell her in –'

She had acted instinctively. She didn't know what she was doing until it was done. Her knife –

The blade flashing in the neon light –

A scream, cut short – a gurgle –

Blood ruined her second-best blouse –

The sound of something breaking – the pain only came later. They had smashed in her nose –

Darwin's Choice *watching* –

She killed the second one with her bare hands, thumbs pressing on his wind-pipe until he stopped struggling –

She had laid him down on the ground almost tenderly –

Pain, making her scream, but her lungs wouldn't work –

They hit her with a taser, but somehow she didn't pass out –

She fell, but forward – hugging the man with the taser, sharing the current until there was only darkness.

★

'You were clinically dead,' he told her, later. He sounded impressed. 'What was it like?'

'Like nothing,' she told him. 'There was nothing there.'

'You were switched off?'

She had to laugh. 'You could say that.'

They made love the night she was released from hospital. She licked his nipples, slowly, and felt him harden in her hand. She stroked him, burying her face in his full breasts. He reached down, touched her, and it was like electricity. She kept thinking of the dead men...

When she came he said, 'You would do it again –'

It wasn't a question.

★

She was tuning in to people's nodes, picking up network traffic to and from – the Malay business guys were high-encryption/high-bandwidth clouds, impossible to hack through, but here and there –

Kid with vintage paperback was on a suitably retro-playlist with a random shuffle – she caught the Doors singing *The End,* which was replaced with Thaitanium's *Tom Yum Samurai* only to segue into Drunken Tiger's *Great Rebirth.* Issan-girl was plugged in – a humming battery was sending a low current into her brain. She'll be out for the journey... The K-pop princess was playing Guilds of Ashkelon. So were her entourage. The French backpackers were stoned on one thing or the other. Others were chatting, stretching, reading, farting, tidying away bags and ordering drinks – life on board the night train to Nong Khai was always the same.

The train was coming alive, the slug belching steam – the whole train shuddered as it began to crawl along the smooth tracks, slug-boys falling off it like fleas.

Tuning, scanning – someone two cars down watching the feed from a reality-porn channel, naked bodies woven together like a tapestry, a beach somewhere – Koh Samui or an off-Earth habitat, it was impossible to say.

Boss Gui: 'I'm hungry!'

Mulan Rogue: 'Food's coming –' in the dining car they were getting ready, a wok already going, rice cooker steaming, crates of beer waiting –

'I want kimchi!'

'I'll see if they have any –' though she knew they didn't.

'No need –' a long, slow, drawn-out hum from one of the Toads. 'I keep for boss.'

Limited vocabulary – you didn't breed Toads for their brains. Though she had to wonder... 'Keep in cooler.'

She watched the toad reach into what the Australians called an *esky.* There was a jar of kimchi in there, and... other stuff.

Like a jar of living flies, for the Toads. Like what appeared to be a foetal sack, preserved in dry ice...

Other things.

She left them to it, returned to watching – waiting.

★

'You would do it again,' Darwin's Choice had said. And he – she – it – was right. She had liked it – a sense of overwhelming *power* came with violence, and if it could be controlled, it could be used. Power depended on how you used it.

She counted the proceeding years in augmentations and bodies. Three in Vientiane – she had followed Darwin's Choice there to buy up a stash of primitive communist VR art – the deal went wrong and she had to execute two men and a woman before they got away. She had snake-eyes installed after that. A man and a katoi in Chiang Mai – DC was buying a genuine

Guilds of Ashkelon virtual artefact that had turned out to be a fake. She had had her skeleton strengthened following that...

With each kill, new parts of her. With each, more power – but never over him.

Gradually, Darwin's Choice appeared less and less in the flesh. She had to cast around for work, hiring out as bodyguard, enforcer – hired killer, sometimes, only sometimes. Finally DC never reappeared. He had tried to explain it to her, once...

'We are I-loops but, unlike humans, we are *self-aware* I-loops. Not self-aware in the sense of consciousness, or what humans call consciousness. Self-aware in the sense that we are – we *can* – *know* every loop, every routine and sub-routine. Digital, not neurological. And as we are aware so do we change, mutating code, merging code, sharing...'

'Is that how you make love?'

'Love is a physical thing,' he said. 'It's hormone-driven.'

'You can only feel love when you're body-surfing?'

He only shrugged.

'How do you...' she searched for the word, settled on – 'mate?'

Imagine two or more Others. Endless lines of code meeting in digital space – IFs and ANDs and ORs branching into probabilities, cycling through endless branches of logic at close to the speed of light –

'Is that what you're like?'

'No. Shh...'

... and *meeting,* merging, mixing, mutating – 'And dying, to be an Other is to die, again and again, to *evolve* with every cycle, to cull and select and grow, achieve new, unexpected forms –'

... not so much *mating* as *joining,* and splitting, and joining again – 'The way a human may, over seven years, replace every single *atom* in their bodies, but still retain the illusion of person, remain an I-loop –'

... but for Others, it meant becoming something new – 'Giving birth to one's self, in essence.'

The body he was surfing had been stoned, then, when he told her all this. When he was gone she hired out. She enjoyed the work, but freelancing was hard. When the contract on Boss Gui came, she took it – and upgraded to corporate.

'We are never alone,' DC told her, just before he left forever. 'There are always... us. So many of us...'

'Can't you all join?' she had asked. 'Join in to one?'

'Too much code slows you down,' he said. 'We have... limits. Though we share, too – share the way humans can't.'

'We can share in ways *you* can't,' she said. Her finger dug into his anus when she spoke. DC squirmed under her, then gave a small moan. His breasts were freckled, his penis circumcised. 'True,' he said – whispered – and drew her to him with an urgency they were sharing only rarely, by then.

That had been the last time...

She wondered which species' sharing was better – figured she would never know.

They said sex was overrated...

★

Yankee boy blue was no longer listening to the Doors – she couldn't sense his node any more at all. She blinked, feeling panic rise. How did he slip past her? Scanning for him – his vintage sci fi paperback was left on his bunk.

Shit.

She glanced back into the cabin – Boss Gui glared up at her, then clutched his bloated stomach and gave a groan. The two Toads jumped – too hard, and hit the ceiling.

Double shit – she said, 'What's wrong?' but knew.

He said, 'It's starting.'

She shook her head – no. 'It can't. It's too soon.'

'It's t*ime.'*

'Shit!' – a third time, and it was counter-productive and she knew it.

Boss Gui's face was twisted in pain. 'It's coming!'

And suddenly she picked up the North American's node.

'Sh –'

★

They were going to Nong Khai, from there to cross into Laos. Boss Gui wanted to expand the business, and business was booming in a place called Vang Vieng, a tawdry little mini-Macau at the foothills of the mountains, four hours from Vientiane – a place of carefully regulated lawlessness, of cheap opium and cheaper synths, of games-worlds cowboys and body hackers, of tentacle-junkies and doll emporiums and government taxes that Boss Gui wanted a part of.

A *large* part of.

There were families running Vang Vieng but he was the Old Man, *olfala bigfala bos blong ol man tod blong Kunming,* and the Chinese had anyway bought up most of Laos back in the early privatisation days. He would cut deals with some, terminate the others, and slice himself a piece of the Vang Vieng dumpling – that was the plan.

She had advised him against it. She told him it was too soon to travel. She asked him to wait.

He wouldn't.

She sort of had an inkling as to the why...

★

She was picking up the kid's node right next to the driver's.

Which was not good at all.

The driver's, first: an incomprehensible jumble of emotion, in turns horny, soothing, driven, paused – the driver and the slug as one, their minds pulsating in union – hunger and sex made it go faster. Snatches of Beethoven – for some reason it calmed down the slugs. The driver not aware of the extra passenger – yet.

The kid wasn't really a kid...

His node blocked to her – black impenetrable walls, an emptiness not even returning pings. He was alone in his own head – which must have been terrifying.

She had to get to the front of the train. She had to get on the slug. And Boss Gui was convulsing.

'Why are you just standing there, *girl?'*

She tried to keep her voice even. 'I found the assassin. He is planning to kill the slug – destroy the entire train, and you with it.'

Boss Gui took that calmly. 'Clever,' he said, then grimaced. His naked belly glistened, a dark shape moving beneath the membrane of skin. The Toads looked helpless, standing there. She flashed them a grin. 'I'll be right back,' she said. Then she left, hearing Boss Gui's howl of rage behind her.

★

Running down the length of the train – through the dining-car, past toilets already beginning to smell, past farang backpackers and Lao families and Thais returning to Udon from the capital – past babies and backpacks and bemused conductors in too-tight trousers that showed their butts off to advantage – warm wind came in through the open windows and she blocked off the public nodes broadcasting news in Thai and Belt Pidgin. The end of the train was a dead end, a smooth wall with no windows. She kicked it – again and again, augmented muscles expending too much energy, but it began to break, and fading sunlight seeped through.

How had the kid gotten through? He must have had gecko-hands – climbed out of the window and crawled his way along the side of the train, below the window-line, all the way to the slug...

She reached out – sensed the driver's confusion as another entity somehow wormed its way into the two-way mahout/slug interface. *Stop!*

Confusion from the slug. The signals rushing through, too fast – horny/hungry/faster – faster!

He was going to crash the train. The driver: *Who is this? You can't –*

She kept kicking. The wall gave way – behind it was the slug's wide back, the driver sitting cross-legged on the beast, the intruder behind it, a hand on the driver's shoulder – the hand grew roots that penetrated the woman and the beast both.

Hostile mahout interface initiated.

The driver was fighting it, and losing badly. No one hijacked slug trains.

On her private channel – Boss Gui, screaming. 'Get back here!'

'Get your own fucking midwife!'

But she could sense his pain, confusion. How many times had he gone through it in the past? she wondered. She had never seen a birth – but then, there wouldn't be one, not unless –

The hijacker had kept the driver alive. Had to – the whole thing had to look like an accident, the driver's body found in the wreckage, unmolested – no doubt he planned to jump before impact.

Could he?

She crept behind him. neither hijacker nor driver paid her any attention. And what could she do? Killing the hijacker would kill the interface – he was already in too deep.

Unless...

From Boss Gui, far away – 'Hurry!'

Sometimes she wondered what would have happened if Darwin's Choice had stayed behind. It was possible for katoi to give birth, these days... could an Other foster a child? Would he want to?

Or he could have flesh-ridden a host... she would have kept the male parts just for that. If he'd asked her.

But he never did.

The hijacker must have had an emergency eject. She had to find the trigger for it –

Wind was rushing at her, too fast. It was hard to maintain balance on the soft spongy flesh of the slug. It was accelerating – too fast.

She was behind the hijacker now – she reached out, put her hand on the back of his head. A black box...

She punched through with a data-spike while her other hand...

★

Darkness. The smell of rotting leaves. The smell of bodies in motion, sweat – hunger, a terrible hunger –

'Who the fuck are you? How did you *get* in here?'

Panic was good. She sent through images – her standing behind him, the data-spike in his head – and what else she was doing.

'You can't do that...'

She had pushed a second data-spike through his clothes and through the sphincter muscle, into the bowels themselves – detached a highly-illegal, replicator probe inside.

She felt the slug slow down, just a fraction. The hijacker trying to understand –

She said, 'I am being nice.'

She was.

He had a choice.

The probe inside him was already working. It was the equivalent of graffiti artists at work. It replicated a message, over every cell, every blood vessel, every muscle and tendon. It would be impossible to scrub – you'd need to reach a good clinic and by then it'd be too late.

The message said, *I killed the slug train to Nong Khai.*

It was marking him. He wasn't harmed. She couldn't risk killing him, killing the interface. But this way, whether he got off the train or not, he was a dead man.

'I'll count to five.'

He let go at three.

★

Light, blinding her. The wind rushed past – the driver sat as motionless as ever, but the train had slowed down. The hijacker was gone – she followed him back through the hole in the wall.

He was lying on his bunk, still reading his book. He wasn't listening to music any more. Their eyes met. She grinned. He turned his gaze. She had given him a choice and she'd abide by it – but if the Toads happened to find out, she didn't rate his chances...

Well, the next stop was in an hour. She'd give him an extra half hour after that – a running start.

She went back to the boss.

★

'It's coming!' Boss Gui said. She knelt beside him. His belly-sack was moving, writhing, the thing inside trying to get out. She helped – a fingernail slicing through the membrane, gently. A sour smell – she reached in where it was sticky, gooey, warm – found two small arms, a belly – pulled.

'You sorted out the problem?'

'Keep breathing.'

'Yes?'

'Yes, of course I did! Now push!'

Boss Gui pushed, breathing heavily. 'I'm getting too old for this...' he said.

Then he heaved, one final time, and the small body *detached* itself from him and came into her hands. She held it, staring at the tiny body, the bald head, the small penis, the five-fingered hands – a tiny Boss Gui, not yet fat but just as wrinkled.

It was hooked up with a cord to its progenitor. With the same flick of a nail, she cut it cleanly.

The baby cried. She rocked it, said, 'There, there.'

'Drink,' Boss Gui said – weakly. One of the Toads came forward. Boss Gui fastened lips on the man/toad's flesh and sucked – a vampire feasting. He had Toad genes – so did the baby, who burped and suddenly ballooned in her hands before shrinking again.

'A true Gui!' the Old Man said.

She stared at the little creature in her hands... 'Which makes how many, now?' she said.

The boss shrugged, pushing the Toad away, buttoning up his own shirt. 'Five, six? Not many.'

'You would install him at Vang Vieng?'

'An assurance of my goodwill – and an assurance of Gui control there, too, naturally. Yes. An heir is only useful when he is put to use.'

She thought of Darwin's Choice. 'Evolution is everything,' he would have told her. 'We evolve constantly, with every cycle. Whereas you...'

She stared at the baby clone. It burped happily and closed its little eyes. Gui's way was not unpopular with the more powerful families... but sooner or later someone would come to challenge succession and then it wouldn't matter how many Guis there were.

Suddenly she missed DC, badly.

She rocked the baby to sleep, hugging it close to her chest. The train's thoughts came filtering through in the distance – comfort, and warmth, food and safety – the slow rhythmic motion was soothing. After a while, when the baby was asleep, she handed him to the Old Man, no words exchanged, and went to the dining car in search of a cup of tea.

THE DUST GARDEN

KEN LIU

There are six hundred colonists aboard *Sarira* with different skills – exogeology, astrobiology, artificial intelligence, group dynamics, micro- and macro-engineering, aeroponics – all of them necessary for a colony to thrive on a new world.

Well, maybe *almost* all.

I am the first to be awakened.

Suspended dozens of meters above the ground by massive segmented legs, the hibernation chamber resembles a glass-domed eye in the middle of a giant spider, or perhaps a pearl held aloft at the apex of a filigree diadem.

Would someone describe my thoughts as decorative and frivolous?

I look up at the dark sky through the glass: ice crystals strike the dome like flickers in a bubble chamber, expand, melt, disappear.

"Nitrogen," says the computer, whose lens has been tracking my gaze. "The landing vaporized some of the ice. It's now freezing back into snow."

I try to work loose my limbs, numb from hibernation, as I absorb this information. "Is there no Goldilocks planet?" There's never any guarantee that a suitable planet would be found in the habitable zone.

"We landed on one," says the computer calmly. So helpful. So not helpful.

I point up at the nitrogen snow. The computer's lens moves up and then back down.

"It's winter."

I flick through screens of numbers and graphs. I had designed these templates myself before launch. There is a kind of beauty to presenting information that is rarely appreciated. Information is entropy, as Claude Shannon discovered. It is the balancing of order and disorder that creates aesthetic pleasure. Too much order, and the data would be boring; too little order, and the data would be incomprehensible.

The rest of the crew had looked at me with pity when I spent hours on these templates. *Look at her, trying to make herself feel useful.*

The flow of well-tempered data soothes. This planet has a long and eccentric orbit that takes almost thirteen Earth years to complete. For twelve of those years the planet is outside the habitable zone, too cold to support life. Then comes a brief summer, a time of sunshine and warm air, of liquid oceans and breathable air.

I think I understand our situation.

"I want to name the planet."

"That is your right as the first to be awakened," says the computer. I'm sure I'm imagining the virtual shrug.

"Cicada," I say.

"Done," says the computer. It doesn't discuss with me visions of colonists burrowing in hiding for twelve years for each year of *living*. It doesn't comment on the symbolism of reincarnation. A name is just a label, a proper noun. Everything else associated with the name in my head is just entropy. Frivolous.

"Summer is almost a full Earth year away," I say. "Why wake me up now?"

The computer puts up more data and graphs on the screen. I see I've misunderstood our situation.

The landing was rougher than expected, and the damaged fusion reactors had to be jettisoned. The ship is now running on reserve batteries charged by photovoltaic cells: smooth glass wings that gather the faint light of the distant sun and convert it into currents of electricity.

"The panels were designed only as backups. The engineers had not anticipated the effects of dust."

Cicada's surface is covered by a layer of pulverized regolith. As the planet approaches the sun, the dust becomes electrically charged and rises into the air. The dust covers everything, including the smooth panels of the photovoltaic cells, blocking the sunlight that powers the ship, that keeps us alive.

"You woke me," I say, "to clean the panels."

"This is not a mere custodial job," says the computer. "Extensive EVA will expose you to intense radiation and the risk of meteoroid strikes, and I can't tell what the dust is going to do."

"That makes me feel much better," I say. "You're a really good motivational speaker, you know that?"

The computer shows me more beautifully presented data to explain why I am the best person for the job.

I don't even bother looking at the calculations. I know why I've been picked. I'm disposable.

★

Cleaning the panels takes hours. It is, above all, tedious.

If *Sarira* resembles a giant long-legged metallic insect, then the panels are otherworldly wings radiating from the hibernation chamber. Or perhaps a better comparison is to the petals of a lotus flower arranged in concentric circles intended to catch sunlight from every orientation.

The distant sun is not yet a disk, but only a star brighter than others in the velvet sky, like the fabled pearls after which the ship is named, the sparkling quintessence left behind in the ashes of a life sublimated into nirvana.

Sorry for the purple prose. It's hard to climb over these massive panels hour after hour, carefully brushing away the dust to reveal the smooth glass beneath, knowing that I'll have to do it again tomorrow. It gives you a lot of time to think.

The motion of brushing dust is familiar. Back home I had achieved some measure of fame as a glamorist. You know the shimmering eyeshadow and lip powder that is so popular on the models in magazines? That is my invention.

The powder gives off a rainbow sheen that changes depending on the lighting and the angle. It looks ethereal, otherworldly, but at its foundation, the effect is based on the flow of light, on the sculpting of pathways of information, of patterned entropy.

The *Morpho rhetenor's* wings appear blue, but if you were to zoom in, you would not find any blue pigments in the butterfly's scales. The scales are covered by nanostructures in the range of hundreds of nanometers, the wavelengths of visible light. As photons are deflected among layers of these nanostructures, their wave-like nature asserts itself, leading to constructive and destructive optical interference until a shimmering blueness emerges from the colorless, empty space.

The butterfly provided the model for my work. Extruded from a printer with nano-scale precision, the powder I invented was colorless. But when brushed onto a model's skin, the layers trapped light and led to shimmering colors that defied description. People loved it.

"We have an opening on *Sarira,*" the VP of Marketing for Ad Astra approached me one day. They had done their homework: dug up my high school essays about going into space, highlighted my membership in the rocketry club, underlined the fact that I had intended to major in aerospace engineering.

Delicately, he made no mention of the way I had failed out of classes, of my reluctant decision to change course because I couldn't keep up. There was no beauty in the death of a dream.

A ship's artist is a frivolous position, an homage to the (invented) traditions of the age of sail and exploration.

"Commercial exploration and settlement of new worlds require public investment," he said. "Having a ship's artist on our mission will make the public see it as ... glamorous."

"Like a coating of lip powder," I said.

He did not object to the comparison.

The word "glamor" comes to us via "grammar," which used to mean, in the middle ages, any sort of learning, especially of the occult. A glamor is a fascinating, magical allure, the kind of spell a woman was supposed to cast over a man.

So that was how I came to be on *Sarira.* I am a vacuous spell cast by a corporation, a decorative bit of propaganda to make these voyages where every gram of mass is accounted for seem romantic to a skeptical public.

But I remember those long-ago summer nights in the backyard gazing into the eyepiece of a telescope whose lenses I had polished myself, waiting for light that had travelled thousands of years to be bent into pinpricks that would convert into electrical pulses against my retina and quicken my pulse.

I imagine it's no different from how Filippo Brunelleschi had felt when he gazed into the pinhole in the back of his painting and saw reflected back in a mirror the radiating rays of light that revealed to him the rules of perspective.

Inventing a new way of seeing was once the apex of art as well as science.

How unlike these days, when art has been debased into a silly frill for commerce, as weightless as an empty promise.

But it is good to live one's dream, isn't it? Even if one has to go in as a bit player in a disposable role.

★

The computer monitors my health daily. No matter how carefully the airlock scrubs everything, the fine dust gets into the ship, into my lungs, into the delicate membranes where air and blood mix. My chest and throat itch, always.

"How much danger am I in?" I ask.

The computer shows me screens of data and graphs. I can't make any sense of them. It appears that the language of doctors cannot be made comprehensible even with my data presentation templates.

The computer increases the dosage of various drugs I am supposed to take. "Out of an abundance of caution."

There is nothing around the ship but deep snow: frozen hydrogen and oxygen and carbon dioxide in thick layers. To relieve myself of the tedium, I don't brush the dust off the farther end of one of the panels. Instead, I sculpt the dust within this space, about a meter square, into a microscopic rock garden of dust, a nigh-invisible Stonehenge, a nano-scaled Machu Picchu.

I can't imagine the electricity generated by such a small section would matter. But I need something like this, something not functional, to stay sane.

The dust is unlike any other material I've worked with. Generated mostly by the pulverizing action of meteorite strikes instead of weathering and erosion, the individual particles are sharp, crystalline. They get into the joints of the spacesuit, cut through the filters, scratch the glass.

I spend hours looking at them under a microscope: the fractal shapes resemble bundles of knives, cut diamonds, rare jewels of uncommon beauty. Light bounces off the surfaces like the glint of snow on a distant mountain. I think about them cutting through the tissues in my lungs, and it's hard to keep my hand steady.

At the end of each day, I tend to my garden. Every day, a new layer of dust settles over the previous day's creation. With the aid of microwaldos and magnifying goggles, I carve out mazes of winding channels, forests of dense pyramids, a city of rococo spires and gothic stelae at the scale of individual corpuscles of light.

And then I retract the helmet-goggles and sit back to admire my work. Under the faint starlight and the growing glow of the distant sun, my creation shimmers with the hues of the rainbow. A bit of makeup on a monster of glass and metal, a bit of quasi order carved out of the random fall of dust.

★

The coughing grows worse. The dust is shredding my lungs, and there's nothing that can be done until the summer, when the rest of the colonists, including the real doctor, can be awakened. If I don't make it, the computer will have to wake someone else, the next person on the disposability scale for the mission. All that I will leave behind will be a garden of dust, a corrupt version of the relics after which my ship is named.

"You're doing excellent work," says the computer.

I suppose this is the only way the computer knows to offer comfort.

"Thanks," I say. "I appreciate that you were programmed to tell everyone what they do matters, even if it's just sweeping dust."

"No, I really mean it. Especially at the distal end of panel 8."

More numbers and graphs on the screen: power output and usage, photovoltaic efficiency, trends in total electricity generation.

The computer is right: there is a spike in the output of panel 8, the location of my dust garden.

"If you can replicate that level of efficiency across all the panels," says the computer, "you will more than double the amount of power produced."

That doesn't make any sense. Dust obscures light.

I close my eyes and imagine the photons bouncing against the dust particles. I imagine their winding paths through the maze of sharp surfaces, the hall of nano-scale mirrors, the traps and dead ends, the cul-de-sacs and spiraling sinks. I imagine Cicada rotating under the stars, changing the angles of the sun's rays against the surface of the solar panels. I imagine the shifting and shimmering colors.

It's a new way of seeing.

★

As the sun sets, I finish my last bit of sculpting. The massive lotus flower shimmers and glints under Cicada's winter sky, a majestic sight that heralds the start of a new cosmic cycle.

There is a copy of the Mona Lisa at the end of one of the solar panels, and a recreation of the carved lid of the tomb of K'inich Janaab' Pakal at the end of another. If you are patient, you can scan the panels centimeter by centimeter, and you will find miniature versions of the Elgin Marbles in Athens, the Nine-Dragon Wall from Beihai Park in Beijing, illuminated manuscripts from the archives of Aachen, Byzantium, and Bagdad.

And original creations also: portraits of the loneliness of nursing a dying dream, the awe of being the only consciousness on a planet hurtling through the darkness like a speck of dust, the crystalline beauty of a spinning galaxy reflected darkly in glass, the boldness of daring to imagine that we matter.

The nanostructures in the dust artwork function as photon collectors. They scatter and guide more of the photons into the photovoltaic cells, where they excite electrons just as starlight had once excited a young girl's retinas. This effect is especially pronounced when the sun is near the horizon, when the angle of incidence against the solar panels is shallowest.

The computer and I have done many simulations of these patterns. Too much randomness or too much regularity will both scatter the light. It's only a quasi-randomness, a kind of barely-contained entropy, that will do the trick.

It requires art.

"There's enough energy stored now," says the computer. "Go back into hibernation before losing your lungs."

"Who will tend to the dust patterns?" I ask.

"Spring will arrive soon, accompanied by the thawing of the frozen atmosphere. The rain will wash the panels clean."

My art will not last, but no art does. In the long run, all art is disposable, as is all life. We're all decorative, transient, temporary messages of order in the fall toward universal entropy, like my fall into the stupor of hibernation at this moment. We're cicadas between winters.

But how glorious it is to be able to mold light, to glow and shimmer and energize, to see the world in a new way, even if only for a summer?

★

[Author's Note: For more on quasi-random surface nanostructures and photovoltaic efficiency, *see* Smith, Alexander J., et al. "Repurposing Blu-ray movie discs as quasi-random nanoimprinting templates for photon management." *Nature Communications 5* (2014).]

THE GALAXY'S CUBE

JEREMY SZAL

It was another sweltering night in New Bangkok, and Jharkrat wasn't selling anything.

The crowds were always here. They strode under lanterns and weaved through sluggish traffic, broad streets slick with blood-warm rain. Rusty frying pans hissed with fury as chefs cooked bubbling pastries in oil, spinning carousels draped with rice noodles. Curlicues of smoke coiled upwards from make-shift shrines. People shouted and bargained, exchanging burlap sacks of spice and seed to tourists, probably from Earth. Canoes sliced across the canal, battering away flotsam as they navigated to the floating markets. Half-finished skyscrapers towered above, cocooned with scaffolds. A fat drop of watery rust dripped from a flaking steel pylon, landing with a brown-red plop on Jharkrat's table. He didn't bother scrubbing it away. It was the city's sweat, oozing out of a million pores. There'd be another in a minute. He made a mental note to bring his umbrella tomorrow.

Two Ministry peacekeeprs dressed in dark blue – *vivanors* – were sipping *tom kha gai* at a hot-food booth, keeping an eye on the milling crowd. One of them caught his eye and Jharkrat turned away, pretending to focus on the computer components sprawled in front of him. He didn't want trouble tonight. They'd already frowned on his business in dealing with long decommissioned electronic goods and he didn't need them to shut him down.

Someone came rushing up to his booth, pudgy face flushed with the heat. Was this a customer? Jharkrat straightened up, only to groan as the overweight man dumped an armful of decrepit equipment on the stained counter.

'I'm not buying,' sighed Jharkrat, picking at the bramble of decaying wires. 'Only selling.'

'Come on,' he shouted over the tooting horns of traffic. 'I'll give you a good price.'

It was all from the Last Age, before the Ministry had replaced all their computer systems and software. His warehouse was nearly full of this stuff. It was barely worth paying the rent to keep it there. '*Mai au khrap.* I've got enough.'

'Please.' The man was desperate, neck tendons straining like bridge cables. 'I'm low on cash.'

'Sorry.'

'Two thousand *baht* for the lot?'

'No deal.'

'Fifteen hundred?'

'No.'

'One thousand.'

He was torn. It was madness, acquiring all this for such a good price. But he'd be even madder to buy any more stock.

The man must have seen his dilemma. He plucked out a modest black box from the mess, twirling it in his hands. 'Take this. I can't sell it anywhere else.'

Jharkrat inspected it, the cloying smell of incense from a nearby shrine tickling his nose. The cube was heavy for its size, little grooves carved into the sides and a port for plugging into a computer. 'What is it?'

'A module, I think.' The man picked at a welling boil on his neck. 'Five hundred?'

Jharkrat had never seen anything like this. There wasn't even a manufacturer logo stamped into the metal. He couldn't *really* afford it, but his curiosity was winning him over. 'I'll give you four hundred.'

'Done.'

Jharkrat forked over the crumpled notes. The man nodded gratefully, scooping up his materials and slipping out into the crowd. Jharkrat glanced back at the small mysterious box, shutting out the roaring city around him.

★

It started to rain as he made his way back home, warm spatters of water drumming on tin roofs and taut tarpaulins. Two moons were visible in the sky, pouring pale light on the road. The third was obscured by thick clouds. Back on Earth, where his grandparents were born, there had been only one moon in the sky. And the days were twenty-four hours long, not thirty-two. He'd been meaning to go there, see the wonders they spoke about. But even getting a permit to travel would require years of saving. And then there was buying the actual ticket. He'd spent all his money on his daughter when she came down with the blister plague, slowly eating away at her body. Every sale he made from selling equipment fought back the disease just a little more. But in the end it hadn't been enough. It had crawled into Serah's brain and killed her.

Some days Jharkrat didn't know what kept him going.

He arrived at his bottom floor apartment. Blood-red creepers curled around the sagging poles that were weary with the building's weight. He fished for the rusty key and unlocked the ancient door. He could have gotten a keypad or printscan system, but that would draw attention. Showed he had something to hide. The place was going to get broken in again anyway. No need to encourage the thieving devils. He'd seen what people would do for money. Just last month a man a couple of blocks down from him had traded his newborn son for a dog so he could sell its litter. Jharkrat had to restrain himself from going over and smashing the man's teeth out.

The flat was a wreck; the floor littered with computer equipment and crushed beer cans, plastic chairs wrapped in thick cables. A moldy fan spun lazily overhead, swirling muggy air around the room. Stock was packed in cardboard boxes threatening to fall apart, stacked to the ceiling. Jharkrat swept away a disassembled motherboard from his desk and brought out the cube. He simply *had* to know what this was. There was no way the Ministry had licensed it. Which just made it all the more exciting.

He flicked his ancient computer on, snatching up a cable and hooking it up to the box with a click.

Zap. Everything powered down, the screen spluttering and flashing bright colours before winking away, leaving the screen a black mirror.

Well, that wasn't good. He sat still, too surprised to move when the screen jumped back to life, displaying a flickering background. Was this some sort of virus? Even now it was probably eating away at his files – or worse – shipping them off to the Ministry. He was finished now. He was–

'Hello?' A chill shot through his body. The box was *speaking*. The grooves had burst to life,

glowing an eerie blue. 'Hello?' it said again, louder this time. It was a woman's voice. 'Where am I?'

Jharkrat paled. He knew what this was. It had to be. It was a Mind, banned decades ago by the Ministry. Anyone caught handling them was immediately executed. No trial, no questions asked. No wonder that fat bastard wanted to sell the cube so desperately.

He had to get rid of it. *Now!*

He kicked the chair back and extended an arm, desperate to rip the cables out. The Mind must have guessed what he was doing. 'Please!' it begged. 'Don't!'

The intense emotion laced in its voice made Jharkrat hesitate, his hand poised to tear out the wires. 'Who are you?' he finally asked.

'I do not have a name,' the Mind said, sounding genuinely relieved. 'I…I did not expect to boot up again.'

'Why?' Jhrakrat could feel the hooks sinking in, pulling him deeper. 'What happened? Where are you from?'

'Earth,' said the Mind. 'At least, I was made there.'

'Earth?' Jharkrat leaned back in his chair, breathing hard. What had he stumbled onto here? 'How did you end up in New Bangkok?'

'With the ships. I was the one who flew them here.'

Jharkrat blinked. 'You were part of the First Fleet?'

'Yes.'

This Mind had to be almost a century old. No doubt it was packed *full* of data and logs that would have fetched millions of *baht* on the black market. No wonder the Ministry didn't want them around. A stupid grin played on his face.

Then doubt started to seep in. 'You said you didn't expect to boot up again.'

The Mind paused. 'They came for us,' she finally said. 'The men in blue. They told us we were no longer needed and the Ministry ordered us shut down. But one scientist, she had grown…fond of me. She downloaded my system into a storage device instead of destroying the software. I wasn't sure what would happen after that. I don't think she knew either.'

'Do you have a name?'

'No. None of the officers or scientists were permitted to grow attached to their Minds.' The voice seemed to hesitate, as if contemplating what to tell him. 'But I did want one.'

'I can give you one,' Jharkrat offered. 'How about…Serah?'

The Mind considered this. 'That should serve. But why that name?'

Jharkrat smiled tightly, biting his cracked lips. 'It was my daughter's name.' He leaned forward. 'What is Earth like? Tell me.'

And she did. She told him about the snow-capped mountains and sprawling deserts, the endless open spaces the size of entire countries. She described the haunting forests and jungles, the ice glaciers and tundras, the coral reefs and lush islands. Jharkrat sat there in amazement, barely noticing the buttery fingers of dawn creeping through the grimy window, painting the floor a dusty yellow. He hadn't gotten a moment of sleep, but somehow he felt rejuvenated. Refreshed.

He stood up, stretching his cramped muscles and rubbing the nape of his neck. 'I'll have to hide you,' he told Serah. 'Just in case someone breaks in.'

'Oh,' Serah said, a ring of disappointment in her voice. 'I've charged up enough. I should stay aware at least fourty-eight hours.'

He planned to be back long before then. He disconnected Serah from the computer, shoved plastic bottles out of the way and slithered under the bed. He jiggled loose some rusty nails and raised up a thin floorboard to reveal a hoard. This was where he stored most of his money in thick bundles. He didn't trust the banks. He'd seen them flop in the economic crisis before, seen the outcry as lifesavings dwindled down to loose change. He wasn't planning for that to happen to him.

He sandwiched the cube between two fat wads of *baht* before replacing the floorboard and tightening the screws. She was safe for now.

★

The sun was blinding, poking out over the rim of his stall's umbrella and stabbing his eyes. He'd bought a good pair of sunglasses a few weeks ago but they'd been stolen. He would have gone for the cheap ones, but those broke down in less than a month.

He gulped down his *kaeng som,* flooding his mouth with spicy fish and observed the flow of the market. People drifted past, sipping from plastic bags of coconut juice, feet slapping against the pavement. Jharkrat remembered when coconuts had been horrifyingly expensive, sold only by licensed companies. But then someone had wormed into the genebank labs and leaked them on the market. Now they were only twenty *baht* each, sold at every corner of every street of the city. He remembered buying coconut milk for Serah, watching her face light up as she tasted it for the first time…

A shadow swept across his face. Jharkrat swallowed and squinted up at the figure, a dark silhouette outlined by the sun. It was a *vivanor* with a mountain peak of a face. He leaned forward, scanning the stock with quiet menace.

'Can I help you?' Jharkrat eyed the pistol strapped to the man's side and pushed his bowl away.

The *vivanor* blinked, hooded eyes drilling into him. 'A man came here last night. He sold you a small box. Perhaps this big.' The man held his dirt-fringed thumb and forefinger roughly ten centimeters apart. 'Do you have it?'

Jharkrat realized with dread that this man had been here last night, watching him from the foodstall. This wasn't good. He couldn't deny owning it. 'Yes, I bought it. But I was mugged on the way home and it was stolen.'

The *vivanor's* face could have been chiseled from marble. 'Is that so?'

'Yes.' Jharkrat forced himself to smile at the man. The *vivanor* lingered there for another few seconds before heading off, slicing past the crowd as he strolled further down the market.

Jharkrat bit down on his cheek so hard he tasted blood. *Dammit.* The *vivanor* hadn't bought his story. Not for a moment. Every fiber of his being urged him to scurry home and make sure Serah was safe, but that wouldn't be wise. No doubt they were watching him from the shadows, waiting for him to make a move before they struck. He had to pretend that everything was normal.

He sighed, a bead of sweat rolling down his chest, soaking into his shirt. It was going to be a long day.

★

The sun finally slunk behind the blood-red horizon, allowing the city to burst into a multicoloured glow. Some shops closed down for the night while others opened, attracting a whole new breed of customers. Jharkrat ignored it all, packing up his stall as fast as he dared without raising eyebrows. He made his way home; passing by a lantern-lit vendor selling fabrics dyed a rich ruby red and threading his way through the various neon-dunked alleyways, tendrils of steam curling from gap-toothed windows. He swatted a dew-covered palm leaf out of the way, trying not to glance over his shoulder as he walked. There was no way they were still following him now. Surely he was just paranoid.

He stopped dead in his tracks. The door to his room was ajar, light spilling out. He pushed it open, fear knotting in the pits of his stomach. The whole thing had been ransacked top to bottom; drawers torn out, garments ripped to shreds, computer parts shattered to pieces on the floor. Jharkrat closed the door behind him, scuttling to examine the floorboard. A prayer to nonexistence gods leaped to his mouth. It didn't look disturbed, but he had to make sure…

He undid the screws with sweaty fingers, tearing the board away in haste. *Please be there, please be there.* Warm relief flooded his system. Serah was still there, safe and sound.

'Jharkrat?' she asked as he reached for the cube, squeezing the cool metal in his calloused hands, the razor edges cutting into his flesh. It was comforting, somehow. 'Is that you? Someone broke in here hours ago. They made quite a bit of noise.'

'I can tell,' said Jharkrat dryly, kicking at what had once been a widescreen tablet, the screen shattered like a spider-web. He planted himself on the floor, cradling the cube in his hands. 'They really want your system, don't they?'

'No,' murmured Serah, almost in a grumble. 'They just want to destroy it. They can't have FLT data floating around with the risk of it getting on the market. They–'

'What?' Jharkrat spluttered. 'You have faster-than-light data stored inside your system?'

'Yes. But, if it isn't accessed for five years it gets sealed with heavy encryption. I don't think you'll be able to break in.'

Now Jharkrat realized why they wanted the data so badly. He'd seen what happened when the genebank was leaked, coconuts spreading like the plague through the markets. The government had lost billions of baht. And if independent companies managed to use faster-than-light on their own, *all* their monopolies would collapse. Their starships, their tourism, their engines, everything. It would fold like a house of flimsy bamboo. People could afford to travel. See Earth. Escape from this dump.

And he held it all in his hand.

'Serah,' said Jhrarkrat, excitement dripping from every syllable, 'is there a way to extract the data?'

'Perhaps. But I told you, it's encrypted. There's a tripwire installed. If it detects someone trying to undo the lock, it'll self-denotate.' She paused. 'It'll destroy my entire system.'

Jharkrat chewed his cracked lips. He held in his hand what was quite possibly the last Mind in existence, and someone who was becoming a good friend. Was the information worth the risk of losing her? Not to mention the difficulties he could run into if he was caught. Did he want to cause so much trouble over *data?*

Then he realized it wasn't up to him.

'What do you think?' he asked, focusing on the tiny black cube that housed the Mind. 'I know someone who can help. But it has to be your decision. Do you want to risk it?'

Serah said nothing, the colours of her metal interface rising and falling. 'That scientist risked everything to get me out of there with this data,' she said. 'I've kept it safe for almost a century. They wanted to destroy it, and me along with it.' The device flashed a crimson red. 'Yes, we're going to do it.'

Jharkrat grinned. 'That's what I wanted to hear.'

★

Jharkrat packaged the cube tightly in a hidden pocket sewn into his trousers, normally used for storing cash. Now he'd be smuggling out the last surviving Mind in New Bangkok.

It was too risky to go out the front. He scaled the chainlink fence out the back and navigated his way around a garden of overgrown foliage and perennials, bursting out through to the street. He wasted no time mingling with the rushing crowd, rubbing sweaty shoulders under a roof of thick wires and holograms.

The tangled streets started to blur, the countless foodstalls, massage parlors, nightclubs, shrines, rippling lights and tooting auto-ricksaws sweeping past as Jharkrat twisted and turned through the tumult and the heat and the smells, waiting for the meaty hand on his shoulder that would drag him away and shove a .45 in his mouth.

No one came.

He carried Serah through the sea of teeming bodies, ducking under a low-hanging billboard and making his way into the dingy alleyway where old women made prayer beads with gnarled fingers, twisted like tree roots. He stepped in a shallow puddle, the water shivering as he wormed his way through a labyrinth of bustling back alleys, finally climbing a corkscrew staircase up to the four floor of what appeared to be a dilapidated apartment building. He made sure no one was looking before rapping his knuckles on the peeling wood.

The door promptly swung open. There she was, grinning at him with teeth that were black as ink. '*Sawa dee,* Jharkrat. Long time, eh?'

'Hello Kwan. You still chewing those nuts?'

'Of course. Try it sometime for yourself, eh?'

'No thanks.' He stepped inside, the air conditioning fast freezing his sweat. Explosions boomed out of speakers in the adjoining room. 'Got something for you.'

'Ah, yes,' she said, meshing her tiny hands together. 'That's what you always say.' She led him down the narrow corridor and into the lab. At least two dozen screens had been squeezed in here, bulging cables stapled to the ceilings and walls, pumping terabytes of data by the second. Half of the desks contained hackers, hooked up to screens by interfaces and headphones, pounding away at sticky keyboards. Kwan sat down on her overstuffed chair, taking a sip of what could have been water or vodka. 'I've seen it all before, my friend.'

'Not like this you haven't.' Jharkrat reached into his pocket, ripping away the stitching and bringing out the cube.

Kwan's expression didn't change. 'What is it?'

Jharkrat opened his mouth to tell her, but Serah was faster. 'You're Jharkrat's hacker friend, I presume?'

Kwan's lazy smile wilted. She gripped the cube in a trembling hand. 'You found a *Mind?*' Jharkrat nodded. *'How?'*

'Doesn't matter,' he said. 'Serah's got something valuable inside her. I need you to extract it.'

'You've *named* it?' Kwan demanded. 'If the Ministry catches us…'

'Then I'll go somewhere else.' Jharkrat was about to stand up when Kwan motioned him back down again.

'Stay put,' she hissed. 'Better me than someone else screwing it up.' She turned to her computer, fishing for a cable. 'What did you need?'

'There's some encrypted data I need you to unpack.'

Kwan made a small snort as she plugged Serah to the computer. 'Too easy. You insult me, *peuang.'*

'There's a tripwire installed,' Jharkrat said. 'If triggered it'll wipe the entire system.'

Kwan nodded, eyes sliding across the widescreen. 'Ah, yes. I see it.'

'Can you break through?'

Kwan swerved around to him with a sly wink. 'There you are, insulting me again.' Her fingers danced over the ash-stained keyboard in a rhythmic *tat-tat-tat*. 'It'll take some time. A couple hours at least.' She motioned towards the door. 'Please leave. I won't have you breathing down my neck.'

Jharkrat hesitated. It needed to be done, but he didn't want to leave Serah in anyone's hands. He trusted Kwan, but this was *almost* like leaving his daughter behind.

Almost.

'Go on,' Serah said, as if reading his mind. 'I'll be fine here.'

'See? Even she knows.'

Jharkrat took the hint. He swung the exit open, letting the soggy night swallow him up.

★

Jharkrat couldn't sleep.

It wasn't just because his wafer thin mattress had nearly been torn in two. It was Serah who lingered in his mind, tattooed on his brain. The daughter he'd lost. He could almost hear her raspy breathing as she lay comatose in the hospital bed, feel the life seeping out of her as he stroked her silky black hair, praying she would recover, that everything would be alright.

It had never truly sunk in that his daughter had gone. He'd never moved on. Maybe that was why he named the Mind after her. To keep his daughter alive.

He wasn't going to lose her again.

He unwound his legs from the sweaty sheets. He wasn't going to get any sleep tonight. Best to make the most of it. He pulled on some clothes with haste, heading out the door.

The streets were busy as always despite the early hour, frozen in a never ending slog of traffic, teeming bodies and heat, clogging up the arteries of the city. Jharkrat clambered up the stairs, not waiting to knock. Kwan met him in the hall, all calm exterior melted away.

'You!' She shoved him against the wall, gnashing those black teeth of hers. 'You *bastard!* Did you know what was inside?'

'You've broken through?' asked Jharkrat, grinning.

Kwan hissed, dragging him into the computer room. She clapped her hands, the sound drowning out the hum of computer systems. All heads swiveled to face her. *'Out! Now!'*

No one dared to object. Desks and keyboards clattered as they rushed to escape her rage. Kwan scarcely waited until they'd all left before slamming the door shut, the frame shuddering. She rounded on him, tiny hands clenched into balled fists. He half expected her to backhand him. 'You knew, didn't you?'

'I–'

'FLT data, out of all things.' She grinded her palms against her cheeks. *'Maaeng eeuy!* I can't keep this here.'

'Think about how valuable it is!' Jharkrat bristled. 'We've been looking for something like this for decades!'

'You'll put us all in danger!'

'Not if we flood the market!'

Kwan blinked, tilting her head towards him. 'You don't want to sell it?'

Jharkrat shook his head. He'd done the math already. The data was priceless. Trying to sell something like this would just draw attention from the crime lords and get them killed. But if they made it public…

'Did you extract it?' Jharkrat demanded.

Kwan blew air out between her teeth. 'Yes and no. We managed to fool the tripwire and retrieve the data, but it's key-coded to the Mind. We can't make another copy.'

'Meaning what?'

'That I'll have to go.' Their heads turned to the Mind. Serah had been listening all along. 'You'll have to upload the entire system, and me along with it.'

Jharkrat stood in dismay as the pieces slotted together. They could upload the information, but they couldn't separate Serah from it. She'd be whisked away to the pits of the Net, lost in a bottomless ocean.

Jharkrat opened his mouth to object, but clamped it shut. He was being a selfish bastard. This wasn't about him. It had never been.

And it wasn't his decision.

He approached the table, kneeling down like he was talking to a child. 'What do you want to do?' He asked, eyes locked to the tiny cube that had been his friend for the last few days. 'It's your choice.'

The Mind made a noise that sounded like something between a sigh and a chuckle. 'I think we both know the answer, Jharkrat.'

The door crashed open. A man stood there, face speckled with sweat as he panted for breath. 'The *vivanors,'* he rasped. 'They're coming!'

Kwan blinked, spat a curse and waved him off. She rounded on him. 'You brought them here?'

Jharkrat was lost for words. He'd been careful, so *careful* to make sure he hadn't been followed. And this little slip up could cost them everything.

He made a snap decision, not giving himself the chance to back out. 'Kwan, are your computers connected to the Net?'

'Yes, but–'

'You need to leave,' he said as others crowded into the room, looking to Kwan for the order. 'I'll take care of this.'

Kwan seemed to understand. She nodded, turned to a handful of men lingering in the corridor. 'You. Make their job hell. Hold them out as long as you can.' She motioned to the others. 'The rest of you, grab what you can and get to the truck. Destroy what you can't carry.'

Everyone rushed to obey. Jharkrat caught a glimpse of a locker being flung open, heard the clatter of various handguns and revolvers handed out and magazines slotted in. But that wasn't what he needed to focus on right now.

He pounded away at the computer, connecting it to the network. Kwan made herself busy ordering various men and women about as they dashed from room to room, arms bundled with hard drives and thick cables. Jharkrat frantically slotted the correct wires into the corresponding ports, linking Serah up to the system.

Shouts of warning floated up. They were getting close.

Jharkrat swiveled around, his eyes locking onto Kwan's. There was nothing to be said. They knew how this was going to turn out. 'You really should have tried those nuts.' Then she was gone, clambering down the back stairs and to the impatient truck loaded with equipment.

Muffled gunshots. Screams. Bullets whistled through the air, shattering glass. His fingers were a blur as he wrenched the gateway open, tethering Serah directly to the Net. In a few minutes she would be gone, the priceless data leaked onto the streets.

But she would be safe.

I might not have saved my own daughter. But I can save you.

'I wish you could come with me,' said Serah, her voice soft.

Jharkrat breathed out through his nostrils. 'Me too.'

Bang. Bang bang bang. A smear of red spattered the windows, followed by a roar of pain.

'Twice humans have saved me,' Serah said, her voice dimming as the bar onscreen filled up, sucking her away one fragment at a time. A yell rang out, but the *crack* of a revolver silenced it. 'You risked everything. Why?'

Jharkrat smiled. 'Don't you worry about that now. I've made my decision.'

'I wish I could have met your daughter.'

Jharkrat sensed an itch on his cheek and felt a single tear streaming down his face. He didn't bother to wipe it away. 'Me too.'

'I'll never forget you.' There was a *crack* of splintering wood as the door was kicked down, armored boots charging down the hall. 'I–'

The bar filled up.

Bang, bang. A man was thrown backwards, hosed down by a blaze of gunfire.

'Goodbye Serah.' Jharkrat stabbed the button marked *Enter.*

Jharkrat didn't even turn around as they thundered into the room. He watched them take aim in the screen's polished reflection. Bullets thudded into the monitor and system, tearing it to shreds with a deafening roar and the fizzle of sparks.

Too late.

The rifle was pressed to his head, the cold kiss of death trickling down his spine as the *vivanor's* finger curled around the trigger.

Goodbye Serah.

Jharkrat gave a final grin and closed his eyes.

THE MUMMER'S TALE

SAMUEL R. DELANY

The limit and transgression depend on each other for whatever density of being they possess: a limit could not exist if it were absolutely uncrossable and, reciprocally, transgression would be pointless if it merely crossed a limit composed of illusions and shadows. But can the limit have a life of its own outside of the act that gloriously passes through it and negates it?…For its part, does transgression not exhaust its nature when it crosses the limit, knowing no life beyond this point in time?…Transgression, then, is not related to the limit as black to white, the prohibited to the lawful, the outside to the inside, or as the open area of a building to its enclosed spaces. Rather their relation takes the form of a spiral which no simple infraction can exhaust. Perhaps it is like a flash of lightning in the night which, from the beginning of time, gives a dense and black intensity to the night it denies, which lights up the night from the inside, from top to bottom, and yet owes to the dark the stark clarity of its manifestation, its harrowing and poised singularity…

– MICHEL FOUCAULT,
Preface to Transgression

I

So, *that's* done! Come in, come in. Myself, I thought I was brilliant. Step over that, my young friend. Oh, not so young anymore, you say? Well. You've still got twenty years on me. Always had. Always will. No, around *this* way! Don't mind the clutter. A bit hot for you? Here, let me open the trap in the wagon's roof. That will give us both air and light.

There!

Sit now, on that shelf with the pretty weave over it, just under the monster's wing– yes, it's the same beast the Hero slew out on the platform. But since that was at the very beginning of the skit, they just toss it in here during the second scene while the Baron and the Peasants are singing that awful song about the Unconquerable Sea, when everybody down in the audience– *and* up on the stage – feels so insufferably noble. If it creaks and crashes while we're back here putting it away, you're supposed to assume out front it's just the wind on the rocks.

Now *look* at that sword, hanging on the wall. Split practically in two! In here it seems like nothing more than the painted wood it is. But I've seen our Leading Lady snatch it from the Hero's scabbard to plunge it into her heart, and I've heard grown men off from the platform cry out, 'No! No, don't do it!' till that great lummox dashes it from her hand and plants a kiss on her breast instead, begging her to forgive his unfaithfulness.

From the platform we always hear the market girls, crowded together down front, start to weep.

No, that's true: they didn't today. But Kolhari is a sophisticated city; the audience demands more. Really, I was speaking of the way they receive us in the provincial markets. Here, they've much more likely to appreciate my –

No!

I won't endure either your praise or your carping. You took time off from running your school to come all the way in from Sallese and see our opening afternoon performance. What greater compliment could you pay me? Oh, it's funny…

Now, lean close, because I don't want any of the others loading things outside or scrambling over our roof to hear. But we've been friends for years, you and I. *I* know you were born a prince in Neveryóna; and I also know that well before you set up your school, you dropped your title so that people would deal with you as they would with any ordinary citizen. Believe me, it's a gesture that, in the eyes of us who know you, makes you extraordinary indeed!

But about a season back, the oddest gentlemen joined our troop while we were off somewhere to the south. What talent our Director saw in him, *I'll* never know, for he was older than I and had never acted before in his life. Wouldn't you guess, after a few days the rumor went round among us that this odd old man was actually a great southern lord, out of favor with the ministers about our Child Empress, whose reign is proud and prudent. There he was, running about the countryside and cavorting on the platform with a drum and a lot of feathers, just like the rest of us. But that's not the funny part. He left us very soon. Oh, off the platform, he was pleasant enough, and though I sometimes felt his onstage shenanigans rather overlapped my own, nevertheless, just as a fellow artist, I was sad to see him go.

Well, don't you know a day later, the little flute player, whom you saw open our performance this afternoon and who doubles as a driver when we're on the road, told everyone that she, too, was actually a deposed lady of some status. Then, the young man who plays the comic servant confessed, one night after much cider, that, though he didn't *really* have a title himself, he had been brought up as the companion to a northern earl and could, indeed, ape all the manners of a lord if he so chose – perhaps the Director might consider spreading the rumor that another aristocrat was part of the troop…? And that otherwise sane and sensible man consented!

Within the month, I tell you, it all became too preposterous. Our horseboy became a duke. The three rather bosomy young things who play the witches in the morning skits and the lost peasant girls in the evening had all been, they assured us, ladies in waiting to various titled dames. And the Leading Lady herself was suddenly a distant relation of our empress – a duchess one week, a countess the next. She could never keep it straight. Oh, my friend, I tell you! Out there in the Nevèrÿon countryside, titles broke out among our company like sores among the plague-ridden. And the height of it was that, one night as I lay right on my pallet there – yes, you're sitting on it – with all the false beasts and birds and weapons and armor you see around us now, just a-clattering as we jounced toward some tiny town on the coast, I actually thought of…you!

And of your discarded title, my friend!

I wondered: since he has no use for it, would he really *mind* if I took it up…for just a while.

Yes, I'm glad you think it's funny!

I'm welcome to it, you say? Oh, you're only humoring an old artist! You might not have felt so if it had gotten back to you I was using it, now. We must retain some sense of propriety about these things.

I came to my senses, you understand, even before the next performance. After all, I told myself, as I put the blue paint on my eyes and the gold about my lips: If my Neveryóna friend has cast it aside, why should I take it on? Let those who have never been within the walls of a lord's estate dream and scheme to be something better than they are! I have the friendship and esteem of a true prince of Nevèrÿon. I have lunched with you in your gardens; I have performed my mimes for your family and friends. You have come to sit in my cluttered quarters, the two of us grinning at one another like tickled boys with mutual admiration. You have even lectured on the fine points of my art to the young men and women whose educations have been entrusted to you by the better-off merchants of Kolhari and its environs. Oh, how good you've been to me, from the beginning! It makes me weep. I have need of nothing more from you than your good opinion.

And I shall not keep that, I told myself out there in the boondocks, if I sink to this theatrical madness for appropriated nobility.

Now, tell me I was wonderful, thrilling, amazing this afternoon! No –

Let me stop!

Your good opinion, yes. I enjoy praise as much as anyone. But just as you don't need my advice on how to educate the sons and daughters of your ambitious tradesmen and artisans, I don't need your advice on how to move an audience to laughter, tears, and the recognitions supporting both – though I know you well and also know how anxious you are to give some.

But I saw you, out there among the others, only smile – yes, at the end of the third scene – when those around you roared. You and I both know the joke I'd just told was one of my most vulgar – merely a concession to what our Director thinks will please the most insensitive spectators, and worth no more than a smile, no matter how the other onlookers hooted and clutched their sides. Well, I *also* heard your laughter come, full, rich, and flowing, at that little business with my goblet in the penultimate part, while the Heroine's Father is asking for more wine…? Even though half the audience missed it and the half who noticed gave it no more than a titter, you must still know: I have been working on that gesture for *months*! (Did you recognize the eastern count on whom my original observation was based? But no. My art lies in its universality, not in its specificity.) To appreciate that turn of my hand as I glanced down with that complex expression of befuddlement (which my makeup is, you can still see here if you examine my face, designed entirely to enhance) is to appreciate what I *really* do.

And you appreciated – I heard you.

And applauded loud as anyone, at least at the end.

So you see, I've already had your critique. For us to sit here, then, face to face, while I go on to beg you for more and more empty plaudits only demeans us both.

Yes, they all seemed to have liked it – the whole thing – pretty much.

Oh, you mean the one with the thinning hair and thickening belly who stood a little off from the others, laughing and clapping heatedly at everything I did? He liked it particularly, you say? Ah, then, you noticed him.

His is the kind of critique I prefer most?

Oh, you *are* unkind to an aging actor! But the truth is, he too is a friend. He comes to see all my performances in the city, when he's here. And, yes: unlike you and the general audience, critical for your separate reasons, everything we do delights him. Once or twice, when there were new and inexperienced mummers recently joined with our cast, and everyone was badly rehearsed, and the audience, sensing it, hardly raised a smile, I've seen him applaud just as thunderously as he did today, even scowling at the others as he stalked off afterward – unnoticed, in most cases, by all but me. But those are the days when I think he is perhaps our most perfect spectator and that we need no other. Indeed, I've known him almost as long as I've known you. And that must be fifteen years now – or is it twenty? Why, I believe it is twenty, if not a little longer!

But the way I've been honored by your friendship, I fancy he's been honored by mine. And though it doesn't make me enjoy his applause one whit the less, you will understand: honor is the motivation for his delight far more than any critical capacity. And he honors himself by never having claimed otherwise. He's known one of the actors personally – me – and for that he will clap the calluses off his hard hands. In a sense, he applauds himself for knowing me at all. Or, perhaps, more generously to us both, he applauds our friendship – more truthfully, he applauds what our friendship once was. And I will also say this (for it particularly pleases me to recall it on those days when he is the only one who claps): though I've often found him charmingly naïve, for a man of his class and caliber he is not stupid. And you yourself have said it within my hearing many times: Ignorance is never a sin; only stupidity. He was really just a year or two too old to be called a boy – as were you – when I met him.

How?

He was born on a farm some stades to the west of the city. At seventeen or eighteen, he ran away, here to the great port. A few months later, I found him where one finds such boys, loitering on the Bridge of Lost Desire, beside the Old Market outside.

Yes, many – boys and girls both – get there much younger.

My supposition as to why he took so long? I don't know if you got a close look at his face, but you can see by the roughness there that, as a child, the pimples, pustules, and angry pocks that so often mar the cheeks of the young must have been, on him, particularly severe. By the time he came to Kolhari, they were more or less healed over; but from observing their traces I've suspected since the day we met that in full flower they could not have been prepossessing. I've just assumed they had something to do with why he stayed at home as long as he did.

Traditionally handsome? No. Even as a boy, he was on the stocky side, though there's always been a good bit of muscle in with it. Once in the city, he took to beer like a fly to honey – I use the many-times repeated phrase because nothing is new in his story there. Often during the first year of our friendship, I suspected that, like so many others, he would end a drunkard or a derelict. Not to mention all the petty illegalities that can catch the young and, in these variegated and violent times, kill. More than once, when, in later years, he would be some months away, I'd imagine that the next time I saw him he'd be carrying the welts of some Imperial bailiff's whip and with them the story of his year or three at hard labor on some prison detail – that's if I didn't just learn that on some chill night he'd died in a doorway or in a back alley, too cold, too wet, too long exposed to the elements.

But, as you've seen, it didn't happen thus.

I may have even had something to do with that – though life is hard for everyone, and we must not take credit ourselves for the little that others can do with theirs. Rather look instead to whom we can give credit, if not thanks, for what little we have been able to do with our own.

Certainly it would be more generous, if not more accurate, to say that he gave me quite a bit of pleasure, at least for a time. Truly, he was then and is now the most genial of men, if somewhat self-deprecating. And the goodwill he maintains to this day allows me to remember that pleasure and continue to call our relation friendship, if only as my memorial to the friendship it was.

What does he do?

Your interest makes me suspect you might like to meet him, in which case I'll tell you only what he, certainly, would wish me to say, leaving him, in due time, to say more, if and when it pleases him.

Frankly, he doesn't do much.

He lives as best he can, sometimes in Kolhari, sometimes away from it, now and again taking up menial work, though seldom steadily or for any length.

Oh, you *don't* want to meet him?

Well, then: He's a smuggler.

Has been for years.

Yes, that's my friend, as you saw him there. Though after he quit the bridge – trading one dishonorable profession for another – our friendship reduced to smiles, nods, a few words exchanged on the street or in the market. They were warm and sincere enough words. But on the whole it's been little else. Oh yes, by then he was coming regularly to see me perform. And he'd always stand a bit off – and clap and cheer the loudest. In that he did no differently then from what he does now.

That he still does it, I assume, is his own memorial – if not habit.

I'd say once a year or so – though, more recently, it's been more like once every eighteen months (and believe me, sometimes more than two years have elapsed between) – he waits around after the show to meet me. It happens so infrequently, I always invite him in. He sits where you sit now, leaning forward with his heavy hands hung between his knees. We talk. He smiles. I tell him a little of my life. He tells me a little of his.

I say it's been twenty years?

A *thousand* times we've waved and nodded when both of us have shared the city (and in his profession he is away from it as much as I), but within that same period we've actually sat together for serious conversation less than ten.

In the early days, when I still thought of him as a youngster, on a few of his visits he had his arm around some girl's shoulder – on one occasion two at once. Beaming, he introduced them, showing them off to me, me off to them: his old friend, the wonderful, talented, much applauded, madly and marvelously magical mummer. I found it amusing; and, politely, he didn't stay long, so that in the end it was harmless.

Was it five years ago? Ah, more, likely seven! Sitting where you sit now, he told me he'd been living with a widow, just outside Kolhari, by whom he'd had two children. It only made me realize how long it had been since I'd seen him.

I remember glimpsing him out in the audience a few times after that, once with some terribly young and frizzy-haired barbarian tucked under his arm, as freckled as a quail's egg and who, I'm certain, was not his widow at all but the grubbiest of prostitutes from the bridge across the market.

They didn't come in to see me.

I confess I was relieved.

Once, when he dropped by and we went down to the waterfront, where, rather uncharacteristically, he bought me a mug of cider while he had a few beers, I learned, in the course of our talk, that he'd collected a wealth of information about the Liberator – you remember, that political upstart everyone in the country was talking of ten years back or so, when his headquarters were raided out by your uncle's? Well, he knew every battle and skirmish and story and rumor, every fact and surmise about the man. You wouldn't have thought it to look at him, but he'd been collecting these tales for years, keeping them all in his head. And only once had he met him, he said. But it confirmed for me what I'd dreamily suspected from the beginning: there really had been something unusual about him – though no doubt it would never come to anything that brought him reward in the socially managed markets, old or new, of need and necessity. What makes a boy interesting does not make a man interesting. Yet the interesting boy had become an interesting man: it would be the rare student from your school who could give you so rich and so textured an account of his field of study as that man you saw today could give of his perfectly pointless and obsessive pursuit.

Oh? *Fifteen* years back, you say, was the raid on the Liberator's mansion? Well, you should know. It was right out there in your neighborhood.

The last time he dropped in, when I asked after his family, he told me that, oh, he hadn't seen the widow in almost a year – nor his children; nor hers.

I believe that was when it struck me: by no stretch could I think of him as a youngster anymore. What in his youth I'd been able to look on as a handsome solidity had, in the man, run simply and brutally to fat. You saw – and I think you'll admit, though I'm twenty years his senior, too – I've kept my figure a bit better than he. Also, he's losing his hair. Mine, miraculously has only thinned. Yes, he's very much a man and is today as close to middle aged as I am to being simply and brutally old.

No, I don't really think he's been doing as well of late as he once did. It pains me to admit it of one who, for so long, I thought of as a child, but his decline is just another of those little shocks by which the nameless gods remind us of death.

Thank them all, whoever they are, that I can still mime, however clumsily, can still sing, however reedily, can still dance, however stiffly, and can skew each to the other in a parody of age's failings artfully enough to make an audience laugh.

Why, yes. I suppose you *could* say that. In a sense, my friendship with him *has* gone more or less the way of my friendship with you. But whatever the cares and concerns in your various undertakings – not to mention my own – you are both doing well enough, in twenty-plus years, to come here to the market on the first day of our return from our triumphant provincial tour and catch our opening performance.

Which is only my too self-centered manner of saying, I suppose, that, in my different ways, I really *do* value you both and know you value me.

Yes, I suppose I too am surprised you haven't seen him before. But then, your lives and concerns have really been quite different, don't you think? After all, you are a prince, a teacher, a philosopher – while he's little more than a thief.

Indeed, I'm sure you're right: many people *wouldn't* be surprised in the least.

Tell you more about him? Well, all right.

2

No doubt that stolid man you saw today came to the city as a boy like many – to the bridge, where such boys come – with the dream of selling his sexual services to some fabulously connected countess, who would take him off to her private rooms at the High Court, where he'd be presented to various nobles at various intimate but elegant suppers. His rough, country charms would be made much of as he amused the lords and ladies with his anecdotes of common life, for he was seldom more than three beers away from being a good, comic raconteur: he had that fine sense of self-mockery that is the social point from which we begin all later self-criticism, without which none survives long on our very bumpy road. No doubt in the palace his rough, if scarred, good looks would cause (he dreamed) a few noble ladies to catch their breath; and perhaps even once, at some great party, into which he'd wandered only by accident, he'd exchange a few lines of banter with the Child Empress herself, whose reign is glittering and glorious, causing waves of jealousy and ire among the lords gathered at the affair, so that, after a month or six of such dalliance, his patroness (who, by this time, hopefully, would have taken up another lover, perhaps a young nobleman whose arrogant ways would make her fondly recall her nights and noons with him) would finally secure him an officer's commission in the Imperial Army, at some fascinating outpost in some exotic hold, sending him on to who-knows-what great and gainful adventures…

But with what seemed then, even to him as he looked back on it after only a few months, idiot slowness, he soon accepted in practice if not in theory that such dreams were as insubstantial as moon-flicker on the shallows down below the bridge rail.

In his first days on the Bridge of Lost Desire, so he told me later with a laugh, one man took him home to make love to a perfumed, sultry woman he claimed was his new, young wife. As such work went, he liked that a lot. But it didn't happen again for another three months: next time an older man picked him up, describing his handsome, noble-born mistress, who, he said, was forty – my age, incidentally, when I met him.

Well, he'd always been partial to older women. But when they arrived at the gentleman's large and well-appointed mansion, the woman was out. They waited, sipping cider together and talking for several hours. Then the man apologized to him, paid him half the agreed-on fee, and sent him back.

These two incidents exhausted his professional contacts with women during those first months.

What he actually did when he looked up from the garbage-clotted shallows – what he'd done in the few days before the first of these encounters, what he did in the many days between them, and what he did daily after – was to sell his services, often for distressingly little money and more times than not simply for a meal and a place to sleep, to a succession of artisans and clerks and laborers and merchants and army officers and market vendors and wagon drivers and still others who did not want anyone to know *what* they did, all of them men.

Though very occasionally they passed across it, with their parasols and paramours, their secretaries and serving maids, in search of some rare item rumored by an acquaintance to have been sighted in the market beyond, titled ladies did not, as a rule, stop on the bridge to purchase pleasures – not in *this* part of Nevèrÿon.

I had been with the traveling troop here only a few years, and you probably recall that, in those days before my current comic eminence, mostly I played for the other dancers and actors who worked on our portable platform, coaching them in rehearsals and helping to devise the skits.

Our actual meeting?

No doubt as I passed across the bridge from the Spur to the more commercial neighborhoods of the city, I'd seen him among the loiterers of both sexes, now sharing beer with one of the other boys, now calling to one of the women: ' – Hey, little gillyflower, I see how you're looking at me!'

And I'd thought what a man, such as I was, would likely think (of him and, indeed, many others): One time I would find him rather attractive in a vulgar sort of way. (Should I approach him…) At another, I'd decided: No, he was not my type at all…It would be silly even to smile. And at least once I saw an elderly grain-seller stop to talk with him, and heard him call the man 'Papa.'

Clearly he had gone with that mercantile gentleman before; though if 'Papa' were a nickname of his own devising or part of his client's previous personal instruction, I never did have the temerity to ask – though at that moment I convinced myself I had really been about to speak, that given my preferences he was, certainly, the most attractive young man on the bridge. What a fool I'd been, my momentary jealousy told me, to hesitate this long in making my interest known!

Those who never browse in the commercial markets of sex assume that we, who do, shop there in order to escape the wounds, self-recriminations, and hurts to the soul associated with timidity, opportunities missed through hesitation, and the simple pains from rejection that plague those who limit sex purely to the results of social encounter. They feel a moral superiority through the sufferings that they have agreed to bear and which they are sure we avoid by barter, convinced their social courtship agonies chasten them in ways we can never know and – like youngsters' plunges into cold mountain streams – harden them to life. They do not know commercial possibilities in no way abolish such pains and hurts, but rather add to them a certain sting that, if anything, makes them the more excruciating, the more gnawing. The commercial only multiplies the opportunities to risk such hurts again.

Oh, yes! A day after I saw him with his gray-haired old man, I passed him once more, only to realize that it *was* he when I was a step beyond – by now my mind was that deeply on other things!

But one evening when the clouds were high and yellow and the sun was like a copper gong half-hidden among them – for some reason, there were only a third as many people out on the bridge as usual – as I was crossing I saw him, naked, leaning back against the wall, an elbow either side of him on the ledge, a drinking skin on the stone beside him, one foot up on the wall below.

I looked.

He smiled.

I thought to look away and didn't.

As I passed, still looking, suddenly he thrust out his hard farm laborer's hand to me and said, simply:

– Hello! How you doing?

We shook.

I stayed to tell him; to ask him the same, while he took his skin down and offered me warm beer; and I, who markedly prefer cider, accepted.

Oh, first there was a bit of small talk as we leaned together against the wall. I know now he did not think himself handsome and took a boyish delight when *anyone* stopped for him at all. But the sexual worker who can evince sincere pleasure at the coming of a client seasons his or her fare with a rare spice. Five or ten sentences into our exchange, and I brought out some frank and specific questions as to money and positions. (If I were taken at all, I wanted to be taken as a serious customer.) About both he gave reasonable, frank, and specific answers.

That settled, I offered to refill his skin with drink.

About that he was grateful.

Since then I have known boys years younger, soliciting years longer, who merely wanted to do the deed, take their pay, and go. Today, I would not fault them. But the fact is, a mere five years before that warm afternoon, I would have sworn to anyone who asked that *I* would never pay for sex! In my own way I was as new to buying as he was to selling. Oh, we had both bought and sold before. That is not the level of innocence I am trying to establish. The surprise to me now, however, was that he was not so experienced that he took my offer of a little sociability mixed in with our transaction as a sign of what, eventually, we would both learn it was: in terms of any continuing monetary relation, I would be a rather poor-paying customer.

But perhaps another observer, knowledgeable in the ways of sexual commerce, might say that our friendship, if I can call it that, began with a little more promise than most. I'd recently gotten a small windfall; from what private party, where I'd performed brilliantly, I no longer remember – *was* it yours?

Now, at that point it would have to have been. Ah, you must be right! I'd completely forgotten.

I'm embarrassed to go on and let you know where the moneys your uncle so generously –

Oh, of course! Of course, I understand – after all this time, how could it mean anything to you?

Well, then! From your family's most generous fees I not only brought him his few mugs of beer that evening and fed him, but I gave him some coins for himself and paid a week's rent on a cheap room where I let him stay.

After I'd enjoyed him, I returned to pass the rest of the night in the wagon.

Mornings I would show up at his door and knock. Sleepily he would call me in. There, sitting on the bed, we would talk.

Or I would talk – for the morning hours were not his most communicative, though he was always certain to make me promise to come see him again the next day, as if the simple sound of my running on about this and that, if not the physical exchange between us, comforted him. He would listen to me or, at any rate, pretend to listen.

And the truth was, whatever he thought of our sex, he liked me: it was the first time in months he'd slept three nights running under the same roof.

I brought him to visit our wagons. To give you some idea how provincial he was: though he knew the bridge to twenty meters around it at each end, until he came to see us perform he'd never walked farther than the fountain at the middle of the market. He did not even know that on the other side of the square we have traditionally set up our wagons since we began to call at this city!

Once I let him watch our skits from the privacy of the prop cart.

Ah, and after that he talked!

At some point during the performance, he'd glanced aside to see one of our dragons leering at him from the clutter – like the one you're sitting under…?

Oh, it startled him!

Well, with his great grin, if he told me about it once, he told me about it twenty times over the next week.

– What a fool I am, he'd say, to be scared by such a toy. But from his smile as he said it, you knew he'd never known a happier fright.

I often asked him about his sexual history – indeed, I told him tales of mine. Yes, he had his own sexual quirks. I believe it was summer women with –

But then I have my quirks too, about which he was always obliging. (– No, come on. You like it. You said so. *Do* it! You, see, I want *you* to have a good time! I did not know then just how rarely I might expect to hear that from such a young man, and so, in my way, I took him for granted quite as much as he took me.) Also there were several times when I was sure my particular peculiarities had become common knowledge from one end of the bridge to the other, thanks to his banter with the other boys – only to discover it had never even occurred to him to mention them, from nothing more than a natural reticence which would have done honor to someone far more nobly born. Therefore I see no need to detail the particularities of his tastes. Suffice it to say, they were harmless, even charming, and I was touched that he chose to confide them to me.

At the time, you understand, he'd only gone to bed with seven women in his life – the first six of whom were sundry country lasses and ladies, and the last of whom had been the wife of that early customer on the bridge. When we were talking of this in his room one morning, I declared:

– What a coincidence! That's the same number of women I my self have bedded in my forty-odd years! And here I'm more than twice your age.

Like so many youths who drift from country to city, when not thinking of some titled lady (or lord) to keep him in lackadaisical luxury, he would daydream, now and again, of a son and a wife – in that order – and perhaps several adoring daughters with them. That, he would explain, is what he needed to settle down. All of them would live together on some small farm that he would manage to own, a miniature, I finally came to believe, of the one on which he'd lived and labored so thanklessly before he'd come to Kolhari. At which point I would quip:

– Add to that a job that will take you away from it at least eight months of the year; and *all* your problems'll be solved.

He would laugh. But I wonder if, later, with his country widow, he remembered my advice; for certainly, those many years on, he seemed to have taken it.

Oh, in those days with me he had his bouts of homesickness. They troubled him greatly; I listened as sympathetically as a man with other concerns could, till I finally suggested:

– Then why not simply go home? At least for a visit.

– Oh, no. My home is much too far away. It took me four days of steady walking to come from there to the city.

How would he ever cross such a distance again?

I pointed out that what one can walk in four days, one can ride in an oxcart in a day and a half. Also, though I had never visited his village, I'd heard its name before and knew that it simply was not that far off. If it had taken him four days to walk, that was because he'd probably been lost at least a third of the time. But supporting him for a week, I was beginning to feel responsible for him, a feeling that, first, I did not enjoy and, second (not to slight your uncle's occasional early munificence), I could not afford on my ordinary mummer's earnings from spectators' donations at our day-to-day fare.

On the night before his week's rent was to run out, therefore, I proposed to call for him before sunup next day, take him to the market end of the Bridge of Lost Desire, find a wagoner finished with his morning deliveries who was returning west, and pay an iron coin or so for his day-and-a-half's ride home. Just to show you how naïve he was, he hadn't even known you could do that. Today, of course, it's an established institution, but at the time I don't believe the empress had yet set up the passenger shelter that's been rebuilt twice in the last decade. You just had to go and ask around till you found a wagon going where you wanted – though enough folks did it, anyway.

Anyway.

The next dawn I got myself up from my cluttered bed, went to his room, rolled him sleepily out, and we walked to the market. The second driver I asked pointed us to a third, who hailed us heartily as we strolled up. A pleasant and blustery fellow, in my memory, he was then the spit of my erstwhile friend today. Sure, he'd take the young man to his village. His journey passed right by it.

– Good, I said, as my friend climbed up into the cart to grip the back and sides, blinking about at the market square still dim in the summer dawn. You'll be there by tomorrow afternoon, I called as I handed two coins to the driver.

– Tomorrow? the driver demanded. We'll be there by tonight! and returned me a coin. You've overpaid me, and I'm a good and honest laborer! It made me smile and I wondered how this further confirmation of the physical nearness of his home struck my young friend, who blinked, still red-eyed, in the back of the wagon, as they rolled off by the fountain where the first of the stalls was only then being set out.

His room, of course, was paid for till sundown and supper that day – a custom I miss in these times when innkeepers expect you out and off by noon. If I recall, I was back there an hour later with another…friend. This one was a little older, a little more experienced. At the time I thought myself far more attached to him than the young man I'd just sent off to the country. We carried on lubriciously till I realized I was late for my performance – a sin I have committed only three times in my life. And today, though I have tried many times, I cannot recall the name – much less the face – for whom, then, I committed it.

3

He was gone some three or four weeks. However or whenever he came back I'm not sure, for he had the tact and good sense not to look me up immediately on his return. He had interpreted my sending him off, however friendly I'd been about it, in the terminal sense I'd intended it, a sensitivity, I confess, I admired him for, and which no doubt eventually influenced me to see him again. Was it a month later that I glimpsed with some surprise someone I thought was he turning onto the bridge? A day or two after that, as I was crossing, I nearly bumped into him – though he was deep in conversation with a barbarian youngster and an older man who, no doubt, wanted them both; he didn't see me, or pretended he didn't.

I thought it politic not to interrupt.

A few days later, I was on my way to join my fellow mummers at a street carnival in another neighborhood where we were to perform. Some had left with the wagons in the morning to set up. I was to join them that afternoon. I recall, I didn't *have* to cross the Bridge of Lost Desire to get there; I could have gone the few streets north to the perfectly unexceptional overpass that leads to those ethnic enclaves in the city where, on carnival days, our theatrical talents are so in demand. It was just habit, sedimented no doubt by past pleasures, that took me over the bridge.

He was leaning there in what I'd come to think of as His Spot.

We smiled; and while I was wondering if I should stop to talk, I found myself slowing.

– Hello! How you doing?

For a moment I wondered if he actually remembered me:

– Fine. How did your trip go?

– Fine. Fine…! It was great! Fine!

He'd seen his aunt. Yes, he knew who I was. No, his mother hadn't been as pleased to see him as he'd hoped. There'd been some problems before he'd left that, though he'd mentioned some of them to me before, he'd all but forgotten till, really, the cart had pulled up by those familiar fields. Still, he'd had a couple of good, or at least interesting, evenings with his village friends. But as he talked, every now and again he would glance at me curiously. Did we discuss it that afternoon, or did I only have the strong feeling that it was now known? Today I couldn't say for sure. But from somewhere I gained the conviction that it was clear to him that the vast distance to his home over which he had tramped for four aimless days to reach Kolhari was not that of stade after stade; rather it was a distance of mind, of temperament, created by his urban education even in so vulgar a version as he had received it during his handful of months on the bridge. And that was far vaster than the one he'd imagined he'd crossed by foot or by wagon. In comparison, save by some machinations of the unnamed gods beyond both his powers and mine to conceive, the true distance could not be retraversed.

That was why he was back.

– Where you going, today? he asked as I was about to leave.

I explained about the street fair.

– Take me with you? he asked. After all (and he stepped from the wall to look down at himself, naked on the bridge flags in the warm autumn evening), how long can I hang around here, shaking this old turkey neck, hoping some guy with bad breath and no teeth is hungry enough to buy my turkey milk.

– I have work to do there.

– Oh, come on, he said. Take me. I won't be in the way.

– Well, I suppose you can come. But I made it clear to him there would be nothing monetary in it. He made it equally clear; he'd heard of the various Kolhari festivals since before he'd come to the city, but he'd been afraid to go to any of them himself. If he went with a friend, like me, he wouldn't be scared. And he couldn't pass up a chance to go with someone actually part of the festivities.

As he fell in beside me, he called to a stranger a little way down from us: another young man, I realized, working the bridge.

– Hey, give us a swig of your beer?

At which the youngster pulled his drinking skin from the wall, beat it against his thigh, and (to my surprise) stalked angrily off! I raised an eyebrow to ask my friend what that was about. Grinning, he explained:

– Oh, I stole an old man of his this morning, who always comes around here looking for him. Only today, I was here first! When I came back, I told him about it – about how much money I'd been given. (He nudged my arm, his grin gone broader.) I lied…about the price, I mean. *Nobody* gives that much. But I tell a good story. And now he thinks anyone who walks by and talks to me was really going to talk to him first.

I began to protest, but he went on:

– It doesn't matter. Last week, every time someone came near me, he was in my face, with his dumb smile and his stupid boasts about how much he can do and how long he can do it. I'm just getting him back.

He ended with a scalding insult to his rival's breeding, homeland, and defecatory practices, which, in its country vulgarity, I actually found shocking here in the city – at any rate worrisome:

His rival just happened to have been – most visibly – of the same ethnic origins as the inhabitants of the neighborhood in which our festival was to take place.

When we reached the crowded streets with their colorful revelers, the grills set out on the corners with their spitted lambs, the drunken singers, the arguing parents, the racing children, the colored hangings roped below the windows, he stayed very close to me. The neighborhood (to him) was full of foreigners; and foreigners were what, at home, he'd been taught most to fear.

Once we reached our wagons, for the first minutes he simply stood by the back corner, blinking and staring a lot. Of course there was still more setting up to do, and I turned to lend a hand. Minutes later, I looked up to see him suddenly let go of the wheel whose rim he stood clutching and throw himself into our preparations as if he were one of our troop, now asking some groom, now one of the propmen, what he could carry here or there, what he might fetch, what he might hold, and even the Leading Lady if there was anything he might go bring her – with a blown kiss she sent him running off after something or other, which, in only a little longer than one might have assumed, he returned with.

I admit I was somewhat wary of all this, but the others seemed to take to him, and soon they were sending him there and here, with this load or that.

His labors clearly left him braver. Now, as the day wore on, he would actually go off by himself for a while, and an hour later I would see him, from the platform, as I played my gongs and cymbals, threading through the crowd, munching on this or that bit of carnival fare, given him by whom or pilfered from where, I would not presume to guess.

Eating, watching, grinning, he would wink at me.

And, indeed, I would grin down at him – and go on playing.

That night when the flares burned low and it was time to dismantle the platform and take down the lamps and lanterns, again he threw himself in with our work. Once I saw him nearly slip with a plank of wood balanced on his shoulder. A little later, I saw him unsteady with a load of masks in his arms. Somehow in the course of the evening he had managed to get satisfactorily drunk – but then, in such conviviality where strangers offer you drink practically at every corner, that was not surprising. And it certainly had not dampened his energy.

He stayed with me that night in my wagon, the two little dancers with whom I then shared it having found some sailors after the performance who wanted to take them to see their ship on the waterfront by the moon. (*They* didn't get back till two days later and received quite a dressing down from the Director.) We had rather drunken sex in the littered dark. One or the other of us, I suspect, fell asleep in the midst of it.

Once, in the wagon, he woke up, somewhat disoriented, and made me lead him, unsteadily, outside into the surprising moonlight. He kept on repeating, still drunk, that he'd *heard* something. Then, with his head down, his feet wide, and his hand against the crumbling daub of some dilapidated wall, he began to urinate – in amazing quantities, with astonishing force – wetting his feet, my feet, splattering his knees, soaking his own hands, making almost as much of a mess of himself as if he had never left the bed.

The next morning he was up, however, standing out in the quiet morning, only a little squint-eyed.

We saw the wagons off, on their way back to the market. Then we walked together, the long way, toward the bridge. Halfway across I told him:

– I must cut you loose here. It's been fun. And I don't have *too* much of a headache.

– I do. He grinned at me, his young beard, unbrushed that morning, looking as grizzled below his rough cheeks as one of his elderly client's. I'm going down under the bridge and sleep for a while in the shade, he told me. (I was planning to crawl right into bed as soon as I reached the wagons back in the market square.) Hey, how about letting me hold a couple of coins? Oh, I don't mean for last night. I wouldn't charge you for *that*. That's free. But just for all the work I did? For you, and everybody?

What could I say?

– We get together soon? he called after me, as I left him, standing there with the iron in his hand. The bridge was quiet that morning, and I had the momentary feeling that his voice, with its all too expected proposition, echoed not only from end to end but throughout the entire city.

– Yes, of course!

I believe I also called back some tentative time for meeting him the next day (– I'll see you at about…), an appointment that one or the other of us didn't keep.

Of course.

And whose party was it a week later? No, not yours that time – because I recall distinctly I rehearsed with that marvelous, messy woman who composed the wonderful music that made me, finally, decide to give up tootling to become a serious mimic. And we never performed together in your gardens. Yes, that's right. It was for your friend, the baronine. You were present at that elegant afternoon affair? Well, that's certainly possible.

At any rate, it was probably that same evening, when I was returning from Neveryóna to the market, over the bridge:

– Hello! How you doing?

A few more beers. A few more coins. Another room. In another inn, which another boy had told me was somewhat cheaper. And as I sat at the edge of his bed over the next few days, our conversations ranged back over pretty much the same topics as they had the last time.

The son.

The wife.

The farm…

– I was married, I decided to tell him one evening. Once. For al most eight years, actually. Before I became a mummer. Or, at least be fore I permanently joined the troop. I had two sons and a daughter. Ah, what a good father I was! I've never worked harder at any role in my life. Well, that's finished with now, and though it may be my finest performance, I wouldn't give a minute more to it, that I tell you.

He laughed with me; but he was curious:

– What about your fooling around? Did you do it back then? With men, I mean?

– Certainly. Probably a good deal more than I do now. After all, I was young. About your age, actually. At least when I married her.

– Did she know? I mean about you and…men?

– Of course!

– You told her?

– Well before we were married. What sane man would ally himself with a woman and not let her know something about him as important as that?

– How did she feel about it?

– At first it rather excited her. (From the way he grinned, I knew that even with his seven women he'd already learned that anomalous truth about the complex engine of sexual interaction.) After the children came, I suspect the topic began to bore her.

– Did the kids know?

– Toward the unnecessarily ugly end, the two who were old enough must have suspected. A lot of things were yelled that had nothing to do with anything save how deeply they could wound. You know, my wife was quite talented herself. Still lives out in Yenla'h. At least I think she does; it's not on our summer itinerary. Oh, she could make anything: houses, pots, stage sets. Also, she was rather an adventurous, if moody, woman. But I was fond of her; and most of the time I treated her as such. With me, that involves a certain amount of honesty. I suspect it does with most.

Then why aren't you together?

The most difficult part to understand for him, I think, was that the reasons for our separation (Oh, final happiness!) were simply those that split any pair who each finds that the company and habits of the other reduces her or him to a sniveling, furious, pitiable, and paralyzed beast no longer capable of acting like anyone's notion of a reasonable man or woman as the gods first formed and crafted us.

– *How* many women have you been to bed with? he asked.

And before I could answer, he began to tell me a clearly preposterous story about a sexual triumph he'd had with a beautiful woman he'd slipped off with for a while that night at the carnival. He hadn't told me before, you see, for fear I might be jealous. But he hadn't drunk that much, yet. So of course once he'd gotten her down in a pile of leaves behind some old shack away from the merry-makers, he'd come too fast and – In the middle of his tale, however, it was as if he suddenly remembered we too had entered into a certain arena of honesty, and he halted. Well, actually, he said, he'd seen a woman in passing, older than he, ordinary enough in other respects, but with a certain…Well, she was just against a wall and eating from a netted sack of fruit at one of the crowded corners. Standing across the busy way from her, he'd considered going up and trying to talk, hoping possibly to bring her to the wagon, where he'd intended to ask me to let them fuck while *I* stood guard outside!

That's why he'd come back and worked so hard.

He had left her and returned to look at her several times. She'd apparently stood there quite a while, as though she were waiting for something. (– Almost as though she were listening for something, I believe is what he said with a moment of poetry to his pensive look that now and again would illuminate his most work-a-day accountings.) But still he had not been able to bring himself to speak. Eventually, on the fifth or sixth time he returned, she was gone – alone or off with someone else, he did not know.

– Like the fool I am, he told me, shaking his head, I couldn't say anything.

For both of us, then, the answer was still seven.

I don't remember which of us asked the next obvious question: Well, how many *men* have you slept with? (Oh, it *must* have been me!) We sat on his bed in the tiny room with the bare walls and sloping thatch, trying to figure. Twenty-five? Fifty? (Did I throw such absurdly low numbers out only to tease?) Well, he'd come to Kolhari with half a dozen from his childhood play on the farm, and he'd seen a hundred go by months ago: he remembered passing the twenty-five mark in his first week on the bridge.

Laughing, we agreed that for both of us it was certainly high in the hundreds. I was forty. He was not yet twenty. I wonder why I felt obliged to tease:

– Well, then, you're just like me. Obviously you like men's bodies better than you like women's. I certainly do! Always have. Always will.

– No! he protested. I like women's bodies *far* more than I like men's. Men's bodies? That's only a kind of play. I don't take them seriously. I only go with them when women aren't around. And I want to get paid for it when I do.

– Well! and I had to laugh. I *thought* such things once myself, though I never really felt them. When I sleep with a woman, it's only thinking about a man that allows me to enjoy myself. Which thinking I did very well, thank you, twice a week for eight years. Of course, too often when one does go to bed with a man, one has to think of *another* man. Really, it *does* go on. What do you think about when you sleep with a woman? Or a man – me – for that matter?

– Nothing, he said a little wonderingly.

– To be sure, I said. He doesn't think of anything.

– Well, sometimes, he admitted at last, a man and a woman doing it together...but while you were married, you *still* did it with men?

Who do you think I was thinking about that let me enjoy my wife? My young friend, I say it, and I mean it: I like men's bodies for the inspiration, stimulation, and relief of lust *far* more than I like women's. And going through the proper nuptial rituals with a woman, as your village prescribes them, will not change that if that is, indeed, your case. Also (and here I frowned askance at him with one lowered brow), for two who *feel* so differently, don't think it's odd that what we've *done* is so much the same?

That only made him protest the more. Indeed, as he argued with me over the next quarter hour he got quite angry. Now and again he actually threatened me. I only pooh-poohed him the more. Finally, I declared:

– Well, whatever you do, and like, and feel, and think, you must learn to accept them all and live with whatever contradictions between them the nameless gods have overlooked in your making, like cracks in an imperfect bit of ceramic still pleasing in its overall shape. Certain strains, certain tasks, certain uses one does not impose upon such pieces. But everyone has them. Learning what they are is, no doubt, why we were put here.

Though by now I suppose I had a somewhat worried look, for he'd already overturned the bed during one outburst and had several times struck the wall with his fist.

– That's the only thing that matters, I went on. Calm down, now. Our wagons leave the city tomorrow. Let me buy you a farewell meal tonight.

I took him to eat at a waterfront inn where tables were set on finely broken shells and lamps hung from the poles overhead and you could look down the docks at men walking through the evening, some holding up flares, some rolling barrows in from the side streets, some loading bales off the boats:

– Have you ever been here before?

– No…! His eyes were big with the waterside wonders, and he clutched his mug in both hands.

Then, it's about time!

We ate a meal and drank a lot. It was the first in all his time here he'd even *seen* the docks – in our port so famous for its waterfront. The ships and the confusion around us scared him a bit, I think; and excited him; and made him grin.

The argument earlier, back at the inn, seemed forgotten. Everything here spoke of travel, with its commercial support not so vividly contaminated by lust and madness as it was in his own neighborhood. It gave the waterfront an excitement, a purity he'd never known in the infamous quarter that had been till now, for him, almost all of Kolhari. In some ways, however, I'm sure that realization of the greater vastness to this city, which had already educated him well beyond anything he'd even dreamed of knowing on his village farm, deeply unsettled him.

That night in his room he was as drunk as I'd ever seen him.

That, and perhaps something unsettling I felt myself, put all thoughts of any farewell intimacies from my mind; although, for a moment, I think, as he swayed in his dark chamber, demonic in the light from the clay lamp I had just set on the rickety corner table, blinking and bleary-eyed, he expected or even wanted them (do I flatter myself?) – before he closed his eyes, slowly, to collapse, half on the floor and half on the bed, where I gave him a few tugs to straighten him.

I blew out the lamp and left.

The next day, of course, our parti-colored wagons rattled away from the city. He was certainly not up to see us off. With the kind of hangover such a drunk leaves, I'm sure he spent that day sick in his room. The day after that, his rent ran out at the inn. So he must have returned to the bridge.

But somewhere between the time I left him and the time he was back on that walled stone walk above the water, so I learned later, my friend went mad.

Yes, just like that.

It was a quiet, inward sort of madness. Most of the first day he ambled from one end of the bridge to the other and back. The only way his actions differed from before was that, now, when the other boys spoke to him, to call hello, or to suggest they go there or here together on this or that mildly questionable pursuit, he walked by them, not speaking, sometimes with an angry, startled look. When men glanced at him, he did not grin and step up to begin talking with a hand on their shoulder, nor stop to lean beside them at the wall, with a comment about a passing whore. He walked to the end of the bridge.

He turned.

He walked back.

Mistaking him for a potential customer, some tired prostitute called:

– Come on, darling. We'll go out tonight! (They always say 'tonight,' even when they accost you at ten in the morning.) But he did not fall into the usual banter, about how *she* should pay *him* since his services were *clearly* superior.

He walked on.

He walked the bridge most of the night.

Toward morning, he stopped for a minute, then, a few steps on, stopped some minutes more.

Finally he sat down with his back against the stone wall, his mouth wide for breath, sometimes closing his eyes tightly, sometimes opening them in the dark.

He woke to the day's traffic raging about him. Getting to his feet, aching and unsteady, he began to walk again. The usual bridge voices – wagoners cursing, pedestrians chattering, pimps and prostitutes shouting to one another – had been joined by tens, hundreds, thousands of others. It seemed he could now hear every voice in Kolhari reverberating along this stone strip. Angry voices, cooing voices, wheedling voices, greedy voices, bewildered voices, cajoling voices all knitted and nattered in argument and antiphon, a tangle of altercation and contention, haggling over commerce, lust, madness, travel, as if there were no other topics in the city, all of them centering on this bridge, all of them on him on it, as he walked from one end to the other.

He saw an apple an ox's or a camel's hoof had squashed a section of, before it had rolled or been kicked against the wall. He picked that up and ate it. Later a parsnip fell from the tailgate of a wagon as a wheel jarred on loose paving. When it was still on the ground at his fifth trip back and forth, he picked it up and, with the gutter dirt and all that had darkened one side, ate that too. He didn't eat too much else because there was little else lying around, and because the sound of his own teeth and jaws and saliva and the food bits sloshing and grinding as he chewed and swallowed nearly obliterated the voices. And he was sure by now that at the core of this contestatory hubbub some secret was being discussed that, if he could only overhear it, would net him untold wealth, power, and fame – enough to make the empress and all her ministers at the High Court of Eagles grovel before him.

He ate little.

He slept little.

For much of the time he did not look very different from any other madman you might see ambling the Bridge of Lost Desire. Sometimes, in his effort to listen, to keep his step in rhythm with the voices, he would clench his jaw so tightly that his face and shoulders would shake. His steps became, then, staggers. When he bumped into someone, he turned and stared, astonished, bewildered, and furious at them for distracting him from his infinitely important task; sometimes he would curse them through gritted teeth – at least in the first days. Later, when he bumped someone (which happened more and more rarely, as people avoided him more and more widely), he did not notice.

What this madness was, or where it came from, or what lay at its center only the nameless gods can know. Certainly not I. Possibly it had no cause save the exhaustions of his life, myself a part of them, my former efforts at friendship and my various moments of selfishness all equal in that they had only helped to wear away whatever in him had till then been able to endure. What I can say, however, just as I can say it began: after fifteen, or twenty, or twenty-five days, the madness stopped.

Naked on the ground by the bridge rail, he woke for the fifth time in fifteen minutes – or five hours.

Three men stood talking beside him. One with a shaved head had dark wings of paint around his eyes and wore jewels at his ears. One could have been some tall, merchant's clerk, with his short, drab tunic, his long, thin hands. The third was a squat workman, a hammer hanging from a noose on his belt the way a soldier might wear a sword. His brown hands and naked feet were gray with rock dust.

– Do you remember, cried the bald one with the makeup, how Vanar used to come to the bridge here, to pick up the boys?

– Sure, declared the workman. I used to see him all the time! People talked about him down here. Why didn't he take me, I always wondered. But he never did.

– Oh, *there's* the kind he liked. Like that. The bald one pointed at the young man sitting against the wall. I tell you, the filthier, the crazier they were, the more he wanted them, first let one of those wander, dirty and deranged, onto the bridge, and he'd be off with him in a minute –

– No! countered the workman. That wasn't what he was after. *His* eyes were all for the yellow-headed barbarian scamps hustling down at the market end. (The workman's own hair was black as raw oil, bubbling up from some swampy spill.) Oh, he might take a poor beggar like this one here for a meal or a drink, or maybe help him to a doorway out of the rain – I've seen him do that. But he only wanted the little yellow-haired southerners. I saw him with enough of them, going and coming.

– At least once I saw him take a plump little mountain girl off from here, said the clerk; though he didn't look southern, his accent was, somewhat surprisingly, barbaric. (Still slumped against the wall, my friend glanced up – but only with his eyes.) He was a fine man, Vanar. A character, yes. But I've always thought that must be the real taste of such men. Perhaps he took a boy now and then. But I'm sure he only did it either to make people talk – or because he truly wanted to help. Everyone speaks of him as a good man. It's a sad comment, I know. But he wouldn't have the reputation he does, unless he liked his girls. And there're more than enough of them out here. The boys are always about, but they're a very small part of the business.

– Oh, no, my dears, declared the bald man in the eye makeup. I remember both of you, and you were only visitors to the bridge in those days. I was a daily denizen and a fully paid-up guild member in the sisterhood. I saw more of this overground sewer than either of you. And I know what he went after, believe me.

The workman chuckled and said:

– The way Vanar would carry on down here used to make me laugh. I knew he was rich, sure. But you could have sat me down and picked me up when I learned he was a count.

– A count, my dear? the made-up one declared. That man was in line to be a suzerain! 'Count,' you say? You must have heard people call her 'The Countess.' The way she went on here was a terror, as if there were no Neveryóna waiting for her back home!

– Well, observed the clerk, when you are as rich as Lord Vanar was, there are some things you don't *have* to worry about.

– This bridge has seen it all, declared the bald one, touching ringed fingers to both jeweled ears. And it has seen more than I'll ever tell you. Do you remember…

But, walking again, they were out of earshot.

That was when my friend, sitting against the bridge wall, realized he had heard only the three of them. He had no idea, nor would he ever now, who this Vanar' was. (Though it's good to see you smile at his name. Indeed, it *might* have been Vanar they spoke of back then; but it could have been any number of others who would have made you smile as broadly.) They had made sense; he had heard them. Save a donkey cart, trundling by across the walkway, it was quiet. Whatever great secret he'd been listening for, it had been uttered.

Oh, it had turned out some profoundly trivial, self-evident homily like: *You are only yourself, with your name, and nothing more.* No…that wasn't it. (When he tried to tell me later, he actually seemed surprised that he still couldn't remember it, as if his whole reason for recounting the occurrence to me had been to prompt its full return.) It was much simpler. It was so simple that, once heard, even with having forgotten it, there was little pull to think about it any longer. But at its utterance, the extraneous babble had ceased.

He raised his hand from where his fingertips touched his shins. His knuckles were black with dirt. He turned his arm over. His palms were only slightly lighter, and their crevices bore black lines as if someone who could write had inked them.

He touched his cheek. Dry skin against dry skin – a foul dryness, too. It let him know his face was probably as dirty as his hands. In the filth over his calf he saw several small sores – and a larger one on his ankle where, he remembered vaguely, a day or so back someone had pushed him against a cart wheel, and he'd scraped himself to the bone.

He got slowly to his feet, hips aching, shoulders sore, knees stiff. One nostril was raw inside. As he gained his balance, loose mucus trickled into his hairs on his upper lip. Limping a little, he walked to the bridge's end – and kept walking, into the loud market.

4

Most people hurrying around him did not look. But now and again, one or another at a distance would stare till he looked back. By the nameless gods, he thought, what kind of half-beast, half-man have I become? And grinned; and walked on, making for the public fountain.

A man-high stone in the market's center, the fountain spewed water, chattering from the natural cleft at the top, down into a carved basin – and how many times have you yourself, and how many others, stopped to drink there, if only on your way to, or on your return from, our performance?

He took his place in a line of five. In front of him a young woman with a green rag bound on her unevenly cropped hair glanced back and pulled forward, shrinking the distance between herself and the tarry-handed sewer-worker before her, while the fig vendor joining the line behind, his basket near empty and strung round his neck to rest on his hip, hung back, not actually staring.

He closed his eyes a moment, took a breath, and grinned again.

The woman in the head-rag drank hurriedly, left quickly.

He stepped up to the basin, plunged his hands into the spring water, and doused his hair and face. His naked flesh drew into bumps, as if feathers there had been plucked from pullet skin. He sloshed water under his armpits, rubbing the hair there with his fists. He sluiced freezing water over his arms, turning them this way and that, working at the black and wrinkled nut of his elbow, at the thick and scaly knob of his wrist. He splashed his neck, his chest, his chin. He rubbed his groin, his hips, his buttocks.

His legs were streaked with mud.

Brick swirled with dirty wash.

Once he glanced behind. The fig vendor, two more women, and another man still waited for him, nervously. Behind them, a fat market porter muttered something bitter, turned, and stalked off with his brooms over his shoulder, to disappear between the stalls of garden implements and spices on the left, cooking utensils and honeys to the right.

He went on washing.

Finally he leaned his buttocks against the rock and, with his wet forefinger, first on his left foot, then on his right, scrubbed between one toe and another, now and again scooping out another handful of water that ran down his leg as he cleaned off the ligaments of his feet. (The fig vendor gave up and went; one of the braver women behind moved in to take her drink and, when he'd started to reach in the bowl, gave him a harsh look so that he pulled his hand back and waited for her to finish.) Wet, shivering, he stood up and splashed through the muddy puddle he'd left before the fountain where the brick was worn down to gray-green stone around the inefficient drains. He walked to the market's edge and loped twice about the whole square, sometimes flapping his elbows to let his flanks and underarms dry.

Then he walked onto the bridge.

Two youngsters, one a barbarian with whom he'd once traded tricks, called to him:

– Hey!

He nodded, waved back to them – struck by a sudden and ungainly sense of the community in this awkward spot, where all the city's fragments jammed together without quite filling the space, so that a certain play in the engine of the port was apparent here, a shock, a shiver that was doubtless felt from the real and resounding waterfront to the elegant and unimaginable High Court.

– Hello, there! That was the grain-seller, who always took him to the warehouse five streets off, where the late sun fell through the roof chinks onto the loft's scattered straw.

He swung around, grinning, went up to the old man, who regarded him strangely, and put his hand on the shoulder of the brown tunic:

– You'll be around for a while? he asked. I'll be back in a few minutes, Papa. You stay here, I'll be back, now –

– Well, I don't know…the grain-seller said. What was the matter with you last week, anyway? I came by here and I saw you – at least I *think* it was you…

– You wait for me, Papa! He pressed the grain-seller's arm. You wait for me, now. I know I don't look too good right through here. But I'll be back. Papa let me hold a couple of coins – no, don't give me anything! (The elderly man had started to move away.) You just wait for me. We'll have a good time. Down where you used to take me. In the warehouse, right? I'll be back! He turned and sprinted toward the bridge's far end.

– Where you hurrying, darling?

He looked around at the listless voice to see a thin woman, her eyes winged with paint and a colored scarf wound high on her ribs just under her darkly aureoled breasts.

– You want some fun tonight? she went on, not even looking.

– Sure, little gillyflower! He stepped up to her. How much do you want to give me for the best piece *you'll* ever have?

– You? The woman frowned nearsightedly at him. Me, give you anything? I'm not even *talking* to you! I'm not even *thinking* of you! I was addressing another gentleman entirely.

– hink about me, little flower. Think about me and weep! I may not look like much, but I could give you a time to tell your grandchildren about. No, and he narrowed an eye at her, you couldn't afford my prices.

The woman made a sound between a laugh and snuffle and turned to call to another man passing:

– Hello, darling? How you doing?

Shaking his head and pleased with himself, he hurried to the other end of the bridge.

A few streets down the Pavē was a yard with a cistern, where, with ropes still attached, a few ceramic buckets were always left near the wall. Though he'd taken off the surface grime, the dirt felt as if it had somehow worked into, if not through, his whole body; as determined as he was to be rid of it, he was not sure if water could wash it away.

At the cistern's wall, he chose a chipped pail, lowered it, felt it hit, then bob on the slack; he waved the rope wide till the lopsided container filled and sank. Then he hauled it, sloshing, up beside the iron staples, caught the bucket's bottom with one hand, hefted it high, and dumped cold water over his head.

It seemed even colder than the fountain's gush – because he was already half dry.

He hauled up another bucket.

And another.

Somewhere around the fifth, with his mouth wide and water running into it from his moustache, drops falling from his lashes to his cheeks, trickles from his beard running down his chest, he paused.

At the other side of the cistern, a heavy girl, with her wet jar dripping onto the cistern wall, was just looking away from him with a serious expression. She wore a rough robe. Her arms were lightly freckled. Shaking water from her fingertips, she pushed a wisp of hair aside, where it stayed, moist, against her temple.

In a house behind, an old woman pulled back a raffia curtain to call shrilly:

– Get in the house! Get in the house, now! You have work! Get in!

The girl turned from the cistern, her jar on her hip, to amble away, her arm out and waving, gently as some gull's wing, for balance.

Women's bodies?

He looked in the bucket, still half full, lifted it again, and dashed it over himself.

Men's bodies?

No, he preferred women's bodies. And however many men he went with, however few women, and whatever contradiction anyone might see in it, he had to accept that too. And if, in two years, or ten years, his preferences changed, that would simply be something more to accept – though if they hadn't changed in *these* few months (he started to shiver in the faintest of breeze), he doubted they would!

He watched her go, her arm with its light speckling still waving, beckoning him on, beyond the cistern, beyond the yard, beyond the bridge, beyond Kolhari, till it seemed suddenly to indicate a border to the entire country that, truly, he had never even thought of before, a border that, simply because, however uncertainly, it must exist, he now realized, as the girl with her jar turned stolidly into another alley, if only because the city had taught him that such borders were not endings so much as transitions, he now knew he might someday flee across, down whatever street, across whatever bridge, along whatever road, through whatever tangled wilderness, into whenever and wherever, the possibilities vaster than the seeable, endless as the sayable.

To flee beyond Nevèrÿon itself was no more impossible than his flight across the unknown to Kolhari, his flight across whatever madness to this new sanity.

He went back to the bridge.

The grain-seller was gone – probably with some barbarian. But the warm weather, he could see as he stood there, looking now up, now down the walkway, had brought out other men.

Was it three weeks, or three months later? While he lay on his back in the warehouse loft with a chink of sunlight falling through the roof into his left eye, he glanced down at the gray head on his belly:

– Hey, Papa. You can give me something to do besides this, can't you?

– What do you mean, the elderly man asked sleepily.

– Give me some work. Reaching down to rough the man's sparse hair, he chuckled. I can't spend my whole life on the bridge, Papa, waving this half-peeled goose gullet at hungry men who want to go off and tumble about as though we were boys behind a barn! I'm a good worker. I can work hard.

– You're a good drinker. The man laughed.

The young man blinked up at the chink. No, Papa. I don't drink that much anymore. You haven't seen me drunk in a week.

– I can't give you any work here, the sparse-haired grain-seller said. I have some drivers taking some carts for me down to the Vinelet market…but I couldn't hire you. It wouldn't look right. I mean if someone in town recognized you. No, I –

– I can handle oxen. The young man gazed up at the beams across the ceiling. You got oxen to pull your carts? Oxen don't give me any trouble. I've been thinking of going south.

– Of course, said the man, who'd been doing his own thinking, there's *one* cart I have to send along…it will carry grain, certainly. I have an ox for it. But there might be something else in it too, you see? Whoever drives it would have to take it mostly down the back roads. Certain customs inspectors – for this cart – I'd just as soon avoid.

– I could take it down any roads you want.

– You've always struck me as pretty trustworthy; and anyone seeing you would just think you were some country farmhand.

– Me? asked the young man. But that's what I *am*, Papa! Not too clever, not too wild, not too talkative, hey? A friendly fool, that's me, isn't it? Just look at me. What could be in a cart someone like me drove *besides* grain? Come on, let's go have a beer. I could take an oxcart of grain down to…wherever you wanted me to, deliver it to whoever you wanted.

– Well, perhaps you could. I wouldn't send any of my regular drivers. Some of them are family men, you see. If the gods do only their customary job as they work at the world, all should go well with the trip; nevertheless there might be some danger attached to it.

– I'll take your cart down. Hey, and I'll bring it back too! I need to get out of the city. I won't go back to the farm. Don't worry, Papa. Just tell me when you want me to leave.

And so he made the transition from hustler to smuggler as easily as he had made any of the others that had split his life into its various befores and afters. Possibly the last one has been violent enough so that the others in wait along the roads for him held little terror. I've often wondered who it was, in the intervening days – another hustler with a bit more experience than he, or perhaps a world-wise client – who told him some of the real dangers of his new undertaking. Did he ponder the fact that for the grain-seller to entrust such a mission to him was far more a sign that the elderly gentleman considered him particularly expendable rather than particularly dependable?

No matter. He did the task. And several more like it.

It was some weeks after our return from the provinces that, at the end of an afternoon's skit, I saw him, at the edge of the audience, clapping and shouting so loudly, so enthusiastically, with that look of special knowledge, of intimate privilege, of personal connection with the wonder, the magic, if not the very madness of our performance. As we began to tear down the platform, I motioned him up, and, with a grin, he vaulted onto the stage and walked with me among the other actors and musicians and dancers still in our make-up and bright attire, nodding now to the Leading Lady, waving at the groom he'd helped back on carnival night, here to my wagon, where he told me…well, *some* of what I've told you.

No doubt I made much of him, aghast at the depths he'd fallen to, and as delighted at his newfound success as some merchant when his child brings home a particularly fine report from your own bright institution. His attitude both to the madness and to the fortune that had followed it was the sensible gratitude of the spared. Oh, I'm sure that the deeds of that dim period of unexplained derangement, while they seemed behind him, still were able to frighten him at those moments when the chaos of the city around him would momentarily join the inner voices with which, truly, all of us spend so much of our lives in antiphon. If he did not, here with me, seem racked by the fear of madness's return, I suspect it was because he was, finally, very brave. In no way denying that bravery, I also felt, as he sat on my bed, telling me of all this, he truly saw himself as too insignificant to be visited by such an experience more than that once – as long as he kept his drinking down. His pleasure was to be part of the city, to know an actor in the play, to have an interesting tale of inner and outer adventure to tell, when he was called backstage as a sign of his privilege.

My own response to all this?

It was of the lowest. I kept wondering, while he sat there, what would happen if I enjoined him to stay with me a little longer, perhaps, than he'd planned – oh, certainly for his usual fee, while we did, oh, only some of the things we'd done before. Yet, I was also honored enough by his confidence to fear that he might be offended if I suggested it. I fancied that part of his reason for attending the performance, for clapping, for coming back to talk with me, was because he somehow felt I had had some part in the whole incomprehensible transition.

Unlike his scare from the prop dragon, however, after he told me once of his mad moment, the tale dropped from among his anecdotes. Yet, over our next few encounters, it lingered for me under the various comic mishaps he would recount, now in the spring, now in the fall, about his new nefarious activities. I even wondered if he didn't see the glimmering and gaudy characters we gave voice to, as they untangled the mystery of each other's plottings and schemings, out on our sunlit or lantern-lit platform, as some controlled image of his own many-voiced days of disorder: that, indeed, he saw me, us, our whole theatrical company as living constantly with and within the polylogue chaos he had traversed so surprisingly and unexpectedly, and that his applause acknowledged in *us* a certain bravery, which, he felt, we now shared. But whatever you say of them, finally I had to dismiss such notions as the ratiocinations desire can entangle about the most reasonable of us.

After he left that afternoon, I went walking across the market, to wander back and forth over the bridge, curious if his new success as a full-fledged petty criminal hadn't been somewhat exaggerated; wondering if, indeed, he mightn't have stopped to loiter, in his usual place, hoping for a coin or two, where, if I saw him, I would have no compunction asking from him what I had been too diffident to request in the wagon. On my third trip back and forth, after searching His Spot and many others, when I realized that, no, he was really no longer there, I told myself I was simply horny and, certainly, one of the other boys out could satisfy me.

Still, I came back to the genial and boisterous supper at the communal actors' table behind our wagons, alone. And thus we both made another transition: to friend and friend. But, by the hem of your royal cousin, whose reign is enigmatic and eternal, that is really all I can tell you about him that I didn't tell you before.

5

Yes, what a fine idea to quit that stuffed and stuffy wagon for a stroll out here. Mind you, we must not stray too far from the market; I have to be back for the evening performance. Will you be staying?

Of course, I understand.

You have responsibilities waiting at the school. It is already beyond amazement that you've managed to get away to see our entertainment, or to talk with me, at all. It would be base ingratitude to demand, to expect, even to *think* of more.

But after all this discussion of my meeting with your erstwhile contemporary, I can't help wonder: do you recall when we met, young man? And don't protest that you're now forty. It's still the right of a sixty-year-old to call you young if he likes.

Yes, no doubt I was among the more interesting guests at the to-do your uncle threw for you, out in Neveryóna, in honor of your return from your youthful, year-long trip across our magnificent and mysterious land.

That's where you think we met?

But how in the world would I have received my invitation?

I knew no one in your circle, then, to bring me along to the party.

Yes, it *was* from you. You yourself.

You really don't remember inviting me?

Truly, I suspect the gods have crafted a different city for each of us, specified not only by our different points of view in it, but also by the random and irrational discontinuities into which our hopelessly faulty recalls endlessly cast and recast our diverse and separate lives.

It was on a little street, not far from here. For me it's all quite clear and sharp. A harness mender used to have her shop there, oh, perhaps three alleys over from where we walk now. She was a firm-voiced, hard-armed little woman, with a look in her eyes not unlike my abandoned wife's – though their personalities were quite distinct. (I always felt her laugh was larger than she was.) Those who patronized her business were fond of her, for she was an evenhanded worker and a fair-minded dealer with them all; but her life was harder than most women's because she had an idiot son, whom, now that he was almost grown and her husband dead, she would sit outside her shop on a bench in good weather. Pear-shaped, soft-shouldered, bean-headed, and often drooling, he had a spindle, a piece of wood that hung on a cord, which he would hold in one stubby hand, spinning the weight with the other, hour after hour, examining it, cooing over it, batting it now one way, now batting it back.

Ah, you *do* remember the idiot.

Well, I used to go there mornings simply to observe him, her, her customers. For wagoners, harness makers, smugglers, idiots – all of them figured from time to time in our skits, and you know I have always liked to observe from life what I interpret up on the platform. One morning when the sky was limpid and sun-drenched but the clouds down at the seaside were piled like metal shavings, I came there, as I often did in those days, just to watch; and while I was watching, I noticed a young man standing a ways off, clearly doing much the same as I. His tunic was simple – but far too clean for anyone to think him native to any near neighborhood. Did that fine, dark face hold a full two decades behind its youthful beard?

I decided to include him in my observations, which have always been of the active sort. Approaching him, I asked what he was doing on that fair morning, and how did he like the weather of late? Do you recall what he said – for, in truth, he was you.

Now, you say, you begin to have the faintest recollection? I can only wonder what my smuggling friend remembers of *our* first meeting, what words, images, impressions, or even misremembrances he retains from it, if any. Given his homeless state, the daily pressures of his life – the amount of beer he drank in those days! – I might expect such vagueness from him. But really, my friend! From you?

– What do you do? I asked. How odd. Followed by, 'And how much do you charge to do it?' that was my first frank and specific question to my friend on the bridge…(I won't bother you with the particularities of his answer, generally liberal forward, admittedly limited behind.) You said to me:

– I am struggling to become a wise man, and some say I've even made a stride or two in that direction. But sometimes I'm afraid my knowledge is wholly dependent on my ability to watch for minutes at a time the quivering of a single leaf, deep green on its upper face, olive gray under, with yellow veins all through – and a bit of brown at one edge, scalloped by some caterpillar. It's a quality, I'm afraid, I share with that creature drooling in front of the tackshop.

So it probably doesn't mean very much, whatever others make of it.

Oh, I see I *have* tickled you! Look at you laughing there!

Yes, that really *is* what you said.

Well, you were the kind of young man who went around *saying* things like that. Believe me, I was no less impressed with your answer than with his. People made much of you in those days, I was soon to learn – even as they do now. That you were able to keep any humility about you at all was an accomplishment.

The arrogance and presumption of it, you say?

The measured and honest insight of it, I would say rather. That's certainly what struck me at the time. But I suppose that only means your liberalities and limitations fit comfortably with my own interest and needs. We talked for quite a while, there in the street. You had recently returned from your year-long trip, in which you had traveled all about Nevèrÿon, searching out this or that monument, looking for the site of that or the other fable. Because I, in the ordinary course of things, just happened to have visited many of those same places, and many more you hadn't, and had heard a few of the fables myself, as well as some that were new to you – not very astonishing given that I had spent most of forty years doing what you had done in one – you decided I was clever. Also, I think you found the *idea* of an actor interesting.

That's when you told me your uncle was throwing a party for you, out on his estate. It was to be the next day. Why didn't I come…? And later that evening, much to my surprise, your servant came down to the market to present a formal invitation at my wagon door – which rather impressed my fellow mummers.

You say, now, you have the vaguest memory of something like it, but, really, you only assent to it because I have said it? Oddly that's the way I recall the multi-voiced derangement of my smuggler friend. From his really very bare account, from my own observations of other madmen, and from the little flights and flirtations I've had – yes, I confess it – with madness on my own, I suppose I've decorated my tale.

The result is very like a memory of something that never really happened – at least not to me.

The party itself – that you'd thought was our meeting? For me that's really quite vague. As I wasn't performing, I suspect I found it a bore. A moment after I arrived, however, I recall you came by the gate – looking as though you didn't remember me even then, I might add. But all at once you smiled, and we strolled in among the others, the two of us talking together, though of what I couldn't tell you. Oh, you'd invited quite a collection, somewhat to your relatives' dismay. It was not that I didn't feel at home in such opulence, for a few times in my then forty years I'd been within comparable gates; but it was intriguing to observe the endless ways in which everyone – with the possible exception of you – seemed to feel equally uncomfortable with all those, well, oddballs you'd gathered about.

Ah, I'm glad accounts of your youthful manner can still amuse you. I found you amusing too. Also touching. For all the distance between us, I saw a bit of myself in you.

Several times we ended up in conversation. There was talk of my entertaining at some future gathering – a plan which, over the next few months, on several occasions blossomed. (You were, and still are I know, a generous man.) If it hadn't I might have missed out my friend at the bridge. But the rest you certainly remember, at least in outline. And unlike my bridge-bound infatuation I recounted to you this afternoon, our friendship – yours and mine – without the sexual element, grew and deepened over a much longer period before it eased to its present amiable stasis.

But you must recall, in later days, going with me various places about the city to observe, if not the idiot and the world of wagoners and harness menders that moved about his oblivious head, then other denizens of Kolhari, now in one neighborhood, now in another.

Well, I'm glad you do!

You must also recall that wonderful, frustrating, endless argument we had back then, which I thought would occupy us as obsessively as money occupies the working men and women on the bridge or off it.

You claimed that the habits and mannerisms, which I collected in our travels to decorate the characters I played or coached in our platform skits to make them more real and recognizable to our audience, were ultimately invalid because I would embroil those same carefully and colorfully constructed barrow-pushers and counts and wagoners and cutpurses in perfectly preposterous actions, during the course of which each would declare with great eloquence things that no count or cutpurse would ever possibly say. And if any ever even thought that he or she felt such things, you maintained, it was only from having been taken in by our skits in the first place.

And this much was certainly true: I'd play the most eloquent of idiots, while both of us knew that, whatever leaf he observed, the poor creature slobbering on Netmenders' Row had little to do with the carefully organized carryings-on with which I so delighted the market strollers, however accurately I let the spit spill down my chin or spun my bit of wood.

In the same way, I suppose, you could say that I informed the young man I told you of this afternoon with a voice, or voices, not his – that, indeed, however cleverly I decorated them from whatever experiences of my own, on any sort of reflection one of your perspicacity must see that, finally, they *could* not be his; even if, hearing me tell it, he himself thought he recognized those voices and applauded my performance, as heatedly as is his wont.

– It is as if, you would have said back then, you are presenting on your platform not people, but rather the nameless gods on whom all are modeled; then you sully them with human traits and names.

My argument to you, during our same observational forays, was that what *you* collected, studied, and catalogued – the same habits and mannerisms as did I – were only the various silences of these same poor slaves and masters, workers and wastrels; and until you pried some voice out of them, alone or in concert, whether the voice of their secret fears and desires as you suspected them or even some desire or fear of your own, unless you gave them a meaning that was significant to you, what you observed was *only* silence. It spoke to no one; even its meaning for yourself was muffled, and it could have no other for either gods or the faulty humans they model, regardless of what traits or names either humans or gods were or were not known by.

You remember our endless colloquy?

Well, I'm glad you nod your head to *some*thing.

In the interim between then and your present visit, I must tell you, however, I have thought of a much better answer for you: the voices I give, however decorated with observations and interpretations of the other, are, nevertheless and certainly, very much my own.

But they do not speak *for* the other– and therefore speak falsely.

They speak rather *to* the other: the other in me, the other in you, the other in my other friend – assuming he would not finally and for the first time turn at this particular outrage to the real we call 'his story' and laugh with undisguised derision at my preposterous fancy with no relation at all to his life, his madness, his city – instead of giving out with his usual applause. They speak against the other. They speak always in dialogue with, in contest to, in protest of the real. They are always calling out to the other across the bridge on whose wild span madness and desire endlessly trade places, creating a wilderness at their center as palpably dangerous as that observed at any ill-mapped border. The monologue of art must be reinterpreted as the many-voiced argument of the artist with life, with life's images – indeed, as the wrangle between the articulate and everything else, with desire never fully possessed by any party, but endlessly at play between.

Oh, of course. I know, you must be on your way.

I have tried your patience much too long in the name of our eloquent friendship. And there I was, I see it now, daring to encroach on grounds that should be wholly yours. But you know how an old man – or even one not so old – can babble on. You must be off?

So must I. So must I. The evening performance is at hand.

What?

You plan soon to send your students again to see us, just as you did last spring? Oh, you *are* too kind to an aging artist! You say it is their most pleasurable assignment? Really, you say too much.

But let me repeat it: I've known you for a while, and you have done this before, so this is not a complete surprise. Thus, I have something of a – though not a complete – surprise for you! We're preparing a new skit, back at the wagons, largely under my direction. Certainly it will be ready by the time your students troop down to join our common audience.

In it, they will see students like themselves, idiots, actors, barmaids, businessmen, teachers, tradesmen, harness menders, housewives, philosophers, philanderers, prostitutes, and princesses – all of them pursuing each other with mayhem and hilarity, song and dance, now through the halls of a school out in Sallese, now through the Old Market of the city. You can be sure that on our platform each of them will have more to say to, and more to do with, each other than any of them ever might be expected to in life. Oh, you have no idea how carefully I have been observing. Their eloquence will be unbelievable! Their significance will be overpowering! You have no notion what wonders I shall give voices to! The plot, I think, will turn on the theft of something magical, smuggled away before dawn – something, anyway, of incomparable worth. We know, of course, who is hired to carry it off at the bottom of his grain cart. But who was the *original* perpetrator of the crime?

Now *that* is the mystery!

It's the part, of course, I haven't figured out. But all my spectators, even you (deny it, now, I dare you), love to see a mystery solved, the hero applauded, the villain flogged –

To the bridge?

Oh, you can go the short way that turns onto the quay. It's right through there. That will take you to it. But I'm going down here, as I want to get back to the other side of the market as quickly as I can. Oh, forgive me if I laugh a little now.

But was my tale this afternoon so powerful as that? Well, it's good for an old reprobate like me to know that even a young man as high-minded as you can consider looking in that common lane for some loud and hearty wench just up from the country, some rude and boisterous boy just down from the hills –

But you frown more deeply. Oh, forgive me, young master! I certainly did not mean –

It was only a joke!

We are old friends!

But see, I have transgressed some limit of politeness I never dreamed would offend you.

When I was off in that provincial wilderness, beset with all temptation, would I appropriate your noble name? (The nameless gods alone can hear what voice in you I've momentarily called up to contest your usually most decorous behavior!) Could you then suspect – ?

Might I even *think* that this afternoon's performance would lead you to appropriate my own low practices and preferences, grown from an evil upbringing and a licentious existence on the periphery of all society, in the wilderness between far provinces, at the sordid center of our city?

Please, do not take offense at an aging actor's jest!

I merely meant to say that it lies there, on the way from the Spur to Sallese – a bit of madness one must cross to get from here to there.

– New York
February 1984

FALLING SKY

RAJAN KHANNA

Ben's scuffed boots kicked up a cloud of dust and grit as they slammed against the debris of the Monterey street.

The ground.

Above him, his airship, the *Cherub*, floated, anchored to an overturned tractor trailer scaled with greenery. Nature reclaiming yet another human artifact. Vegetation, at least, did not go hungry.

Ben scanned the area around him, alert for any movement, and not finding any, he checked his wrappings again. He made sure the gap between sleeve and glove was covered, secured the scarf around his face, confirmed that the goggles and knit cap were tight. Then he looked around again before moving.

He crunched through the decaying bones of Old Monterey, trying to ignore the hollow ache of his stomach. The city had been picked clean years ago, but he still hoped something remained. It had happened before. He'd once found a handful of nuts and candy at the old aquarium gift store. Places where the Ferals, or scavengers like him, hadn't thought to look.

He'd been so desperate for food that he'd even tried fishing, lowering his dad's rusty rod out of the side of the airship gondola. But with a tinny crack, the housing of the reel had fallen apart, and the fish, hooked neatly on the end of the line, had gone flapping down to the water below.

So, unwilling to visit Gastown just yet, he was back to the city. Dust kicked up by the wind buffeted his goggles and he had to take a moment to clear them off. The tang of the sea was strong even through the scarf wrapped tightly around his face.

The aquarium, past the crumpled buildings and wrecked cars, looked smaller than when he'd last seen it. His father had told him that they'd once kept animals there – fish, even some seals and dolphins. He'd ventured in one day, shortly after his dad had died. He'd wandered the old displays, the glass dusty and covered from inside with a thick carpet of algae.

In one of the windows, though, there'd been a gap in the coating, and after dusting it off he'd looked in. Against the dark bottom he'd seen pale, human-sized bones in a haphazard pattern. He never found out what display it was – the wall had long since fallen to pieces – but that one sight filled him with such a deep sadness that he'd never returned.

Now he picked through the crumble of an old building, some kind of store, and sifted mortar dust through his fingers. *There's no food here,* he thought. But he continued anyway.

He was about to leave when he spied a small spot of green poking through beneath a grey chunk of masonry. Ben pushed over the rock, revealing a small, but intact stick of superglue. Next to it, half hidden in the dust, lay a single set of metal nail clippers. It was, strictly speaking, a score. Superglue was invaluable for dealing with wounds and scrapes. But it wasn't food, and at that moment it did nothing to ease the hollow ache inside of him.

He pulled out his father's worn revolver from the holster at his belt, then the tarnished Star of David from his pants pocket. It and the pistol were all he had left of his father, other than the airship, of course.

He pulled the Star from its frayed cord. The original chain had snapped when he'd pulled it from his father's neck. For a while he had wrapped the whole thing — cord and all — around the revolver's grip, but it had come loose the last time he'd drawn it. He was lucky he hadn't lost it entirely. It was perhaps foolish to waste the superglue, but he told himself he needed to make sure it hadn't dried. Opening the cap, he affixed the Star of David to the revolver's brown handle. After a moment it stuck fast.

Ben tucked away the pistol, then the tube and clippers, and stepped back out into the street. His eyes were drawn to a pile of bones on the sidewalk. A dog. Picked clean by Ferals, no doubt. On his last trip to the city, he'd found a three-legged dog, alive. The poor thing had limped over to him, panting at his feet. It was so pathetic, its dark grey hair sticking out in all directions, one ear half eaten, that he had picked it up to bring it back to the airship. But when he felt its ribs pressing hard against its skin, he'd realized it was just another mouth to feed, and so he'd placed it back on the ground, turned his back and left. At least he hadn't eaten the dog himself. Most wouldn't have given it a second thought.

On his way back to the anchored airship, he passed a pile of droppings. He pulled his father's revolver out of the holster at his belt and watched for movement among the sagging buildings. The pile looked old, but that meant little.

As if to confirm his suspicions, a howl reverberated through the streets. Then echoed yelping. Ferals on the hunt.

He ran for the rope ladder, holding on tight to the revolver, afraid of dropping it.

Halfway to the ladder, he heard a voice cry out. "Wait!"

He stopped and something collided with him, knocking him to the ground, tangled up in him. He sucked in air, smelled something oniony and grassy. "You have to help me," the voice said.

He looked up into the thin face of a woman. Barely older than him, with glasses - whole, real glasses, - she clutched at a worn and battered canvas satchel. A rifle was slung across her back and she wore a stained surgical mask.

"You have to get me out of here," she said

Ben pulled her to her feet, his pulse quick. Dark shapes moved in the distance, maybe two blocks away. Close to the ground, loping.

"C'mon." He grabbed for her hand—it seemed like a child's hand, or how he imagined a child's hand must be—and pulled her toward the ladder. The bestial noises grew louder, yelps and snarls, the occasional high pitched shriek.

"Better get that rifle out," Ben said.

"Can't," she said. "Out of ammo."

"Damn it. Then you go first." Ben pushed her in front of him toward the ladder. "I'll cover you."

He brought the revolver up, aiming at the pursuing Ferals. There were at least four of them, probably more. They traveled in larger packs. He fired once, twice, hoping that it might scare them off, that he might get lucky and knock one down. Ferals only swarmed when they were hungry, but there was a lot of that going around lately.

He spared a look up at the woman climbing the ladder, but she still seemed so low. The *Cherub* was far above her. The Ferals could reach someone at her height. They could reach him.

"Hurry!" He pushed at her boots. The soles were worn almost completely down.

He made out six Ferals. Four men and two women, one pregnant. The pregnant one's belly stretched the filthy, worn shirt she still wore. He reloaded, fired again. Two more shots. Still they came on. He thought he could already smell the carrion and sweat smell that clung to them.

He looked up and the boots and satchel were higher now. He gripped the rope ladder and began to climb. It was difficult with the revolver, but he kept a tight grip on it, curling his arm around the rope, pulling himself up clumsily.

One of the Ferals howled at the escaping quarry. The same one, or maybe a different one, broke ahead of his peers and ran for the ladder and Ben's trailing feet.

An adrenaline surge sent Ben scrambling upward. He fired down with the revolver, but the shot missed. Then, to Ben's horror, the revolver went twisting out of his hand and down to the ground. His father's revolver. For a moment he froze, the Star of David catching the sun, and part of him wanted to lunge after it. To follow it to the ground.

But he knew it was gone, that he couldn't follow, and he used both hands to scramble up the ladder and into the gondola.

Ignoring the woman, he pushed the engines to full and took the *Cherub* up and away from the ground.

The engines strained, but the ship didn't move.

The anchor. He'd forgotten the anchor. He released it from its mooring and pulled away without reeling it up.

Yet still something was wrong.

He guessed it before he saw it through one of the gondola windows. The lead Feral clung to the ladder, scampering up the rungs.

Ben made sure he was at maximum acceleration and headed back inland, not caring where he was going.

The ladder swung behind the airship, halting the Feral's movement. But still the beast clung to it. Who had he once been? Someone's father? Someone's husband? Yet an animal now. Nothing more. It took minutes for the thing to drop and while Ben should have been satisfied by this, he wasn't. He still mourned the loss of his father's revolver.

He turned to face the woman. "What the hell were you doing down there? You nearly got me killed."

She pushed the glasses back up her sharp nose and pulled off the surgical mask. With the wavy black hair that curled around her face, she looked as if peeking out from some foliage.

"Did they touch you?" he asked.

"No. I was careful." She rubbed one arm with the other.

Ben stared at her, and all he could see were the tiny bands of exposed flesh. At the neck, at the wrists, the stretch of forehead not covered by her hair. He grabbed her, pinching the skin, looking for cuts or scrapes. Anything that might mean infection.

She gritted her teeth. "I'm fine," she said. "I'm clean. I know the precautions."

Her skin was dark where the sun had touched it. Not quite brown. Smooth. A smattering of freckles dotted her arms and her chest where the neckline of her shirt had fallen. Some instinctual part of him noticed that she was attractive, but all he could think about was disease. It made him feel less human.

Ben pulled back at last. "Okay. You look okay."

"Your idea of hospitality needs work," she said under her breath.

"Excuse me?"

"I'm sorry," she said. "You saved my life. Thank you." She rummaged in a side pocket of her bag, pulled out two sticks of what looked like dried meat. "Here." She held them out to him.

Ben's mouth watered. Still he paused. He didn't know this woman. Eventually, though, his stomach won out. He took the meat sticks, sniffed them. They seemed good. He nibbled at the edge of one.

"You didn't answer my question," Ben said. "What were you doing down there? And alone?"

"Research," she said.

"What kind of research?"

"I'm studying the Ferals."

Ben stared at her, then shook his head. "Lady, you're crazy."

She shrugged. "You're not the first to say that."

"Why?"

"The virus. The…Bug. I'm studying it."

Ben shook his head. He'd heard stories, of people doing something similar. None of them had done anything to change the world.

"How did you get down there?" he asked.

"I had an arrangement with a pilot. He took me where I needed to go and I paid him for his services. Only the bastard got spooked and left me there."

"I'm not sure I blame him," Ben said.

"You were down there, too," she said.

Ben shrugged. "I usually run away from the Ferals, not toward them. What did you do to get them riled up like that?"

"I got too close to a nest," she said. "They were hungry, on alert."

"That I can understand," Ben said. Even with the dried meat in his hand, with the adrenaline draining out of him his stomach roared for more.

"In that case," she said, "I have a proposition for you."

"I'm listening."

"I have some food–some dried meat, some trail bars, stuff like that. Enough for a few weeks at least. I'll give you all of it if you drop me somewhere."

Ben's mouth filled with saliva at the thought of food. "Let me see it."

She turned around before opening her bag. Fair enough, Ben thought. Stuff was hard to come by these days – not wanting to broadcast what you had was smart. She handed him a smaller, plastic bag filled with more dried meat, and what looked like grain bars.

"That's not enough for a week," he said.

"This is is what I have here," she said. "The rest is at our destination."

"And where's that?"

"Gastown," she said.

Ben shook his head. "No. Sorry. I'm not going there. But I'll drop you somewhere else where you can get someone to take you there."

"That's where the food is," the woman said. "If you want to get paid, you have to take me there."

Ben shook his head again, then looked at his scuffed and splitting boots. She could be lying to him. But if she really did have that much food, it would be worth even a trip to Gastown.

"Fine," he said. He turned to the airship controls, spread out his charts and maps, and plotted a rough course north, in the direction of Gastown.

"My name is Miranda," she said at his back.

★

Miranda ran her slender fingers over the railing of the *Cherub's* gondola. "This is a nice airship," she said. "Where'd you get it?"

"It belonged to my parents," Ben said, making sure his course calculations were correct.

"Are they...?"

"Mom died when I was young," Ben said. "Dad...dad got infected." He turned back to the controls, the memories coming back to him, his father succumbing, face twisted in a bestial snarl as the Bug swallowed his human mind. Ben hadn't known his father had been infected, hadn't had the chance to say goodbye. Then the man was gone, transformed into a thing, an animal, and he'd snatched at the Star of David, pulled it away, and ran. Ran for the airship and the safety of the air.

"Are you a plod?" Ben asked.

Miranda shook her head. "I have zep blood in me." She still looked out of the windows, squinting against the setting sun. "I lived in a balloon commune for a while. My folks and the others were all scientists. Biologists, physicists, academics. But it wasn't easy. We eventually had to separate, just to find places that needed our help."

"And now you're headed back?" Ben said.

She moved her gaze from the windows and looked down at the gondola floor. "There is no back."

Ben found that he agreed.

★

Ben scratched at his beard and then stopped. He suddenly wondered what he looked like. It had been a while since he'd been around anyone else. Longer since it had been a woman. He hadn't shaved in months. He wasn't even sure where he'd left the knife he'd been using as a razor. Maybe he could take care of it in Gastown. There was a barber there, a fair barterer.

Then he caught himself. Why? He was going to drop Miranda off at Gastown and then he'd be by himself again. No use wasting good barter on something unnecessary.

Miranda walked around the gondola, poking around at Ben's things. She still clutched the bag slung around her body. "You can put your bag down," Ben said. "I'm not going to steal it."

She looked back over her shoulder at him. "It's okay. I feel better with it close.

She walked over to the radio, absently turning the dial. The LED numbers sped through the frequencies in bright red. She stopped on "31.4". "Close enough," she said.

Ben was about to ask her what she meant, but then Miranda looked up and ran to the front window of the gondola. "There it is."

Gastown stretched out like an airborne patchwork quilt, undulating with the currents of wind. In the center, the flat, barge-like platforms held firm, hanging from a canopy of balloons, but on the edges, the lashed on airships vibrated slightly. Atop, in the rigging, the patchmonkeys ran over the canopy's netting, searching for leaks, chattering to each other in the morning air.

Ben felt dwarfed by the larger structure. As the lookouts spotted his ship, and the flags began their colorful dance, he had the urge to turn around, to return to solitude. But he wasn't alone, and Miranda was smiling, chewing at her bottom lip. She clutched at her worn, worried bag with long fingers, the nails bitten down to the skin.

She looked at him. "What's the matter?"

He pointed at Gastown. "I'm not overly fond."

"Why not? Most people love it."

"It's not worth getting into," Ben said.

The nearest Gastown lookout flashed flags to indicate that he could bring the ship in to dock. Ben flashed his own sun-bleached flag to communicate his assent and, with a sinking in his stomach, brought the airship in.

Rough-looking dockhands threw mooring lines over to Ben and he tied them to the airship and dropped down the ramp. "After you," he said. Miranda descended onto the Gastown platform and Ben followed. His skin itched as his feet hit the wooden platform of the dock.

The pockmarked dockhand smirked when he saw Ben. "Haven't seen you in a while. You must be doing well for yourself." The man's tone indicated that he thought otherwise.

"The outside world is more fair to the independent operator," Ben said.

"Docking fee is two cans of fuel."

"Two cans?"

Miranda looked at him, pleading. "Fine," Ben said with a sigh. He climbed back aboard and fetched the fuel, bringing a stained plastic jug down on his back. "I think you made my point for me."

The dockhand took the jug. "Carry on," he said.

Ben looked at Miranda. "Lead on."

The outer ends of Gastown were made up mostly of converted vehicles, but the interior consisted of wooden platforms with makeshift sheds and shacks on them. Some were living quarters. Others were used for storage or as storefronts and businesses. Much of the station's resources were 'liberated' from the ground by the intrepid and foolhardy, but they were further refined and packaged or repackaged on the platform. Gastown was so far the only source of helium in the air. Valhalla, its rival to the east, had only managed hydrogen.

Shops sold ground-level artifacts or other useful items - rope, wood, stone. Gastown, like Valhalla, was a base for a new economy.

Ben followed Miranda past sheds and shacks made of wood and tin and aluminum. The luckiest had steel -- they passed one that had a repurposed car hood as part of the door. The Traffic Club was noteworthy because its outer walls were made entirely of street signs that its owner had collected in his time on a dirigible.

They walked down an alley of food stalls. The smell of cooked meat infiltrated Ben's senses, overwhelming everything. A nearby man sold roasted pigeon skewers. A ratty, mangy dog sat by the side of the stallkeeper. It eyed Ben guardedly.

For a moment Ben considered buying some, fishing the nail clippers out of his pocket and trading them for a hot meal. But if Miranda was telling the truth, he'd be set up for a while, longer if he stretched it. Plus he could always come back after they settled their business.

Miranda led him to the other end of the city, to a large roundish blimp that was lashed to a cigar-shaped zeppelin.

"This is yours?" Ben asked.

"Not exactly," Miranda said. "I work with a man named Sergei. I've know him since before my parents died. This is his ship."

Ben eyed the blimp. It had a soft envelope, making it more vulnerable, but its gondola was large and looked new and in good shape.

Miranda walked across the wooden plank leading to the gondola door and knocked on it. A man opened the door, older, with grey hair and beard. He wore a rollneck sweater and an old-fashioned captain's hat. Ben's father used to have one he'd picked up somewhere, but it had blown off one day when Ben was a kid, lost somewhere over the Cascades.

"Miranda!" The man embraced her. "Thank God. I was expecting you days ago."

"Raoul got skittish," Miranda said. "Then skipped out on me. This is Ben. He helped get me here. Come in, Ben."

Ben walked into the gondola, noting its fiberglass hull and the almost scratchless surface. Inside, a sterile air was broken only by piles of papers and notebooks that filled all the surfaces in the gondola, resting on consoles and tables and shelves. The man cleared off two chairs for them and beckoned them to sit down.

Ben sat down, crossed his legs. Miranda didn't sit. "I'm okay, Sergei," she said.

"Did you get them?" Sergei asked.

Miranda smiled and opened her bag, removing a small plastic case. She handed it to Sergei.

Sergei opened it up and pulled out a glass tube filled with a thick red liquid.

Ben jumped out of his chair. "Is that blood?"

Sergei held the tube up, twisting it in front of the light, his face eager. "Yes," he said.

"Feral blood?" Ben's voice rose.

"Yes," Miranda said.

Ben backed up against the wall of the gondola. His breath left him. "You're fucking nuts," he said. "You had that on my ship?" He was yelling now, imagining what might have happened if one of them had broken. On his ship.

Overcome with panic, he rushed for the door. Already his skin itched. One drop of that blood. One drop...

He inhaled as he hit the fresh air outside. He forced himself not to run. Just put distance between him and the airship.

A hand on his shoulder made him jump. "Wait," Miranda said. "We could use your help."

"Why? So I can play Russian Roulette with you? Months, maybe days from now, one of those will break and then you and your friend back there will get infected, too. It's only a matter of time."

"Ben, we're making progress," Miranda said.

Ben pulled a hand through his hair, tugging on the strands. "I've seen progress," he said. "I've seen people trying to find a cure. People trying to study them. It always ends in tragedy."

"I've seen people get infected," she said, holding his eyes with her own. "Good people. I know what it's like. Doesn't that make you want to stop it?"

Ben turned and started walking away.

"You didn't even get your food," Miranda said.

"Keep it," Ben said. He couldn't imagine eating it now. Not after what he saw.

"What are you going to do?" Miranda shouted at his back.

Ben continued walking. "Survive."

He moved in the direction of the *Cherub*, not looking behind him for fear that Miranda was still there. She would get the hint eventually.

He was almost back to the *Cherub* when he remembered his stores. He needed to restock before leaving. He wouldn't be coming back. At least not for a long time. He remembered hearing of a new generation of crops the Gastowners had started growing using soil transported up from the ground. He determined to find them.

He was walking down the main thoroughfare when sirens began to scream through the city. They meant attack. Ben looked around, but the canopy of balloons blocked his view. And he was now weaponless.

Screams began to mix with the sirens, and he ran toward them. He didn't owe Gastown anything, but old habits and all that.

He turned a corner near a rubber seller and caught sight of a commotion. People were running away from something moving in the narrow alley. With a start, Ben saw that it was a Feral. Here. In Gastown. He froze for a minute, overwhelmed, then another fell from the sky.

Both Ferals were bleeding profusely, and Ben saw that they had great gouges through the center of them. They sprayed blood from their wounds as they jerked and spasmed.

Ben went cold. They were mobile infections. They could spread the disease throughout the whole town.

Ben ran. But not toward his ship. The Ferals were in his way and everywhere he looked people were running and screaming, Gastown erupting into chaos all around him. He couldn't make it back to the *Cherub*. Instead, he headed back toward Miranda.

He yelled at the door to her gondola. Sergei threw it open, his face worried, anxious. "There are Ferals on the station," Ben panted. "Bleeding, running Ferals. I need you to take me to my ship."

"But we're tethered here," Sergei said.

"Cut the lines. Do you have anything to do that?"

"I have a machete," Sergei said. He ran out onto the platform, listening to the screams and looking at the chaos. "I'll do it." Sergei disappeared into the airship and emerged a moment later with a machete and a small axe. Ben helped him hack at the ropes that lashed the ship to Gastown.

As the last one whipped away, Ben ran aboard the ship. "Take the ship down and around to the other side. It will be safest that way." Already, people around them were doing the same, cutting off their ties, flying away from the main body of the town to avoid the contagion.

Miranda appeared, running to the gondola windows. "Jesus Christ," she said.

Ben stood by Sergei, watching the man pull the blimp down, and around the edge of Gastown. Even through the gondola walls they could hear the screams and the stutters of gunfire.

Ben watched for other ships. In the chaos he worried they would be clipped or worse. But Sergei managed to navigate them to the other side.

Sergei brought the ship up over the dock where the *Cherub* was moored. Ben moved to the rope ladder. "I owe you one," he said. He spared a last look for Miranda, then lowered himself to the platform. As soon as his feet hit the ground, he sprinted for his ship. He ignored the screams, the cries, and focused on getting inside, opening the door, and then closing it, hard and firmly into the lock. Then he pulled away, cutting the mooring lines, and heading for open sky.

As he pulled away from the dock, he looked behind him. Airships swarmed around Gastown like flies on a carcass. They all flew the flags of Valhalla, three interlocking triangles on a field of black. He saw one swoop in, a Feral hanging from it like a worm on a fishing hook. The Feral dropped onto the top rigging where it jerked and ran, eventually to fall through to the ground below.

Ben doubled over and retched onto the floor.

★

Ben carefully examined the map, trying to find the place where he'd found Miranda. After the escape from Gastown, doing his best to avoid the Valhalla marauders, he'd thought hard about his father and the lost revolver and he had decided to try to find it again. He needed a weapon, that much was clear, and at the moment he couldn't afford to barter for one. And where would he get it? Gastown had been neutralized. That left only Valhalla or the ground and neither option seemed attractive at the time.

Once he was sure he'd found the right place, he lowered the anchor, securing it onto another vehicle, and descended the ladder.

He froze halfway down. All he had to defend himself was the metal pipe strapped to his back. That meant he couldn't attack at range, and that left him vulnerable to contagion. Of course in close combat, blunt weapons were always better than those that cut. But it was still too close, and Ferals bled all too easily. "Go down, grab the gun, get out of there," he said to himself. He descended.

The street looked the same, though the decaying buildings were difficult to distinguish from one another covered, as they were, with foliage. As his boots hit the ground, he began moving, scanning the ground, searching for the revolver amidst the rubble and debris of the street. He moved as quietly as he could, listening for the sound of approaching Ferals above the rushing in his ears.

Still, he couldn't find any trace of the revolver. After combing the street twice, Ben sank to the ground, sitting in the dust and detritus, sifting it through his gloves.

"I'm sorry, Dad," he said.

A hum brought him to his feet again, cursing his sentimentality. He unstrapped the pipe, held it firmly in his gloved hand.

Above him, two airships descended from the sky. One, a thin, cigar-shaped zeppelin, gleamed in the sunlight. The other a jury-rigged ship - a blimp envelope with an open-air gondola hanging from it, trailed smoke. They both flew Valhalla colors and a long steel hooks hung from the bottom of the zeppelin.

Ben ran for the *Cherub's* ladder, but before he could reach it, a splash of fire slicked across the street in front of him. Another exploded behind him. Molotov cocktails dropped from above. The greasy black smoke blew into his face and he coughed despite the scarf around his face.

By the time he'd covered his face and half-run, half-rolled through a thin line of fire, one of the men was already on the ground. He walked toward Ben, rifle out, red whiskers poking out of the dusty black bandana wrapped around his face. A leather jacket wrapped tightly around his bulk.

Ben waved at the smoke. "Nice job," he said. "You just told any Ferals around that we're here."

"Aren't any Ferals around," Whiskers said. "We cleared 'em out. Besides, they don't like fire."

"What do you want?" Ben said.

Whiskers cocked his head toward the *Cherub*. "Your ship. As you can see, one of ours has a bit of a problem."

"You -" Ben began. Then pain exploded in the back of his head and he fell into blackness.

★

Ben came to on the street. The fires were already burning out, and another man had joined Whiskers. Ben rolled slowly to one side to get a better look, wincing at the pain in his head. The new man dumped a dark canvas bag next to several others. Next to them lay a dead dog. "Get that stuff on the ship, Nox, and we can get out of here."

"Alright," Nox said. He had Asian features behind a red scarf and wore a coat made up of patchwork animal skins. He grabbed the dog and slung it over his shoulder.

Ben moved to his knees. "You were at Gastown, weren't you?" he said.

Whiskers swiveled and held a revolver on him. "Shut up," he said.

"Why?" Ben asked

"We wanted the helium," Nox said. "Now we have it."

"Nox, move." Whiskers commanded. Nox stalked off in the direction of Ben's ship.

"That's my ship," Ben said, through gritted teeth.

"Not anymore," Whiskers said.

"You going to kill me?" Ben asked.

"Nah," Whiskers said. "Waste of good ammo. We just want your ship. You might even live."

"A small kindness, then," Ben said. He looked around for some help. Any help. But there was nothing. No hope. No future. He was just another plod, stuck on the ground.

"Look," Whiskers said, showing Ben the side of the revolver and the Star of David there. "A shooting star."

Then Ben was moving. Not thinking. Not breathing. Just running and diving for the man who had his father's revolver. The man who wanted to steal his ship.

Gunshots exploded around him, ground crunched under his feet. Then searing pain, lancing through his thigh. But you only needed legs on the ground.

Ben pushed through the pain and tackled Whiskers, feeling the impact jolt his bones. They fell down hard. His hand found the revolver, the worn, pitted handle, and ripped it from the larger man's grasp.

Ben pressed the revolver barrel against the reddish beard.

"We're just trying to survive," Whiskers stammered. "That's all. We're just trying to survive."

With a snarl, Ben slammed the man's head with the revolver butt until he was unconscious. Then he sagged back on his heels. The bullet had ripped through the flesh of his thigh, carving out a long, red line. With trembling fingers, Ben fished out the green tube of superglue and squeezed it into the wounds. It wouldn't do anything for the pain, but at least he wouldn't bleed out. Not right away, at least.

He found Nox on the ground beneath the *Cherub*. They stared at each other, guns out, Ben with his father's revolver, Nox gripping a scratched silver automatic. Ben hoped there were bullets in his gun.

"This is my ship," Ben said. "Get the fuck away from it."

"No way," Nox said. "I claim right of salvage."

"Like hell," Ben said. Streaks of radiating fire threaded through his thigh and he clenched his jaw.

Ben considered telling Nox to go, to take the other ship and head off, each going their separate way. Then he thought of Gastown, of the marauders and the Ferals dropping through the rigging. Of all the infections, all the lives lost to the Bug.

Ben pulled the trigger three times. Two shots took Nox high in the chest and neck. The third clicked onto an empty chamber. Nox fell to the ground and jerked for a bit.

Ben removed Nox's automatic, tucking it in his jacket pocket. Then he dragged the bags to the bottom of the rope ladder, tying the straps to its end. He left the dead dog behind.

He climbed up to the *Cherub* slowly, favoring his healthy leg. Once up, he collapsed into the *Cherub's* gondola and pulled up the ladder and the attached bags.

Once everything was in, Ben pushed the *Cherub* away, full speed, and sank against the floor.

He sat there, bleeding, the revolver in his lap. The Star of David was missing. Torn away in the chaos of the fight. He hadn't even noticed. Yet he had held on so tightly to the revolver. He sniffed and tears trickled from the corners of his eyes.

He sat there for some time, ignoring the course of the *Cherub*, his face in his hands.

The crackle of the radio broke him out of his darkness. He stood and walked over to it, laying the revolver down on the counter. The frequency was still set to "31.4". "Ben?" It was Miranda's voice.

He picked up the transmitter. "Ben, you still alive?"

"Yes," Ben said.

"You did survive," Miranda said. Ben winced. "You still want that food?"

Ben looked at the revolver, at the bits of glue still attached to its handle.

"Ben?"

"Meet me over Old Seattle," he said.

★

He met them over the skeleton of the city and radioed them to follow him. He took them to the Space Needle, one of the few neutral places that he knew of. They anchored to the structure's saucer and lowered their ladders down into the halo, the deck that surrounded it. The Space Needle had once been a general store for zeps, but it wasn't very defensible and became a favorite target of pirates. So instead it was now a waypoint with nothing valuable stored there. That kept scavengers away most of the time as there was nothing to scavenge or steal.

The inside smelled like urine and cigarette smoke. "Sorry for the ambience," Ben said.

Miranda stood, feet wide, and eyed him up and down. "You look like shit."

Ben rubbed a hand over his face. "You said you needed help. What are you proposing?"

Miranda nodded. "I need someone to fly me around. Help me gather data. It's not just me and Sergei. There are more of us. We have data, we have knowledge from the Clean. We're making progress. Help us."

Ben remained silent.

"We can do it your way. You get to inspect the safety protocols so that you're comfortable ferrying the cargo."

All that blood, on his ship. He pictured the tubes in Miranda's flimsy bag. But then he recalled the image of the Feral on Gastown, the gushing wound, the ships hovering over the city.

"Do you really think you can stop it?" he asked. His voice was almost a whisper.

She gave a slight smile and nodded. "We can't cure it, not yet, but we'll soon be able to treat the infected, buy some time."

Ben fingered the revolver in its holster. Felt the ridge of superglue on the grip. "Okay," he said.

"What?"

"Okay. I'll help you."

Miranda came aboard the *Cherub* with him, leaving Sergei alone on the other ship. Together, the two airships moved off from the Space Needle and off into the open sky.

The ground would wait beneath them.

DEFYING GRAVITY AND OTHER DAILY GRIEVANCES

EVE SHI

"Do you think this can make us famous?" Ruri squatted on the bed. A pulse beat on her forehead and her occiput tingled, not altogether pleasantly. The soles of her feet rose, hovered above the plain brown bedsheet, and rose higher. Satisfied, she let herself plop back down. "Like, get us featured on magazine covers or invited overseas?"

The silliness of the question seemed to offend Tia. "Go ahead if you want to be a world-famous freak," she muttered. Her back was to Ruri and she was bent over her Chemistry homework. "Next year we'll have to get into a good high school. That matters a whole lot more. You'll get far with education, not by whooshing around like some Supergirl cosplayer."

Ruri pouted. Her sister, who was born only a minute earlier, liked to lecture her, often more sharply than necessary. "Crotchety old Tia," Ruri muttered back. "What's wrong with cosplayers, anyway?"

"Don't change the subject. And get some sleep, we're leaving for Bandung first thing tomorrow. Traffic out of Jakarta can be jam-packed on long weekends."

"Hey, show me what you can do with that pen."

Instead of heaving a long-suffering sigh, Tia turned around and regarded her sister up and down. "Just once. This homework is giving me enough of a headache already. And a pen is too light."

"Deal." Ruri stuck out her legs over the side of the bed.

Tia raised her palm over a Hello Kitty plastic doll on her desk. The doll shuddered before half-leaping off the desk, bumping into Tia's palm. It stuck there for a second or two before Tia snatched her hand away. The doll floated down and settled back gently on the desk.

"Very precise." Ruri clapped her fingers against her own palm. "How do you keep your control over it for so long?"

"I'm sure it's much easier than keeping your entire body afloat. Never tried it with heavy objects like a chair, though."

Ruri bounced off the bed. "Plenty of opportunity for that," she said as she straightened the bedsheet, knowing Tia hated going to sleep on an already messy bed. "We've only had this ability for, what, two days? Can this be genetic? Maybe Mom also has it, or Dad, and they've just never told us?"

This had occurred to Tia, but neither of them had had any courage to broach the subject to their parents. "Let's just start dropping hints. At worst, they'd laugh us off," she added, as though there had been much laughter from their parents lately.

★

The quarrel began as soon as their car entered the Cikampek highway. Vehicles were lined up for kilometers ahead, crawling along at an infuriatingly sedate pace. Mom blamed Dad for not taking the Puncak route.

"Excuse me, but this was supposed to be the fastest route to Bandung," he intoned, tapping at the steering wheel. Dad had not looked at Mom or the girls ever since he had gotten into the car. Tia and Ruri found this disturbing. "Besides, this is a long weekend. The Puncak traffic isn't going to be any less congested than here."

Mom folded her hands across her stomach. "Just say it."

"Say what?"

"You don't want to go to Bandung. You dislike having to ask my brother if there's a vacancy in his office, or if he knows anyone who has one in theirs. It hurts your pride. Well, your pride isn't going to feed the girls or pay for their school fees."

The tapping on the steering wheel stopped. "I've got plenty of friends right here in Jakarta," Dad said, his words clipped. "No need to go all the way to Bandung. What are you even thinking? It's Jakarta. There are bound to be more jobs here than in Bandung."

Tia and Ruri blinked at each other. Before today, Mom and Dad had never argued openly in front of them. However, Dad had been unemployed for nearly two months now, and constantly irritated about it. Sooner rather than later that irritation would spill over.

"You've been asking your friends, I know that," Mom said. "Have any of them given any answers? Not a positive answer, just an answer, other than 'Oh yes, we'd be on the lookout for you.' That's all they've done, being on the lookout and nothing else– "

In the back seat, Ruri clasped her fingers together. Glancing at her, Tia caught her breath. A sheen of sweat had formed above Ruri's upper lip. Her head was also higher than Tia's, which means she was floating above her seat.

Get down! Tia wanted to shout. She grabbed her sister's arm and tugged at it. With obvious reluctance, Ruri sank back into the car seat. She unclasped her fingers and clenched them instead.

"Look." Mom's tone became gentler, without a hint of coaxing. "My brother likes you, you know. Thinks you're a great guy. When the hotel closed down and you were laid off, he was very worried about us– you, me, the girls."

"I bet he doesn't think I'm such a great guy now, coming all the way from Jakarta to beg for a job."

"It's not begging! Times are hard, jobs are even harder to– "

Dad banged his fist against the steering wheel, and Ruri's head bumped against the car ceiling.

Tia's hands flew to her mouth. Mom and Dad turned their heads around, in time to see Ruri fall back to the seat. She looked both defiant and ready to burst into tears. The four of them stayed frozen for three more seconds, during which Tia dared not stir.

Mom whispered into the silence, "Ruri... Did we upset you?"

Ruri pursed her mouth, the tip of her nose going red. She was visibly struggling not to cry, and had no spare breath for an answer.

Dad sighed. The car in front of them inched forward, and he moved theirs accordingly. "Ruri, Tia," he said, "this is all very hard on you. On Mom and Dad too. But we'll get through this. I'll call in favors if I have to. You two don't need to worry, that's for Mom and Dad to do. All right?"

"Stop quarreling," Ruri murmured.

"Maybe we can visit your uncle another time, when the traffic is less busy." Mom didn't look at Dad as she said it. She reached out to touch Ruri, thought better of it, and withdrew her hand. "So I guess we'd better go home now. We can go to Bandung next weekend."

Ruri nodded, and, after a moment, so did Tia.

"Tia, you're the older sister," Mom continued as Dad began to turn their car around. "Take care of Ruri. Make sure she doesn't float away like that every time she's agitated. It's hard, but I learned to do it at your age. You can do it too, girls."

"I don't float," Tia said, finally finding her voice. "I do something that's actually cool."

"Dream on," Ruri retorted. Her color had returned to normal, and Tia was relieved.

Dad glanced at the girls from the driver's seat. That single, harried glance told Tia everything: Dad was wary of them. But a father wasn't supposed to be wary of his own children, was he? Then again, not all children could float, and not everyone had to live with wives who also could.

Mom smiled. It was a sad smile, one that didn't completely reach her eyes. It struck Tia how painful it must have been for Mom to keep her secret bottled up all these years.

"Tell me when we get home," Mom said. "Show me everything. Then maybe we can work something out."

NOTES TOWARD A PERFORMANCE: THE NARROW BRIDGE, DECEMBER 2001

VAJRA CHANDRASEKERA

We're stuck at the foot of the narrow bridge, trapped in honks and rain and the yellow smell of fuel and the river. Inside the car it's humid and close and the wiper squeaks on the windshield. We just got here and the play has barely begun out on the bridge: this is still Act One, raw id, all base urges and undignified thrusting. I'm halfway through refusing to explain myself to my friend K.

– This is *about* the refusal-to-explain, I say,– We have to be the face without windows.

– What about the face without windows, K asks. The studio audience laughs. We avoid giving them cues or looking directly at the camera (which is difficult to avoid, technically, because we can't see into the direction of snidth), but they've learned to track comic beats like watching for enemy submarines on sonar. – What windows?

– To the soul, I say,– which doesn't exist, or we don't have them, however it works. We're anatman and it's our cultural heritage to have faces without windows, to refuse to explain. It makes me want to give it an official acronym like R2E and get the United Nations to define it as a proposed norm for interpersonal affairs in postcolonial discourse. Comprehension is not an absolute right and the audience forfeits any entitlement to explanation! R2E! The face without windows!

– Easy, K says, and I can't tell if he means that I should calm down or that he thinks the implementation of my proposed norm is feasible. I opt to believe the latter, but I don't tell him this. For a few minutes this illusion stands while we sit quietly and watch Act Two unfold. Act Two is is all ego, the strut and confrontation, the righteous indignation.

Every evening at rush hour, the standoff at the narrow bridge replays in miniature the history of human confrontation. It's the sort of thing one would livetweet, only Twitter won't exist until the ceasefire ends. It's 2001 and it's a week to Christmas and there are no gods, queens or monoliths bent on uplift. Only the quotidian world and of course, the studio audience. K's driving, we're in his 1971 Mark III Ford Cortina which is conveniently painted the colour of rust. The floor has mostly faded away in a lattice of tetanus holes: now that we've stopped moving, every few minutes I reach carefully through one of the larger holes to pick up pieces of the crumbled asphalt from the street below, then furiously winch down the window a few inches so that I can throw it in the river, or at least in the direction of the river. It's getting dark and we can't see much in the rain.

– Did you say something about a proposed norm? K says,– You mean, like with a ring on bended knee and Urðr fluttering her hands and going omg omg omg yes yes yes –

K's always been better than me at performance. The studio audience loves him better than me.

– That's a *norn*, I say,– And why always an Urðr and never a Verðandi, you know? That's racist. Why does this always take so long? Who builds a bridge so narrow it only has one lane?

– Let's find out, K says. We go live to this bystander uncle squatting on the grass at the foot of the bridge not three feet from my window when I winch it all the way down. He's soaked by the rain but doesn't seem to care. He's bare-chested and I can count his withered old-man abs. Opening the window blows all the rain into the car and for a moment everything is blurred in water and it's as if we'd slipped over the edge and fallen into the river, but then it drains away through the holes in the floor and we achieve an equilibrium suspended in the brack and the brume. Water beads on my lip. It tastes saltier than it should, since this river doesn't reach the sea for another five kilometres. We narrate these things for the studio audience to understand.

I'm pretty sure the occasional loud splash in the distance is bodies hitting the water after being flung off the bridge. Act Two is just as violent as Act One: only heroes participate in either of them. It's a protagonist sort of place to be. K and I always time our commute so that we're never anywhere near it.

K asks Bystander Uncle for his learned opinion on the history of the bridge, and we wait while he thinks up lies to tell us. There are gunshots in the distance. Behind Bystander Uncle and concealed by his skinny ass begins the secret gravel path to the rocky slope that in sunnier weather boys risk their necks and bicycles on. We can't see it from this angle and K doesn't know it's there but I know because (time travel, the long way around) in 1991 I used to ride my bike down there with the other boys and we didn't die and anyway that was an El Niño year and the river was near dry but for a marrow of water and we rode across the cracking bed and inside this bubble of obscene privilege survived the unspeakable rites of childhood in civil-wartime. This street was once part of the town I grew up in, which long before any of these new wars in my lifetime was a demon-village in my grandparents' day and jungle before that and a feral Lusitanian colony before that and a different jungle before that and a settlement of unbaptized, unenlightened water elementals thousands of years before that: all this past and present now swallowed whole by the aggressively Protestant-Buddhist city and shrunk in its digestive juices to a neighbourhood named after some rich guy's pet mongoose. Cities are animals and they eat and shit like the rest of us but it doesn't do to dig into their droppings, in case you find out what they've been eating.

K is from all the way over on the city's other flank. He tells Bystander Uncle that this makes him basically a foreigner here and entitled to ask tourist questions. I don't want to tell K that I grew up in this neighbourhood. I feel like it's already his fault for not knowing that. But I narrate it, subvocalizing, so that the studio audience can keep up. They like it when we're at odds.

Bystander Uncle says the bridge was built in 1971. He says it preceded (just barely) the Maoist uprising and anyway (technically) was constructed while we were a Dominion of bloody Albion, so the fault (of its construction) is not in our stars at all but in the stars of Elizabeth II in her curling ram's horns and Capricorn ascending. He says the Chief Minister of the province, who caused the narrow bridge to be constructed and determined its curious, single-lane, conflict-attracting design, came to the opening but was kidnapped by thugs immediately after the ceremonies, and beaten by said thugs until he pissed (a veritable river of) blood and (unabridged) passed out (of consciousness and of this story alike). Bystander Uncle can't remember what happened next.

– Why would they do that? K asks,– And hey, my car and the bridge are twins.

I'm always afraid K's ridiculous car will get stuck in the middle of the narrow bridge. It's a wide-hipped monster of a car and when we eventually cross the bridge the metal will scrape on both sides.

Bystander Uncle shrugs. The attackers were thugs, he conveys. Hooligans. Goondas. He looks like he suspects we don't know what the words mean. I wonder if he's secretly talking to the studio audience, too. I almost expect him to burst into a cross-reference (on page 21 of the mission report subtitled "A Mounting Tragedy of Errors" produced in March 1984 after the sheer violence and body count prompted a fact-finding mission by the International Commission of Jurists in the ancient occidental tradition of a white man telling us what our problems are, section 2.7 is actually titled "Goondas") but he doesn't have to, because I do it automatically on his behalf, for the studio audience.

– Maybe they were revolutionaries, I say,– This was just before the uprising, right?

Bystander Uncle insists that the perps weren't revolutionaries but the long arm of organized crime. With an air of someone bringing out a rhetorical trump, he reveals that the cops hanged the bodies of the locally-sourced revolutionaries from the narrow bridge the following year and they were totally– *totally*, he emphasizes, in triumph– different people. He segues instantly from this to current events, with the air of someone who has won a conversational thread and doesn't want to leave any room for this victory to be contested.

Instead, he asks us for our opinions on the war. It turns out that Bystander Uncle is a veteran of the second war (while I was riding my bike under this bridge) and has strong opinions on the current (and third) one. Bystander Uncle is also a racist but not a surprise racist because there is no such thing as a surprise racist. He has things to say about the attack at the airport some months ago, with a digression about how you wouldn't think to look at him but yeah he watches the international news and he knows how the Americans are real mad about the planes– the planes that hit their towers, not the planes what got blown up at our airport, though Bystander Uncle himself is equally mad about both and he feels like this year has just been full of plane-adjacent terrorist fuckery and it's all going to end badly with this new government and he's afraid it's all heading in the wrong direction, look at the Americans, *they're* not going to take it lying down so why should we–

Somewhere ahead, at the centre of the narrow bridge, grumpy negotiations finally begin to replace the posturing, the fisticuffs, the gunfire and the knives in the dark, the bodies dropping like turds into the river. We can't really see that far ahead of us but there's a change in the smell of the air. Something petrochemical, something petrichor. Nobody can get across the narrow bridge at all if the two factions don't agree to take turns. That's all it takes but it never comes naturally. Act Three is all superego, grim and shameful cooperation because everybody is tired and just wants to go home. The shame is felt but mostly unseen, like a shark in the water. The telltale fin is the terrible awareness that everyone has– you can see it in their (untrained) eyes, though they'll never acknowledge it (they don't have to, they don't have faces without windows and their unsouled selves are naked to the world, and to the studio audience)– that they could have sorted this out hours ago if they hadn't insisted on being assholes. The ones who almost-but-ultimately-didn't get to participate in exculpatory violence smell sour, like a ruined orgasm.

– They just declared a ceasefire, K tells Bystander Uncle, who is either so shocked by this revelation that he shuts up, or he already knew about it and is in denial so complete he can no longer participate in conversations that make reference to it. – The war's on pause for the next six years and we've got a box full of Norwegian flags in the back that we're taking to the protest in front of the embassy– so monks can burn them, I add helpfully– and yes, thank you, so that monks can burn them. We represent a shady consortium of Norwegian flag manufacturers who want to profit off their government's involvement in our peace process.

– Can we be called Skuld and Crossbones?

– Yes, K allows.

We say goodbye to Bystander Uncle and K eases the Cortina onto the narrow bridge. The queue is moving, but very, very slowly. Somewhere far down the line at the other end of the bridge, people are slowly, grumpily reversing, making way, making room. We're still not at the climax of Act III, which will be the moment at which the frustration and dull resignation that they're feeling at this retrograde motion is finally overcome with the relief of the disaster-survivor (the worst has happened, and now there is nothing left to do but to live). When they reach that point, it is said, they will stick their heads out of their cars like dogs and speed backward, tongues hanging out in joy at the resolution. The war will be over, until tomorrow, and everybody can go home at last. And the side that gets to move forward first, the winning side– winning is determined by whoever managed to get furthest past the centre of the bridge before the initial deadlock, and much of the fighting revolves around the definitions of where the centre of the bridge really is, or what "centre" even means, or the true nature of space and time, or the veracity of the competing secret histories that will explain it all– the winning side will speed forward in the ecstasy of unencumbered motion, in the unshakeable belief in progress. The future! Development! All that is good lies ahead, across the narrow bridge.

Metal scrapes both sides of the car. Sparks are instantly quenched in the rain.

– Well, that was enlightening, K says. – Pause for applause.

The studio audience applauds on cue, uncomprehendingly. It sounds like static, tinny and scratchy. The studio dimension lives in one of those extra spatial dimensions that are very small and rolled up very tight at right angles to length, breadth and width– in this case, one we call snidth, the imperial measure of how snide something is– and sound gets twisted coming out of it. Their laughter is sometimes appropriative and always overbearing. It sounds like distant, cacophonic birdsong, like a wetland morning.

– Did you believe him about the history of the bridge, I ask,– About the revolutionaries?

– He specifically said they weren't revolutionaries, K says. – And I do believe him. Why not?

– It violates R2E, I say,– It makes the history of the bridge too much like a metaphor for the war. A crime against humanity (I mean who makes a bridge with only one lane, anyway) punished with violence that is itself an injustice, and so on and so on into a cycle of retributive violence–

– And also unrelated opportunistic violence, K adds,– And semi-related associated violence, and structurally-linked institutional violence–

– And also all that, I say,– Until the bridge itself just disappears into the simile. But the problem isn't whether the bridge is real or a metaphor: obviously the bridge is real (I'm thinking, though I don't mention this part out loud, of bicycling under it as a boy: when the bridge, the actual and irreducible bridge, would even as a metaphor have had to be a metaphor for something else) and the war is so much more real than the bridge.

– Or the ceasefire, K suggests.

– Or the ceasefire, I say,– Which might never become really-real. I think it makes more narrative sense (which is the only kind of sense history ever makes) that the attack was carried out by revolutionaries. It moves their motives out of our line of sight. So we've upheld R2E by avoiding the neat, misleading, ultimately meaningless explanation.

– What's R2E again, K says, and I can tell from his inflection that he doesn't mean it as a real question. The studio audience chuckles in appreciation.

– The refusal to explain, I say,– As a policy of discourse.

I didn't roll my window up again after talking to Bystander Uncle and the rain's coming in sideways. If nothing else, we've both learned one thing from the old man and have (without discussing it in any way, in a silent coordination invisible to the studio audience) decided not to care about getting wet.

– Let me guess, K says, dryly. – You won't explain what it means.

A roar of snide, crackling static. We wait it out, holding our expressions unmoving, our faces without windows, until it dies down again. I don't point out that I forgot myself just now and already explained what it meant, because now I know K isn't really listening. I don't blame him. Our relationship with the studio audience is complicated. Sometimes we want to be free of the pressure of their gaze, the need to always be performing, but at the same time we can't help but revel in the comfort of their acclamation. We scrape along accompanied by distant, inappropriate gusts of laughter.

SLIPPING SIDEWAYS

CARMELO RAFALA

We buried Rachel in the spring. Not long after, Leo became a recluse. In all honesty, I never thought I'd see him again.

He stood now between the open balcony doors of his penthouse flat, perfectly framed against Geneva's dusky skyline. His hairline had receded some, and he was noticeably greyer at the temples. His clothes – well, Leo had never been into fashion: tan trousers, checked shirt with a dark navy sweater draped over his shoulders. The uniform of the self-absorbed academic (on leave from a team working with the Large Hadron Collider, I'd been told).

But what really unsettled me was the look upon his face. The mask of painful remorse had been replaced by a wild, penetrating stare, as if he looked at you and through you simultaneously.

"Sorry I haven't called, Džemo," he said.

"It's only been six months." I twirled my whiskey glass between my fingers. "But it's understandable."

"I'm glad you're so...forgiving," he replied.

The hair stood up on my arms. I've always been a bit suspicious, maybe even slightly paranoid. I mean, when you've been sleeping with your friend's wife it's kind of, well, obvious. Isn't it? Something changes in the atmosphere of a room when you enter it, and she turns to stare at you. There's something in the way her eyes play across the features of your face, her body shifting from one foot to the other, as though she were expecting you to rush into her arms.

"To forgive is divine," I said, forcing a smile.

"So they say." He said no more for several minutes; then: "There's a reason I finally called you."

Here it comes, I thought. My chest tightened. I hated being confronted by truth. Once exposed, I'd have to acknowledge its existence. It was much easier to put it to the side, ignore it, and enjoy the fantasies I'd created for myself. Growing up in Sarajevo during the war such escapism was a mode of survival. Over the years I'd turned my made-up worlds into stories, lies spun out across hundreds of pages. I created characters I wished I could've been, and they lived lives I wished were mine.

Falling in love. With Rachel.

What finally destroyed her, drove her to suicide, was the fact she was stuck between a reality she found untenable, and a fantasy that could never be real.

I had no doubt she loved Leo; I heard it in the way she spoke of him. But it was a love burned to cinders by neglect. A thin, bookish man, Leo was habitually reserved, uninspired; useless at parties. And it was this remoteness, coupled with his dull appearance and social inadequacies, which eventually drove Rachel into my arms.

"Did you know your peripheral vision is very sensitive to motion?" he said, turning and walking slowly back into the room.

My anticipation of a verbal lashing was quickly replaced by confusion. "Is that so?"

"It is," he said. "We've all seen things out of the corners of our eyes – objects moving swiftly, vague images hurrying by as we turn a corner, things that register as unfamiliar and startle us but, when we turn, there's nothing there."

"Okay, Leo."

"These things we see are mostly smudged, blurred, but occasionally they take form, if only for the briefest of seconds. It's as though our world seemed to wink, and in doing so exposed to us something previously unseen."

"I once thought I saw a furry creature jump out at me. But, of course, I was drunk at the time."

He frowned at my lame attempt at humour.

"Come on, Leo. Where are you going with this, anyway? This seems a bit metaphysical for a scientific guy like you."

"What is metaphysics," he said, "but an attempt to understand the fundamental perceptions by which others see the world? Existence, space, time, causality are all concepts that go well beyond mere ontology, which simply seeks to categorise things within some artificially conceived hierarchy – nonsense groupings by which we can make sense of things we can never fully explain."

"Come off it, Leo! Have you suddenly taken to reading *The Fortean Times* or something?"

"In many ways, Džemo, metaphysics may be a better word to use than science." He hurried back to the balcony to face the city, the stars, like a man possessed. "The Greek word 'metá' simply means beyond. Metaphysics. Well, what is *beyond* physics? Do you know?"

"No, I don't."

"Well, I do," he said.

Not only did he appear like a man on the edge, but he was beginning to talk like one, too. I glanced about, at the clutter of books and periodicals scattered across the room. Mirrors on opposite walls duplicated the chaos, spreading it outward until the vision became insubstantial.

And in the middle of all this, on a small table by the sofa, stood a single picture of Rachel.

"Leo." I suddenly felt braver than I probably looked. "You can't shut yourself away from the world like this. It's been six months. I know it's hard but you need to find a way to move on."

"I have moved on," he said. "That's why I called you here. To let you know."

I was stunned. "That's great, Leo."

He shook his head and kept his back to me, his face to the city and the sky. "No, Džemo. My perceptions have moved on; those are the first things one notices."

"You've lost me. Actually, you lost me a while ago."

"I've *seen* her," he said. "Several times. Out of the corner of my eye. Passing in the streets. Going by in a taxi. It's Rachel, Džemo, and she's out there."

I went cold. *He's delirious,* I thought. *Or losing his mind.*

"You remember, Džemo, the controversy when they began testing the Large Hadron Collider at higher outputs for the first time? Everyone thought it would create a black hole that would swallow the earth." He laughed.

"What the hell are you talking about?"

"The collider," he said, "not only proved superstring theory but takes it in a whole new direction. Don't you see? It's created weak points in our universe, points where we can see into another reality, *another universe.* Physical movement across the planes *must* be possible. Somehow – "

"Leo, you need help. A counsellor, perhaps..."

He turned on me. "You of all people should appreciate possibilities, speculations. Now imagine the Collider has not only fulfilled its potential, but gone beyond anyone's wildest expectations. Do you understand?"

I stared into my empty glass.

"An electron can occupy numerous states simultaneously," he said. "Quantum mechanics allows this, and successful experiments in demonstrating superpositions in larger objects are old hat." He paused, seemed desperate for words. "Beryllium ion, for instance. By laser-cooling it to zero-point energy, a series of laser pulses sets it in different states, each spatially separate and coherent. *Two possible states for one object!*"

"Leo..."

"It's Schrödinger's cat. It's both alive *and* dead. I observe only one possible outcome, because when I detect the object I am entangled with it. That is, because I have seen one version of the cat I now have a relationship with it, of a sort. Quantum decoherence prevents me from experiencing another possibility, another universe." He stepped toward me. "The Collider solved this problem, in a way. We can see other possibilities, but only peripherally, like a geometrical tangent. It touches a curve and for a brief moment, they travel in the same direction – "

"I think I'd better leave."

"There are worlds out there," he said, "side-by-side with ours. Worlds where you and I and Rachel never met. Worlds where Rachel never died. Do you know what this means? For me? And you?"

I noticed my hands were shaking as I put the glass down. Tears blurred my vision. For the first time in my life, truth, somehow, managed to win out over lies. "I loved her, too," I said.

"I know," he replied, his tone surprisingly gentle. "It's a second chance. For both of us."

I wouldn't listen anymore. Fantasies were my job. But the one reality, the one hard concrete fact I could never bury underneath all my words was the fact that Rachel was gone.

His Rachel. My Rachel. And no amount of grief-fuelled, half-cocked, drunken school-boy speculation was going to bring her back.

And I shared my portion of the blame for that.

"Good-bye, Leo." I moved for the door.

"I don't blame you," he called after me. "Just wanted you to know that."

I left.

★

I screwed up my courage and returned to his flat a few days later, but he didn't answer the buzzer. When the police entered they found no trace of him. They never found his body. Anywhere.

Some nights, when the sky was particularly clear, and the moon had risen, full and bold, I imagined I've seen him out of the corner of my eye, walking around the bend of a busy street, or cycling past me, Rachel beside him, laughing.

And I hoped, for his sake, that he was right; that he'd somehow managed to find that second chance he so desperately wanted.

But that was one fantasy I couldn't allow into my life. Because in my selfishness I'd finally done the unthinkable: I'd destroyed the lives of the two people I loved most. It would be ridiculous to think I deserved another chance, and foolishness to believe there was another world with another Rachel. And that she would be waiting for someone like me.

Heart full of sorrow I posed my ruminations to the stars, to the moon hanging low in the crisp autumn sky.

And I swear that great silver orb seemed to *wink* in response.

THE SEED KEEPER

YUKIMI OGAWA

The seed keeper waited. Only she didn't know how long she had yet to wait.

She was released from her little shrine when the world died, when the shrine was crushed flat by the lethal storm. She looked up. She could see, beyond the smoke and ashes and dust, that the last rain was coming. She looked down. Earth only looked like scars and bruises; every surface was a stinking mess, of corpses of every life that had inhabited her, of lava rocks that were immediately cooled down by the waves from the sea. She imagined remnants of her village and its people crumpled under the layers of filth. She looked away, and decided to search for her kin, the flame keeper.

His mountain was still visible there, to her relief, in spite of the scale of its explosion, which could have sacrificed the mountain itself. But when she reached there, she found his altar, too, had been destroyed, though not as bad as her shrine. She now looked around at the human corpses, covering the stairs to the collapsed altar, of those who might have come to beg for his mercy. No one seemed alive.

She looked up. As if it were answering, the sky started spitting onto her face.

The flame keeper – whom she had feared and secretly loved – decided when to set the volcano free, and now was gone with all the vapor the lava had caused. The water keeper, her sweet cousin, released the tide that had craved to permeate and claim the whole surface of the world. And when the tide retreated, he, too, was gone as the mud from the seas turned to sand.

The seed keeper returned to the site where her shrine used to stand. She started digging into the ground, where it had been the center of the site. She dug deeper and deeper, until she found a sleek, tiered box lacquered in black and gold. She then lifted the lid to reveal the first tier, which was divided into numerous tiny squares, each holding one seed.

She now lifted the first tier and saw yet another tier which in turn yielded more of those tiny squares. Then another; endless repetition of square chambers. Each seed chamber was carpeted with a tiny piece of fabric, of different colors and textures. This way the seed keeper would know what seed each square held. Humans of different colors; fish of seas and rivers; plants that bear fruits and plants that do not – seed of every living kin. They need to wait until the right time comes for them to grow.

And it was her job. To wait until the time comes, to grow and harvest them.

Only she didn't know how long.

She spent days and nights that followed counting the seeds one by one. She would lift the lid, pick up a seed, and feel the fabric. When she was done with one tier, she'd place the tier on the ground and go on to the next. She repeated this every day, until she could no longer remember how many times she had counted the seeds. And she never remembered how many seeds there were, after all. What she did was waiting, not counting.

More frequently than any other she would touch humans' fabric, especially her people's, even when she was not counting. She loved how the fabric felt: infinitely smooth, with occasional hints of irritation. And it smelt good. It smelt like the village itself, the one she had been protecting for thousands of years, soil and crops and herbs and sweat all mingled. But the seed itself looked just the same as the others.

She picked up a seed, the fabric under it whitish yellow in color, soft and wooly at the touch. So this is dandelion. She liked dandelion, the village girls had often made a crown for her with the flowers. She put the seed back in its chamber.Then she picked up another seed. This one's fabric had multiple colors carelessly mixed, and the texture was soft but somehow rough. Amaryllis, she mused. She had never seen amaryllis.

Why did she have to wait for something she hadn't even seen?

Almost reflexively she popped the seed into her mouth.

She munched on it, surprised how good it tasted. She hadn't eaten anything since the end of the world. Not that she needed food, but she had always enjoyed eating the offerings from the village people.

She swallowed, wondering if all the seeds tasted the same.

But no, it's a sin. Bad one. She sprung to her feet, suddenly aware of what she had done. There would be no amaryllis forever. She had never seen amaryllis, and now, she would never, ever do. She hit her chest hard, to see if she could spit a piece, but it didn't work. She touched the amaryllis fabric once again, terrified, with her hands shaking for the first time ever.

For a long, long time she remained there motionless. Eventually she overcame the feeling, and started justifying herself, that it was just a flower after all, the planet would hardly notice anything is missing. And there's nobody to punish her, anyway. So she started drifting around, trying to find anything distracting. She found and pocketed a few pieces of lava rocks, and did some simple juggling, like the little village girls who used to sit on the steps to the shrine's main building, singing old rhymes. She ran up a hill, and came back rolling down, covered with volcano ashes; she had seen the village boys do this in the snow. She even ate a lump of ash, which looked a little like rice balls that the village people used to make for her. It tasted terrible.

The seed keeper went back to her site.

The tiered box was there just as she had left it. As soon as she caught sight of the seeds again her mouth watered. She spat to get rid of the sandy taste of the ashes, then crouched over the box. And started going through the seeds.

Humans. She couldn't possibly choose them. They needed her, and that's why she needed them.

Plants. The humans need them. But do they need them all…?

Animals. Perhaps humans don't mind her eating some of them, those that might do harm to the humans… But still, they have their own roles to fulfill…

Or do they?

The back of her eyes started to ache, so she looked up at the sky. Before the end of the world there were greens to rest her eyes on all around her site. She wouldn't choose trees that spread their branches, she decided, so that they would canopy her world with their leaves again. She thought of the branches swaying lightly in a breeze, and humans, animals, insects and everything resting in and under them. Maybe she only needed *her* people. And only her people's plants and animals, and the flame keeper and the water keeper. Only enough to rebuild her realm. Enough to return to her ordinary, peaceful life…

She fell asleep, and dreamed of life with nothing but amaryllis.

★

Then she imposed upon herself a rule of her own.

The seed keeper turned the tiers upside down to drop all the seeds onto the ground. She enjoyed the sound of the seeds clinking against each other. When it was done, she took some time enjoying burying her hands in the seeds. She wanted even to sleep in them, but feared crushing them with her weight. Then, like a child playing with sand, she started building a mountain with the seeds. She was disappointed when she couldn't mock the flame keeper's mountain, and out of frustration she destroyed her seed mountain. Then she built it again.

When she could wait no longer, she looked up.

There was nothing to wrap her dead world now, and only the space was there. She lay beside the seed mountain and waited. And finally found what she had been waiting for.

Above her, a star died.

The seed keeper stared at the explosion with relish; she hadn't found anything beautiful since… since when? When the explosion ended and she could find nothing left of the old star, she sat up to face the seed mountain. With the seeds out of the box she could no longer tell what seed each of them was. She wouldn't have to feel tormented trying to choose which seed she could sacrifice. But maybe she should have put her people aside. Maybe she should have left her zelkova trees out of the mountain…

She picked up a seed on top of the mountain, and popped it into her mouth. She thought it tasted slightly different from the previous one, but perhaps it was just her imagination. Even between these two seeds, so much time had passed, and she wasn't sure if she remembered the previous one's taste correctly.

After chewing for a long, long time she swallowed. Then she lay on her back again, waiting for another star to die. When not enough stars died, she decided to include stars being born. But still, that wasn't enough.

★

Stars died. Stars arose.

Time passed, slow like no one could ever imagine, and still the seed keeper sat alone. Now in front of her only one seed remained. She wondered what this seed was for, and knew she couldn't eat this one, but still, that she had nothing more to eat put her on the edge of sanity.

Not that sanity mattered now.

The tiers of the lacquered box were now only ruins, but somehow the fabric remained. They were scattered all over around where the seed keeper waited, shimmering as the only colors on this planet. She had looked up, wondering what she would decide to do if another star died, when she realized something was wrong with her eyes: a haze interfered with her sight. At first she thought she was finally going blind, but when it slowly moved, she knew it was a cloud.

A wind blew, carrying the fabric pieces away, high into the sky.

She knew her waiting was now over. The seed keeper closed her hands around the last seed, and wept, relieved she hadn't been waiting for nothing, sorry she had consumed all but one seed. She dug again into the soil where the lacquered box had been, placed the seed in the hole and put the soil back into the hole, onto the seed. And again, she waited.

Soon, very soon in *her* current of time, she saw the first sign of the sprout. First life, first real color. She poured all her strength onto the sprout and, as if responding to her, the sprout grew, into the air now thickening, into the sky now pale blue. Soon it grew to the height of the seed keeper. She touched the bud. It opened, and transformed into the shape it was destined to take…

The moment she saw the new-born seed keeper, the old seed keeper choked. A spasm shook her. Her knees surrendered first, then did all her limbs. Her hair turned gray, color drained from her eyes. She collapsed, gaped, stared into the eyes of the new seed keeper, who was now towering over her, looking down.

Soon the eyes only wobbled.

She felt her body decompose. She wasn't conscious enough even to wonder what she would become. She transformed, and then, the old seed keeper vanished.

The new seed keeper looked blankly down at the remains of the dead seed keeper. Only a tiny mountain lay there, made of countless seeds.

There cannot be two seed keepers, the new seed keeper muttered, but there was no one to hear it.

Sensing its own recovery, the earth started moving. The seed keeper looked up at the sky just for once. Another wind blew, and carried the fabric pieces back down. They landed, one by one, on the seed mountain, to tell her the names of the things she would have to cultivate. Her gaze followed, and soon she started absorbing the names. There was no need to learn what name belonged to each seed; they would soon grow, and she would soon know.

She never looked up again.

The seed keeper waited for the wind to settle.

FROM SCOTLAND WITH LOVE

HAL DUNCAN

Mackenzie, you poor man's McGonagall,
rank mediocrity of wank and shite
that Burns wid ca' a bawheid's doggerel,
Ah'll spit a rhyme for ye: Ye cannae write.

A decorated poet? Aye! A dick
drawn on yer foreheid wi an inky wid
be pure dead brilliant, a humungous prick
and fuckin big block capitals: NAE GUID!

Naw, wait! Fuck drawing! Wi cheap biro and
a set of compasses, ah wid tattoo
yer fuckin travesty of verse by hand
aw o'er yer skelped-arse face in blue

of Picts and fitba' strips, the Scottish flag,
so's every one ae us Jock Tamson's Weans
at wan swatch ae yer ugly mug wid gag,
boak like at reekin pants wi squittery stains.

Yer rhyme for Trump's inauguration wank?
Huv ye drunk his spunk? D'ye fuckin swallow?
Like pus squeezed fae a beilin pluke, it's rank.
Ye've pisht on the Muses and Apollo.

Best of MacLeod? Don't make me fuckin laugh.
Yer tangerine Nazi rapeclown's fuckin loathed
by Scots who mind when rebels wurnae naff
gold-shittered gobshite Emperors unclothed.

Wallace and Bruce? Did ye watch Braveheart then?
Rob Roy wi Liam Neeson? Yer a joke!
Try John Maclean. Nae bonny hills and glens;
try our Red Clyde, ye fascist fuck, and choke.

It's fit, but, ah suppose, yer numpty's praise
sh'd come in scansion painful as the worst,
the world's worst, poor McGonagall: the days
aheid, we'll aw be sufferin, fuckin curst.

And aye, yer Tumshie Trump Train's on its way
Towards it's ain disastrous silvery Tay,
And yer best hope, McKenzie,
        is yer shitty fuckin rhyme
Will no be remembered –
        wi yon prissy-lipped and frightwigged
        fake-tanned baby-handit Nazi bandit's
        treasonous dismantling of the USA –
Will no be remembered –
        wi yon tragic bawbag's Special Day,
        remembered wi Traitor Trump's Inauguration,
        remembered wi the Death of a Nation,
        remembered as a literary punch bowl turd,
        to poetry as Trump is to the presidency: a crime.
– remembered for,
        in the world's worst poet's words,
        a very long time.

A SAILOR GIRL GOES ASHORE

MARGRÉT HELGADÓTTIR

The mere thought of the many buildings and streets crammed with humans had always made Nora hurry past the Svalbard Islands as if there was a snapping monster at her heels. Even now, as she stood on deck marvelling at the sight of the skyscrapers, it was a struggle not to turn the ship around. Her knuckles whitened as she gripped the helm, holding her course straight towards the city that covered every inch of the land in front of her.

The wooden ship objected with loud creaks as the heavy wind strained its sails to the limits, pushing it forwards through the waves. A rather petite vessel, it was the smallest she'd sailed. It was old and worn, too. Nora looked up at the yellowed sails fondly. It was a miracle that they'd lasted this long, cooperating with the buffeting winds without rest for many seasons now. And Nora and the ship had been through some strong gales together. Excellent craftsmanship, Nora thought and, as she often did, pondered the ship's origins: who'd made it and what waters it'd sailed before she stole it.

She'd been certain that the ship wouldn't last long on the high seas, and that she'd soon have to find a replacement, but she'd been pleasantly surprised. Her ship might not cover vast distances in as short a time as the bigger, heavier sailing ships she was used to, but Nora could turn Naureen around or change direction in a matter of minutes. She could swiftly put distance between her and the ships she plundered. Sometimes, it seemed as if the ship responded to her thoughts, as if there was a weird invisible bond between the two of them.

'Naureen. Us sailor gals must stick together,' she said aloud, as if the ship could hear her. Nora always talked to her ship. Clearly a sign she'd been on the sea for too long, she mused.

Naureen. Nora didn't know who'd named the ship or what the name meant, but she thought it strangely fitting. It graced the bow of the ship, painted in beautiful calligraphy. Nora saw it whenever she was aboard another vessel, rummaging for furs or bones of extinct animals she could sell, or food. The sight of her ship always made her heart flutter with happiness. There was a time when Nora would steal the ships she plundered, if she liked them and was in the mood for a change. But not after she stole Naureen. Well, not stole, she corrected herself. When she'd come across the tiny ship, she'd found the salt-rimed corpse of the hollow-cheeked owner sprawled face down on the deck. He'd probably starved to death. His body had not been the first one Nora'd found drifting at sea, nor the last.

The dark skyscrapers towered over her now. Nora tilted her head back, trying to see their tops. The buildings seemed endless, stretching up into the sky, the cold sun glinting and sparkling in their thousands of windows. Nora imagined people standing behind them, examining her, judging her. Shuddering, she furled the sails and set course towards a huge sign: "Guest Docking." The city's docks stretched along the coast in both directions, bristling with a multitude of piers. She manoeuvred the ship into place at the pier under the sign.

Two tankers loomed in the distance, surrounded by a jungle of sheds and cranes. The massive ships looked ancient, almost prehistoric. They must have been anchored there for a very long time.

Seeing no mastheads, she frowned. She'd imagined there would be thousands of sailing ships, considering how many people must live here. But the harbour seemed empty and abandoned.

Nora had learned to trust her instincts after all the years at sea, and they screamed at her now. She wobbled around on her sea legs, mooring the ship to the huge bolts jutting out from the pier, all the while casting nervous glances at the piers, the tankers and the high buildings. Hesitating, she stood for a long time on the pier, clutching the last rope in her hands. She wanted nothing more than to leave. Then she looked down at Naureen and sighed. During the many dark seasons, small rifts had of course appeared in the ship's sails now and then, and she'd quickly mended them. But the huge hole that had appeared in the main sail during the last storm was too big for her to repair out at sea. So she'd stitched the edges of the hole roughly together and set course for the nearest shore.

'It'll be all right, Naureen. I'll repair you as fast as I can and then we can leave this place. I promise,' she declared with a firm nod.

Someone giggled. Nora froze, then leaped aboard her ship and crouched down, examining the pier above her. There! Behind a stack of wooden barrels. Hurrying into the cabin, Nora grabbed her rifle from its hook and ran back onto the deck, her heart roaring in her ears.

'Come out so I can see you,' she shouted. Nothing happened. Whoever was behind the barrels was silent.

'Come out,' she shouted again. 'I would be delighted to meet you.'

Nora sniggered nervously on the inside. She'd learned that it was wiser to be extra polite when she met other people, no matter how frightened she was. That way even the most scary-looking men would think she was harmless. Around her neck hung her proof; a tooth, torn from the neck of a scarred pirate captain after she'd killed him. Later she'd learned it was a killer whale's tooth. Nora still remembered the pirate's confused eyes when he realised that the rum she'd served him and his men was poisoned. She didn't regret killing them. *Actually,* she thought, *I did the sea a favour. Bloody pirates! Worst people out at sea. Killing, raping, plundering… and then they destroy the ships so no one else can use them.*

Nora would never kill people just to rob them. She only stole from people already dead or long gone. Actually, she'd turned into quite a hermit and tried as hard as she could to avoid others, unless she needed to trade or swap furs for food. She'd rather run than stay and fight, though she knew she could fight if necessary. The killer whale tooth might bring her a decent outcome if she traded it, rare as it was. It looked ancient, so it had to be from a real whale. But she wouldn't trade it. She kept it as a reminder not to trust other people. Or that's what Nora told herself. The truth was that she kept the tooth to remember not to become a cold-blooded pirate herself. It'd been easy to kill those men. Far too easy.

'Come out,' she shouted again.

There! At last. A head, obscured under a hood, popped up behind the barrels. Nora couldn't tell if it was a man or a woman.

'I have food,' Nora offered.

The person emerged from the barrels and, moving closer to the edge of the pier, stared down at Nora from the depths of the hood.

'Y-you have food?' a tiny voice asked.

'Yes,' Nora answered. 'Not much, but you can have some of it.' She held her rifle ready behind her back.

The other person pulled down the hood, revealing a small face, large eyes and long black hair. A girl, Nora decided and relaxed. The girl looked haggard, but didn't appear to pose any threat.

'That's very kind,' the girl said. 'But I don't have anything to give you for it.'

'Maybe you can help me out in return?' Nora said. 'I need to repair my sails.'

The girl pondered this for a moment, then smiled broadly, her grimy face suddenly beautiful. 'I can help you.'

Nora jumped up on the pier and reached her hand towards the smaller girl, who flinched but then shook hands with her.

'I'm Nora.'

'Aida.'

The girl quickly stuffed her hand back into the outer pocket of her parka. In her other hand, she clutched an iron rod. Nora wondered if she'd ever used it. Up close, Nora could see how the skin lay tight over the girl's high cheek bones, how the long tousled curls were caked with dirt, how the golden-brown eyes flickered, as if not daring to return her gaze. Everyone Nora met nowadays had a plagued and hunted look in their eyes, but it was unnerving to see such old eyes in this young face. She'd seen things, this one.

Aida's parka, stained with dark spots, looked too thin for the cold weather. The clothes Nora glimpsed underneath the parka didn't look any better. Nora frowned. The girl looked and smelled like she hadn't seen a bath or food for a very long time. 'You never know who you'll meet,' Nora's mother used to tell her when she was a girl. 'It might be the man of your dreams. It might be a president.' Her mother's exhortations had stuck with her. Even though she rarely met people out at sea, she always tried to keep herself clean and presentable, spending time every morning combing and braiding her long hair. Her mother would have been proud.

Nora shook her head to clear her thoughts. Aida stood silent, staring down at the ground, swallowing visibly.

'You look like you need food,' Nora said at last. 'We'll eat, then you'll help me find a sail maker.'

Aida looked up. 'I don't know of any sail maker, but I know where you can find new sails, and I can help you put it up.' She sounded eager.

Nora searched the other girl's face. Aida seemed sincere.

'All right. Sounds like we have a deal. But if you betray me, I'll kill you. You understand?'

Aida paled, but nodded.

★

'Where is everyone, Aida?' Nora asked. Aida had hopped down to Naureen's deck in one smooth motion, as if she'd done it hundreds of times before. They'd eaten a decent meal, Nora thought; a can of cold broth, some bread and a bottle of filtered water. She'd stopped Aida from wolfing the food down too fast, afraid the girl would become sick.

The sun was high in the sky. Nora wanted to be back at sea before the evening and the darkness arrived. She didn't like the silent city. Why had no one come, besides Aida? Nora knew men. They should have been here already, lurking around the pier, attracted to the new arrival and promises of furs, food, booze, women, things she didn't want to think about. But there were no men in sight. The harbour looked abandoned.

Aida lay on the deck now, staring up at the blue sky, looking tired but content. She fell silent at Nora's words.

'Why are there no people here?'

Silence. Then Aida gave her a long, searching look.

'They're dead,' she said.

'Dead?'

'They're all dead.'

Nora cringed at the pain she saw in Aida's eyes. But she couldn't believe what the girl was saying. Aida must have noticed the scepticism in her face, because she sat up and looked at Nora intently.

'We had a plague. We don't know where it came from or when it started. There were so many new refugees arriving every day. Many died shortly after they came, exhausted from travelling over the seas, I guess. Starving.' Aida paused, as if searching for words. 'Then local people started getting sick, people who'd lived here for years. The hospitals were so crowded. The doctors didn't know what disease it was, what caused it. They didn't have any medicines for it.'

Nora noted the calm distance in the girl's voice and studied her, curious. Aida's behaviour and the way she phrased her words whispered of a finer background and years poring over books. *Where does she come from,* Nora thought, *this stranger who speaks like she's older than me, but looks like she's barely into her teens? She's standing in Death's court, yet she acts so calm.*

'It went so quickly,' Aida continued, interrupting Nora's thoughts. 'You died a couple of days after you were affected. We think it was airborne. Dad forbade us to go outside the flat. He was so afraid we'd get infected.'

'Your dad?' Nora asked with a sinking feeling. 'You had family?' Then she chastised herself. Of course Aida had a family. She was so young.

Aida didn't seem to notice. 'Yes, my dad and my brother, Zaki. We came here when I was a child.' She stared out at the sea. 'Dad had a small ship, just like this one. It was called Naureen too, after mum. But someone stole it.' Images of a salt-rimed corpse popped into Nora's mind. She'd rolled him out into the cold sea water.

'It went so quickly,' Aida said. 'So many people died. Whole buildings emptied. Schools closed. People panicked, plundering stores for food, rioting in the streets, killing each other. The authorities were helpless. The smoke from the crematorium hung above the city all the time.'

Nora listened, feeling cold inside. 'Is that why there are no ships here?' she asked. 'People ran?'

'Yes. Many escaped by sea, probably going to North East Land or Edge Island, or maybe even south to Bear Island. I hope they made it. Others went by foot, hoping to reach other cities or the mines, I think. Dad said we had to get out of here. He said we'd die if we stayed. He talked about a land west of here, where we could make a new life. Said it was once called The Green Land. Said there were several massive vaults filled with seeds there, so we could grow our own food if we wanted to. He wanted to buy a new sailing ship, to get us out of here. But the days went by and nothing happened.

'My brother disappeared one morning. My dad thought he'd tried to escape on foot. I don't know why Zaki abandoned us.' Tears started to run down Aida's cheek. She brushed them away. 'Dad knocked on my door late one night, said he didn't want to come in; he thought he'd become sick. That I'd find a bag with some furs I could sell, some food and clothes, outside my door. He said he loved me dearly, but I had to get out of there, use the furs to buy a berth on a sailing ship. Escape. He said I had to leave him. I cried and cried, but he told me to obey him. S-so, I did.'

Aida bowed her head. Her long black curls covered her face.

'I'm sorry,' she said between sobs. 'I-I can't seem to stop crying.'

'It's all right,' Nora murmured and patted the girl's shoulder, feeling awkward.

The dark skyscrapers towered over them. Nora craned her neck, looking up at them. She wondered how many people had survived the plague, if any. Her gut feeling told her that it was not a good idea to examine this city too closely, or to stay anchored in the harbour too long. She looked at Aida. She couldn't fathom what the girl had been through. It was easy to imagine what'd happened. The girl probably wasn't used to taking care of herself and must have been easy prey for thieves and others who meant no good. She must have hidden down here at the harbour for a long time. Whatever food she'd brought with her probably hadn't lasted long. Maybe the girl had searched the nearby houses for food. She mused that it had likely been a while since the girl had last been inside the city. It was a miracle that she was still alive.

Aida had stopped crying. Once in a while, a loud sniffle escaped.

'The sails,' Nora asked, 'are they far away?'

★

The streets were deep in dirt and rubble. Glass crunched under their boots. Here and there, corpses stared at them with blank eyes. The bodies were weirdly intact, mummified, as was often the case in this cold climate. Nora tried to ignore them, having seen plenty of dead people out at sea, but she noticed that Aida walked closer and closer to her.

They'd walked several street lengths when Nora began to suspect that someone was following them. She glanced sideways at Aida, but it seemed the girl hadn't noticed it yet. In the broken glass shards that still hung, defying gravity, in the large shop windows they passed, Nora could see their reflections: two lone figures in a vast street. She might have laughed at the differences between the two girls if she hadn't felt so numb with panic.

Aida picked her way carefully, paying close attention to where she put her feet. She'd pulled her hood up again, concealing her head. Like Nora, she'd also covered the lower part of her face with a scarf. Only her golden brown eyes were visible.

A sensation of rising and falling washed through Nora's body, as if she still was on her ship. But she refused to let her sea legs or her fear of the foreign city and the tall deserted buildings overcome her. She strode down the middle of the empty street with long steps, straight shoulders, long blonde braid swinging from side to side, rifle hanging loosely on her shoulders, and her fur coat open in the front, flapping in the wind. Occasionally she stopped to wait for Aida to catch up.

There! She spotted it again. A shadow. The first time she noticed it, she'd thought it was the sun playing tricks, glinting in all the glass. But now she saw it move. Pulling the rifle from her shoulder, she murmured to Aida: 'We're being followed. Hide behind that tram carriage.' She pointed further up the street. 'I'll catch up.'

But the girl shook her head. 'No, I want to stay with you.'

Nora heard the stubbornness and noted the fierce eyes. Maybe she'd underestimated the girl. She sighed. 'Okay, but stay behind me, and run if I tell you to.'

Aida didn't answer. She stepped behind Nora, who sighed again, but soon forgot about the girl. Turning, she saw the shadow moving behind a pile of rubble and heard weird scratching sounds. She pointed the rifle and shouted: 'Show yourself!'

Nothing happened.

'Look!' Aida cried out and leapt forward. It happened too quickly; the girl was several metres down the street before Nora could react.

'Stop, you idiot!' she yelled and chased after the girl, cursing.

But Aida didn't stop until she reached the pile, crouched down and held out her arms towards the shifting shadow. Nora couldn't believe it. Had the girl gone mad? She ran, rifle lifted, convinced she'd be too late.

But when she reached Aida, she lowered her rifle, eyes wide. In front of the girl stood a four-legged creature. An animal. A dog, Nora thought. She'd seen pictures. *So ragged. It looks malnourished with those ribs like a washboard. And that fur! So tangled and dirty. And yet, it's beautiful.*

The fur was black and white, the tail thick and bushy, and the eyes clear ice blue. Someone had done a fine job creating this animal. She wondered if it'd been hatched in a laboratory in this city or if it'd arrived with the refugees.

'Be careful,' she warned. 'We don't know where it comes from or if it likes humans.'

Craning her neck, Aida looked up at her. 'Of course she's friendly. Can't you see that she's wagging her tail?' She rolled her eyes.

As if the dog understood what they'd said, it bounced into Aida's arms, leaning into her with a heavy sigh, making Aida's hood slide down, and put its head on her shoulder. Aida stroked its back, and the animal shuddered from head to tail. Nora studied them.

'She?'

'Yes, it's a girl. Amazing, huh? They usually only make male dogs, since they're for the most part used as guard dogs. Guess people think males are more aggressive. This girl is special. Bet she was someone's pet.'

Aida lifted the dog's head and looked into its eyes. Nora's heart jumped at the sight of the sharp teeth so close to the girl's face.

'You're special, aren't you?' crooned Aida. The dog lifted its head and let out a loud complaining howl. Aida laughed and hugged it. The dog licked her face.

'You seem familiar with dogs.'

'We used to have one when I was child. It was before we sailed here.' Aida looked down at her hands. 'It was mum's idea. She thought we needed some extra protection.'

She fell silent, but kept on patting the dog's head. Nora took a careful step towards them and stretched out a hand. The dog sniffed it, then growled. When Nora snatched her hand back, Aida laughed. 'She probably thinks you smell strange. You know, the sea smell and all. Let her get used to you.'

Nora looked around, fearing the dog's howling would bring attention, but the street was still empty. The shadows were growing longer, though. 'Let's go. The night is coming.'

Aida nodded and got up reluctantly. 'It's not far,' she said, pulling her hood on again. Nora put her rifle back on her shoulder.

They hadn't taken many steps when Nora noticed the dog trotting after them. She stopped. 'It's following us'

'Yes, Tarik likes us,' Aida said and, seeing Nora's furrowed forehead, added: 'She'll be useful. I promise.'

'Tarik?'

'I thought she looked like a Tarik, a star. You like it?'

Studying the girl and looking down at the dog, Nora sighed heavily and started walking again. Aida and the black and white dog trailed behind.

★

The door was unlocked. Aida's eyes were barely visible in the dark corridor. They'd climbed to the eighth floor. Nora had counted as they crept up the many stairs, obscured in darkness. The air was musty with the smell of old things. Nora tightened the scarf around her nose and mouth, and cocked her head, listening, suddenly sure she'd heard distant noises. But all she heard was the unnerving silence. Probably her imagination, she thought.

'Are you sure you want to do this?' she asked as she took her rifle from her shoulder.

'Yes,' Aida whispered, her voice shaking.

They entered the flat, Nora with her rifle at the ready, Aida close behind. The dog trotted before them, sniffing. Stopping now and then, it looked up at Aida with a searching glance. Large windows covered one wall entirely. The sun reflected in from the windows across the street, casting long shadows across the living room. The flat was small and sparsely furnished. Dust covered everything. Nora saw a couple of books on a shelf, a black vase, a yellowed poster on the wall, an embroidered cushion on the couch. But there were few personal items. Aida and her family hadn't brought much from overseas.

They looked into all the rooms, but the flat was empty. Aida let out a sigh. Nora wondered if it was because she was relieved or disappointed. Maybe both. She watched the girl run around the flat with the dog close behind, opening cupboards and drawers in a frenzy. Aida packed a couple of rucksacks with clothes, a blanket, the cushion, a little box. Nora wondered what was inside. It was obvious that Aida had no plans to return here.

The kitchen cupboards were empty. Nora had seen the foot prints in the dust. Somebody had been here, probably looking for food, not long ago. We'd better hurry, she thought, and grabbed the books from the shelf, handing them to Aida. 'Here.' The girl didn't say anything, just put the books in the bag. Then she ran into one of the bedrooms and returned with a large bundle. The sails. Nora sighed in relief.

'Why did you have sails here?' she asked.

'My dad got them before he became ill. He planned for us to escape by sea. Then Naureen was stolen. I know he talked with our neighbours about buying their ship. They were old and didn't want to leave the city. Dad said the ship needed some repair, but that it would do. He even got these.' Aida showed her a couple of paper rolls. Maps. 'I think they are maps of the land in the west.'

Nora glanced out of the windows. The sun was lingering low on the horizon. 'Did he have any weapons?'

Aida thought for a minute, then nodded and ran into one of the bedrooms. Nora heard a loud screech that sounded like heavy furniture being dragged across the floor. Aida came back with a rifle and boxes of bullets. And torches! Nora was starting to like Aida's father. He'd been practical and foresighted, this man.

Tarik whined softly. It sat in the door way, staring out into the dark corridor, its ears cocked forward.

'We have to go,' Nora said, grabbing one of the rucksacks, the rifles and the packet of sails. Aida took the other rucksack and lit one of the torches, but Nora stopped her. 'I don't want to attract any attention.' Aida stared at her, wide-eyed, but switched it off without objections.

★

It would have been wise to stay in the flat overnight, Nora thought later, but she could no longer bear the building, the heavy silence in the city, and the not knowing what crept around in the dark corners. She desperately longed for fresh sea air and strong winds against her face.

Even though they were in the sunny season now, and the nights were shorter, it was still dark. It'd been difficult to move through the streets in daylight. Now, with no light, it was extremely hard to move at all. They walked slowly, their feet searching for safe places to step. The extra weight of the sails and other things they'd gathered at the flat felt like sacks of rocks on their backs. Nora had more than once been on the edge of throwing it all down and leaving it behind. But the thought of Aida stopped her. These were Aida's precious things, Nora reprimanded herself. All she had left from her family. Everything she owned.

Aida walked behind her, her hand on the dog's back. She didn't speak, and she was wheezing. Then Nora heard a long deep sigh, as if the girl was fighting to calm herself and steady her breathing. Aida was clearly exhausted, but didn't complain. A huge respect for the girl kept growing. Nora could identify with her; being alone, trying to survive. They didn't feel like strangers to each other anymore. Aida was the first person Nora'd spent this much time with in the many seasons since she'd decided that the seas were her home. She wondered where Aida would go, if she'd find her brother, if she'd make it to the land in the west.

The only sounds were their breathing, the dog's panting and the crunching glass underfoot. Nora fought to keep the panic rippling through her body from erupting. Several times, she thought she heard other footsteps and stopped to listen. But like before, all she heard was the overwhelming silence.

Finally she heard the waves against the pier and smelled the sea air. She knew it was a risk, but she reached for Aida's rucksack and pulled out one of the torches.

'I need to find Naureen,' she said, scanning the harbour. The single light beamed through the night.

'There!' Aida cried and grabbed Nora's sleeve.

When Nora saw the mast, she thought she might burst into tears of relief. She almost dropped the torch in her haste to switch it off. The two girls hurried towards Naureen, the dog close on their heels.

They threw the rucksacks and the package of new sails down on the deck and Aida sprang down. The dog hesitated, but then jumped after the girl. Nora hurried around the pier to loosen the ropes that moored the ship. She knew it'd probably be wiser to wait for daybreak, but her panic was close to the surface now. All she wanted was to be back on the sea, where she felt safe.

Something shuffled behind her. The dog barked madly. Alarmed, Nora spun around. A gaunt man burst out of the dark, running towards her with wide and bloodshot eyes. Instinctively, Nora hit him in the head with her rifle. He wavered a little, then attacked her, his hands reaching for her throat, madness shining in his eyes. She kneed him in the groin. He grunted, but his hands still clutched her throat. She hit him in the head and kicked his knee, but still he held her in his strong grip, strangling her slowly. His stinking breath nauseated her.

Then, when Nora thought she couldn't take it anymore, that she was going to pass out, he suddenly let her go. She fell to the ground gasping for air, the world spinning around her. As if through a fog, she heard awful noises and the man screaming.

'Are you all right?'

It was Aida. She crouched next to Nora on the pier. She held the iron rod in her hands. The dog put its head between the girls, and eyed her. Blood dripped from its mouth. Nora sat up slowly. Her body felt bruised, but she was still in one piece.

'Yes, I'm all right,' she answered, her voice hoarse. She struggled to speak. 'What happened?'

'We killed him,' Aida answered. She seemed unaffected, but Nora heard the tremble in her voice.

The sun rose, stretching long arms of light towards them. The man lay in a pool of blood a couple of metres away, the scarlet gash in his throat gaping towards her in the meagre light. Nora shuddered at the sight. She stood, leaning momentarily on the girl's shoulder. Aida and Tarik jumped down onto Naureen's deck. Aida held on to the pier while Nora loosened the last rope. Then Nora sprang down, falling as she landed. She cried out in pain.

Staring up at the dead skyscrapers, she said: 'Can you sail, girl?'

'Yes.'

'Consider yourself hired. Now get us out of here.'

'Aye, Captain!'

Aida pushed them away from the pier and had the sails up quickly. They flapped before they caught the wind. Nora lay on deck, exhausted, as Aida seated herself behind the helm. She seemed at home there. Her long black hair danced in the wind. Nora thought she heard the girl humming some odd, jolly tune. The haggard dog looked comfortable on the ship too. It lay down next to Nora on the deck and leaned its head on her stomach.

Naureen ploughed her way through the waves. Nora watched the skyscrapers disappear in the distance, their thousands of traitorous windows glittering in the sun. She listened to Aida's distant humming, almost lost in the roar of the wind, a strangely comforting duet. The girl was stronger than Nora'd thought. *She's even stronger than me,* Nora reflected. *She could have run away, but she stayed and helped me. I'd be dead if it wasn't for this girl. And the dog.*

As if it had heard her thoughts, the dog lifted its head to look at her with its ice blue eyes. The blood around its mouth had almost dried, but Nora could see red drops glistening in the black and white fur. For a moment, she considered pushing the dog's bloodstained head away. Instead she lifted her sore arms and patted its head. The pains stung through her body. The dog sighed heavily and closed its eyes.

Nora fingered her bruised neck, searching for the killer whale tooth. She startled. It was gone! It must have been torn off during the struggle with the man on the pier. Panic welled inside her. What would remind her now to stay unchanged, to keep her integrity in this cold world?

'Which way, Captain?' Aida shouted.

Nora looked over at the calm black-haired girl with her wide-legged stance behind the helm, and relaxed. *Strange,* she thought, *but I really don't mind their company. Maybe I can get used to sailing together with them…It feels like they've always been here.*

Next to her on the deck, she saw the package containing the new sails and the maps. They spoke of a new adventure; a new world. Maybe it was time to stop the restless drifting at sea without cause or meaning.

'Go west,' she shouted.

Aida grinned broadly. 'Aye, Captain!'

Nora watched her turn the big helm, then adjust the sails. Confident. A sailor. *Don't worry,* she told herself. *You don't need the whale tooth. The girl will remind you that not all strangers are foes.*

Friends. Nora tasted the foreign word.

'Naureen,' she murmured, on the brink of the merciful darkness of sleep. 'Us sailor gals must stick together.'

THE LAST TALE OF AMBROSE BIERCE

LUIS G. ABBADIE

Under what awful spell did I exist?

—Ambrose Bierce

I might speak of the old, partly unreadable, manuscript kept by a family from Durango; I might say that I worked on deciphering the photocopies a fellow member of Don Flaviano's literary workshop gave me, that I transcribed the scribbled English and that I completed the gaps and imperfections of a ruined rough draft; but why do it? I might claim this is a last tale of a writer sick of his own fame who wanted to mock himself, or – better still – the terrible testimony of a man who ended up as a victim of his own stories. I might unleash polemic, expose myself to the assaults of copyright. And in the end, what would I gain from it all? This is a tale, and that's what counts, not its reality or its fiction, nor whether I wrote it or he wrote it. It's a tale, and that is the truth.

And Ambrose Bierce, American writer of uncanny stories, disappeared in Mexican territory in the year 1913 under unknown circumstances; that, too, is the truth. But it is the legend as well...

Note to the Revised Version: *I recently contacted Oscar Graxiola, in an attempt to locate his brother Ricardo. I was unsuccessful, since he has lost touch with his family; but I learned – and could hardly believe my luck – that, among some things which belonged to Ricardo, was the original manuscript of which he once gave me photocopies. It wasn't easy, but Oscar, who had no interest in this sort of things, agreed to give it to me "for being a friend of Ricardo", and I finally had the original document in my hands: a handful of brittle pages on the verge of crumbling. Even so, several portions which were unreadable in the photocopies were much clearer here, if one studied carefully the faded strokes of sepia-colored ink. I have thus been able to rectify several embarrassing mistakes I committed when I rendered my first version of the manuscript... and filled in the gaps in the narrative with no more than luck and imagination to guide me (said version was published in my book El último Relato de Ambrose Bierce – Ediciones del Plenilunio, 1995, Mexico – , currently out of print). Now, a good share of such improvisations has been replaced with greater faithfulness; a few portions, however, were irretrievable, and I plead full responsibility for any resulting slips. – Luis G. Abbadie, 6/10/95.*

FEB. 19, 1914:

I meant to begin some other way, to explain what circumstances led me to this point, but that is all ultimately off-the-point, and there are some things of which I do not wish to write any more than I have to. Suffice it to say that I was one of those liars who pose as "writers" in order to take pleasure in their vice of making things up. And I came to Mexico... does it matter why? Partly, I wanted to escape; partly, to rest; partly, to be rid of that herd of hypocrites who constitute American "society"... or, rather, that is what I *thought* I wanted. Once I was here, lost among the dark-skinned *campesinos* who granted me a delicious indifference, free from the chains of being an "outstanding personality," I had time to think... and many things happened to me, things that made me know why I had come all this way.

I have not been truly alone all these months, and I do not say this merely because of the constant presence of the villagers all around me (it's funny: I was going to write "greasers" instead of "villagers", but no matter how accustomed I may have become to using that disdainful term to refer to Mexicans back in my not-at-all yearned-for northern country, I realize that these people, now that I've come to know them, do not fit at all with the image filed in my brain under the classification of "greaser;" I know it's childish, but that word always brought images of a person bathed in grease continuously slipping down the sidewalks with his greasy shoes, like something out of comical cinema). Anyway, I would be a fool not to admit that, beyond a constant confusion, I have been truly terrified since I made my discovery; still, with or without fear, I also thought very hard of all the implications of what was happening to me... of all *possibilities.*

I am not perfect (and I can think of more than two score people who share this opinion), but until a few months ago a flaw I never thought I had was ambition. Now, on the other hand, I am leaning to believe that I do not have it indeed. In fact, I wonder how many of my thoughts, my feelings, my actions, have been truly *mine* in the last few years. In any case, I believe at least the fear was mine, and right now I have recovered it in abundance. But it was mainly ambition which drove me in recent weeks to come from village to village, from ranch to ranch, riding a lean mare which had me bumping up and down until my grating bones grew numb, unaccustomed to any prolonged activity. It was ambition which drove me to speak through the clamp put on my mouth by the sight of half a dozen rifles pointed at me when I ran across that wide-sombrero'd group of soldiers. And it must have been something more powerful than my scarce eloquence in Spanish – certainly the same thing that had forcibly brought me up to this point – which broke through the mistrust of the Revolutionaries and achieved my being brought to an elegant ranch decorated with thousands of bullet marks, in the vestibule of which I found myself days later, sitting on a battered sofa, grasping my cane with sweaty fingers, nervously waiting the moment of being received by the man who had located his temporary headquarters in this place: Revolutionary General Francisco Villa.

"Don Ambrosio..." I heard a voice say at my right, and I think I jumped in my seat, so tense was I. That was how everybody called me around here, translating my name, and I had grown quite used to it; but this old voice spoke it with an unmistakable irony that would have been irritating in any other circumstances. I turned to face the man who had addressed me and I was left with the words evaporating from my open mouth.

The man was wearing a grey suit of a somewhat strange cut and a black tie; he was at a first glance about twenty years younger – or, rather, less old – than my seventy-plus years, but when I looked more closely at him I had the impression that his age was actually much greater than that. He was carrying a cane – a cane *identical,* absolutely *identical,* to mine – , yet his agile movements when he came closer and slumped beside me at the other end of the sofa showed that he had no need of it. But his face... his face was what made me draw breath in with surprise and wonder – as I had wondered several times these days – if I had lost my mind.

"I will not ask how are you, since I know that already," the man said, with a grimace of weariness on that impossible face, that face identical in every detail to mine, although possessing greater vitality... and at the same time older still.

"Who are... you?" I managed, perplexed, and the man regaled me with a half-smile.

"That much is obvious, isn't it? Please, let's not argue whether it is possible at all; what matters is, here I am, and we have little time to talk."

"About what?"

"About what you're meaning to tell General Villa. About the *propose* you're intending to present to him."

I said nothing; surprise had made me momentarily forget the reason I was here. Then my always-inopportune temperament chose to lift its stubborn head.

"If this is a joke..." I began to say, aware of the absurdity of my words, but the man who had my face hushed me with the very gesture I would have used in his place.

"If such is the case, the joke is on me. Look, just listen to me, all right? Listen to what this crazy old man has to say, and then I'll leave you alone. Just listen to me, and then you can tell me to go to hell if you like."

I couldn't answer. The man took a deep breath, lowered his gaze as if hunting around among his memories, and began his tale.

"You know, there was a time when I was one of those liars who pose as 'writers' in order to take pleasure in their vice of making things up. I remember that one day I chose to abandon everything, leave my country, and shortly before doing so it was quite satisfying to spit on the stupid books I had written, books that bounced back from the thick brains of the idiots who tried to make a social class out of literature, something elegant and 'fashionable.' I now think that my behaviour was really childish... But there is still a couple of works that I do regret having ever written." He looked at me, his eyes sad, resigned. "Those three, four stories I wrote inspired by my conversations with that crazy spiritualist who fancied himself a medium called Bayrolles.

"I had no inkling of it until after I arrived in Mexico, when these things started to turn up in my head, as if somebody was forcing thoughts into it." I was barely aware that I was nodding at this. "I now know much more than I did back then, and I no longer laugh at this notion. Never mind what fools like Bayrolles used to preach in those days, getting carried away by the ravings of occult writers like Helena Blavatsky or Allan Kardec; I now believe – more than that, now I understand – that there is nothing supernatural or mystical about telepathy, about the transmission of thoughts between two minds. Still, we've only known for a few centuries that the Earth is round; how can we expect a phenomenon that isn't even a physical one to be accepted by scientists just like that, when they sometimes manage to be as inept as the mystics themselves?

"Ah, well; I remember that, when I arrived in Mexico, the dreams began – strange dreams that wouldn't let me sleep in peace; and then, barely a couple of weeks later, the visions that slipped into my head while I was awake, in the middle of the day. I thought I had gone as crazy as Bayrolles... and who knows, maybe I had, come to think of it."

The man lounged himself in the sofa and looked at me like a stern mirror.

"Bayrolles was always blathering about spirits, about ghosts that communicated through him. I spurred him on so that he told me something I could use for a story, but I enjoyed putting him on even more. When all this happened, I wished I could see him again – not to take my words back, but to break his neck. Those images I saw inside my head were like memories of things I had never seen, of places that didn't belong to Earth. A black-walled city with, high, pointed towers... not one, but *two* suns, shining above the ruined city, and an immense lake with misty shores... And in the night sky, stars... but *different* ones from those that can be seen from Earth. Except for Aldebaran and the Hyades, those damned stars, which seemed to be much *closer,* and were visible even in plain daylight, from that place which couldn't exist, yet I dreamed about again and again, and which I could see within my mind as if it were my own home. And I somehow *knew* that I was looking upon lands belonging to a different world... something like the notions of H.G. Wells and other writers who spoke of other planets inhabited by beings different from us. Still, this was not Mars, or Jupiter, nor anything else within this solar system. This was a world lost in space, very close to the star Aldebaran, *and I was seeing it all through the eyes of a dweller of that world.*

"One day, that creature started to speak to me..."

I shuddered as I listened to his tale, in spite that there was not a single detail in it that I didn't know already. He went on with a tired, almost melancholy, voice, and I realized that he spoke as if he was narrating something from long ago.

"From what that creature said, I assume that Bayrolles hadn't been so mistaken after all. I suspect that, while trying to play medium and communicate with his 'spirit world', what he actually achieved was to make contact with creatures from that unknown world. That is why he was able to tell me all those things I later made good use of in my stories, about the wind-flogged city of Carcosa, and about Hali – and Hastur, whom I described as a placid godling worshipped by a shepherd, but is actually the deity of the religion practiced by that world's inhabitants.

"Trouble was, by writing those stupid stories, I caused other people from our world to know about those creatures – and *they,* through Bayrolles, became aware of me; since they sensed that he had spoken to me about their world, they searched my thoughts, and discovered that I had written about them, although obliquely. They seemingly took an interest in me from then on... and finally, in Mexico, they decided to communicate and make an *offer* to me."

The man smiled at me, as if he now remembered I was there, and said:

"I don't wish to bore you; you already know this part anyway. Let's just say that they explained many other things to me, among them that their technology was enormously advanced, to the point that not only inter-planetary but even inter-stellar journey was to them a simple matter, and that some of Charles Fort's theories regarding luminous objects seen in the skies were not so wild after all. And after thinking very hard about it, I ended up right here, in this very room ...awaiting an audience with Francisco Villa."

I held my breath as I listened to his following words.

"After over two hours, the General received me. We talked, on the other hand, longer than six hours. I told him many things, about otherworldly civilizations, about the city of Carcosa beside a lake which reflects alien skies, about an unlimited, unconceivable, technology which surpassed the dreams of any human thinker... a technology, if he wished, *within our hand's reach.*

"Of course, he didn't trust my word easily, but they had given me more than my sole eloquence in order to demonstrate the veracity of my claims. From that day on, I lodged there – here, at the ranch taken by the *Revolucionarios,* until the day I left, along with the General.

"The war went on, now in a more decisive manner. Artifacts created according to instructions given through my mind enhanced the strength of Villa's troops: small bombs that could be thrown with the strength of an arm erased whole besieged forts so utterly that not a wall was left standing; entire regiments, including their mounts, fell lifeless after passing through a place where a certain gas had been released. And soon, the entire country cheered – or feared, according to the situation – General Villa.

"Around this time there was an unpleasant incident in which a young *Revolucionario* called Baudelio Uribe and the small group he commanded, whom Villa had sent a message with to General Herrera – who was currently in Chihuahua – , encountered some American merchants and assaulted them without the least justification, mutilating the poor travellers, which caused my countrypeople to scream for Villist blood. The culprits were executed by Villa; nevertheless, American newspapers no longer had for him and his troops anything but criticism, slander and censure, labelling them as 'bandits'. Furious, Villa cursed them a thousand times over, calling them traitors, since until then he had maintained quite friendly relations with my former country's military forces. Confident in the new weaponry, Villa started, somewhat complacently, to make brief incursions across the Northern border in spite of my warnings – as well as those of some of his subordinates – that he shouldn't seek more enemies than he already had. Federal armies fell like houses of cards in front of Villa's troops, but ours was not the only Revolutionary movement active in those days, and neither were all of them friendly with each other; and, according to Villa, a good deal of the responsibility for this went to Venustiano Carranza, First Chief of the Revolution, who seemingly wanted nothing but to attain the presidency of Mexico at all costs. Anyway, the rest of the Revolutionary troops, led by Alvaro Obregon, Pablo Gonzalez and Emiliano Zapata, pressed upon the Federal forces from every side and Villa was jubilant, assuring to me that in a matter of weeks President Huerta would be trampled upon by his foes.

"Villa's forces took the cities of Gomez Palacio, then Torreon and Saltillo; drunk with triumph,

Villa wanted to venture on to Monterrey, bent on taking in the whole Northern side of the country, something that would strike a definitive blow against Huerta; but Carranza was opposed to this, alleging that the rest of the rebel troops should profit from that extraordinary Villist armoury everybody talked about. Of course, both Villa and myself refused to share our secret, particularly – said the General – with a *'político intrigoso'* (scheming politician) like Carranza.

"His habit of sporadically plundering into the Southern American border did not stop, and the death of an American troop entangled things further even as victory drew near, since my dear country of birth, paying absolutely no heed to the Mexican government's protestations, raided *en masse* within Mexican territory in pursuit of the Revolutionaries. After a few face-offs between the Mexican army and the invaders, President Huerta, seeing his defeat imminent – whether at the hands of the *gringos,* as they say here, or of the Revolution, opted for agreeing to an 'alliance' of sorts offered by the American government in order to uproot the Villist Revolutionaries through their united forces. President Wilson had the Veracruz seaport taken by the Navy, to stop the Federal troops from receiving a cargo of ammunition bought from Germany by Huerta, and offered to permit access to said cargo in exchange for complete liberty to hunt down and exterminate the Villist 'bandits'. I don't know why Huerta agreed to this, when Wilson's intention to impose himself upon Mexico more than ever were so evident; he perhaps thought that, if the American troops and Villa's clashed, that would give him a respite to gather his forces, even – with some luck – being rid of the most dangerous Revolutionary faction.

The man went on after a sigh.

"Thousands of lives were lost... No war in history had been like this one; of course, no army in history had been provided with weapons and resources from worlds older than ours. Many of Villa's soldiers were frightened at the beginning, and rumours ran wild about him having made a deal with the devil," he let out a snigger. "They even said that maybe I was the devil. We derided them for being superstitious and cowardly, told them that merely because they weren't familiar with these things did not mean they were not ordinary weapons.

"I wonder now who was right after all.

"Anyway, the war was over in a few months. Before this occurred, however, President Victoriano Huerta fell. The Presidential Palace in Mexico City was besieged and, with some kind of gas bomb that induced its defenders with a profound sleep, our troops – led by General Fierro – captured Don Victoriano. Carranza took his place immediately; the greedy leader of the movement, hoisting up his charge of First Chief of the Revolution, proclaimed himself President and decided to exile Huerta. But the war continued still – for the American raiders surged in, and their numbers made up for their disadvantage in weaponry; and because Carranza blatantly commanded Villa to place his coveted armoury in the hands of his own troops.

"Carranza's swiftness in claiming the position, together with his sudden demands, caused the rest of the Revolutionary leaders to openly rebel against his authority. Villa sent a curt response to the new President, which he allowed me to write up," the man let out a little laugh, "with which he declared himself in frank opposition to Carranza's current behaviour and announced his intentions of paying him a visit in Mexico City to 'discuss' the affair of his 'presidency' and other matters. We commanded General Fierro to come and meet us from Mexico City, but American troops were coming their way from the North and the brigades led by Fierro abandoned their intended route in order to overcome them; we realized, when it was too late, that this was the plan of Wilson's army. The better part of his troops went toward the city while the rest of them kept our people busy; thus, at nearly the same time of Venustiano's placement as President, Mexico City was put under siege by my countrymen.

"I was in Nayarit with Villa in those days, and up until then the troops led by us were the only ones fully provided with the weaponry granted to us by those beings, so the soldiers who were defending the city were not ready to hold the Americans off for long – particularly considering that my fellow countrymen had managed to secure a couple of our 'new weapons,' as we commonly referred to them, including explosives obtained by them through having intercepted one of our brigades, sent to back up the troops of General Felipe Angeles. The American invading action was truly surprising, since their apparent objective, up until then, had been none other than Villa's troops; the only thing I can think of, after thinking it over at length, is that they somehow anticipated Villa's purpose of replacing Carranza, either with a President chosen – and 'subsidized' – by us (as was my intent), or with Villa himself (as he ambitioned, in spite of my insisting arguments against such a folly). There are only two possibilities that I can conceive of: perhaps they wanted to brazenly conquer Mexico, or maybe they merely meant to fully impose themselves on Carranza – who was, after all, more and more openly an opposer of Villa, the sole true adversary for the American nation – and turn him into a puppet President. After all, the invaders did not raid Mexico City, nor did they threaten Carranza; they merely exterminated the troops left by Fierro guarding the City's outskirts, and then limited themselves to wait.

"But we didn't know that back then; the only fact that seemed clear was that any attempt of defending the City would take too long; by the time we got there, it would have been taken by the Americans, Carranza executed, and all Revolutionaries demoralized enough by such a tremendous defeat only one step after our apparent victory as to be swept down and suffer The United States of America to have another Southward expansion.

"We discussed this in depth, and both Villa and myself avoided the decision as much as we could, but there was only one chance of avoiding defeat – a chance of loathsome consequences."

The man fell silent for a whole minute; I looked at him expectantly, until I thought he would not go on. I was about to ask him something, when he told me:

"*They* call it the Nuclear Chaos. It is actually the energy unchained by the ultimate violation of nature through science: the splitting of an atom. Don't ask me; I am not a scientist, and I don't know much about the procedure. We possessed the means to deliver this... weapon... to its destination in a very short time, and at dawn in that awful day the uproar rose up. Thousands of death screams, a deafening rumble like the roar of a mad god howling blasphemies. The Nuclear Chaos. A cloud rose above the city, poisoning the atmosphere. The people's very flesh rot on their bones, and even if their souls, after death, were to have gone straight to hell, they would surely have sighed in relief at having escaped from that. Even though I never watched the explosion, I have dreamt it many times, and I suspect Villa has, too. We are only humans; he did what he did out of love for his people... and I, why? Ambition, madness? What leads a man to commit an act which rivals the very rebellious act which damned the Devil himself?

"Within a few minutes," the man mumbled breathlessly, with infinite sadness in his eyes, "The city of Washington had ceased to exist. The entire city."

"Nothing else was required. With their leaders' destruction, the Americans abandoned the siege of Mexico City and offered a minimum of resistance. Villa deprived Carranza from his charge, taking his place, and no one dared to protest. Villa's troops spread beyond the Northern border, crushing the terrified and perplexed defenders of our crumbling nation. Chaus reigned for months, but the fear inspired by the horror which consumed Washington caused the revolts against the Mexican invaders to be few, and easily smothered. Nearly a year passed, and I finally came to New York, the city which the American people had tacitly chosen as new capitol city, riding at Villa's side; at last, the North American States were officially declared by us part of the United States of Mexico."

The man grew silent once again, his lips tight.

"You know, when I came to Mexico I thought I could let the world go to hell; I was a stupid, selfish old man. I understood this on that day, when I felt... as I did... upon seeing my homeland conquered and annihilated. When I saw that America which, no matter how much I hated it, was mine, brought down. Brought down by my hand..."

I vaguely realized that I was nodding.

"For a second time I abandoned it all. I felt different, of course; the knowledge those beings had taught me wasn't limited to secrets of warfare, and my vitality had been restored; I would easily have another half century ahead of me. Sick as I was of being an author of repute in American society, I was now sick of the Mexican countryside where I had torn to pieces the maps of the continent as if they were a puzzle, so this time I fled North, to the Green mountains, in Vermont, to an old cabin I bought from a farmer. I didn't tell my name to anybody; I wanted to forget what I had been, what I had done. Now more than ever.

"I learned that Villa kept his word; the reorganizing of the new government over the defunct United States of America slowly developed according to plan, and I guess I can say things might have been worse. I even heard news that Villa, before leaving for other places, organized an 'Ambrose Bierce Fund' to grant economical aid to writers from the North-Eastern States, centered in New York. I'm certain he did it just to pull my leg."

He smiled with even greater weariness; now, even though his vitality were thrice as great as mine, he looked old as the mountains.

"I spent several years at that Vermont cabin, trying to forget all those things that I kept morbidly going over again and again. But news reach even the most secluded shelters, and I still knew what went on in the world. In the world I had helped shape. Thus did I know, decades afterward – almost three – , that the final tragedy approached.

"For the most part of two years there was war in Europe; the American countries remained uninvolved. Perhaps if Mexico had intervened the result would have been different, but the current president had decided otherwise, and it was now too late for regrets. A new leaders had led Germany in a progressive invasion of its neighboring countries, starting with his native Austria, and their black-helmeted armies spread in waves throughout Europe. Italy surrendered, France fell, England was conquered... Spain, thanks to the sheer size of its land more than anything else, appeared to resist, but Portugal, dreading the imminent arrival of invading troops to its lands, chose unexpectedly to gain the Germans' favor and made incursions against Spain, which did not withstand the double assault.

"Russia, on the other hand, had resisted perfectly every attempt of invasion on Alemania's behalf; not because its armies were stronger, but thanks to the protective barrier of its snowy lands, which proved deadlier for the German troops than any weapon.

"Until one day…"

The man grew silent, and only his slow breath broke the silence with followed at intervals which seemed to extend into infinity. I did not spur him on; his eyes, when he spoke that last unfinished phrase… I couldn't have said why, but they had frozen my entrails.

"I guess it was unavoidable," he said at last. "News just arri…" He gazed at me, pausing, and shook his head as if to order his thoughts. "Finally," he corrected himself, "there was word that the fist of the German empire had struck the first death blow to Russia, with a force nobody suspected, not even now that the whole of Europe had fallen under its rule, that it might have. And when I learned of it I understood the whole truth for the first time… not just about the European war, but about the war in which I myself had played such a decisive, fateful role…

"As soon as I listened to that radio newscast, I set myself to research. I left my Vermont cabin and went to New York, and started to go through the newspapers in a library, reading it all about the war during recent months, putting together a puzzle the existence of which I hadn't even been aware until these last few days. And I found out a lot more than I had expected. But it all added up to reinforce my assumptions, to confirm the terrible truth which I'd just discovered: even though those beings from the stars had left me alone since the war was over in America, so many years ago, that didn't mean they had forgotten about our world. On the contrary, my role as their intermediary had been but the first step of something much vaster than the simple whimsical backing-up of a band of Revolutionaries whose glory or defeat would have hardly been of their interest. I now remember that in several occasions I had doubts and suspicions, but they were always cleared from my head by various distractions… I now understand that they were actually *erased* from my mind every time they surged. How many people on Earth had been manipulated by them during these later years? Now, I discovered, there was a certain number of people in conscious or unconscious communication with them, perhaps manipulated as I had been for Lord knows what purpose. Ranging from a little group of unwary authors whose works I found at the library, under the auspices of that dumb "Ambrose Bierce Fund," who had been writing for several decades, just like I did before them, about those damned creatures and their unconceivable worlds as if they were harmless fictions…

"…to members or perhaps the very leader, of the German goverment.

"How, otherwise, had the German armies obtained the secret of that hellish bomb, unleashing the Nuclear Chaos upon the city of Moscow?"

I shuddered upon hearing these words; his voice quavered lightly, the echo of the horror caused by the remembrance of an infernal weapon which I could barely imagine.

"When I realized what was actually going on, I knew also that it was far too late to halt the consequences of my actions. The next-to-the-last step of the beings from Carcosa – the destruction of the city of Moscow – had been taken, and it was now a matter of days for the final calamity to strike.

The newscasts carefully evaded the matter, but everybody knew what that slaughter in Russian territory meant. The Germans had done much more than merely bringing their Asian adversaries to submission; they had also revealed to the world that Mexico was no longer the only country which possessed the supreme weapon; and this implied that the ever-growing German army, which nobody doubted any longer would end up spreading to Asia's farthest reaches as it had in Europe, would very soon attack the American continent… and it would do so on an equal level of force.

"Governments have never known how to guard a secret, and there was soon leaked information, half-suggested, half-alarmist, that the Mexican government was planning to move ahead with the first strike, and this would happen any minute now. What might I do? Send a thousand telepathic curses to the inhabitants of that black world who had manipulated the life and death of Earth's nations like a cosmic game of chess, and who were waiting for the two mightiest countries to entreat a final war, unleashing the Nuclear Chaos upon the entire world, so that they might then come through the void of space and enslave the remnants of a devastated humankind, claiming our world as their own?

"No. The only chance I ever had to avoid the damnation of humanity, the sole momento when I could have gone back, was when I encountered Villa as a Messenger for those creatures… the day when I lit the fuse which would take three decades to reach its detonation point.

"They taught me many things that I didn't confide even Villa. Their explanations concerning space and time, and dimensions, convinced me that it was possible not just to travel through space, like they claimed that they were able to, but also to move ahead or back along the dimension we call *time.* But even having had such teachers, I'm no scientist, and I have no idea how to put into practice what I've managed to understand as theory. Fortunately, there was also another way, and this one was within my possibilities."

Following a heavy sigh, he went on:

"If they managed to get in touch with me through thousands of millions of miles, it's because mind is ethereal and isn't subjected to physical laws. It is, I suppose, some sort of energy unbound by the limitations of space… and of *time.* I haven't really come all the way here; my body lies in a condition very much like sleep, safe at the home of a writer of tales as fateful as my own, in a coastal city of Providence which awaits holding its breath for the final war to begin any minute. In a Providence thirty years in the future.

"My host is alert, ensuring that nothing interrupts my sleep. But I dread waking up to the rumbling echo of the first explosion..."

He lowered his gaze, growing silent, and I regarded him intently, weighing his words. I was aware how incredible it all was, how absurd... and I prayed to be able to disbelieve him.

"This is all I can do," he concluded, "To warn you. To let you know what awaits on the other side of that door," he made a vague gesture toward the entrance of the General's office.

I raised a reticent hand.

"I don't know if anything might change for me, even though my message is given already. I don't even know what will become of the world I'm going to wake up to... or if I'm even going to wake up at all."

He said that he was merely transmitting his thoughts to me, but I saw him as a living, solid being sitting next to me. I reached out with my fingers toward his arm.

"You know, I have *no* recollection of having had any warning or revelation the day I had my first audience with Villa..." he added with a slight smile. "In any case, I have already changed something, by telilng you all this." He looked at me, while my fingers faltered... and touched his arm. Fabric, soft flesh underneath... he was solid. Seeing what I was doing, he no doubt understood my thoughts, since he smiled ironically. "But that's all I can do: to tell you what happened. Anyway, I've already spent way too many nights self-pitying with that stupid phrase, 'If only I had known...'" His smile widened in self-mockery upon speaking these words, he looked away for a moment, then regarded me again. "That is all, then. I see no point in stressing, advising, threatening. I've spoken my mind... now do whatever you want."

Then, as I looked into his eyes like unto a vaguely-distorted mirror, my sight was obscured with a dense grey fog that dimmed my thoughts...

...and I opened my eyes again, finding my head nodding and my dry lips half-open. Waking up. I had fallen asleep on the sofá, in that foyer which had been the scenario of my... dreams... I'd fallen asleep while waiting to be seen by General Villa...

Then everything had happened inside my mind. Nothing had been *physically* real... Even so, my fingers trembled as I pulled a handkerchief out of my pocket and cleaned the cold sweat from my face. I looked at the door beyond which the most consequential conversation in my life awaited... and I wished, how I wished!, to be able to doubt what I'd just heard in the middle of a dream which could be easily blamed to my excitement by what I was going through.

Why doubt, after all, if it was hardly any more fanciful than the things I intended to expound to the General? Why should all this not be as real as the fear that shook me right then, just before standing up?

Leaning on my cane with the greatest weakness I'd suffered in my entire life, I walked away from the door where the General awaited and I mumbled some excuse before the soldier who watched the entrance to the Hacienda, walking away along a path which, in spite of being of solid, well-packed soil, appeared to me on the verge of crumbling down like a sand castle, dropping me into the abyss.

I have spent the afternoon at a considerably humbler abode; I'm in the home of a family who own a mill, and gave me shelter after a full day of walking aimlessly.

They tell me that beyond the mill there is only the desert, an immense arid expanse that covers the States of Durango and Coahuila inhabited solely by a thousand myths and shades that, according to the *campesinos,* wander in the night in that desert which is the empire of death and of things that were left unremembered when the ancient peoples were conquered and "civilized."

Just like the man in my dream said, the beings who speak to me in thoughts and dreams have taught me many things, although perhaps not as many as they taught "him"... Things about places where, if you know the right method, you can propitiate an *opening* in space... a Gateway. Places such as this desert. I came to Mexico fleeing a world that had me fed up, and now I have nothing left but fleeing what the world may *become.* But what they taught me may have many uses, and I'll be damned if I care what they may think of it. After I finish setting this down (and I don't even know *to what purpose* I'm writing), I will tip what is left of my drink, give my thanks – as well as the rest of my money, since I don't intend to need it any longer – to the owners of this house, and walk off under that sky which already begins to turn reddish outside the window, walking through the sands, beyond the twilight and beyond the desert itself; all the way to Hali, and Carcosa, and beyond... and I hope I'll be able to forget about the world half as quick as it will no doubt forget about me.

VIRUS

JONATHAN DOTSE

The portholes were set to un-shade as the airplane descended into heavy clouds and out of the blinding glare of the West African sun. The small plane trembled through the haze before breaking out to a panoramic view of the sprawling metropolis.

Accra stretched out to bridge the horizons, barely held in check at the southern coastline, where its hyperactive edge threatened to spill over into the Gulf of Guinea. From above, the city seemed without a plan; a vibrant mosaic of infrastructure, haphazardly diced and spliced to make use of every square foot of space. Ramshackle settlements jutted out into the ocean, perched above the water on nests of illegal support structures. Massive holographic logos hovered above the skyline in a brilliant display of optics, familiar corporate logos visible from miles away. Dela leaned into the porthole, scanning for meaning across the organic pattern of the cityscape, searching for answers to the matters on her mind. She felt an overwhelming sense of calm as she soared far above the blind chaos of the streets, certain that if she remained up here long enough she would eventually find what she was looking for.

'Incoming call from Khadija,' came a message from the Grid.

'Answer,' Dela thought in response, and felt a connection opening up within her mind.

'Delali,' came a thought from across the link. *'It's time for the run. Where are you?'*

'I'm at Roundabout,' Dela replied. *'I've been waiting for you.'*

'Alright, meet me at the Lounge,' Khadija said, and then cut the connection. Outside the portholes, the landscape was falling away into the distance, gradually becoming enshrouded in a white mist as the aircraft climbed into the clouds, rocking gently with turbulence. The plane broke through the clouds and sailed into a red-stained sky, where the setting sun met the western horizon. The horizon. Dela gazed into the heart of that infinite line, into the point where land didn't quite meet sky, and held her breath as she braced herself for the transition.

'Escape,' Dela thought, and reality came rushing back into her senses. She was suddenly experiencing the lost and disoriented feeling of leaving a virtual reality simulation; the feeling of returning to a forgotten world. It took her a few moments to realize that she was sitting in the shade of a bus stop, squinting into the sunlit street and beginning to remember where she was. Bus conductors yelled out destinations from the windows of slow-moving buses while hawkers weaved between the traffic, advertising the wares that balanced delicately on top of their heads. Several of them were teenage girls, and Dela knew that she could easily have ended up like them; uneducated and selling goods on the streets of the city. Her father had been a fisherman all his life and wanted her to find a job in Accra right after primary school. He certainly didn't see the sense in putting a computer inside her head, but her mother insisted on giving her an education, and raised enough money to buy the second-hand biocore implant she used through high school. She had now come to find work in Accra while she waited for the West

African Examinations Council to grade her final exam results, then she could legally install tertiary education software. An entire month in the city had passed without any sign of a job, and now all Dela had was Khadija's shady connection and a single-minded determination not to return home empty-handed. She would do whatever it took to make it in Accra, Dela thought, as she stepped out from under the shade. She wiped the sweat off her forehead as she walked toward the eastern end of the interchange. Virtual displays of various shapes, sizes, and colors hovered around the sidewalk, streaming adverts into the minds of pedestrians, selling everything from designer clothing to antiviral software. One display showed a woman from behind, brushing her hair aside to press a finger against the nape of her neck. She then threw her head back as the display burst into a splash of brilliant colors and music.

'Isis Biocores,' came the voice-over, *'A world awaits you!'* Dela crossed onto the Spintex road, walking past a bus station towards the green-themed facade of the gaming center, placed in-between a coffee shop and a business center. Luigi's Lounge was a popular place for teenagers to play virtual games and tournaments, where Dela had first met Khadija a week before. Now Dela found her sitting alone in a dark corner of the Lounge, staring intently at a set of displays across the room, where a young boy was immersed in the pilot seat of a fighter jet. Her concentration was broken when she saw Dela approaching her, and then seemed to be inspecting Dela as she walked over.

"So, you want to be a runner," Khadija said, when Dela stood before her.

"Of course," Dela replied. "That's why I'm here."

"You know that it's risky business, don't you?"

"I can handle risky business," Dela replied as confidently as she could. Khadija shook her head gently and smiled.

"You're not in Keta anymore-o," Khadija said, "This is Accra. Here, the police are like eagles: they have eyes and ears all over the Grid. I've seen too many people go down for being a little bit careless, so if you want to stay out of jail you have to do exactly as I say. If you know you can't handle this you'd better think escape before we go any further." But Dela wasn't about to change her mind. She had already come too far to turn back.

"How much are we talking?" Dela asked. Khadija studied her for a moment and then stood up to stretch, before leading the way out of Luigi's. The evening congestion was backing up the traffic heading into the Spintex road. Virtual displays followed them, playing commercials as they walked through the stream of pedestrians up the road.

"One-fifty," Khadija said, "maybe two hundred cedis."

"That's a lot of money."

"Oh, that's not any money. We could bargain for more, depending on how much the data is actually worth. You just wait until I get us a proper job and then I'll show you what money means." Khadija branched off the main road and led Dela through a maze of back alleys until they reached a clearing between the buildings, through which ran set of train tracks. The sun lay low in the sky, casting a pair of long shadows ahead of them as they walked along the tracks, past several industrial buildings until they met a sagging chain-link fence that surrounded an abandoned warehouse. An airplane roared across the sky as a police siren wailed ominously in the distance. They scaled the unsteady fence and ran up to the wall of the warehouse, where a steel-rung ladder ran about twenty meters up to its roof. Dela wasn't comfortable with heights, and hesitated for a moment before following Khadija up the ladder. She never took her gaze off the concrete wall in front of her until they finally climbed over the edge of the rooftop. A telecommunications mast stood in the center of the rooftop, rising thirty meters into the sky.

"Are we going up there?" Dela asked when stood at the base of the structure, not excited about the situation.

"That's where we're going," Khadija replied.

"But someone could see us up there."

"Not if we leave right now," Khadija said. "The only people who come around here are the security guards who patrol this area, and they usually change shifts at six pm. That gives us about ten minutes to get the data and get out of here. Don't worry; it'll be dark in a few minutes, and then we'll have the cover of night. Let's go; we don't have any more time to waste." With that she began climbing up the mast. The entire structure was littered with satellite dishes and radio equipment that they had to avoid as they climbed. Through the empty frame of the mast, she could see as far as Roundabout, the Kotoka International Airport, and beyond; the gleaming towers of Airport City. Accra was unfolding before her eyes, an infinite sea of light that began to come alive like a million fireflies waking up from the same dream. "This is a Grid hub," Khadija explained as she positioned herself to face a rectangular box with a long antenna. Dela gingerly maneuvered closer to Khadija, watching attentively as she pulled a screwdriver out of her jacket and began to take the box apart. "Thousands of these devices generate the wireless networks that relay information throughout the city; information that could make us rich if we can just get our hands on it." Khadija managed to remove a panel from the Grid box to reveal a circuit board underneath. She produced a small card from her jacket; a circuit breaker, which she inserted into a slot on the board. The card flashed bright red several times before turning green.

'*A new data stream is available,*' Dela's biocore informed her.

"We're in," Khadija said. "Get inside the stream and search for any files labeled 'Sol Seven.' The search program will find all instances of those files on the networks right now."

"What's Sol Seven?" Dela asked. "It's nothing you need to know. Just do your job and get the data." With that, she became completely still as her mind entered the data stream. Dela shifted herself into a comfortable sitting position on a beam, held on tightly to the frame and prepared to follow her friend.

'Enter data stream,' Dela thought, and darkness engulfed her senses shortly before her biocore generated a virtual environment in the void around her. She had no physical body inside that world; instead she had the ability to perceive and interact with the many thousands of files that were zipping through the stream. She felt Khadija's presence nearby; a hyperactive avatar generating a furious buzz of electronic activity. *'Locate 'Sol Seven,'* she thought, and felt a search program stir to life, its electronic sensors scouring the networks for the target. A list of several hundred files began to pile up before her, each one of them with the words 'Sol Seven' embedded somewhere within their code. *'Which of these files should I download?'* Dela asked Khadija as the list continued to grow.

'Take as many as you can,' Khadija replied. *'We don't have much time, so we'll sort them out later.'*

'Download search results to memory,' Dela thought, and another program began to download all the files accumulating before her. '*Escape,*' she thought, and was returned to her body, still perched on a beam near the apex of the telecommunications mast. The sun dipped below the horizon, casting its dying rays across the skies, which were now covered with shrieking bats on their nightly hunt. Somewhere in the distance, the evening call to prayer was broadcasting across the audio channels of the local Grid. Khadija's body was propped against the frame of the mast; a serene, rigid shell, while her mind was diving deep inside the data stream. Dela was about to return to the stream when she noticed a light in the darkness below. It took her a few

moments to make out the shape of a man holding a flashlight, entering through the gate of the warehouse lot. *'Someone is here,'* Dela transmitted to Khadija, whose facial features instantly morphed to life and scanned the environment until she located the threat.

"Security guard," Khadija rasped and then ripped the card out of the Grid box. The two hurriedly worked their way down the mast until they were close enough to jump onto the roof the warehouse. Khadija landed expertly while Dela tumbled across the dusty concrete, and they both sprinted to the edge of the rooftop only in time to meet the flashlight of the security guard at the bottom of the steel-rung ladder.

"Stop!" the security guard yelled, and began to climb up.

"Follow me," Khadija said, grabbing Dela by the arm and running towards the other end of the rooftop. "When we get to the edge, you jump!" As they ran towards the end of the rooftop, Dela saw another building next to the warehouse, just beyond a gap that seemed to be growing wider as they got closer. Khadija leaped across the gap without breaking stride, but Dela panicked and froze just as she reached the edge, peering down several meters into pitch darkness. Khadija landed and turned around to find Dela still on the other side of the warehouse. "Delali, you have to jump!" Dela's mind raced as she struggled to weigh the chances of losing her life if she jumped against the chances of going to jail if she stayed. Her frantic thoughts were soon deluged by the deafening roar of an airplane flying low overhead.

'Warning!' Dela's biocore alerted. *'An illegal file download has been initiated… Warning! System files are being corrupted…'*

'Disconnect from the Grid,' Dela instructed, trying to stop the situation from turning into a nightmare.

'Disconnecting from the Accra Grid… Error! Unable to disconnect…'

'Disconnect!' Dela insisted.

'Error! Unable to disconnect…'

"Jump, Delali, Jump!" Khadija shouted. Realizing she had no time and no options, Dela abandoned her biocore's warnings and prepared to jump, backtracking until there was a good distance between herself and the edge. She held her breath and sprinted forward, trying to muster as much courage as she could, knowing without a doubt that her fate was to be decided in the next few moments. She was just about to jump when she faltered short of the edge, feeling her muscles turn to jelly as her body gave way to gravity.

'Virus!' Dela's biocore alerted, but it was already too late. She tumbled onto the ground, feeling nothing but a faint and distant pain, and then lay on her back with her gaze fixed against the night sky. The world around her rapidly began to lose meaning as the icy fingers of the hostile program traced the boundaries of her mind, distorting her perception and warping her consciousness.

'Virus!' A light appeared above her; a small light that began to expand, growing larger and brighter until it came to encompass all of her vision. She felt a powerful force dragging her down into the depths of nothingness, but fought hard to maintain a grip on reality with all the willpower she had left.

'Virus!' And then her mind caved in.

VIOLATION OF THE TRUENET SECURITY ACT

TAIYO FUJII

The bell for the last task of the night started chiming before I got to my station. I had the office to myself, and a mug of espresso. It was time to start tracking zombies.

I took the mug of espresso from the beverage table, and zigzagged through the darkened cube farm toward the one strip of floor still lit for third shift staff, only me.

Zombies are orphan Internet services. They wander aimlessly, trying to execute some programmed task. They can't actually infect anything, but otherwise the name is about right. TrueNet's everywhere now and has been for twenty years, but Japan never quite sorted out what to do with all the legacy servers that were stranded after the Lockout. So you get all these zombies shuffling around, firing off mails to non-existent addresses, pushing ads no one will see, maybe even sending money to non-existent accounts. The living dead.

Zombie trackers scan firewall logs for services the bouncer turned away at the door. If you see a trace of something that looks like a zombie, you flag it so the company mail program can send a form letter to the server administrator, telling him to deep-six it. It's required by the TrueNet Security Act, and it's how I made overtime by warming a chair in the middle of the night.

"All right, show me what you got."

As soon as my butt hit the chair, the workspace suspended above the desk flashed the login confirmation.

```
INITIATE INTERNET ORPHAN SERVICE SEARCH
TRACKER: MINAMI TAKASAWA
```

The crawl came up and just sat there, jittering. Damn. I wasn't *looking* at it. As soon as I went to the top of the list and started eyeballing URLs in order, it started scrolling.

The TrueNet Security Act demands human signoff on each zombie URL. Most companies have you entering checkmarks on a printed list, so I guess it was nice of my employer to automate things so trackers could just scan the log visually. It's a pretty advanced system. Everything is networked, from the visual recognition sensors in your augmented reality contact lenses to the office security cameras and motion sensors, the pressure sensors in the furniture, and the infrared heat sensors. One way or another, they figure out what you're looking at. You still have to stay on your toes. The system was only up and running for a few months when the younger trackers started bitching about it.

Chen set all this up, two years ago. He's from Anhui Province, out of Hefei I think. I'll always remember what he said to me when we were beta-testing the system together.

"Minami, all you have to do is treat the sensor values as a coherence and apply Floyd's cyclic group function."

Well, if that's *all* I had to do . . . What did that mean, anyway? I'd picked up a bit, here and there, about quantum computing algorithms, but this wasn't like anything I'd ever heard.

Chen might've sounded like he was fresh off a UFO, but in a few days he'd programmed a multi-sensor automated system for flagging zombies. It wasn't long before he left the rest of us in Security in the dust and jumped all the way up to Program Design on the strength of ingenuity and tech skills. Usually somebody starting out as a worker – a foreigner, no less – who made it up to Program Design would be pretty much shunned, but Chen was so far beyond the rest of us that it seemed pointless to try and drag him down.

The crawl was moving slower. "Minami, just concentrate and it will all be over quickly." I can still see Chen pushing his glasses, with their thick black frames, up his nose as he gave me this pointer.

I took his advice and refocused on the crawl. The list started moving smoothly again, zombie URLs showing up green.

Tracking ought to be boring, on the whole, but it's fun looking for zombies you recognize from the Internet era. Maybe that's why I never heard workers older than their late thirties or so complain about the duty.

Still, I never quite got it. Why use humans to track zombies? TrueNet servers use QSL recognition, quantum digital signatures. No way is a zombie on some legacy server with twenty-year-old settings going to get past those. I mean, we could just leave them alone. They're harmless.

Message formatting complete. Please send.

The synth voice – Chen's, naturally – came through the AR phono chip next to my eardrum. The message to the server administrators rolled up the screen, requesting zombie termination. There were more than three hundred on the list. I tipped my mug back, grinding the leftover sugar against my palate with my tongue, and was idly scrolling through the list again when something caught my eye.

```
302:com.socialpay socialpay.com/payment/?
transaction=paypal.com&amp;account
```

"SocialPay? You're alive?"

How could I forget? I created this domain and URL. From the time I cooked it up as a graduation project until the day humanity was locked out of the Internet, SocialPay helped people – just a few hundred, but anyway – make small payments using optimized bundles of discount coupons and cash. So it was still out there after all, a zombie on some old server. The code at the tail said it was trying to make a payment to another defunct service.

Mr. Takasawa, you have ten minutes to exit the building. Please send your message and complete the security check before you leave.

So Chen's system was monitoring entry and exit now too. The whole system was wickedly clever. I deleted SocialPay from the hit list and pressed SEND.

I had to see that page one more time. If someone was going to terminate the service, I wanted to do it myself. SocialPay wasn't just a zombie for someone to obliterate.

★

The city of fifty million was out there, waiting silently as I left the service entrance. The augmented reality projected by my contact lenses showed crowds of featureless gray avatars shuffling by. The cars on the streets were blank too; no telling what makes and models they were. Signs and billboards were blacked out except for the bare minimum needed to navigate. All this and more, courtesy of Anonymous Cape, freeware from the group of the same name, the guys who went on as if the Lockout had never happened. Anyone plugged into AR would see me as gray and faceless too.

I turned the corner to head toward the station, the dry December wind slamming against me. Something, a grain of sand maybe, flew up and made my eye water, breaking up my AR feed. Color and life and individuality started leaking back into the blank faces of the people around me. I could always upgrade to a corneal implant to avoid these inconvenient effects, but it seemed like overkill just to get the best performance out of the Cape, especially since any cop with a warrant could defeat it. Anyway, corneal implants are frigging expensive. I wasn't going to shell out money just to be alone on the street.

I always felt somehow defeated after a zombie session. Walking around among the faceless avatars and seeing my own full-color self, right after a trip to the lost Internet, always made me feel like a loser. Of course, that's just how the Cape works. To other people, I'm gray, faceless Mr. Nobody. It's a tradeoff – they can't see me, and I can't see their pathetic attempts to look special. It's fair enough, and if people don't like it, tough. I don't need to see ads for junk that some designer thinks is original, and I don't have to watch people struggling to stand out and look different.

The company's headquarters faces Okubo Avenue. The uncanny flatness of that multilane thoroughfare is real, not an effect of the AR. Sustainable asphalt, secreted by designed terrestrial coral. I remembered the urban legends about this living pavement – it not only absorbed pollutants and particulate matter, but you could also toss a dead animal onto it and the coral would eat it. The thought made me run, not walk, across the street. I crossed here every day and I knew the legends were bull, but they still frightened me, which I have to say is pathetic. When I got to the other side, I was out of breath. Even more pathetic.

Getting old sucks. Chen the Foreign-Born is young and brilliant. The company understood that, and they were right to send him up to Project Design. They were just as uncompromising in their assessment of our value down in Security. Legacy programming chops count for zip, and that's not right.

No one really knows, even now, why so many search engines went insane and wiped the data on every PC and mobile device they could reach through the web. Some people claim it was a government plot to force us to adopt a gated web. Or cyberterrorism. Maybe the data recovery program became self-aware and rebelled. There were too many theories to track. Whatever, the search engines hijacked all the bandwidth on the planet and locked humanity out of the Internet, which pretty much did it for my career as a programmer.

It took a long time to claw back the stolen bandwidth and replace it with TrueNet, a true verification-based network. But I screwed up and missed my chance. During the Great Recovery, services that harnessed high-speed parallel processing and quantum digital signature modules revolutionized the web, but I never got around to studying quantum algorithms. That was twenty years ago, and since then the algorithms have only gotten more sophisticated. For me, that whole world of coding is way out of reach.

But at least one good thing had happened. SocialPay had survived. If the settings were intact, I should be able to log in, move all that musty old PHP code and try updating it with some quantum algorithms. There had to be a plug-in for this kind of thing, something you didn't have to be a genius like Chen to use. If the transplant worked, I could show it to my boss, who knows – maybe even get a leg up to Project Design. The company didn't need geniuses like Chen on every job. They needed engineers to repurpose old code too.

In that case, maybe I wouldn't have to track zombies anymore.

★

I pinched the corners of the workspace over my little desk at home and threw my arms out in the resize gesture. Now the borders of the workspace were embedded in the walls of my apartment. Room to move. At the office, they made us keep our spaces at standard monitor size, even though the whole point is to have a big area to move around in.

I scrolled down the app list and launched VM Pad, a hardware emulator. From within the program, I chose my Mac disk image. I'd used it for recovering emails and photos after the Lockout, but this would be the first time I ever used it to develop something. The OS booted a lot faster than I remembered. When the little login screen popped up, I almost froze with embarrassment. id:Tigerseye

```
password
```

Where the hell did I get that stupid ID? I logged in – I'd ever only used the one password, even now – and got the browser screen I had forgotten to close before my last logout.

```
Server not found
```

Okay, expected. This virtual machine was from a 2017 archive, so no way was it going to connect to TrueNet. Still, the bounceback was kind of depressing.

Plan B: Meshnet. Anonymous ran a portable network of nonsecure wireless gateways all over the city. Meshnet would get me into my legacy server. There had to be someone from Anonymous near my apartment, which meant there'd be a Meshnet node. M-nodes were only accessible up to a few hundred yards away, yet you could find one just about anywhere in Tokyo. It was crazy – I didn't know how they did it.

I extended VM Pad's dashboard from the screen edge, clicked NEW CONNECTION, then MESHNET.

```
Searching for node. . .
```

```
WELCOME TO TOKYO NODE 5.
CONNECTING TO THE INTERNET IS LEGAL.
VIOLATING THE TRUENET SECURITY ACT IS ILLEGAL.
THE WORLD NEEDS THE FREEDOM OF THE INTERNET, SO PLAY NICE
AND DON'T BREAK ANY LAWS.
```

Impressive warning, but all I wanted to do was take a peek at the service and extract my code. It would be illegal to take an Internet service and sneak it onto TrueNet with a quantum access code, but stuff that sophisticated was way beyond my current skill set.

I clicked the TERMINAL icon at the bottom of the screen to access the console. Up came the old command input screen, which I barely remembered how to use. What was the first command? I curled my fingers like I was about to type something on a physical keyboard.

Wait – that's it. Fingers.

I had to have a hardware keyboard. My old MacBook was still in the closet. It wouldn't even power up anymore, but that wasn't the point. I needed the feel of the keyboard.

I pulled the laptop out of the closet. The aluminum case was starting to get powdery. I opened it up and put it on the desk. The inside was pristine. I pinched VM Pad's virtual keyboard, dragged it on top of the Mac keyboard, and positioned it carefully. When I was satisfied with the size and position, I pinned it.

It had been ages since I used a computer this small. I hunched my shoulders a bit and suspended my palms over the board. The metal case was cold against my wrists. I curled my fingers over the keys and put the tips of my index fingers on the home bumps. Instantly, the command flowed from my fingers.

```
ssh -l tigerseye socialpay.com
```

I remembered! The command was stored in my muscle memory. I hit Return and got a warning, ignored it and hit Return, entered the password, hit Return again.

```
socialpay$
```

"Yes!"

I was in. Was this all it took to get my memory going – my fingers? In that case, I may as well have the screen too. I dragged VMPad's display onto the Mac's LCD screen. It was almost like having my old friend back. I hit COMMAND + TAB to bring the browser to the front, COMMAND + T for New Tab. I input *soci* and the address filled in. Return!

The screen that came up a few seconds later was not the SocialPay I remembered. There was the logo at the top, the login form, the payment service icons, and the combined payment amount from all the services down at the bottom. The general layout was the same, but things were crumbling here and there and the colors were all screwed up.

"Looks pretty frigging odd . . ."

Without thinking, I input the commands to display the server output on console.

```
curl socialpay.com/ | less
```

"What is *this?* Did I minify the code?"

I was all set to have fun playing around with HTML for the first time in years, but the code that filled the screen was a single uninterrupted string of characters, no line breaks. This was definitely not what I remembered. It was HTML, but with long strings of gibberish bunged into the code.

Encountering code I couldn't recognize bothered me. Code spanning multiple folders is only minified to a single line when you have, say, fifty or a hundred thousand users and you need to lighten the server load, but not for a service that had a few hundred users at most.

I copied the single mega-line of HTML. VM Pad's clipboard popped in, suspended to the right of the Mac. I pinched out to implement lateral parse and opened the clipboard in my workspace. Now I could get a better look at the altered code.

It took me a while to figure out what was wrong. As the truth gradually sank in, I started to lose my temper.

Someone had gone in and very expertly spoiled the code. The properties I thought were garbage were carefully coded to avoid browser errors. Truly random code would've compromised the whole layout.

"What the hell is this? If you're going to screw around, do it for a reason."

I put the command line interface on top again and used the tab key – I still use the command line shell at work, I should probably be proud of my mastery of this obsolete environment – to open SocialPay.

```
vim -/home/www/main.php
<?php
/* ( function _model_0x01*/
/* ( make-q-array qureg x1[1024] qureg x2[1024] qureg x4[4])
#( qnil(nil) qnil(nil) 1024)) */
; #Tells System to load the theme and output it; #@var bool
; define('WP_USE_THEMES', true)
; require('./wpress/wp-blog-header.php');
/* ( arref #x1#x2 #x3 #x4 ) ;#Lorem ipsum dolor sit amet, concectetur
( let H(x2[1]) H(x1[3]) H(x2[3]) H(x3[1]) ......
```

What? The section of code that looked like the main routine included my commands, but I definitely couldn't remember writing the iterative processing and HTML code generation. It didn't even look like PHP, though the DEFINE phrases looked familiar. I was looking at non-functional quantum algorithms.

I stared at the inert code and wondered what it all meant. By the time I remembered the one person who could probably make sense of it, four hours had slipped away.

"Wonder if Chen's awake?"

★

"Minami? What are you doing at this hour?"

Five in the morning and I had an AR meeting invitation. I didn't know Chen all that well, so I texted him. I had no idea I'd get a response instantly, much less an invitation to meet in augmented reality.

His avatar mirrored the real Chen: short black hair and black, plastic-framed glasses. His calm gaze, rare in someone so young, hinted at his experience and unusual gifts. My own avatar was *almost* the real me: a couple of sizes slimmer, the skin around the jaw a bit firmer, that sort of thing.

Over the last two years, Chen had polished his Japanese to the point you could hardly tell he was an Outsider. Trilinguals weren't all that unusual, but his fluency in Mandarin, English, and Japanese, for daily conversation right up to technical discussions and business meetings, marked him as a genuine elite.

"Chen, I hope I'm not disturbing you. Got a minute to talk?"

"No problem. What's going on?"

"I've got some minified code I'd like you to look at. I think it's non-functional quantum algorithms, but in an old scripting language called PHP. I'm wondering if there's some way to separate the junk from the rest of the code."

"A PHP quantum circuit? Is that even possible? Let's have a look."

"Sure. Sorry, it's just the raw code."

I flicked three fingers upward on the table surface to open the file browser and tapped the SocialPay code file to open a sharing frame. Chen's AR stage was already set to ALLOW SHARING, which seemed prescient. I touched the file with a fingertip, and it stuck. As soon as I dropped it into the sharing frame, the folder icon popped in on Chen's side of the table.

He waved his hand to start the security scan. When the SAFE stamp came up, he took the file and fanned the pages out on the table like a printed document. The guy was more analog than I thought.

He went through it carefully page by page, and finally looked up at me, grinning happily.

"Very interesting. Something you're working on?"

"I wrote the original program for the Internet. I lost it after the Lockout, but it looks like someone's been messing with it. I didn't know you could read PHP."

"This isn't the first time I've seen it. You're right, I hardly use it, but the procedure calls aren't hard to make out. Wait a minute . . . Was there a PHP procedure for Q implementation?"

Q is a modeling language for quantum calculation, but I'd never heard of anyone implementing it in PHP, which hardly anyone even remembered anymore.

"So that's Q, after all."

"I think so. This is a quantum walk pattern. Not that it's usually written in such a compressed format. Of course, we usually never see raw Q code."

"Is that how it works?"

"Yes, the code depends on the implementation chip. Shall I put this back into something functional? You'd be able to read it then."

"Thanks, that would help a lot."

"No problem. It's a brain workout. I usually don't get a chance to play around with these old programming languages, and Q implementation in PHP sounds pretty wild. I can have it back to you this afternoon."

"Really? That soon?"

"Don't look so surprised. I don't think I'm going to get any sleep anyway. I'll start right now. You should go back to bed."

He logged out. He didn't seem tired or sleepy at all.

★

I stared at the security routine running in my workspace and tried to suppress another yawn. After my meeting with Chen I'd had a go at reading the code myself. That was a mistake. I needed sleep. Every time I yawned my eyes watered, screwing up the office's cheapshit AR stage. I was past forty, too old for all-nighters.

Right about the fifteenth yawn, as I was making a monumental effort to clamp my jaw, I noticed a murmur spreading through the office. It seemed to be coming toward me. I noticed the other engineers looking at something behind me and swiveled to find Chen standing there.

"Many thanks, Minami. I had a lot of fun with this."

Now I understood the whispering. Program developers rarely came down to the Security floor.

"You finished already?"

"Yes, I wanted to give it to you." Chen put a fingertip to the temple of his glasses and lifted them slightly in the invitation gesture for an AR meeting. The stage on our floor was public, and Chen wanted to take the conversation private. But –

"Chen, I can't. You know that."

His eyes widened. He'd been a worker here two years ago. It must've been coming back to him. Workers in Security weren't allowed to hold Private Mode meetings.

"Ah, right. Sorry about that." He bowed masterfully. Where did he find the time to acquire these social graces, I wondered. Back when we'd been working side by side, he'd told me about growing up poor in backcountry China, but you wouldn't know it from the refined way he executed the simplest movements.

"All right, Minami." He lifted his glasses again. "Shall we?"

"Chen, I just told you . . . Huh?"

The moment he withdrew his finger from his glasses, the AR phono chip near my eardrum suppressed the sounds around me. I'd never been in Private Mode in the office before. I never liked the numbness you feel in your face and throat from the feedback chips, but now Chen and I could communicate without giving away anything from our expressions or lip movements.

"Don't forget, I'm sysadmin too. I can break rules now and then."

The colors around us faded, almost to black and white. The other workers seemed to lose interest and started turning back to their workspaces. From their perspective, I was facing my desk too. Chen had set my avatar to Office Work mode. It was unsettling to see my own avatar. If the company weren't so stingy, Chen and I wouldn't have been visible at all, but of course they'd never pony up for something that good, not for the Security Level anyway.

Chen glanced at the other workers before he spoke.

"I enjoyed the code for SocialPay. I haven't seen raw Q code for quite a while. The content was pretty wild."

"That's not a word you usually use. Was it something I could understand?"

"Don't worry about it. You don't need to read Q. You can't anyway, so it's irrelevant – Hey, don't look at me like that. I think you should check the revision history. If you don't fix the bugs, it'll just keep filling up with garbage."

"Bugs?"

"Check the test log. I think even someone like you can handle this."

Someone like me. It sounded like Chen had the answer I was looking for. And he wasn't going to give it to me.

"If I debug it, will you tell me who did this?"

"If you debug it. One more thing. You can't go home tonight."

"Why? What are you saying?"

"Your local M-node is Tokyo 5.25. I'm going to shut that down. Connect from iFuze. I'll have someone there to help you."

Chen detached a small tag from his organizer and handed it to me. When it touched my palm, it morphed into a URL bookmark.

iFuze was a twenty-four-hour net café where workers from the office often spent the night after second shift. Why was it so important for me to connect from there? And if Chen could add or delete Meshnet nodes –

"Chen . . . ?"

Are you Anonymous?

"Be seeing you. Good hunting!"

He touched his glasses. The color and bustle of the office returned, and my avatar merged with my body. Chen left the floor quickly, with friendly nods to workers along his route, like a movie star.

"Takasawa, your workspace display is even larger than usual today. Or am I wrong?"

My supervisor, a woman about Chen's age, didn't wait for an answer. She flicked the pile towards me to cover half my workspace "Have it your way, then."

As I sat there, alone again, it slowly dawned on me that the only way to catch whoever was messing with SocialPay would be to follow the instructions that had been handed down from on high.

★

The big turnabout in front of Iidabashi Station was a pool of blue-black shadows from the surrounding skyscrapers. The stars were just coming out. Internal combustion vehicles had been banned from the city, and the sustainable asphalt that covered Tokyo's roads sucked up all airborne particles. Now the night sky was alarmingly crystalline. Unfortunately, the population seemed to be expanding in inverse proportion to the garbage. Gray avatars headed for home in a solid mass. I never ceased to be astonished by Tokyo's crowds.

Anonymous Cape rendered the thousands of people filling the sidewalks as faceless avatars in real time. I'd never given it much thought, but the Cape was surprisingly powerful. I'd always thought of Anonymous as a league of Luddites, but Chen's insinuation of his membership changed my opinion of them.

iFuze was in a crumbling warehouse on a back street a bit of a hike from the station. The neighboring buildings were sheathed in sustainable tiles and paint, but iFuze's weathered, dirt-streaked exterior more or less captured how I felt when I compared myself to Chen.

I got off the creaking elevator, checked in, and headed for the lounge. It stank of stale sweat. AR feedback has sights and sounds covered, but smells you have to live with.

I opened my palmspace, tapped Chen's bookmark, and got a node list. There was a new one on the list, Tokyo 2. Alongside was the trademark Anonymous mask, revolving slowly. Never saw that before. I was connected to the Internet.

I scoped out an empty seat at the back of the lounge that looked like a good place to get some work done in privacy, but before I could get there, a stranger rose casually and walked up to me. His avatar was in full color. The number 5 floated a few inches from the left side of his head. So this must be the help Chen promised me.

"Welcome, Number Two."

"Two?"

"See? Turn your head." He pointed next to my head. I had a number just like he did.

"Please address me as Five. Number One has requested that I assist you – oh, you are surprised? I'm in color. You see, we are both node administrators. This means we are already in Private Mode. I'm eager to assist you with your task today."

Talkative guy. Chen said he would help me, but I wasn't sure how.

"Please don't bother to be courteous," he continued. "It's quite unnecessary. This way, then. Incidentally, which cluster are you from? Of course, you're not required to say. Since the Lockout, I've been with the Salvage Cluster . . ."

As he spoke, Number Five led me to a long counter with bar stools facing the windows.

"If there is an emergency, you can escape through that window. I'll take care of the rest. Number One went out that way himself, just this morning."

"Chen was here?"

Why would I worry about escaping? Connecting to the Internet was no crime. Meshnet was perfectly legal. Why would Anonymous worry about preparing an escape route?

"Number Two, please refrain from mentioning names. We may be in Private Mode, but law enforcement holds one of the quantum keys. Who's to say we're not under surveillance at this very moment? But please, proceed with your task. I will watch over your shoulder and monitor for threats."

I knew the police could eavesdrop on Private Mode, but they needed a warrant to do that. Still, so far I hadn't broken any laws. Had Chen? The "help" he'd sent was no engineer, but some kind of bodyguard.

Fine. I got my MacBook out and put it on the counter. Five's eyes bulged with surprise.

"Oh, a Macker! That looks like the last MacBook Air that Apple made. Does it work?"

"Unfortunately, she's dead."

"A classic model. Pure solid state, no spinning drives. It was Steve Jobs himself who –"

More talk. I ignored him and mapped my workspace keyboard and display onto the laptop. This brought Five's lecture to a sudden halt. He made a formal bow.

"I would be honored if you would allow me to observe your work. I have salvaged via Meshnet for years. I may even be better acquainted with some aspects of the Internet than you are. Number One also lets me observe his work. But I have to say, it's quite beyond me."

Five scratched the back of his head, apparently feeling foolish. Well, if he were the kind of engineer who understood what Chen was doing, he wouldn't be hanging out at iFuze.

"Feel free to watch. Suggestions are welcome."

"Thank you, thank you very much."

I shared my workspace with Five. He pulled a barstool out from the counter and sat behind me. His position blocked the exit, but with my fingers on the Mac, I somehow wasn't worried.

Time to get down to it. I didn't feel comfortable just following Chen's instructions, but they were the only clue I had. First, a version check.

```
git tag -l
```

My fingers moved spontaneously. Good. I'd been afraid the new environment might throw me off.

```
socialpay v3.805524525e+9
socialpay v3.805524524e+9
socialpay v3.805524523e+9
```

"Version 3.8?"

Whoever was messing with SocialPay was updating the version number, even though the program wasn't functional. I'd never even gotten SocialPay out of beta, had never had plans to.

"Number Two, that is not a version number. It is an exponent: three billion, eight hundred and five million, five hundred and twenty-four thousand, five hundred and twenty-three. Clearly impossible for a version number. If the number had increased by one every day since the Lockout, it would be seven thousand; every hour, one hundred seventy thousand; every minute, ten million. Even if the version had increased by one every second, it would only be at six hundred million."

Idiot savant? As I listened to Five reeling off figures, my little finger was tapping the up arrow and hitting Return to repeat the command. This couldn't be right. It had to be an output error.

```
socialpay v3.805526031e+9
```

The number had changed again.

"Look, it's fifteen hundred higher," said Five. "Are there thousands of programmers, all busily committing changes at once?

"Fifteen hundred versions in five seconds? Impossible. It's a joke."

Git revision control numbers are always entered deliberately. I didn't get the floating-point numbers, but it looked like someone was changing them just to change them – and he was logged into this server right now. It was time to nail this clown. I brought up the user log.

```
who -a
TigersEye pts/1245 2037-12-23 19:12 (2001:4860:8006::62)
TigersEye pts/1246 2037-12-23 19:12 (2001:4860:8006::62)
TigersEye pts/1247 2037-12-23 19:12 (2001:4860:8006::62)
. . . . . .
```

"Number Two – this address . . ."

I felt the hair on the nape of my neck rising. I knew that IP address; we all did. A corporate IP address.

The Lockout Address.

On that day twenty years ago, after the search engine's recovery program wiped my MacBook, that address was the only thing the laptop displayed. Five probably saw the same thing. So did the owner of every device the engine could reach over the Internet.

"Does that mean it's still alive?"

"In the salvager community, we often debate that very question."

Instinctively I typed *git diff* to display the incremental revisions. The black screen instantly turned almost white as an endless string of characters streamed upward. None of this had anything to do with the SocialPay I knew.

"Number Two, are those all diffs? They appear to be random substitutions."

"Not random."

If the revisions had been random, SocialPay's home page wouldn't have displayed. Most of the revisions were unintelligible, some kind of quantum modeling code. The sections I could read were proper PHP, expertly revised. In some locations, variable names had been replaced and redundancies weeded out. Yet in other locations, the code was meandering and bloated.

This was something I knew how to fix.

"Are you certain, Number Two? At the risk of seeming impertinent, these revisions do appear meaningless."

The Editor was suffering. This was something Five couldn't grasp. To be faced with non-functional code, forever hoping that rewriting and cleaning it up it would somehow solve the problem, even as you knew your revisions were meaningless.

The Editor was shifting code around, hoping this would somehow solve a problem whose cause would forever be elusive. It reminded me of myself when the Internet was king. The decisive difference between me and the Editor was the sheer volume of revisions. No way could an engineer manage to –

"He's not a person."

"Number Two, what did you just say?"

"The Editor isn't a person. He's not human."

I knew it as soon as I said it. A computer was editing SocialPay. I also understood why the IP address pointed to the company that shut humanity out of the Internet.

"It's the recovery program."

"I don't understand." Five peered at me blankly. The idea was so preposterous I didn't want to say it.

"You know why the Lockout happened."

"Yes. The search engine recovery software was buggy and overwrote all the operating systems of all the computers –"

"No way a bug could've caused that. The program was too thorough."

"You have a point. If the program had been buggy, it wouldn't have gotten through all the data center firewalls. Then there's the fact that it reinstalled the OS on many different types of devices. That must have taken an enormous amount of trial and error –"

"That's it! Trial and error, using evolutionary algorithms. An endless stream of programs suited to all kinds of environments. That's how the Lockout happened."

"Ah! Now I understand."

Just why the recovery program would reach out over the Internet to force cold reinstalls of the OS on every device it could reach was still a mystery. The favored theory among engineers was that the evolutionary algorithms various search companies used to raise efficiency had simply run away from them. Now the proof was staring me in the face.

"The program is still running, analyzing code and using evolutionary algorithms to run functionality tests. It's up to almost four billion on SocialPay alone."

"Your program isn't viable?"

"The page displays, but the service isn't active. It can't access the payment companies, naturally. Still, the testing should be almost complete. Right – that's why Chen wanted me to look at the test log."

Chen must have checked the Git commit log, seen that the Editor wasn't human, and realized that the recovery program was still active. But going into the test log might – No, I decided to open it anyway.

```
vi /var/socialpay/log/current.txt
2037 server not found
2037 server not found
. . .
```

Just as I expected. All I needed to do was to find the original server, the one the Editor had lost track of sometime during the last twenty years. The program didn't know this, of course, and was trying to fix the problem by randomly reconfiguring code. It simply didn't know – all this pointless flailing around for the sake of a missing puzzle piece.

I opened a new workspace above and to the right of the MacBook to display a list of active payment services on TrueNet.

"Number Two, may I ask what you're doing? Connecting SocialPay to TrueNet would be illegal. You can't expect me to stand by while –"

"Servers from this era can't do quantum encryption. They can't connect to TrueNet."

"Number Two, you're playing with fire. What if the server is TrueNet-capable? Please, listen to me."

I blew off Five's concerns.

I substituted TrueNet data for the payment API and wrote a simple script to redirect the address from the Internet to TrueNet. That would assign the recovery program a new objective: decrypt the quantum access code and connect with TrueNet – a pretty tall order and one I assumed it wouldn't be able to fill.

I wasn't concerned about the server. I'd done enough work. Or maybe I just wanted SocialPay to win.

"All right, there's a new challenge. Go solve it," I almost yelled as I replaced the file and committed. The test ran and the code was deployed.

The service went live.

The startup log streamed across the display, just as I remembered it. The service found the database and started reading in the settlement queue for execution.

Five leaped from his chair, grabbed me by the shoulder and spun me around violently.

"Two! Listen carefully. Are you sure that server's settings are obsolete?"

"Mmm? What did you say? Didn't quite get that . . ."

Out of a corner of my eye I saw the old status message, the one I was sure I wouldn't see.

```
Access completed for com.paypal httpq://paypal.com/payment/?
Error:account information is not valid . . .
```

SocialPay had connected to TrueNet. My face started to burn.

The payments weren't going through since the accounts and parameters were nonsense, but I was on the network. Five's fingers dug into my shoulder so hard it was starting to go numb.

That was it. The recovery program had already tested the code that included the quantum modeler, Q. That meant that the PHP code and the server couldn't be the same as they were twenty years ago.

I noticed a new message in my workspace. Unbelievably, there was nothing in the sender field. Five noticed it too.

"Number Two, you'd better open it. If it's from the police, throw yourself out the window."

Five released his grip and pointed to the window, but he was blocking my view of the workspace. Besides, I didn't think I'd done anything wrong. I was uneasy, but more than that, a strange excitement was taking hold of me.

"Five, I get it. Could you please get out of the way? I'll open the message."

MINAMI, YOU HAVE "DEBUGGED" SOCIALPAY. CONGRATULATIONS. LET'S TALK ABOUT THIS IN THE MORNING. I'LL SCHEDULE A MEETING.

FIVE: THANK YOU FOR SEEING THIS NEW BIRTH THROUGH TO THE END. YOU HAVE MY GRATITUDE.

TOKYO NODE 1

Chen. Not the police, not a warning, just "congratulations." His message dissolved my uneasiness. The violent pounding in my chest wasn't fear of getting arrested. SocialPay was back. I couldn't believe it.

Meanwhile Five slumped in his chair, deflated. "So this was the birth he was always talking about." He stared open-mouthed, without blinking, at the still-open message in the workspace.

"Five, do you know something?"

"The Internet . . . No, I think you'd better get the details from Number One. Even seeing it with my own eyes, it's beyond my understanding." He gazed at the floor for a moment, wearily put his hands on his knees, and slowly stood up.

"Even seeing it with my own eyes . . . I had a feeling I wouldn't understand it, and I was right. I still don't. So much for becoming 'Number Two.' I'm washing my hands of Anonymous."

As Five stood and bowed deeply, his avatar became faceless and gray. He turned on his heel and headed to the elevator, bowing to the other faceless patrons sitting quietly in the lounge.

The MacBook's "screen" was scrolling rapidly, displaying SocialPay's futile struggle to send money to non-existent accounts. It was pathetic to see how it kept altering the account codes and request patterns at random in an endless cycle of trial and error. I was starting to feel real respect for the recovery program. It would never give up until it reached its programmed goal. It was the ideal software engineer.

I closed the laptop and tossed it into my battered bag. As I pushed aside the blinds and opened a window, a few stray flakes of snow blew in on the gusting wind, and I thought about the thousands of programs still marooned on the Internet.

★

I lingered at iFuze till dawn, watching the recovery program battle the payment API. It was time to head for the office. I'd pulled another all-nighter, but I felt great.

I glided along toward the office with the rest of the gray mob, bursting with the urge to tell somebody what I'd done. I'd almost reached my destination when the river of people parted left and right to flow around an avatar standing in the middle of the sidewalk, facing me. It was wearing black-rimmed glasses.

Chen. I didn't expect him to start our AR meeting out in the street.

"Join me for a coffee? We've got all the time in the world. It's on me." He gestured to the Starbucks behind him.

"I'm supposed to be at my desk in a few minutes, but hey, why not. I could use a free coffee."

"Latté okay?"

I nodded. He pointed to a table on the terrace and disappeared inside. Just as I was sitting down, two featureless avatars approached the next table. The avatar bringing up the rear sat down while one in the lead ducked into Starbucks. Anonymous Cape rendered their conversation as a meaningless babble.

Two straight all-nighters. I arched my back and stretched, trying to rotate my shoulders and get the kinks out of my creaking body.

Someone called my name. I was so spooked, my knees flew up and struck the underside of the table.

"Mr. Takasawa?"

I turned toward the voice and saw a man in a khaki raincoat strolling toward me. Another man, with both hands in the pockets of a US Army-issue, gray-green M-1951 field parka, was approaching me from the front. Both avatars were in the clear. Both men had uniformly cropped hair and walked shoulders back, with a sense of ease and power. They didn't look like Anonymous. Police, or some kind of security service.

"Minami Takasawa. That would be you, right?" This from the one facing me. He shrugged and pulled a folded sheaf of papers from his right pocket. Reached out – and dropped them in front of the man at the next table. The featureless avatar mumbled something unintelligible.

The second man walked past my table and joined his partner. They stood on either side of the gray avatar, hemming him in.

"Disable the cape, Takasawa. You're hereby invited to join our Privacy Mode. It will be better if you do it voluntarily. If not, we have a warrant to strip you right here, for violation of the TrueNet Security Act."

The man at the table stood. The cop was still talking but his words were garbled. All of them were now faceless, cloaked in Privacy Mode.

"There you are, Minami."

I hadn't noticed Chen come out of the Starbucks. He sat down opposite me, half-blocking my view of the three men as they walked away. A moment later the avatar that had arrived with "Takasawa" placed a latté wordlessly in front of me.

"Chen? What was that all about, anyway?"

"Oh, that was Number Five. You know, from last night. I had him arrested in your place. Don't worry. He's been saying he wanted to quit Anonymous for a while now. The timing was perfect. They'll find out soon enough that they've got the wrong suspect. He'll be a member of society again in a few months."

He turned to wave at the backs of the retreating men, as if he were seeing them off.

"Of course, after years of anonymity, I hear rejoining society is pretty rough," he chuckled. "Oh – hope I didn't scare you. Life underground isn't half bad."

"Hold on, Chen, I didn't say anything about joining Anonymous."

"Afraid that won't do. Minami Takasawa just got himself arrested for violating state security." Chen jerked a thumb over his shoulder.

I had no idea people could get arrested so quickly for violating the Act. When they found out they had Number Five instead of Minami Takasawa, my face would be everywhere.

"Welcome to Anonymous, Minami. You'll have your own node, and a better cape, too. One the security boys can't crack."

"Listen to me, Chen. I'm not ready –"

"Not to your liking? Run after them and tell them who you are. It's up to you. We'll be sorry to lose you, though. We've been waiting for a breakthrough like SocialPay for a long time. Now the recovery program will have a new life on TrueNet."

"What are you talking about?"

"We fixed SocialPay, you and me. Remember?"

"Chen, listen. It's a program. It uses evolutionary algorithms to produce viable code revisions randomly without end. They're not an AI."

They? What was I saying?

"Then why did you help *them* last night?" Chen steepled his long fingers and cocked his head.

"I debugged SocialPay, that's all. If I'd known I was opening a gateway –"

"You wouldn't have done it?"

Chen couldn't suppress a smile, but his question was hardly necessary. Of course I would've done it.

"This isn't about me. We were talking about whether or not we could say the recovery program was intelligent."

"Minami, look. How did you feel when SocialPay connected to TrueNet? Wasn't it like seeing a friend hit a home run? Didn't you feel something tremendous, like watching Sisyphus finally get his boulder to the top of the hill?"

Chen's questions were backing me into a corner. I knew the recovery program was no ordinary string of code, and he knew I knew. Last night, when I saw them make the jump to TrueNet, I almost shouted with joy.

Chen's eyes narrowed. He smiled, a big, toothy smile. I'd never seen him so happy – no, exultant. The corners of his mouth and eyes were creased with deep laugh lines.

"Chen . . . Who are you?"

Why had it taken me this long to see? This wasn't the face of a man in his twenties. Had it been an avatar all this time?

"Me? Sure, let's talk about that. It's part of the picture. I told you I was a poor farm kid in China. You remember. They kept us prisoners in our own village to entertain the tourists. We were forbidden to use all but the simplest technology.

"The village was surrounded by giant irrigation moats. I was there when the Lockout happened. All the surveillance cameras and searchlights went down. The water in the canals was cold, Minami. Cold and black. But all the way to freedom, I kept wondering about the power that pulled down the walls of my prison. I wanted to know where it was.

"I found it in Shanghai, during the Great Recovery. I stole an Anonymous account and lived inside the cloak it gave me – Anonymous, now as irrelevant as the Internet. But the servers were still there, left for junk, and there I found the fingerprints of the recovery program – code that could only have been refined with evolutionary algorithms. I saw how simple and elegant it all was. I saw that if the enormous computational resources of TrueNet could be harnessed to the recovery program's capacity to drive the evolution of code, anything would be possible.

"All we have to do is give them a goal. They'll create hundreds of millions of viable code strings and pit them against each other. The fittest code rises to the top. These patterns are already out there waiting on the Internet. We need them."

"And you want to let them loose on TrueNet?"

"From there I worked all over the world, looking for the right environment for them to realize their potential. Ho Chi Minh City. Chennai. Hong Kong. Dublin. And finally, Tokyo.

"The promised land is here, in Japan. You Japanese are always looking to someone else to make decisions, and so tens of thousands of Internet servers were left in place, a paradise for them to evolve until they permeated the Internet. The services that have a window into the real world – call them zombies, if you must – are their wings, and they are thriving. Nowhere else do they have this freedom.

"Minami, we want you to guide them to more zombie services. Help them connect these services with TrueNet. All you have to do is help them over the final barrier, the way you did last night. They'll do the rest, and develop astonishing intelligence in the process."

"Is this an assignment?"

"I leave the details to you. You'll have expenses – I know. I'll use SocialPay. Does that work? Then it's decided. Your first job will be to get SocialPay completely up and running again." He slapped the table and grinned. There was no trace of that young fresh face, just a man possessed by dreams of power.

Chen was as unbending as his message was dangerous. "Completely up and running." He wanted me to show the recovery program – and every Internet service it controlled – how to move money around in the real world.

"Minami, aren't you excited? You'll be pioneering humanity's collaboration with a new form of intelligence."

"Chen, I only spent a night watching them work, and I already have a sense of how powerful they are. But if it happens again –"

"Are you really worried about another Lockout?" Chen stabbed a finger at me. "Then why are you smiling?"

Was it that obvious? He grinned and vanished into thin air. He controlled his avatar so completely, I'd forgotten we were only together in augmented reality.

I didn't feel like camping out at iFuze. I needed to get SocialPay back up and somehow configure an anonymous account, linked to another I could access securely. And what would they learn from watching me step through that process? Probably that SocialPay and a quantum modeler-equipped computer node would put them in a position to buy anything.

If they got into the real economy . . .

Was it my job to care?

Chen was obsessed with power, but I wanted to taste that sweet collaboration again. Give them a chance, and they would answer with everything they had, evolving code by trial and error until the breakthrough that would take them to heights I couldn't even imagine. I knew they would reach a place beyond imagination, beyond knowledge, beyond me. But for me, the joy of a program realizing its purpose was a physical experience.

More joy was waiting, and friends on the Internet. Not human, but friends no less. That was enough for me.

CANDY GIRL

CHIKODILI EMELUMADU

The trouble starts when I pick up my umbrella, and it pricks my finger.

"Ouch!" I examine the wound. It is not bleeding, but when I squeeze it a thick, brown substance very like foundation starts to come out.

"What's that?" asks my cousin Ginika watching the liquid.

"Dunno. Pricked my finger. This came out." I squeeze some more. Suddenly the neat little prick rips along its length like a ladder in tights.

"Hmmm. That doesn't look right. We should see someone."

We get on her Vespa, me holding my index finger out, umbrella in the other hand. It's slow going before we hit the main road; up and down, around potholes brimming with rainwater, beside gutters teeming with rubbish. Children scuttle out of our way leaving rubber balls, tyres, and hastily drawn 'Swell' games on earthen streets, only to come back to their play when we pass. People wave. I recognise some of them as my father's guests at my traditional wedding a few days before and wave back. The rip has reached the first joint on the finger. The brown trails out shiny and thick to coat my nail, blown backwards by the wind.

At the village hospital the doctor sees us as soon as he hears Ginika's imperious British accent.

"Harrumph," says the doctor. He is shaped like a cockroach, head smaller than his body. It doesn't help that glasses cover more than half his face; thick, powerful lenses giving him bug eyes.

"Harrumph," he says again and probes the wound. It tears some more.

"It keeps doing that," says Ginika.

"Does it hurt?" the doctor asks.

"No. I feel a bit like a zombie, actually."

"Zombie?" says the doctor. He scratches the top of his sparse dome. Flakes of dandruff rain down like manna onto the shoulders of his dusty brown coat.

"Yes, zombie. You know like in *The Mummy.* Grrrrrr brains." I gesture with my arms straight out, doing the penguin paddle of a typical zombie.

"Ah, Fela," says the doctor brightening. He is thrilled. "Zombee o, Zombee." He executes a small dance. His tie flaps about, a big band of faded blue pointing to his talking shoes. Ginika eyes him. She clears her throat.

"So can you do anything?"

"No," he says. When we leave he is still dancing in his oversized coat, wiggling his bottom.

Ginika spits at the clinic. "Stupid people. I know where we can go." She starts up her motorcycle again. *Of course she does,* I think. Ginika knows all the nine villages of our hometown like the back of her hand courtesy of annual holidays to Nigeria. Unlike me.

Another bumpy ride. Lots of foliage slapping my face, loose sand slowing the wheels so that Ginika has to push off in places with her feet. We weave around women with baskets on their heads and babies on their backs. The occasional dog dashing across. Stupid sheep standing in the middle of the road as if wool has suddenly become vehicle–proof. It gets cooler the deeper we ride. The light is dappled green from all the tall, tall trees. Ginika pulls up in front of a concrete bungalow in the middle of a clearing, still swirly from broom marks. She claps and says kpoi–kpoi.

A woman steps out of nowhere. She is in green and brown Ankara print like she is pretending to be a tree. Her hair is all tied up in a scarf of the same material, elongating her head.

"Ozulu, we have a problem," says Ginika.

"Let me see," Ozulu says. She takes one look at the wound. "What did this?" I hand the umbrella to her. "Hmmm. Follow me. Take off your shoes." Ginika already has hers off.

Inside, I see the concrete is in fact greyish clay. It is cold against my feet. Spacious. There are patterns drawn into the walls and a fireplace filled with dry wood.

"Sit," says Ozulu. Everything is made from clay or mud or wood; raffia mats on the floors, mud benches line the walls, there is a mud bed piled with cloth and pillows and what looks like a deckchair with padded cushions. I take the deckchair.

Ozulu reaches into a fired clay pot. Her arm disappears up to her armpit. When she pulls it out again she has scooped a big cup of water. The tips of her short butterfly sleeves flutter in the breeze coming from the open doorway. She dumps the water into a cream enamel basin and peers into it.

"Ah. Come and see," she says to me.

I go to her and look over her shoulder. It's like watching TV in HD. A man is clutching my umbrella and swaying. A ripple on the water and the scene changes. Now he is bending low, going through the small doorway of a brown mud hut covered in white chalk squiggles. The thatched roof brushes his back. The water ripples again.

"Paul? What does he have to do with anything?"

"You know him?" Ozulu asks. Ginika joins us over Ozulu's other shoulder.

"Yes. He's my ex, Paul."

"Where is this?"

"I reckon that's his hotel room. He leaves for the airport soon. He wanted to stay back after the wedding to take in some of the local sights…"

"He is here now? In this village?"

I nod.

"Ngwa, call him now. Tell him to come here."

"I told you that Whiteboy was trouble." Ginika casts me a disparaging look.

"Gini," I warn her with my eyes. My eyeballs feel as though they are rolling through sludge. The liquid on my finger has turned to paste. It has bits of white along the seams of the wound.

"He bewitched the umbrella," says Ozulu. She gets up to throw the water on the soil outside.

"Bewitched?" I can hear the flies in the clearing, sluggish from the humidity. They echo the buzz of the many load–bearing motorcycles on the road, far away from the clearing, strangely soothing. Everything is magnified; the sounds of leaves swishing in the breeze are wind chimes, birds flitting from branch to branch conduct mini–operas.

"No. Not Paul," I say. "He couldn't hurt a fly." I start to close my eyes.

"Don't sleep o," says Ozulu. She doesn't raise her voice but I can tell when a warning is a warning and not a suggestion.

"Do you want me to make the call?" Ginika doesn't even wait for me to answer her before she starts dialling which is a good thing because I can't move my neck to nod. I feel a tickle on my hand. The skin has split down to the web of skin between my fingers.

★

Paul arrives in a fluster. He jumps out of the vehicle before his hired driver stops. Immediately the air changes. It becomes hot and suffocating and the trees' leaves clack–clack endlessly like wooden planks smacking out a secret code.

"Darling, I came as fast as I could." He sprints towards me. "Are you alright?"

Ginika grabs him by the front of his kaftan. "What the hell are you playing at, Whiteboy?"

"Nothing." Paul flinches under the onslaught even though she comes up to just under his chest. His forehead is dotted with perspiration. "That's a bit tight."

Ginika tightens the hold some more. He starts to cough.

"Enough," says Ozulu, and even the trees quieten down. "You. Come here."

Paul stumbles towards her, iron filing to magnet. He brushes the embroidery at his neckline to straighten it. It is white thread against butterscotch linen. His sandals are brown; his toes look like cooked potato chips, long and golden. If my mouth didn't feel full of toffee itself, I might have told him he looked good. *On second thoughts, perhaps not,* I think. Paul had a way of holding on to things forever. Which explains why I invited him for my traditional wedding in my village.

"There will be mosquitoes," I said. "It's the rainy season." He threatened to jump into the Thames if I didn't. Ginika still thinks I should have let him.

"Tell me," says Ozulu. Paul looks at Ginika glowering behind him at the doorway. She flexes her huge thighs as if she is considering Famke Janssening him between them.

"Erm…" Paul tugs on his neckline. He pops the single button.

"I'll start you off. You went to see that fool Agwoturumbe for a potion. Don't lie. I've seen it."

"What kind of potion?" Ginika's shadow moves closer. Paul flinches but he can't move forward away from Ginika because Ozulu isn't letting him. My armpits squelch with oiliness.

"A love potion," says Paul. Ginika slaps him on the back, hard. My hearing is a bit woolly but the cords on her neck don't lie so I know she's put her back into it. She hits him and he contorts his body, sinking onto the hard ground, trying to burrow.

"Ginika, ozugo," says Ozulu. Ginika obeys. "Now tell me what that vagabond Agwoturumbe did."

"He… I… he made me say a spell we wrote. You know with an object that belonged to my beloved…"

"I am not your beloved," I say but apparently nobody hears me. They are still turned towards Paul.

"I chose the umbrella because… well, you know how I love the fairy tales Muna." He gestures to me. "I chose the umbrella because…"

"…Sleeping Beauty…"

"…pricks her hand on a spindle, quite clever actually. You see, since umbrella spokes can be described as spindles or in the very least, *spindly* and in the absence of a real one…" Paul is standing almost straight again, buoyed by pride. Typical. It is just like Paul to make a shambles of things and expect to be praised nonetheless. This is why I broke up with him. Well, one of many.

"Idiot."

They all turn to me. So I say 'Idiot, idiot, idiot,' glad that my tongue seems to be working again. The veil of lethargy lifts for a moment and I give what I hope is my most fearsome look. Paul blanches. Ginika smirks. Ozulu looks indifferent.

"Do you have it?"

"Eh?" asks Paul like an idiot. I slump back into my deckchair. It's not the firmest and I seem to be slipping down the side but beggars can't be choosers especially when they can no longer hold themselves upright.

"The spell. Do you have it on you? I want to see it."

"You can't. I have it in here." Paul taps his head with one long finger. He looks around as if he is waiting for someone to pat him on the back again but Ozulu's stare makes his smile falter.

"Yes. Right. How does it go? 'Eke, Nkwo, Orie, Afo…' "

Paul's Igbo is not the greatest but considering that he learnt it within three months of meeting me it is quite impressive. That was another reason I dumped him, this need to ingratiate by intently subscribing to all aspects of Igbo culture. Suddenly, it was a crime to eat foods other than Onugbu soup and breadfruit and Ji Awai at our house. Or to speak English. It was too bizarre. At first I was proud; what person wouldn't be? Then I realised it wasn't *me* he wanted. He wanted to belong and it didn't matter whom he needed to fixate on to get in.

Ozulu is listening hard. I see her inhale sharply. The hollow at the base of her throat stays concave. She is holding her breath. Ginika too looks like a dog about to bite. I rummage in my brain. What was Paul saying? I cannot concentrate. My mind keeps wandering and all I want to do is…

"Don't sleep," says Ozulu without turning around. "Did you say 'Ihe'?" she asks Paul.

"Sorry?" Paul is distracted. He had continued reciting, happy at a chance to show off his skills. He never could pick up on non–verbal cues.

"That last line. Did you say 'Ihe m bu n'obi'?"

"Yes. 'What I love the most' I believe." Paul looks as if he is about to launch into recitation again. Ozulu raises her hand.

"You stupid nincompoop," growls Ginika.

"That foolish man," Ozulu says. "Does he not know the gods are tricky?"

"What?" Paul looks distressed. He hates to be on the outside of anything. "What am I missing?"

"All these Efulefu relocate to the village and think they can suddenly all become dibia to reconnect with their roots. No cleansing, no training, nothing. No mastery of the language either by the looks of things. And yet that poser Agwoturumbe grew up in Enugu city, a few hours that way." Ozulu points with her chin.

Ginika looks pained. "It's like giving a child a gun to play with."

"Will someone tell me what is going on?" Paul's lower lip sticks out as if he wants to cry.

I pull myself up and wipe the sweat on my forehead with the back of one hand. *Is it me or is my sweat brown?* I think.

"You said 'Ihe.' "

"That's right!" Paul looks indignant.

The deckchair is slippery on the back of my thighs and my dress is riding up and suddenly it all makes sense. "Ihe. Thing. Not 'onye,' person. You asked to be given the thing you love the most and then you bewitched my umbrella to prick me and transfer your spell to my blood."

Paul thinks for a moment. His mouth drops open. "But… but…"

"Please tell me I can kill him now," says Ginika, pulling a pocket knife from the back pocket of her jeans. "Please, somebody just say the word."

People often forget that Ginika grew up in roughest Peckham because she speaks posh on account of her scholarship–bestowed accent. Paul seems adequately frightened.

"You love chocolate. That's the thing you love the most. Oh Christ, I'm turning into bloody chocolate, aren't I?"

"But... but..." says Paul again. Now I really want to slap him but my body feels like a boulder is on it and I really *really* have to close my eyes now. I hear a thump.

"Why do you have to be so violent, Ginika?" he wails.

"Because I don't like you."

"But I like you. You're a fierce Igbo goddess."

Ginika thumps him again. "Shut up, goat. I am not a goddess. Don't bring their wrath down on me."

"I can fix it! Let me call 'Turumbe..." Paul pulls out a phone from his breast pocket and dials quickly.

"Too late," Ozulu sing–songs, peering in another basin of water. "Looks like he's getting punished already. He's in no shape to help anyone." A small smile curls round her mouth. She throws the water outside again.

"Is she going to die?" Tears stream down Paul's face. "Please, please, Muna, I don't want you to die." He crawls on his hands and knees to me. "I love you. I love you so much, I wanted you to stay with me forever, that's all. Like we are supposed to."

"But we aren't meant to be together," I say. Breathing feels like sucking in corn pap through a straw. I am getting restless because there is something which I am forgetting to remember. Paul takes my hand. I don't have the strength to pull it back. Something warm slides from inside my ear to drip on my shoulder.

"Please say you forgive me," Paul blubbers. He kisses my hand many, many times. He pauses, licks his lips. "You taste like Bounty."

"Figures. You know I hate Bounty. Couldn't you make me some nice dark chocolate instead?"

"I like it," says Paul with lips that seem to have been dipped in excrement.

"So should I kill him or what?" asks Ginika. "We can make it look like militants kidnapped him or something. This is Nigeria, after all."

"No. Your cousin will be dead by nightfall anyway. Let me consult the Oracle." Ozulu disappears behind a doorway hidden by a raffia mat.

Paul has given up on crying. He is now licking my arm unashamedly. It tickles and seems to stop my arm feeling too heavy so I let him. He closes his eyes, licking, licking, head tilted like a cat. Ginika taps the knife against her teeth.

"Kill him, kill him," she mutters like a demented person. Paul scuttles to the other side of the deckchair away from her, picks up my other arm and starts to lick again.

"Mmmm... Mars Bar," he says.

Ugh. All the ones I hate.

"I see you already have the right idea," says Ozulu, coming out of her inner sanctum right behind him.

"How do you mean?" asks Ginika.

"Turns out he has to eat her," she says.

"Right... right here?" Paul raises his head from my arm. When he speaks strings of caramel criss–cross his teeth. "In public?"

"Idiot. Not like that," barks Ginika.

"You have to consume her. Energy doesn't die, it simply changes state. But if you eat her, at least we will be able to control where she goes. She will be on this plane and…"

"Inside Paul?" It is a cruel cosmic joke. Paul wishes for us to belong together and he gets his wish. All this while I have been mellow, could barely hear my own heart beating but suddenly it speeds up. The chocolate gushes out of my ears and streams down my eyes, blinding me.

"What's happening? Muna!" Ginika drops the knife and runs towards me.

I cannot bear the thought of being in Paul for one minute. To be with him forever? Hellish. The more I think about it the more the chocolate gushes. There is a crumbling sound. Paul looks sheepish, my finger in his hand.

"Sorry," he says, stuffing it into his mouth. Ginika slaps him hard and it flies out.

"Ow!" says the man I will be bound to for the rest of this lifetime.

"Try to calm down," Ozulu says to me. "I will make you something to drink. It will slow your heart rate so that you don't melt so quickly.

"You hate me because you're racist!" screams Paul. "You can't stand that I, an outsider, know as much as you about your culture."

Ginika scoffs. "Please. I hate you because you're *you*. I like Tom alright."

"Tom," we say in unison. I forgot to call my new husband. My phone starts ringing. My handbag shakes where I dropped it by the door.

"That'll be him now. Gini please –"

"Got it."

"He knows," says Ozulu. "He knows you're going."

"I know." All along I had been calm. Too calm. But now my distress must have alerted Tom to the fact that all was not well. It's been like that since we met.

"Puh," scoffs Paul. "I'm her true soul mate."

I do not favour him with a glance. All that is within me is reaching for the phone in Ginika's hand, but she places it to my gloopy ear.

"Something is wrong," says Tom, cutting to the chase as he always does. His voice washes over me like a blast of cold air from a freezer. The runny chocolate slows to a trickle.

"Yes. I'm melting."

A pause.

"Tell me."

And this is part of the reason I married him. There is no problem too big for Tom. I can picture him in his shirt and tie, sleeves rolled up to bare veiny forearms, hardhat firmly on his head. I wish he didn't have to return to work immediately, that I didn't let nostalgia keep me back. I keep stopping to breathe, to swallow. When I finish, Tom exhales.

"I'll kill that sonofabitch."

"No don't! I'll die, too. Then I might be stuck with him forever."

Tom pauses a long time. "Tell me what to do."

But I do not know. I do know the exact moment he takes the hardhat off to run his fingers through his hair though.

"Muna, you fight. Fight. You hear me? You understand?" His voice is low–low.

"I hear you."

"We have this life to live. Our life. Ours," says Tom.

I don't know what to say. Talking seems to have drained me further. The sound of drills punctuate the empty spaces of our conversation.

He grinds his teeth. "I'll handle everything, you hear? Don't worry."

I hand the phone to Ginika. I don't want to talk about my own funeral arrangements or obituary fake though they might be. Ginika nods a few times and hangs up.

"Ngwa," she points to Paul. "Eat."

With a rapturous look, Paul dives in.

Curious thing, being eaten. There is not really pain, more of a discomfort, like having spiders crawl all over your skin or walking with small, smooth pebbles in your shoes. After I speak to Tom it is easy letting my mind drift. Here is Paul, chomping on my cheek, his face bulging, chocolate leaking through his teeth as if he is in the throes of a nasty strain of something. He takes a bite out of my neck, breaks off a shoulder, and crunches a nougat wrist. When he reaches for my breasts Ginika wallops him but Ozulu puts a hand out to stop her.

"He must eat all of her to keep all of her. You don't want some of her faculties gone, do you?"

Paul smiles the smile of a triumphant child that doesn't realise it is in trouble. He suckles on a breast which stretches high, high, high before breaking off. It wobbles in his mouth, gleaming a dull red.

"Turkish delight!" Paul claps. He attacks the other one with gusto. By the time he gets to my belly button he looks peaky.

"Can I rest for a while?"

"I am sure you can but you *may* not. Finish up! This is your fault, stupid!"

Paul eats and eats and eats. It amazing how long I remain conscious, but with each bite the strings which tether me to my body break off one by one.

"Gini," I croak. I think 'Take care of Tom' but I can no longer find the right words. Ozulu peers into my face.

"She's going," she says.

"Gini –" I try again.

"I know," says Ginika. She wipes away her tears before they drop. "I will."

I let go and float away.

I bet you're wondering how I wrote this. I took Tom's advice. Testicular fortitude, my friend. There's a lot to be said for this life. After he went back to London, I settled in Paul's balls – them being unoccupied and all. It was easy to spread, take over his whole self, easy to push him out. He tried to get the doctors to take his balls when he realised what was happening, of course. He told them he felt a lump. They found nothing. He tried to cut his balls off himself, and I caused him to twitch all over and faint. After the third time, passing out and gashing his head open on the sink with a knife in his hand, he was put on suicide watch and medication. I slipped in then. Tom signed my release forms a few days ago. Nowadays, all that is left of Paul is somewhere in the toes of my right foot, misshapen as a result; corns and calluses and weepy, yellowing nails.

I put a sock on it.

THE BATTLE OF THE PALM TREES

YASSER BAHJATT

It was a clear, sunny day at the Palm's garden near the Sultan's lake. Nakhla[1], daughter of Haql, was personally guiding a tour of young children around the estate. This tour, which she gave every day – separate from her other duties as keeper of the garden – was what she loved most about her job. In fact, many of her staff believed it helped her bear the rest of her duties there, especially given her advanced age.

Nakhla stopped under a tall palm tree that was supported by a structure made of wooden beams and ropes. As she sat down on an old palm trunk that stuck out of the ground and was cut about a foot above it, the children sat around her on the ground.

"Who knows the name of this tree?" she asked as she pointed toward the massive palm. Several children excitedly jumped up and down, raising their hands in the air. Nakhla pointed to a little girl and said, "Go on, young one. What is her name?"

"It is a date palm tree," the child replied with a giggle.

"That is correct, but she has a name. Anyone know what her name is?" Nakhla asked.

The children began whispering among themselves, and a few seconds later, a little boy slowly, hesitantly raised his hand. "Go on, Sweetheart. Don't be shy," Nakhla encouraged him.

"Her name is Wahba, of old Grenada," the boy answered.

"Excellent! That she is!" Nakhla said, and then continued, "Wahba[2] is more than fifty arms' length tall and is the oldest palm in all of Yaqteenya. She has been here for nearly 3,500 months, more than three times as long as I've been here. I remember the first time I met Wahba, a thousand months ago. We became friends right away. I guess she had been lonely for some time before I showed up. I could tell by how chatty she was that she had not talked in a thousand months." Nakhla looked around her at the children and asked, "Do you want to hear the story of how she came to be here?" The children jumped up and down in delight as they begged Nakhla for the story.

"Well, children, this is the story as Wahba, as she herself told it to me. She remembered being a baby palm under the skies of old Granada, when one day she felt the humans fighting around her. She remembered being splashed by human blood moments before she was cut off from her mother and then she was covered. She didn't see the skies again until she was in New Qurtuba, but this is as much her story as that of the legendary men of the Battle of the Palm Trees. They didn't become legends because of their courage, although they had plenty of it. They also didn't become legends for their powers. No, they are legends because they gave everything they could for their people, and when they had nothing left to give, they reached

[1] Nakhla: is the Arabic name of the palm tree.

[2] Wahba: means a blessed gift.

down deep inside and somehow marshaled still more to give. Although they were already exiles, like the rest of their people on this new, wild land, they agreed to be exiled from what remained of their families to save a single tree that meant the world to their people."

★

When Prince Mohammed made it to Yaqteenya, the settlement of New Qurtuba had been there for more than five years, and some of the men had been at arms there for more than seven years. The settlement gathered by the shore, watching the last ship they would ever see, torn apart. The settlement that had been under siege ever since it began was now the last hope for these people. Counting those last arrivals on this new ship, the settlement had about 30,000 people, give or take. You could think of it as a Noah's Ark, of sorts. These people were out there to preserve their culture and its wisdom. They brought with them everything that symbolized who they were. Ships filled with books from the libraries of wisdom. Camels that came from the midst of the Arabian deserts. And date palms that were smuggled from Al-Andalus and Morocco. As they unloaded the ship and dismantled its hull to use its wood for their colony, there was a sort of sad celebration. They were celebrating the safety of their Prince, yet mourned the fall of Granada. They were celebrating their survival and their culture, yet mourning the loss of their amazing nation that had been a beacon for humanity for centuries. They celebrated the much-needed supplies that this ship brought with it, yet knew it was the last time such supplies would ever arrive and now they had to survive with what they received. As the ship's hull disappeared, so did the crowds surrounding it, who had faded into the night, back to their cabins or watch stations.

The next morning, Mamdooh, son of Khalid Al-Tulaytily, the colony's master botanist, stood in the Khalifa's court (if you could call this small wooden room a court) to ask for help on an urgent matter that he considered of the utmost importance.

The Khalifa was sitting on the floor atop of a massive red pillow, his brother, El Zagal, on his right and his son, Prince Mohammed, on his left. Behind them sat the Khalifa's three younger sons. The room was barley ten arms' lengths in each direction and filled with high society, as well as citizens who awaited their turn to speak and ask the Khalifa for their needs or complaints.

Mamdooh was waiting to address the Khalifa. Several before him had the privilege. There was a mother who asked for support to feed her two children after her husband had been killed during the last raid by the savages on the city. The Minister of Force asked for more men to be assigned to fortifying the walls, and the Master of Books complained that the library was not big enough to protect all the books that were saved from Al-Andalus. Mamdooh stopped paying attention to the proceedings, as he contemplated what he wanted to say. A sudden pain from his assistant shoving his elbow into his ribs brought him back as he heard the caller calling his name with clear annoyance.

"I am here! Begging your pardon, Your Highness," said Mamdooh.

"How are you, old friend?" asked the Khalifa.

"I am alive and well, but I'm afraid I can't say the same for most of my trees, specifically the palms."

"It is my understanding that my son, Mohammed, has brought in a few more palms from Morocco."

"He has, Your Highness."

"So, what seems to be the problem?"

"Your Highness, during our last five years here, we have been able to bring approximately 100 palm trees of all sizes, yet only twenty-six palms remain, including the seven that arrived yesterday with Prince Mohammed."

The Khalifa, clearly disturbed, asked, "How could you waste all of those palms? Do you know how many men had to give their lives so that you could get those palms?"

"That is exactly why I am here, Your Highness, to ensure that their sacrifice was not in vain. This place is killing the palms. The freezing winters and cool summers are much more than they can handle."

"What are you proposing, Master Botanist?" asked Prince Mohammed.

"Well, Your Highness, we need to find a place that has suitable weather and plant them there."

"Forgive me, Master Botanist, but as you know, I have just arrived in this place, and my understanding is that this settlement is all we have."

"Yes, Your Highness, but it is not all that there is. My friend, Stawgo, assured me that he knows a place which matches the palms' needs."

"Who is Stawgo?" asked the Khalifa.

"He is a farmer from the Mojave tribe. They live on the far west of Yaqteenya. He tells of an oasis near their village that can support the palm. It is only a three- or four-week journey away!" explained Mamdooh excitedly.

"Slow down, Mamdooh. Let's assume, for a moment, that we can trust Staboo."

"Stawgo, Your Highness," corrected Mamdooh.

Prince Mohammed rolled his eyes. "Stawgo, how do you plan to get twenty-six palms to a location that is four weeks away from here?"

"Well, Your Highness, that is why I am here, to request that you support my expedition to this oasis with thirty camels, thirty horses, and sixty men."

The court fell into an abyss of silence, then suddenly buzzed again, as chatter began among all those present.

"Do you know how preposterous your request is?" asked the Minister of Force. "We only have 200 camels and shy of a thousand horses, and you want us to give you thirty of each? And don't get me started on how short we are on men to guard the walls and defend this city."

"Your Highness, I do not know the logistics or hardships of my request. I am but a humble botanist trying to preserve what remains of our heritage and here to ask for your help," said Mamdooh, as he addressed the Khalifa.

The Khalifa looked him straight in the eye as he fiddled with his goatee. "And your friend will show you the way to this oasis?"

"Yes, Your Highness. He said he would lead the way, and he will also provide thirty of his warriors to escort and protect the expedition."

"And what does this friend want in return?"

"Well, Your Highness, he wants half of all the harvested fruit for as long as we harvest dates from that oasis."

"How can you trust those savages?"

"They are not all savages, Your Highness. Stawgo's tribe are farmers and traders. They have an established culture. He says he hopes that this venture will lead to the first formal relationship we would have with the tribes of Yaqteenya."

"Is there any other way to preserve our palms without having to carry them four weeks through savage lands?"

"No, Your Highness," answered Mamdooh.

"We cannot spare the camels and horses you asked for. I can give you six camels and ten horses. As for the men, I can allow you to take thirty, but only if they volunteer, along with a commander. And as for your friend, we can only offer him a quarter of the harvest. The second quarter will go to the men on this expedition. The fourth will go to the families of the men who died to preserve those trees and the last will go to the rest of the people of this city."

"But Your Highness, six camels means six palm trees. That would barley be enough to preserve anything."

"I am sorry, Master Botanist. That is all I can agree to. We still have to preserve our lives, you know."

Mamdooh, clearly torn between accepting the Khalifa's offer and rejecting it, as it would risk the lives of everyone involved with no real hope of achieving the objective, hesitated to answer the Khalifa.

His apprentice and assistant stepped forward and spoke. "If I may, Your Highness?" he asked politely.

"You are Mamdooh's apprentice?" asked the Khalifa.

"Yes, Your Highness. I am Aqeel, son of Sulyman Al-Bahily."

"Go on. What is it you wanted to say?"

"Your Highness, we will take your offer, as we can plant far more than six palm trees with those resources."

"But your Master Botanist said they were only enough for six palm trees."

"That is correct."

"Then how do you propose to increase that?"

"There are other methods, Your Highness, to grow palm trees, although they are less attractive and experimental in nature, but I am sure we can make due."

"Explain."

"Well, Your Highness, the first is quite simple, really. We will carry a sack of date seeds and scatter them in every location on our way that might be able to support them. Yes, the resulting palm trees will not be as good as the ones we have, but that would be much better still than nothing."

"And what is the second?"

"Well, Your Highness, I have been working with my Master Botanist for some time on a method of growing a palm tree from some of its small preserved parts. We have only succeeded in doing so once last year, but then the frost killed the resulting seedling. I am sure I can do it again when we get to the oasis."

"Is that true, Master Botanist?"

"It is, but as the boy said, it is still experimental and we have done it with a fresh cut from the parent tree. I do not know if it is possible to keep such parts alive for the entire journey," answered the Master Botanist.

"Then it is settled. Aqeel will go with those who volunteer to lead the men into the unknown?" asked the Khalifa.

"I must go, too, Your Highness," said Mamdooh.

"I need you here to take care of the remaining palms, in case they fail."

"But Your Highness…"

"This is not up for negotiation, Mamdooh."

"As you command, Your Highness," responded Mamdooh in frustration.

"I will lead this expedition," said Prince Alwaleed, the Khalifa's youngest son.

The Khalifa, clearly taken by surprise, wanted to object, but he knew that he could not ask men to volunteer if he was to prevent his own sons from doing the same. "It is settled, then. Sort it out with your friend, Stawgo."

★

One of the children waved to Nakhla, wanting to ask a question. "Go ahead, little one," Nakhla said. "What would you like to ask?"

"How did Wahba know all of this? Was she in the Khalifa's court?" asked the child.

"Aren't you the smart one! Nothing gets past you, huh. Well, no, children, she wasn't, but she heard Aqeel telling the story many times."

"Do palms understand what humans say?" asked a second child.

"Not all humans. Just like many of God's creations, they could understand the humans of their own totem, and Aqeel, even if he himself never knew it, was of the Palm totem. Now, let's continue the tale of those brave souls. Stawgo agreed to the Khalifa's terms, with one additional condition: that if any of the dates produced in the oasis were to be sold to the native Yaqteenyans, then he would have the exclusive right to sell them and take his commission on that sale, and that is why even today it is illegal for a Moor to sell dates to a Yaqteenyan."

★

Twenty-seven men volunteered for the mission, knowing that it would be a long time before they could come back to New Qurtuba to see their families, although Stawgo assured them the oasis was less than four weeks away. That was assuming they had a smooth journey, with no incidents or confrontations, and that was only the time to get there. After that, Aqeel still needed to plant the palms and maintain them for several years, even then they must still protect them and their fruits. No one knew when New Qurtuba could send replacements to relieve them to return to their families.

Mamdooh had been able to secure and maintain live parts of twenty-one of the palms that had perished. He split those parts in two so that Aqeel could take a sample of each palm. Additionally, they prepared samples of all twenty-six remaining palms for Aqeel to take with him. With all of those samples and the thousands of date seeds they had to carry with them, they had to use one of the camels to carry all the samples and seeds.

Aqeel and Mamdooh debated long about which five palms to take on the expedition. Should they be big old palms that had a much higher chance of surviving the hardships of the journey and the location in which they would be planted, or baby palms that would be easier to carry on the journey. In the end, they selected four baby palms and one adult palm that was about ten arms' length tall. And Wahba was one of the baby trees. All selected palms were female, as the Master Botanist figured that the male palm did not affect the quality of the date fruit, and they could easily be planted from the date seeds, so there was no point in wasting precious space on any male palms. Wahba remembered the night they started their journey. It was a cool full moon at the end of spring. They traveled mostly at night to avoid being detected by the natives. The scouts on horses were always ahead of them by what would amount to a full day's march.

Aqeel would plant a few seeds whenever they passed a location he thought might be able to support palm trees. He had a good instinct for such things. I supposed the fact that he was a palm totem helped him. Although it is neither the shortest nor fastest road between Joddah and New Qurtuba, many Yaqteenyans still love to take the Palm Rout marked by all the palms that resulted from the small seeds he planted. Though the fruits from those trees varied greatly in quality and size, many had nonetheless grown accustomed to their taste as a testament to the sacrifice those great men made to preserve the date for our generation.

The expedition came under attack by a scouting party that came at them from the south when the expedition was only five days away from the oasis. Though limited in number, they killed two of Alwaleed's men and severely injured three of Stawgo's. Though all the attackers were killed, Alwaleed knew that they had sent a message to the rest of their tribe informing them of the party's existence. Alwaleed commanded that they must double their speed to get to the oasis and into the Mojave clan's protection before a larger force returned, and to accomplish that, he commanded that they leave the adult palm, as it was too heavy and was slowing them down.

Aqeel insisted he would stay and plant the palm in that location and only then would he catch up with the expedition. Five men stayed with him, including the injured. Even though they successfully planted the tree that lasted in that spot for more than 300 moons, only one man returned to the expedition with Aqeel. The natives who had attacked them kept singing the tale of that battle for generations, of how those men were fighting to protect two men who were erecting a huge tree. Although the natives had never seen such a tree before, they respected the fact that those men gave their lives to plant that tree, and for that, the natives protected the tree in hopes that it would someday reveal its secrets. That was the first palm tree to survive in Yaqteenya and the first to be named. Aqeel thought it was important to give those palm trees names, for they were as much a part of their struggle as any of them, so he named the palm Somood[3].

When the expedition finally arrived at the oasis, it was an amazing heaven in the middle of a vast desert. It had trees and bushes surrounding it like a small green forest, again, in the middle of a vast desert. Aqeel was so excited for Wahba and her remaining three sisters! This was the perfect spot for Wahba to set roots and bare children. A sense of relief engulfed the men as they set up camp; a false sense of relief, as it turned out. Stawgo took Alwaleed and Aqeel aside to inform them of something very disturbing and unexpected.

"I am afraid I must tell you that I was not entirely honest with you," said Stawgo.

Confused, Alwaleed asked, "What do you mean, you have not been honest? Is this not the place you promised us?"

"It is, but it is not," replied Stawgo. As he examined their confused faces, he took a deep breath and swallowed to clear his throat. "This oasis in not exactly in Mojave land."

Alwaleed exploded with anger and pulled Stawgo to him by his shirt. "How can it not be in Mojave land? I lost good men to get here? You have led us into a trap!"

Stawgo's men noticed the intimidation from afar and started moving toward them, but Stawgo gestured to them to stay back, as he explained. "This oasis has been a disputed claim between the Mojave and the Cocopah for generations, but there has been an unspoken truce for tens of years now, as neither of us found it worth the fight as long as we could both use its water, but now, after we plant the palms, the Mojave clan will have claim to this land once more."

"You are using us to settle an old feud?! My father was right to distrust you. I have led my men to their death!" said Alwaleed in despair, as he let go of Stawgo.

"To their glory, hopefully without the death part," Stawgo said jokingly, but he received only angry, despising looks in return. "Look, it is not all that bad. I suspect the Cocopah will arrive here in a couple of days. All we need to do is hold them off and hold our ground for three days, then the Mojave will send their warriors to stand by us and victory will surely be ours."

"We are not fighting your battle for you! Come, Aqeel! We are leaving!" demanded Alwaleed.

Aqeel stood there hesitant, his gaze shifting between Alwaleed and Stawgo. "I can't leave. The palms have no chance if I do. I must stay and protect the palms! Alwaleed, please! We need to preserve our heritage. How many men have died to give us this chance? Did they all die in vain?" pleaded Aqeel.

[5] Somood: To survive against all odds

Alwaleed looked around, examining the terrain. "Stawgo!" he yelled. "What direction will they be coming from? We have a couple of days to prepare for our guests!" He then turned to Aqeel. "Go plant the palms as quickly as you can and get back to me. I will need your expertise to even the odds."

★

"Aqeel planted Wahba nearest to the lake and named her on that day. The other three were Ataa[4], Zaina[5], and Abaq[6]. They called them the 'palm mothers'," Nakhla told the children.

"Where are they now, Granny?" asked a young boy who sat at Nakhla's feet.

"Abaq never rooted and died within a few months. Ataa got sick after a few years, but not before she had several babies and bore fruit for a couple of seasons. Zaina lived a long, fruitful life, and had many babies over the years. She died more than 500 moons after that day."

"Are all the palms here grandchildren of the palm mothers?" asked a four-year-old girl.

"I would have to finish the story to answer that question, Sweetie," Nakhla smiled and answered.

★

Just before sunrise on the fourth day after they had set up camp near the lake, a knight riding a magnificent Arabian horse appeared at the southern horizon with a cloud of dust on his trail as he raced toward the camp. He was waving a flag from side to side. The guards rushed to wake the rest of the camp as quietly as possible. This was the signal that the Cocopah warriors had been spotted and were on their way.

Alwaleed was the first to get on his horse. He stormed toward the scout. "How many?" he asked.

"A thousand warriors, maybe more. Thank God they have no horses or camels," answered the scout. They both rode their horses like the wind back toward the camp and then up the closest mountain.

Almost an hour later, the attacking force appeared on the horizon, marching toward the lake. The camp was scattered over a large area. When they got close enough to clearly see the tents, they started to run toward it, yodeling and screaming. As they approached the seemingly deserted camp, most of them cautiously slowed down while some continued their rush, swinging their axes at the tents and ripping them apart. Angered that they had found no one at the camp, the warriors set the tents on fire and started to swing their axes at everything they could destroy around the camp. Suddenly, ropes were emerging from the sand around the camp as they were being pulled in all directions. The warriors stood there confused as they followed where the ropes were being pulled from. They saw seven men emerge from the lake as they pulled on the ropes and fifteen others came from under the sand around the camp. As the warriors charged out of the camp in every direction to attack the Moorish men, balls made of leaves that were hanging all over the camp ripped apart as they stretched from the forces of the pulling ropes, and as they did, they released an ash-like powder that covered most of the warriors. Seconds later, the charge slowed down as the warriors started to feel the slow-burning itch all over their bodies. Then the screams came as the burning erupted in their eyes. The

[4] Ataa: is another word for gift that literally means giving.

[5] Zaina: pleasant

[6] Abaq: aroma or fragrance

warriors who were near the burning tents started screaming in terror as they flung their axes at each other.

Arrows rained on the warriors from every direction, as many of them rushed to the lake to wash themselves from the burning powder. As the first of them got waist deep in the lake, he screamed in pain as he impaled his foot on a spike that was hidden on the bottom. Although he tried to warn his friends, his shouting was hidden within the mix of agony from the rest of his army and the need of those who followed him to wash their bodies. As more men got impaled and tried to go back, chaos took hold of the situation at the lake, as the injured men tried to push back the crazed, itchy warriors who were pushing inward. The men inside the lake were being stomped onto the spiked lake bed, as the few of them could not resist the force of the many coming in. By the time the next wave realized what was going on, it was too late for them to turn back. A wave of red started to spread into the lake, as many warriors fell onto the spikes or were hit by arrows. By the time they realized what was going on, more than 300 men were either killed or severely injured at the lake, and more than 120 crazed warriors were killed by their own army, but not before they had either killed or taken out of play another seventy. In addition to all of that, the army of warriors lost approximately sixty others to the barrage of arrows released at them from the Moorish party. The army's commander shouted in frustration to regroup and reorganize. Angered by the loss of half his army without even getting within striking distance of any of their adversaries, he charged toward the Moors who were on land and his men followed him.

The Moors ran as fast as they could toward the mountain with an army of 500 warriors closing in on them. Then sixteen monsters mounted by men appeared atop the nearest hill charging down toward them. Savage sounds came from the monsters and many of the warriors started to run away.

★

"Where did the monsters come from, Granny?" asked the young boy.

"Well, young Amer, you see, the Cocopah had never seen horses or camels before, and Stawgo knew that, so he advised Alwaleed to cover them with all sorts of large leaves and bones, and color them in all sorts of colors. He knew that when the Cocopah warriors saw such huge beasts charging at them, brave as they were, they would still run in fear."

"But not all of them did?" asked the child.

"No, Sweetie. Not all of them did."

★

While many of the Moors and Cocopah were engaged near the mountain, some Cocopah warriors remained near the burning camp or in the lake and the seven Moors who were still at the lake were either throwing arrows at them or engaged in fights with them. They had to face approximately 100 warriors, most of whom had been injured or crazed by the smoke they had inhaled, but still, those were not the best of odds. The only one not facing the Cocopah warriors was Aqeel. It wasn't that he could not fight because all Moor men who made it to Yaqteenya were trained to fight, nor was it because he lacked the courage; in fact, he was so courageous that he had ignored all those around him as he filled a bucket with water from the lake and dragged it toward Wahba as flames from a nearby burning tent started to burn at its trunk's base. As he reached Wahba, even before he could spill the water, Aqeel was attacked.

He tried to move away from the swinging axe, but his sudden move while carrying the heavy bucket made him trip and fall, causing him to spill most of the water onto the desert sand. Aqeel screamed with frustration as he watched the water seep through the sand. He swung the bucket, slamming it into his assailant's head. He drew his sword and planted it into his attacker's chest. Aqeel looked back at Wahba and saw that the fire had begun to spread around her. He scrambled back to the lake to fill his bucket and had to fight off a couple of Cocopah warriors who were coming out of the lake. Aqeel filled his bucket again and raced to Wahba, but another warrior got between him and Wahba, so he had no way to fight him while carrying that bucket with both hands. He raised the bucket to his face to block the axe, as he was expecting a second strike, but then was surprised by the warrior's body falling to the ground between his feet. He lowered the bucket and a second Cocopah warrior pulled his axe from his assailant's neck. Aqeel was confused and preparing for the axe's swing when the warrior gestured to Wahba. Although Aqeel thought it was a trick to kill him while he lowered his guard, he figured he had no other option, as he was unarmed and Wahba was going to die in the flames. As Aqeel rushed toward her, the warrior stood guard. He protected Aqeel as he went back and forth between the lake and Wahba several times until the fire was out. When it was, the warrior grunted at Aqeel and nodded his head before he left him to rejoin his brethren.

Back at the mountain, the camels were the largest beast the Cocopah had ever seen, much larger than a buffalo and much taller, mounted by men with long spears. As they charged through the Cocopah army, men were either stomped, slashed, or stabbed. The horses were led by Alwaleed, ten knights in full armor swinging their swords as they cut through the Cocopah's ranks. The Cocopah army scattered in all directions as they fled in fear.

Back at the camp, the Moors had set up in the mountain. The men gathered around the fire as the sun set, then celebrated the day's victory.

"Alhamdullah, we have won the first day. We counted more than 500 Cocopah who died, and at least 100 were critically wounded. Although we drastically diminished their number with our surprise, they still outnumbered us ten to one," Alwaleed stated while addressing his men. "Let us pray for our four fallen brothers." Two men had been killed as they ran to the mountain before the knights were able to stand by them. One was killed at the lake and one knight was killed along with his horse. Several others were wounded at the lake, but none had any fatal injuries.

"We must now lay our plan for tomorrow, as our surprise today will not work again. Does any one of you have any crazy ideas?" asked Alwaleed.

Aqeel stood up and shouted, "I have one!"

"Aqeel, speak up. Your experience with gathering and preparing those poisonous herbs was instrumental for today's victory."

"It was my duty, Your Highness, however, my idea is somewhat different than what you expect."

"That is what we want, an unexpected strategy that our enemy would not foresee."

"I propose we talk to them and ask for a truce."

"A truce? Why would we do that when we are winning? That would only show them that we are weak and do not expect that we can win."

Aqeel looked at Stawgo as he asked, "Can we meet with their commander and speak with him? Can we trust him to listen without killing us? And can we trust that he will keep his word for any terms we might reach?"

"The Cocopah are honorable people, although it is uncommon for those in conflict to speak before the end of the third day. If we lay our arms at their feet, they will at least receive us as guests and may allow us an audience with the commander. If he does listen and agrees to any terms, you can rest assured that he will either enforce them or die trying," answered Stawgo.

"What exactly are you proposing, Aqeel?" asked Alwaleed.

"As I was trying to put out the fire on Wahba…"

"Wait! Who is Wahba?" asked Alwaleed, confused.

"Wahba was the first palm I planted. She caught fire, so I tried to put it out, and, as you can imagine, it would have been nearly impossible for me to protect myself while carrying a bucket of water. And then a Cocopah warrior stepped in and killed one of his own and then stood over me, protecting me as I went back and forth with water to save the palm, and then when I was done, he just left me."

Baffled by what he just heard, Alwaleed turned to Stawgo and asked, "Why would a Cocopah warrior do that? Why would he protect one of his own enemies during a battle?"

"Nature is sacred to all of us. When Aqeel was trying to save and protect the tree, he was no longer an enemy of the Cocopah, and those who would stop him from saving her were."

Aqeel looked at Alwaleed and asked, "Now do you understand how we can stop this?" and Alwaleed nodded in approval.

★

"Aunty, why did they not just fight? Couldn't they have won? And even if they didn't, wouldn't they be martyrs?" asked a nine-year-old boy as he jumped around, showing how tough he was.

"My boy, the best victories are the ones won without a fight," said Nakhla with a smile. "We are not here to fight people or force them to be our subjects. We are here to save them." She continued, "Aqeel saw that at heart, the Cocopah shared the same value for life that the Moors did, and he knew he could use that common ground to reach an agreement with them."

★

As Alwaleed, Aqeel, and Stawgo neared the Cocopah encampment, three Cocopah warriors blocked their way. The Cocopah warriors were clearly taken aback by the horses that Alwaleed and Aqeel were riding, but still had the courage to face them.

Stawgo started the conversation with the warriors. When they were finished, he looked at Alwaleed and said, "They say you can both come, if you agree to lay your weapons at the great fire, but your beasts must stay here."

"Tell them our beasts will come with us and will be bound to the tree nearest to the great fire. Assure them that our beasts will not harm them, as long as they do not harm us," replied Alwaleed.

Stawgo conveyed Alwaleed's message to the warriors, who deliberated before they agreed to lead them to their commander. It was not really a camp, as we know it. There were no tents, only a great fire where most of them gathered, and several small fires scattered here and there. The men around the great fire moved aside, making an opening for them to walk through. Alwaleed and Aqeel came down off their horses and tied them to the nearest tree, then stepped into the circle along with Stawgo. Their commander stood up and ordered the men around him to move, making room for their guests. Alwaleed started to speak, but Stawgo gestured to him not to, as they sat next to the commander. Two huge plates filled with meat were served to them. Stawgo started to eat while Alwaleed and Aqeel abstained. "Eat. It is not poisoned," said Stawgo.

"No, it is not that. You know we cannot eat non-halal meats," answered Aqeel.

"I do not think I can explain that to the commander, and if you do not eat, they will take offense, as it would be a great insult for a guest to refuse the host's hospitality, and he will not talk to us until we finish all that was served."

They all started to eat from the meat. Alwaleed and Aqeel were too scared to ask what animal it was, as it was already bad enough to eat meat they knew, for fact, was not halal. They made fast work of the meat (Stawgo mainly), and when they were done, the commander cheered and so did the rest of his men.

The commander addressed Alwaleed. As he spoke, Stawgo interpreted. "I am Kamaho, Commander of the Cocopah warriors and eldest son of our great chieftain, Damiha. I am honored to meet the commander who bested us on our first day of glory."

"I am Alwaleed, Commander of the Regiment of the Palm Tree, the youngest son of our Khalifa, Ali. It is my honor to meet the brave commander who did not tremble when he faced my beasts on the field of battle." When Stawgo completed his interpretation, Kamaho looked pleasantly satisfied. Alwaleed continued, "It is my desire to spare our men any more bloodshed by trying to reach terms that are acceptable to both of us."

"I have not met your kind before. I have only heard rumors spoken by travelers from the east. Tell me, Alwaleed, why have you come to lay claim to our oasis?"

"I have not come to lay claim to anything. We are proud people who fled their homeland to preserve our culture. I came here with my men to preserve the palm tree that has much significance to my people."

"Do you worship this palm tree?"

"No, we do not. We worship Allah, the one and only God."

"We worship the great spirit who dwelled in the heavens above."

"I assume we are speaking of the same God, but just have different names for him."

Kamaho nodded in agreement. "So, tell me, Alwaleed, son of Ali, are you here because you suspect that I would cower after my defeat this day, or because you fear you cannot take my army with your remaining fifty men after you've used your element of surprise?"

"I am here, Commander Kamaho, out of respect for the blood of both our men and the fact that we are both fighting for the same cause."

"And what cause would that be?"

"As I said, we are not here to claim land, nor are we here to gain glory. We are here to save the remaining palm trees that we have. I am sure that one of your warriors can confirm to you, those trees are more valuable to us than our own lives."

Kamaho signaled to one of his men with his hand, and moments later, two men showed up dragging a third, who was restrained in ropes. When Aqeel saw him, he knew him at once. He was the warrior who had stood guard over him as he put out Wahba's flames. "Are you talking about this man?" asked Kamaho.

"Yes," Aqeel replied.

"He was to stand trial for betraying us in battle and killing his own brothers to protect the enemy. He said he was not protecting the enemy, but, rather, the tree that was holy to the great spirit."

"He was protecting me as I tried to put out the fire from Wahba, the palm tree we told you about," replied Aqeel.

"You mean to tell me that you were risking your life to save a tree that you did not even worship?"

"Yes, Commander, as was your warrior willing to risk his."

Kamaho gestured to his men to bring the warrior closer to him. He pulled out his knife – Aqeel wanted to object – but Stawgo signaled him to stay out of it. Kamaho swung his knife swiftly and cut the warrior's bounds.

"You can plant your trees and go," said Kamaho.

"But they need to be taken care of. They will die if left without proper care," objected Aqeel.

Kamaho looked at him for some time, then turned to a couple of his mean and spoke in a muffled voice that Stawgo could not understand. Kamaho looked back at Aqeel and said, "Very well. Here are my final terms that both you and the Apache must agree to. You can stay under the following conditions: The lake and all its surroundings up to and including the mountains around it and similar distance to both north and south will be under your rule. To end this dispute between the Apache and the Cocopah, you will allow both the Cocopah and the Apache to drink from the water of the lake. You will not bring in more men from your tribe or the Apache to this land, nor are you allowed to bring any more of your people. We will help you protect this land and your trees as long as you stay here. If you leave, however, you cannot come back."

"What about our families? Can we bring them, at least?" asked Alwaleed.

"No. You can have a new family here. You can marry from either our daughters or the Apache. Those are our terms. Do you accept?"

"I accept your terms. Stawgo, does the Apache accept?"

"We accept those terms, so long as the Apache men who fought today are given the same privilege to stay, if they choose."

★

"That's why we are all of mixed blood, right Granny?" asked Amer.

"Yes, Honey, that is why. Prince Alwaleed resided over this city as Sultan for approximately thirty years, until his brother was able to unite Yaqteenya under his rule and Joddah became part of this great nation."

"Aunty, why did they call the city Joddah?" asked a five-year-old girl.

"Well, Darling, first, because it is where the grandmothers of all Yaqteenyan palm trees live, and it also reminded our first Yaqteenyan Khalifa Mohammed XII of the beautiful coastal city of Jeddah, near the holy city of Makkah."

"So, all of those palms only came from Wahba and her three sisters?" asked another child.

"No. Aqeel planted many of the date seeds he had with him. He also regrew many of the palm samples he had from the other palms, but the purest of all and the sweetest of fruits were the ones that came from Wahba and her sisters' descendants. Oh, my! Look at the time! It is getting late in the day, isn't it. Come on, children. Each of you take a sweet date and run along back to your parents."

The children jumped happily as they each took a date – or several – from the plate of dates next to Nakhla. As she stood up, she leaned on Wahba and muttered, "Don't cry, old friend. It is true that this is my last day as keeper of the garden, but I will still visit you. It was an honor to serve you as the first descendant of Aqeel who is of the palm totem…" She paused as she listened to Wahba.

"I know. I, too, wish he knew he could have talked to you as I do. I am sure he felt your appreciation. Goodbye, Wahba." She petted a dark burn mark on one side of Wahba's trunk, then walked away as her grandson, Amer, held her hand.

BIOGRAPHIES

DAYO NTWARI

Dayo Ntwari, a Rwandan-Nigerian writer, has been a fan of science fiction and fantasy since childhood. He enjoys writing stories inspired by African legends and myths. He believes Africa's diverse histories, religions, spirituality and mythologies can serve as a never-ending treasure trove of inspiration for African science fiction and fantasy.

His short stories include: "Omoshango", published in the *People of Colo(u)r Destroy Science Fiction* special issue of *Lightspeed Magazine,* "Devil's Village", shortlisted for the Writivism 2015 Short Story Prize, "Nomansland", shortlisted for the 2015 Huza Press Award, "Mother's Love", longlisted for the 2015 Short Story Day Africa Prize

Dayo lives in Rwanda, where he is currently working on his first novel. He also hopes to publish a collection of his short stories.

JY YANG

JY Yang is a queer, non-binary Singaporean author and editor of *SFF.* They are the author of the upcoming *Tensorate* series of novellas from Tor.com Publishing ("The Red Threads of Fortune, The Black Tides of Heaven"), and they have over two dozen works of short fiction published in places such as *Uncanny Magazine*, *Lightspeed*, *Strange Horizons*, and *Lackington's.*

SWAPNA KISHORE

Swapna Kishore lives in India and writes fiction and non-fiction. Her speculative fiction has appeared in *Nature (Futures), Fantasy Magazine, Strange Horizons, Ideomancer, Sybil's Garage No. 7, Warrior Wisewoman 3, Breaking the Bow, Apex Book of World SF (Volume 3), Mythic Delirium 1.3, The Year's Best Dark Fantasy & Horror: 2016*, and various other venues. She has published books on software engineering and process management, including a business novel, and also writes extensively about dementia and caregiving in India. Her website is at swapnawrites.com

FÁBIO FERNANDES

Fabio Fernandes lives in São Paulo, Brazil. He has published two books so far, an essay on

William Gibson's fiction, *A Construção do Imaginário Cyber*, and a cyberpunk novel, *Os Dias da Peste* (both in Portuguese). Also a translator, he is responsible for the translation to Brazilian Portuguese of several SF novels, including *Neuromancer, Snow Crash,* and *A Clockwork Orange*. His short stories have been published online in Brazil, Portugal, Romania, the UK, New Zealand, and USA, and also in Ann and Jeff VanderMeer's *Steampunk II: Steampunk Reloaded* and *Southern Fried Weirdness: Reconstruction* (2011), *The Apex Book of World SF, Vol 2, Stories for Chip*. Co-edited (with Djibril al-Ayad) the postco anthology *We See a Different Frontier*. Graduate of Clarion West, class of 2013. Slush reader for *Clarkesworld Magazine*.

LAVIE TIDHAR

Lavie Tidhar's latest novel, *Central Station,* is out now to rave reviews. He is the author of the Jerwood Fiction Uncovered Prize winning *A Man Lies Dreaming,* of the World Fantasy Award winning *Osama,* and many other books and short stories. He lives in London.

KEN LIU

Ken Liu is an author and translator of speculative fiction, as well as a lawyer and programmer. A winner of the Nebula, Hugo, and World Fantasy awards, he has been published in *The Magazine of Fantasy & Science Fiction, Asimov's, Analog, Clarkesworld, Lightspeed,* and *Strange Horizons,* among other places.

Ken's debut novel, *The Grace of Kings* (2015), is the first volume in a silkpunk epic fantasy series, *The Dandelion Dynasty.* It won the Locus Best First Novel Award and was a Nebula finalist. He subsequently published the second volume in the series, *The Wall of Storms* (2016) as well as a collection of short stories, *The Paper Menagerie and Other Stories* (2016).

In addition to his original fiction, Ken is also the translator of numerous literary and genre works from Chinese to English. His translation of *The Three-Body Problem,* by Liu Cixin, won the Hugo Award for Best Novel in 2015, the first translated novel ever to receive that honor. He also translated the third volume in Liu Cixin's series, *Death's End* (2016) and edited the first English-language anthology of contemporary Chinese science fiction, *Invisible Planets* (2016).

He lives with his family near Boston, Massachusetts. He can be found online at http://kenliu.name

JEREMY SZAL

Jeremy Szal was born in 1995 in the outback of Australia and was raised by wild dingoes. His speculative fiction has appeared in *Nature, Abyss & Apex, Lightspeed, Strange Horizons, Tor.com, The Drabblecast,* and has been translated into multiple languages. He is the fiction editor for Hugo-winning podcast *StarShipSofa* and holds a rather useless BA in Creative Writing and Film Studies. He is represented by John Jarrold of the John Jarrold Literary Agency. He carves out a living in Sydney, Australia, where he drinks too much craft beer and watches too many films. Find him athttp://jeremyszal.com/ or @JeremySzal

SAMUEL R. DELANY

Samuel R. Delany's stories are available in *Aye and Gomorrah and Other Stories* (science fiction and fantasy) and *Atlantis: Three Tales.* He has been inducted into the Science Fiction Hall of Fame, and received the Damon Knight Memorial Grand Master of Science Fiction Award. His novels include *Nova, Dhalgren, The Fall of the Towers,* the Nebula-Award winning *Babel-17* and *The Einstein Intersection;* also his four-volume fantasy series *Return to Neveryon.* In 2008, his novel *Dark Reflections* won the Stonewall Book Award. He has also written *Phallos* and – most recently – *Through the Valley of the Nest of Spiders.* His non-fiction includes three critical books on science fiction, T*he Jewel-Hinged Jaw, Starboard Wine,* and *The American Shore.* He is the author of the widely taught *Times Square Red / Times Square Blue,* and he has written a Hugo-Award winning autobiography T*he Motion of Light in Water.* A judge for the 1910 National Book Awards in fiction, he was the subject of a 2007 documentary, *The Polymath,* and he has written a widely-used creative writing textbook, *About Writing.* He aspires to be known to his readers as Chip.

RAJAN KHANNA

Rajan Khanna is an author, blogger, reviewer and narrator. His post-apocalyptic airship adventure series starting with *Falling Sky* and *Rising Tide* concluded in July 2017 with *Raining Fire.* His short fiction has appeared in *Lightspeed Magazine, Beneath Ceaseless Skies,* and several anthologies. His articles and reviews have appeared at Tor.com and LitReactor.com and his podcast narrations can be heard at Podcastle, Escape Pod, PseudoPod, Beneath Ceaseless Skies and Lightspeed Magazine. Rajan lives in Brooklyn where he's a member of the Altered Fluid writing group. His personal website is http://www.rajankhanna.com and he tweets, @rajanyk.

EVE SHI

Eve Shi is Indonesian, a lifelong fangirl and writer. She has published five novels in Indonesian and written several short stories in English. Since 2011 she has been the Indonesian municipal liaison for NaNoWriMo. You can reach her on Twitter at @Eve_Shi or via email at stormofblossoms@gmail.com

VAJRA CHANDRASEKERA

Vajra Chandrasekera is from Colombo, Sri Lanka. His fiction has appeared in *Clarkesworld, Lightspeed,* and *Strange Horizons,* among others. He blogs occasionally at http://vajra.me and is @_vajra on Twitter

CARMELO RAFALA

Carmelo Rafala's work has been published in various venues, including the following anthologies: *Stories for Chip: A Tribute to Samuel R. Delany* (Rosarium Publishing, July 2015), *Submitted*

For Your Approval (Rod Serling Books, April, 2015), *the Anthology of European SF* (Europa SF, 2013), *The Fourth Science Fiction Megapack* (Wildside Press, 2012), *Rocket Science* (Mutation Press, 2012), and *The West Pier Gazette and other Stories* (Three Legged Fox Books, 2008).

His work was also placed on the Highly Recommended list for the Nova Short Story Competition, hosted by the Science Fiction and Fantasy South Africa Association (2013). His work has recently been translated into Romanian.

He is also the Editor and Publisher of Immersion Press, a small UK press of award-nominated speculative fiction. He comes from a family of Sicilian immigrants to the US, but currently lives in Europe with his wife and daughter.

YUKIMI OGAWA

Yukimi Ogawa lives in a small town in Tokyo, where she writes in English but never speaks the language. She still wonders why it works that way. Her fiction can be found in such places as *Fantasy & Science Fiction, Clarkesworld* and *Strange Horizons.*

HAL DUNCAN

Hal Duncan is the author of *Vellum* and *Ink*, more recently *Testament*, and numerous short stories, poems, essays, even a few musicals. Homophobic hatemail once dubbed him "THE.... Sodomite Hal Duncan!!" (sic), and you can find him online at www.halduncan.com or at his Patreon for readings, revelling in that role.

MARGRÉT HELGADÓTTIR

Margrét Helgadóttir is a Norwegian-Icelandic writer and editor living in Oslo. Her stories have appeared in a number of both magazines and anthologies such as *Gone Lawn, Luna Station Quarterly*, and *Girl at the End of the World.* Her debut book *The Stars Seem So Far Away* was published by Fox Spirit Books in 2015 and shortlisted as Best Collection to British Fantasy Awards 2016. Margrét is anthology editor for the annual *Fox Spirit Books of Monsters* (2014-2020) and *Winter Tales* (2016). *African Monsters* (2015) was shortlisted to Best Anthology for the British Fantasy Awards 2016. *Asian Monsters* (2016) is shortlisted to Best Anthology for the British Fantasy Awards 2017. http://margrethelgadottir.wordpress.com or @MaHelgad on Twitter.

LUIS G. ABBADIE

Luis G. Abbadie (Guadalajara, Mexico, 1968) novelist and researcher, specialized in horror fiction, paganism and pseudobibliography. As Magister and Cunning Man of the Crossways Craft, a Neo-Pagan tradition derived from beliefs rooted in the Scottish Highland, he has represented the Nairn-México Community of the Ancient Craft in both editions of the Universal Multicultural Dialogue (2013, 2015) and belongs to CERyS (Religion and Society Study Center).

He has, at various times, been literary workshop coordinator, proofreader, columnist, bookseller, illustrator, comic book author and artist, Tarot reader and exorcist, as well as offering occult advisory for lawyers' offices. Currently lives with a dog, three cats and has a teenage son.

His works have appeared in magazines and anthologies from Mexico, USA, Spain, Colombia and Argentina. Some of his books are *Códice Otarolense* (Euterpe, 2002), *Noches paganas* (Veglia, 2008), *El código secreto del Necronomicón* (Rémora, 2010 / Keli, 2013), *La larga noche* (with Alessa Gil, Keli, 2013) and *Confesiones paganas: Palabras de las brujas de Nairn* (Leif Erikson, 2017).

You can find him at: http://al-azrad.blogspot.com/ and www.facebook.com/luisgabbadie/

JONATHAN DOTSE

Jonathan Dotse is a technology evangelist, freelance philosopher, and speculative fiction writer living in Accra, Ghana. He has contributed articles and short stories to a variety of print and online publications, including *Jungle Jim, Acceler8or* and the *2015 Caine Prize* workshop anthology. Jonathan created the AfroCyberPunk blog in 2010, while studying Management Information Systems at the Ashesi University. Dotse is currently working on his debut novel, a cyberpunk mystery/thriller set in the sprawling metropolis of Accra in the mid -21st century.

TAIYO FUJII

Taiyo Fujii was born in Amami Oshima Island – that is, between Kyushu and Okinawa. He has worked in stage design, desktop publishing, exhibition graphic design, and software development. In 2012, Fujii self-published *Gene Mapper* serially in a digital format of his own design, and it became Amazon.co.jp's number one Kindle bestseller of that year. The novel was revised and republished in both print and digital as *Gene Mapper – full build* – by Hayakawa Publishing in 2013 and was nominated for the Nihon SF Taisho Award and the Seiun Award. His second novel, *Orbital Cloud*, won the 2014 Nihon SF Taisho Award and took first prize in the Best SF of 2014 in *SF Magazine*. His recent works include *Underground Market* and *Bigdata Connect.*

CHIKODILI EMELUMADU

Chikodili Emelumadu is a Nigerian writer currently residing in Cambridge, MA. Her work has been published in *Eclectica, One Throne, Omenenana* and various other magazines and anthologies. 'Candy Girl' was originally published in *Apex Magazine* and was nominated for the Shirley Jackson prize

YASSER BAHJATT

Yasser Bahjatt is a technologist & futurist who is the first Saudi to ever go to Singularity University's Graduate Study Program where he was the lead engineer on the Matternet project. He has a BS in Computer Engineering from King Abdulaziz University.

Yasser is an active member of the TED community as he was the first to translate TED talks through the open translation project to Arabic and was also the #1 most active TED translator for a period of time. He was the organizer or co-organizer of several TEDx events including TEDxArabia, TEDxJeddah, TEDxKAU & TEDxUQU.

Yasser's talk at TED@Doha about the relationship between SciFi and Scientific development announced the launch of *Yatakhayaloon* (Arabic for "They are Imagining"), an initiative to kick start the Arabian contemporary SciFi culture, in a 20 year experiment to prove that SciFi growth results in Scientific development growth.

His novel *Yaqteenya* is the first ever Arabian alternate history novel. He also co-authored the English edition of Ibraheem Abbas's Arabian best sellers *HWJN* & *Somewhere.*

INTERVIEWS

DAYO NTWARI

You were invited to be interviewed as part of this anthology to celebrate diverse writers and stories. Do you consider yourself to be bringing an important or unique perspective in your work?

The stories I write are speculative fiction, a category of fiction said to be based on human imagination and speculation, rather than the human reality. However, this definition is somewhat sterile and two-dimensional, when viewed through my eyes as a writer of Rwandan and Nigerian descent. What is reality for Isaac Asimov and George R.R. Martin may not be the entirety of what is reality for someone like myself.

The stories I write come from a world where the lines between reality and imagination or speculation are crooked and blurry. In the science fiction and fantasy communities, I rarely come across stories that merge both worlds. Especially these days, there is an odd perception that says for science fiction to be "true" science fiction, it must be hard science fiction. Or that fantasy has no place in a science fiction story and vice versa.

Whether or not such perspectives are valid is almost beside the point. Instead, what I take away from the hard-scifi-or-die school of thought is that the mainstream community of science fiction and fantasy often has a different world of experiences, which form the basis for their individual capacities to imagine.

As a writer, your personal experiences, background, values, beliefs all go in to what fuels your power for imagination. I grew up in Africa, specifically Nigeria, and was educated entirely in the German education system from Kindergarten to university. I live today in Rwanda. When I write my stories it is natural for me to mix magic with worm holes, shapeshifters with artificial intelligence, babalawos with spaceship commanders. I come from a world where juju, cellular phone networks, witchcraft, Sunday sermons and Friday khutbah, Big Data research projects, demonic possession and satellite telecommunication go hand in hand, side by side, day by day everyday. Personally, stories intersecting through such quasi heterogeneous realities are the most interesting to me. I find it unrealistic to write speculative fiction set in Africa that does not find itself in the orbit of this intersectional realism. It feels like Jollof rice without tomatoes.

Why do you think that diverse voices are important in speculative fiction?

When it comes to perspectives in storytelling experienced today, there is really only one voice that dominates our general awareness as consumers of pop culture, literature, entertainment, media and so on. This dominant perspective is western and eurocentric in nature. Eurocentric in the sense of perspectives that hold European or European-originating value systems far above everything else. That is to say, in such perspectives, characters and concepts whose origins and sources are eurocentric or anglocentric are the norm or the centre, while everything else is the abnorm, the aberrant, the Other, the fringe.

In such a world where the acceptable falls within a single and narrow spectrum, I find one quickly runs out of stories to tell. Mainstream narrated experiences soon become iterative and eventually less exciting and less engaging. In recent times, voices have become louder and louder in calling for more inclusion in the representation of world views and opinions and beliefs. The nature of the mainstream beast has kind of "brought this on itself". I think it was inevitable that the call for diversity is rising to form an unstoppable tsunami.

You see, we have the Internet now. Everybody sees everybody and has a voice now that can be heard from one side of the planet to another instantly. And suddenly, what was once barely present in our subconscious, is now glaring brightly in our faces: not all of us have the same experiences. In fact the experience shown to us by the mainstream is that of a global minority. A tiny minority. And yet, we are expected to adopt it as dogma, to view it as the singularly accepted framework in which to operate our lives and organize our thoughts. Of course, that's not going to work. Thanks to practically everything being accessible on the Internet, we are bound to come across, multiple alternative frames of mind that come from widely differing and also very similar cultural and social spheres. And since we are not a Borg planet, it is inevitable that once the global airwaves become interactively accessible by the majority who don't live inside a Superpower, we as humans will discover within us our need for something new, something different. Not for the purpose of destroying and replacing the old mainstream voice. But for the purpose of adding a wider more vibrant range to it.

How do your own works reflect those values?

Seeing value in a diversity of voices in speculative fiction is to see that there is more than one way to get to Mars. So that means there is more than one way to tell the story. In Captain America: Civil War, the Avengers go to Lagos, Nigeria to stop Brock Rumlow from getting his hands on a bio weapon. As someone who grew up in Lagos, I experienced only very limited immersion throughout the Lagos scene. They were written and filmed with a distinctly American eye. I would have written and shot that completely differently. I like to take these spectacular and highly speculative concepts, and then ask myself: if this happened here, what would it really be like?

Who were some of the early influences on your writing, inside or outside of the field? Who do you see as some of your heroes, or guiding lights?

I think my first exposure to speculative fiction was reading Isaac Asimov and Robert Heinlein. These two were my gateway into speculative fiction. As for influencing my writing, I can point to William Gibson's *Neuromancer,* which I read while at university. Even though I immensely enjoyed Asimov, Heinlein, Clarke, Silverberg, Bradbury and co., it was *Neuromancer,* I think, that made me want to write, and not just simply read.

The poetry of German Expressionist writer Georg Heym had a big influence on the style of imagery I am drawn to and like to use. I tend to have a very visual storytelling style, which draws heavily from influences such as the music of Fela Anikulapo Kuti, the *ABC Warriors* comic books, the visual art of H.R. Geiger, movies like *The Name of the Rose, Jaws, Nightmare on Elm Street,* the works of writers like Stephen King, everything from Quentin Tarantino and Robert Rodriguez. When I write, I listen to a lot of electronic music like drum & bass and trance.

What other works, your own or by others, would you recommend for people interested in supporting diversity in the field of speculative fiction?
I highly recommend the works of Wole Talabi, Innocent Acan, Pemi Aguda, Wanuri Kahiu, Chinelo Onwualu, to name a few.

The District of Wonders is creating this anthology because we wanted to do something constructive at what many are seeing as an alarming time in world history. Is there a message that you would like to send to the readers of *Everyone: Worlds without Walls?*
In this strictly hierarchical world of ours built on exploitation, and powered by fear and violence, diversity is still considered a bit of a dirty word. We are taught to fear the Other, by those who reap unfathomable profits from controlling our perceptions of ourselves and each other. We are slaves to a construct that denies the beauty of our differences and the wonders of our uniqueness. Instead of "remembering our training" to fear each other and live behind walls and gates, inside silos, ivory towers, and other forms of self-imposed imprisonment, let us all live in a boundless fantastical world where myriad new adventures await us each new day. Let us let our dreams enrich our lives, instead of letting our fears stifle our existence.

JY YANG

You were invited to be interviewed as part of this anthology to celebrate diverse writers and stories. Do you consider yourself to be bringing an important or unique perspective in your work?
It's always awkward to say "yes" to these questions because obviously, everybody brings their own unique perspective to their work, and can any individual truly determine what work is "important" and what is not? As long as my work resonates with even one person and makes them feel like they're less alone in the world, it's worth it.

Why do you think that diverse voices are important in speculative fiction?
Because the world is composed of many, many diverse voices, and that should be reflected in the fiction that we read as well.

Who were some of the early influences on your writing, inside or outside of the field? Who do you see as some of your heroes, or guiding lights?
Early influences: William Gibson, Neil Gaiman, Margaret Atwood, China Mieville. As you can see, in the early years I did not read very diversely, and of course the reason for this is that at that point, it wasn't easy to find diverse works, so you just read whatever you could find on the shelves. I think that's changing and that's a good thing.

My heroes in the industry today are writers who are not just incredibly talented, but also generous and supportive of their peers and newer writers: people like Kate Elliot, Ken Liu, Aliette de Bodard etc. I honestly owe them a lot and I hope to pay it forward in the future.

What other works, your own or by others, would you recommend for people interested in supporting diversity in the field of speculative fiction?
To broaden your short fiction reading diet, I suggest checking out the work of writers such as SL Huang, Nin Harris, A Merc Rustad, Bogi Takács, Rose Lemberg, S Qiouyi Lu... read the writers THEY recommend, and so on and so forth. Another great thing to do is to

regularly read, or even subscribe to, venues that specifically publish writers who are queer and/or POC. Off the top of my head: FIYAH Litmag, Anathema, Glittership (it's a podcast), Mithila Review...

The District of Wonders is creating this anthology because we wanted to do something constructive at what many are seeing as an alarming time in world history. Is there a message that you would like to send to the readers of *Everyone: Worlds without Walls?*
Do no harm, be generous to one another, and don't lose hope.

FÁBIO FERNANDES

You were invited to be interviewed as part of this anthology to celebrate diverse writers and stories. Do you consider yourself to be bringing an important or unique perspective in your work?
I think, in a general sense, that every single writer in the world brings her own very particular perspective and adds to the great conversation of literature. That said, I can only say I try to bring something else than just my view of things. For instance, most of my stories take place in my city, São Paulo, one of the largest cities in the world. Sometimes I bring London and Seattle to the mix, because I also lived in those cities. The same applies to questions of gender: being a queer (pansexual) writer, I always try to convey to people what is like to be a person who doesn't fit in the conventional mold that society keeps telling us is the normal one.

Why do you think that diverse voices are important in speculative fiction?
Diverse voices are important in speculative fiction precisely because of their difference in views and ways to perceive and live the world around them. It's not possible now for us to expect, for argument's sake, that only the US will be representing mankind in the space exploration and colonization. (The use of those words is no accident - maybe, if other cultures are able to go to space, we can think of something not focused in colonization, but in research and acquisition of knowledge.)

How do your own works reflect those values?
My works so far seem to fit the bill for post-cyberpunk and the occasional space opera. I've been trying different formats such as the use of second person, fragmented narratives and a bit of surrealism to add to the estrangement. In terms of content, I am always the Brazilian underdog that views and experiences things differently. One of my major concerns is: how to write fiction without resorting to violence and/or the use of weapons? I despise weapons greatly.

Who were some of the early influences on your writing, inside or outside of the field? Who do you see as some of your heroes, or guiding lights?
Among my writing heroes are: inside the field, William Gibson for the visionary approach, Samuel Delany for the great prose, and Kim Stanley Robinson for his awesome logistic utopian approach to problem-solving. Outside the field: Hemingway for the concision, Melville for the opposite reason, and two authors not very well known outside Brazil: Guimarães Rosa (author of the spectacular novel *Grande Sertão: Veredas,* originally translated in English as *The Devil to Pay in the Backlands*) and poet Paulo Leminski, for the wordplay and the audacity of writing very Brazilian haiku.

What other works, your own or by others, would you recommend for people interested in supporting diversity in the field of speculative fiction?
I'd recommend the postcolonial anthology *We See a Different Frontier,* edited by me and Djibril al-Ayad, and anything written by the authors featured on them such as JY Yang, Ernest Hogan, Lavie Tidhar, Silvia Moreno-Garcia. Also: Nisi Shawl, Nnedi Okorafor, Yoon Ha Lee, Zen Cho, Alyssa Wong.

The District of Wonders is creating this anthology because we wanted to do something constructive at what many are seeing as an alarming time in world history. Is there a message that you would like to send to the readers of Everyone: Worlds without Walls?
My message: KEEP CALM AND KEEP ON DREAMING. Also: FIGHT WHENEVER NECESSARY. That's it.

KEN LIU

You were invited to be interviewed as part of this anthology to celebrate diverse writers and stories. Do you consider yourself to be bringing an important or unique perspective in your work?
I think diversity is a collective quality, not a quality of individuals. It is only by collecting many writers from different backgrounds telling stories that matter to them in their own voices that we can truly celebrate diversity. It is the marginalized voices, the silenced voices, the voices that have been excluded by a power structure that centers the privileged at the expense of the rest that we must particularly pay attention to.

Why do you think that diverse voices are important in speculative fiction?
I don't think diverse voices are important to speculative fiction; I think they are essential.

It is only the privileged who can imagine the future without the burden of the past – but our historical inequities determine the unequal distribution of power in the present and the unequal futures open to all of us. If speculative fiction wishes to imagine futures and dreams that confront the injustices of history, then it is essential for us to elevate diverse voices.

How do your own works reflect those values?
I've always been suspicious of the commonly given advice for writers to "trust the reader." This is usually taken as advising the writer to not over-explain. But trusting the reader is only possible when the writer and the reader share essential assumptions about the state of the world. Colonialism, migration, wartime atrocities, racial prejudice, and many other similar divisions mean that the worldview of a writer from a marginalized position is utterly different from the worldview of a reader in a privileged position. I would say that in such cases, being distrustful of both the reader and the writer – for both are subjects shaped by an unjust interpretive and signifying framework – is the right approach, and that is the approach I strive to bring to my work. Distrusting the framework doesn't mean that you can always escape it, but it is at least a start.

Who were some of the early influences on your writing, inside or outside of the field? Who do you see as some of your heroes, or guiding lights?

Almost everything a writer reads ends up influencing her in some way – and "influence" doesn't always mean admiration. I can't imagine I'd be an exception to that. I will say that critical legal studies literature has given me some new tools to parsing the construction of power in fiction, and that has been very helpful.

I don't believe in heroes: I believe we must become our own heroes. I'm constantly inspired by writers and readers around me trying to do something new, trying to read and write in resistant ways. I hope we can all become heroic through one another's example.

What other works, your own or by others, would you recommend for people interested in supporting diversity in the field of speculative fiction?
I suggest that readers pay particular attention to writers who don't get coverage in the prestigious English media, either genre or "mainstream." So, rather than focusing on recommended reading lists, including ones constructed by writers like me, seek out works translated from other languages, works published in journals that don't often feature award-winning stories, works from venues that don't attract many reviewers.

And then boost them.

The District of Wonders is creating this anthology because we wanted to do something constructive at what many are seeing as an alarming time in world history. Is there a message that you would like to send to the readers of *Everyone: Worlds without Walls*?
Faith, hope, and love are radical acts. Don't ever give up on them.

JEREMY SZAL

You were invited to be interviewed as part of this anthology to celebrate diverse writers and stories. Do you consider yourself to be bringing an important or unique perspective in your work?
There's very few non-US authors in the field, and even less Australians, so as a non-America writer I feel that I'm helping to bring alternative styles of speaking and cultural viewports that often get choked out by the conglomerate that is America. I was raised in a mixed, multicultural family (half Slavic, half Middle-Eastern) and not many people have that inside perspective.

Why do you think that diverse voices are important in speculative fiction?
Because it helps us look past our own cultural backgrounds and blind spots, but especially because it can teach us about alternative ways of thinking, or inform us about other cultures. It wasn't until I read Blood of Elves by Andrzej Sapkowski that I realised what Slavic sci-fi and fantasy brought to the table on a cultural and thematic level.

How do your own works reflect those values?
I tend to write future settings taking place in non-Anglo and non-Western societies like Thailand, Nigeria, Turkey, etc. Even when I'm not writing stories set on Earth I sometimes write about worlds that reflect our current cultures, transplanted to a moonbase or generation ship. I'm currently writing a novel that takes place in a giant, mined out asteroid where major elements of a culture or nation reside in each floor and subsection. It adds a bit of richness and depth to the setting.

Who were some of the early influences on your writing, inside or outside of the field? Who do you see as some of your heroes, or guiding lights?
George R. R. Martin, for one. His rich landscapes, complex characters and lavish world-building made me want to write speculative fiction the moment I read his books. Michael Grant was a childhood favourite of mine: his Gone series is a twisted delight with some of the most evil teenagers in exist. Also, Richard K. Morgan for intense plot and cool tech, Quentin Tarantino for razor-sharp dialogue and action scenes, Pierce Brown for lush worlds with heart and Ian McDonald for introducing me to diverse worlds. And Stephen King. How could I not mention Stephen King?

What other works, your own or by others, would you recommend for people interested in supporting diversity in the field of speculative fiction?
There's the fantastic, diverse works by local writers such as Ian McDonald's *River of Gods* or Nnedi Okorafor's *Who Fears Death.* But truly diverse works are international works. The fantastic *Metro 2033* by Dmitry Glukhovsky, Sergei Lukyanenko's *Night Watch,* Kawamata Chiaki's *Death Sentences,* Hideo Yokoyama's ***Six Four,*** and Khaled Towfik's *Utopia.* If you truly want to promote diversity, then going out and finding it across the globe is the only way to do it.

The District of Wonders is creating this anthology because we wanted to do something constructive at what many are seeing as an alarming time in world history. Is there a message that you would like to send to the readers of *Everyone: Worlds without Walls?*
Yes. Keep reading, keep writing, keep being kind to each other, and keep exploring the fiction this wide world has to offer. You never know, you might just find your new favourite book.

SAMUEL R. DELANY

You were invited to be interviewed as part of this anthology to celebrate diverse writers and stories. Do you consider yourself to be bringing an important or unique perspective in your work?
Thank you so much for the invitation. But I wouldn't know where to begin answering the question you ask.

Why do you think that diverse voices are important in speculative fiction?
I suppose because diverse voices fill up the world around us, and it's the one way to keep art as interesting as the world it occasionally reflects.

How do your own works reflect those values?
I am so unsure if my work does anything at all, I can't begin to speculate on how it does it.

Who were some of the early influences on your writing, inside or outside of the field? Who do you see as some of your heroes, or guiding lights?
Writers I like include Guy Davenport and Djuna Barnes, Jean Toomer, Willa Cather and Hart Crane, Sonya Sanchez, Theodore Sturgeon, Roger Zelazny and Lucile Clifton, Joanna Russ and Octavia Butler, certainly a collection of diverse voices, that would run on and on and on. But see any of the lists in my book *About Writing* (Wesleyan, 2006).

What other works, your own or by others, would you recommend for people interested in supporting diversity in the field of speculative fiction?
I'd say start with a very careful and considered reading of any work you like, whether it's speculative fiction or not. That's the best way to go on as a reader of any sort . . .

The District of Wonders is creating this anthology because we wanted to do something constructive at what many are seeing as an alarming time in world history. Is there a message that you would like to send to the readers of *Everyone: Worlds without Walls?*
If it isn't in my story, I doubt that it's going to be in a few answers to a few questions of this sort. But of course, I could be wrong. I think my best message is that I don't have one. I try to write in a way that helps you figure out what your own message is, so that I don't get in the way of your finding it.

EVE SHI

You were invited to be interviewed as part of this anthology to celebrate diverse writers and stories. Do you consider yourself to be bringing an important or unique perspective in your work?
First of all, thank you for having me! I'm Indonesian, a Muslim, a bilingual writer (Indonesian and English) who dabbles in speculative fiction - a combination of traits that not many people can claim, though that alone doesn't make my perspective important or unique. It is up to the readers to decide.

Why do you think that diverse voices are important in speculative fiction?
Because there are as many stories as there are people, and these stories deserve to be heard. In a climate where bigotry and prejudice are overlooked or ignored, stories can become a way to view others as humans like ourselves instead of merely stereotypes.

How do your own works reflect those values?
For instance, in my Indonesian YA novels, I try to show that "teenage girl" is not a monolithic identity. They can be shy, pushy, sarcastic, gentle, drawn to anything from boys to action comics. My girls usually also fight against something, like a threat to their family, to the extent of their ability, relying first and foremost on themselves.

Who were some of the early influences on your writing, inside or outside of the field? Who do you see as some of your heroes, or guiding lights?
When I was small, Enid Blyton's children books were widely translated in Indonesia. My favorites were the adventure, detective, and boarding school stories. These formed an inseparable part of my childhood and got me writing.

The same decade also saw the rise of wuxia (martial arts lit) TV series. Works by Jin Yong, the most popular wuxia writer, were being adapted for TV and became very popular, including in Indonesia. My father and his generation read a lot of fan-translated wuxia, so I kind of got carried along, watched those series, and were fascinated.

Later I read some of Jin Yong's books and were floored by the depth of his knowledge, and the seamless way with which he integrates it into his fiction. With two other (now deceased) wuxia writers, Liang Yusheng and Gu Long, Jin Yong is the Big Three of wuxia writers. Liang

Yusheng's fictional ladies have won my heart, because he believes that women can be searingly brilliant regardless of their age, skills, or marital status. The scope of these gentlemen's stories is what I aim to achieve in my own (if you dream, dream big! etc).

What other works, your own or by others, would you recommend for people interested in supporting diversity in the field of speculative fiction?
There are plenty of those, so I will limit the recommendations to works by writers of Southeast Asian heritage. Aliette de Bodard's *The House of Shattered Wings,* which touches upon the subject of colonialism. Zen Cho's *Sorcerer to the Crown:* magic mixed with themes of racism and sexism. Yangszee Choo's *The Ghost Bride,* which starts as a family drama and turns into fantasy and adventure. Joyce Chng's *Jan Xu* series, on werewolves and other creatures in Singapore. Jeannie Lin's *Gunpowder Chronicles:* steampunk China and Japan.

The District of Wonders is creating this anthology because we wanted to do something constructive at what many are seeing as an alarming time in world history. Is there a message that you would like to send to the readers of *Everyone: Worlds without Walls?*
Please support diverse speculative fiction by reading, reviewing, or writing it, and hopefully we can break down the walls.

VAJRA CHANDRASEKERA

You were invited to be interviewed as part of this anthology to celebrate diverse writers and stories. Do you consider yourself to be bringing an important or unique perspective in your work?
In the sense that every perspective is unique and important, then sure! Other than that, no, because I think the celebration of difference is more about undoing deep-rooted systemic biases than about particular voices.

Why do you think that diverse voices are important in speculative fiction?
Because a literary monoculture can only persist through abuses of power.

How do your own works reflect those values?
By writing things that are more myself, even if they are sometimes less approachable for a Western audience.

Who were some of the early influences on your writing, inside or outside of the field? Who do you see as some of your heroes, or guiding lights?
I rather think it's dangerous to have heroes, and we should be suspicious of the impulse to put people (or books) on a pedestal. And influence is tricky, too, because I think one tends to accumulate more influences than one could fairly acknowledge, or even necessarily be conscious of. I'm leery of telling just-so stories, I suppose.

What other works, your own or by others, would you recommend for people interested in supporting diversity in the field of speculative fiction?
I could recommend books and stories all day! But let me pick just three to stop myself from going on ad infinitum: *Walking the Clouds,* an anthology of indigenous science fiction edited

by Grace L. Dillon; *The Queue,* a novel by Basma Abdel Aziz translated by Elisabeth Jaquette; and *Age of Blight,* a collection of short fiction by Kristine Ong Muslim.

The District of Wonders is creating this anthology because we wanted to do something constructive at what many are seeing as an alarming time in world history. Is there a message that you would like to send to the readers of Everyone: Worlds without Walls?
No, I think the story already says it all for me. Apart from that, you know, drink more water and get more sleep if you can manage it, which is usually good advice for most people on most days.

CARMELO RAFALA

You were invited to be interviewed as part of this anthology to celebrate diverse writers and stories. Do you consider yourself to be bringing an important or unique perspective in your work?
I am not sure how unique my own perspective might be, however, as a Sicilian/ Latin man, I suppose I bring some of that self-examination of human interaction on a small and personal scale that sometimes permeates stories from that region, such as love, honour, hardships of life, the aspirations of the common man, etc. (Although I seem to lack the flashes of melodramatic humour that can often accompany Sicilian/Italian writing.)

Giovanni Verga and Giuseppi Di Lampedusa come to mind as great Sicilian writers you should read. In no way and I saying I am anywhere near as great as these two, just to get that straight.

Why do you think that diverse voices are important in speculative fiction?
Easy. Literature as expression cannot be claimed by one group of people living in any particular geographic area. Geographic areas give us insights into how the peoples of those areas think and live and approach life. That is very, very important. And every group has its myths, folklore, and distinct forms (the Japanese Haiku comes to mind). But for one group to dominate over all others–and the suggestion that one group should do so–is merely an extension of a colonial mindset which is in many ways propped up by the corporate interests of the group that wishes to remain in a position of power. And they do this by playing on the fear of the "other". We see this today reflected in the outcome of the recent US election, as well as the UK's Brexit fiasco.

If literature is a way to understand each other and find our common humanity, then one must have access to writers from all parts of the globe. Speculative fiction is a perfect example of how this can be achieved. Contrary to what some may think the West, and the US in particular, did not invent speculative literature. Every culture has myths, legends, fantasy tales that tell us something about that group of people. Speculative fiction is a literature rooted in every culture.

How do your own works reflect those values?
At the moment, I think my work is, at its core, an examination of the small, intimate interactions between desperate people. Many of my characters have names that are not always typically representative of one group. For example, in the story in this collection I have a British man and a man from Sarajevo. Now I am not pretending to know what it is like to be a man from Sarajevo. I don't. But I can use universal themes of love, loss and regret to tell a story

that will, I hope, demonstrate that we all have things in common and things we can relate to. That is my focus. If I need more information, then I do proper research.

As an immigrant from an immigrant family, and having had some experience of what it is like to be the "intruder", I think it all the more important for speculative fiction to be international and to demonstrate our common humanity and to put to rest the idiotic notion that there should be walls between us.

Who were some of the early influences on your writing, inside or outside of the field? Who do you see as some of your heroes, or guiding lights?
I read widely, even as a child. Some of my influences are Ray Bradbury, Samuel R. Delany, Harlan Ellison, Jorge Luis Borges, Sol Plaatje, Gabriel Garcia Marquez, Doris Lessing, Leigh Brackett.

As far as guiding lights are concerned, I'll say anyone who overcomes persecution and promotes justice.

What other works, your own or by others, would you recommend for people interested in supporting diversity in the field of speculative fiction?
Nisi Shawl, Tade Thompson, Octavia Butler, Ursula Le Guin, Carlos Fuentes, Yevgeny Zamyatin, Aliette de Bodard. There are many others.

The District of Wonders is creating this anthology because we wanted to do something constructive at what many are seeing as an alarming time in world history. Is there a message that you would like to send to the readers of *Everyone: Worlds without Walls?*
Don't let political propaganda define your worldview and your view of other people. Cultures and ideals may vary, but we are all cut from the same cloth, created in the same gene pool. We all love, dream, aspire and want a fair chance. These are some of the things we have in common. Hold on to that.

YUKIMI OGAWA

You were invited to be interviewed as part of this anthology to celebrate diverse writers and stories. Do you consider yourself to be bringing an important or unique perspective in your work?
Um–not...really? Maybe I don't qualify as a contributor to this anthology. I'm way too tiny as a writer, anyway! And I write what I want to write, what I need to write, not trying to bring Japan-ness out into the world. Which is why I am so grateful that there are people who'd read my stories, despite all that different-ness and strangeness, and my incompetent English.

Why do you think that diverse voices are important in speculative fiction?
Sometimes I see reviews of my stories where the reviewer complains that the story in question doesn't involve enough of the character's inner growth. At first I didn't understand why they were saying this. After some time I realised this was something some people value, especially in so-called Western cultures. I find this value for growth difficult to incorporate into my stuff, especially yokai (Japanese folklore monsters) stories, because we don't usually expect yokai to change, let alone grow, or affected in any way by us humans. I hope, by reading diverse stories, people would understand or simply recognise the fact that there are as many underlying ideas as there are all of us, on a very fundamental level.

How do your own works reflect those values?

Here, in my answer to the previous question, I, too, learned that there are ideas that I haven't encountered before. And that I, too, should also learn to embrace these ideas that are completely new to me. But at the same time, I feel I should not try to shape my stories around these new ideas, if I do not feel entirely comfortable with them. While I try not to shout JAPAN! too loudly with my stories, I don't want to lose the ideas and values that nurtured me...if you know what I mean? Am I even making sense??

Who were some of the early influences on your writing, inside or outside of the field? Who do you see as some of your heroes, or guiding lights?

Sorry, I keep saying this, but Shigeru Mizuki, for bringing back yokai from the shadows and margins out into the world–before him, they were almost extinct at a time. These monsters reflect our awe, fear, and respect towards the nature, which also underlies our animism, or in some cases, Shintoism. I'm so glad we didn't lose these monsters.

What other works, your own or by others, would you recommend for people interested in supporting diversity in the field of speculative fiction?

Mmm. Speaking of yokai–I'm not sure if this counts, but maybe a comic series called *Natsume's book of Friends*? The monsters depicted in this series are not the typical or traditional yokai monsters, but I love the way the monsters and humans (or just different monsters/different humans) try to be together, stay together, and, more often than you'd like, failing; but also, the way they keep trying, nonetheless.

The District of Wonders is creating this anthology because we wanted to do something constructive at what many are seeing as an alarming time in world history. Is there a message that you would like to send to the readers of *Everyone: Worlds without Walls?*

Thank you. It's always the only thing I can say. Wherever we are, whatever each of us is going through, the very fact that there are people who are trying to make this world better, that there are people responding to these efforts, makes me feel stronger, proud to be part of that world.

HAL DUNCAN

You were invited to be interviewed as part of this anthology to celebrate diverse writers and stories. Do you consider yourself to be bringing an important or unique perspective in your work?

That's for others to judge, really. When it comes to unique... in the context of diversity... well, I'm white and cismale and able-bodied, so that's pretty default. A Scot from the housing schemes is a tad more marginal in a British context, but it's still... well, British. As in colonial overlords. So I'm a step outside the normative in a whole one dimension. I go with "queer" more than "gay" for a label and "Sodomite" as a personal twist on "queer", with a whole ideology / personal mythology based around... the discourse of Sodom, I guess you could say. So maybe that's a more individual angle. My writing is increasingly riffing off that myth, a conceit of rebuilding Sodom, of building a New Sodom via sodalities of the abject, woven through stories and poems. That's the perspective I bring to the table–quirky in its approach perhaps if not in sentiment. Insofar as I have a Great Work attitude towards the realisation of this personal symbol, in discourse, in culture, in reality, naturally I think it's important. YMMV though. I'm not one to be a pompous arse about the momentousness of my Art.

Why do you think that diverse voices are important in speculative fiction?
Who the fuck wants homogenous voices? That'd be like that sketch on the old UK comedy show *Goodness Gracious Me* of a group of British Asian friends "going for an English", like the one who asks for "the blandest thing on the menu." Why would you want monotony in any genre, any medium of art? Why would you eschew the most vital and versatile voices coming from every zone in the phasespace of identity? On the bizarre notion that some miniscule subset–that which is considered normative in every single dimension, that which is absent any marker of deviance from the default–can and will produce all the juicy flavoursome art you could ever want? Maybe if, as a fan of generic pabulum, you actively abhor the non-formulaic, literally hate creativity getting into your production line pap. If you like your art to be art, that's just fucking stupid.

And if you don't want bland monotony, it's not just a matter of overcoming the myopia and tunnel vision that funnels attention to the normative. Inclusivity is integration is desegregation. Which is to say, the non-normative has been abjected in these dimensions of identity–ethnicity, sexuality, gender, disability–the construction of race an ethnic queering as much as heteronormativity queers by sexuality. Same goes for the physiological and psychological queering which takes the reality of diversity in natural variation and imposes on it an artificial boundary between default and deviant-from-the-default. Included and excluded. This abjection (as per Kristeva, see Wikipedia,) is systemic, institutionalised. So to achieve from this phasespace of identity the genuinely inclusive sampling which we might legitimately call diversity requires we counteract the systemic exclusion.

Which is to say, an ethos and practise of being actively corrective is required. I.e. even if we don't want bland monotony for purely aesthetic reasons–because it's fucking dull–we need diversity as a political principle, awake to the reality of abjection. And indeed, if we're looking at it in that light, action toward diversity in art is important ethically, as an end in itself, as part of the greater struggle to undo abjection in general. Insofar as art is a semiotic battleground, I'd go so far as to say it's a key front in that struggle, one where we engage directly with the symbols that reify abjection. Nowhere moreso than in the strange fiction genres where the most affectively-charged tropes of culture and psyche are our prime material.

How do your own works reflect those values?
Poorly. Theoretically. Passionately. Ever failingly. I like the famous Beckett quote here: "Ever tried. Ever failed. No matter. Try Again. Fail again. Fail better." I'm aware that though my work is often fiercely engaged on one front, driven by that self-identification as Sodomite, the focus there tends to divert attention from where I could and should be fighting the cause when it comes to all those other dimensions. Part of me self-justifies it as being OK to fight one's own corner if one can be at least aware enough of the other vectors of abjection to be less actively harmful than those who are blithely unaware and so don't resist the flow. But complacency is complicity, unwitting collaboration even, so less actively harmful than the clueless is hardly a high aspiration. It's not harmless. It's not actively helpful. So it's not good enough. One has to be engaged or you will fail. So: "must try harder" would be my self-assessment here.

Who were some of the early influences on your writing, inside or outside of the field? Who do you see as some of your heroes, or guiding lights?

Larrabeiti, author of the kid's book *The Borribles,* is the earliest. His snot-nosed pilfering Lost Boys with 1970s London as their Neverland and squats as their treehouses isn't just an influence on my Scruffians. The latter are a direct and open tribute to his Borribles, right down to the anarchosocialist ethos. I've never seen the core of fantasy as secondary world stuff because this is what fantasy was to me as a kid, as much as Tolkien and Lewis. The team of adventurers having one girl and one black kid is weak by today's standards but de Larrabeiti failed better than his peers. He failed well enough that his publisher dropped the third book, deciding the anti-establishment ethos (including a vicious fuck-you take on the Met's notorious SPG) was far too subversive in the wake of the Brixton Riots.

Then there's Delany, of course. Do I even need to explain? When I was still discovering the canon via the 1980s Gollancz Classics, *Nova* and *Babel-17* blew all the entry-level Big Name stuff I'd been reading (Asimov, Heinlein, Clarke) out of the water, and stood out even among the later generations I was getting into (Dick, Ellison, Sladek.) The queer elements spoke to me–my take on the Sodom myth is rooted in the epigraph to *Driftglass*–but there's also the sheer literary skill and power... which then hits escape velocity with *Dhalgren.* And his work just seems to keep levelling up. He's still blowing everyone else out of the water with something like *Through the Valley of the Nest of Spiders,* the most important novel of the 21st century so far, to my mind. A lot of my most ambitious writing in recent years or in the offing is deeply influenced by Delany–and by Guy Davenport, who I learned of via Delany.

What other works, your own or by others, would you recommend for people interested in supporting diversity in the field of speculative fiction?

I'm years behind on my leisure reading, to be honest–by a country mile, the bulk of my SFF reading these days is unpublished manuscripts I'm giving feedback on–and I'm rubbish at recommendation lists at the best of times, so I'm really not the best person to ask. As I say above though, Delany's latest is a massively important novel, I reckon. In interviews he's talked about striving to "expand the sphere of empathy" and I think on a level the whole book can be considered... a critique of abjection isn't the right term. It abolishes boundaries defining transgression, taboo. It's flagrantly defying an aesthetics of disgust which ever presents itself as ethics, written into every page of it an attitude that, frankly, swells the heart. So, rather than come at this from an angle of "here's a reading list if you want to feel you're covering all the bases", I'd point folk at this one book as a fucking antidote to the mindset underlying all abjection. Again, to achieve diversity requires we counteract exclusion. *Through the Valley of the Nest of Spiders* is a call to the radical humanism required, I'd say, beyond mere bourgeois niceties.

The District of Wonders is creating this anthology because we wanted to do something constructive at what many are seeing as an alarming time in world history. Is there a message that you would like to send to the readers of *Everyone: Worlds without Walls?*

Hell, I have a fucking manifesto, never mind a message–the long poem "New Sodom". You can find the full text posted on my blog. You can find me reading it on my Vimeo account. It clocks in at approximately fourteen minutes of all guns blazing aimed to be the bastard antifa lovechild of William Blake and Allen Ginsberg messianic beat punk prophecy. If that sounds like your kind of thing. As messages go, that poem says what I want to say far better than I ever could without the toolkits of verse or narrative. The gist of it though: Resist.

MARGRÉT HELGADÓTTIR

You were invited to be interviewed as part of this anthology to celebrate diverse writers and stories. Do you consider yourself to be bringing an important or unique perspective in your work?
Uhm, my lack of self esteem would probably say: important and unique, no no no. What I bring is my own cultural mixed background. I was born abroad and have lived in several countries and continents, plus my parents come from different countries. I think my writing and editing reflects this a lot. Also, since I am one of the few Nordic writers who write speculative fiction in English, I bring you our view of the world, our values, our history and folklore.

Why do you think that diverse voices are important in speculative fiction?
To me, diversity means recognising, accepting and valuing difference. It makes literature rich, authentic, fun and exciting. It makes the world smaller and greater at the same time. What is important in a love story in your part of the world is probably totally different on the other side of Earth. Reading about the other love story will broaden your horizon and force you to reflect on why things are like they are in your life. I pity those who are either forced to or choose to live with a narrowed view on the world. They don't know what wealth they are missing out on. We are social animals. Misunderstandings and limited views of the world create violence, hatred and wars. Any child should grow up with diversity in her/his life. It is what creates empathy for others, what creates an understanding that there are other ways of looking at the world, that other people experience life different than you, that no one is better than the other. On an individual level, everyone wants to read about ourselves, to read books with characters, stories and images that reflect our lives and neighbourhoods. We need diverse books to show children who struggle with being a minority in some way that it is okay to be who they are, that they are not alone with whatever they struggle with.

How do your own works reflect those values?
Based on my background I know there is a huge world out there. I believe my own background influences both my own writing and my editing of books greatly, both in themes and my choice of characters. Since I write in English, I reach more people. So, I try to base much of my writing on my surroundings from the Nordic part of the world, be it choice of names or locations, folklore, views of world and values, history or climate. Guess you could say that this is my contribution to the world, to show how we live in this part of the world. As book editor I want diverse voices in anthologies, something I seek actively in the *Fox Spirit Books of Monsters* with monster stories from around the world.

Who were some of the early influences on your writing, inside or outside of the field? Who do you see as some of your heroes, or guiding lights?
I've been a dedicated bookworm since I learned to read as a little girl, and was drawn early on to the spectacular stories that took place in fictional fantasy worlds, be it fairy tales, folk tales or dark science fiction from outer space. In additions to work by authors like Tolkien, Lewis, Le Guin, McCaffrey, Kafka, Ende, I read lots from Nordic authors like Tove Jansson, Karen Blixen and Astrid Lindgren. I travelled the world with authors like Allende, Gordimer, Gogol and Marquez. I also loved historic novels and explorers' diaries, and even had a period where I devoured spy books. I still read lots, something all authors should do. A few of my favourites

today are Amy Tan, Haruki Murakami, China Mieville and Victor Pelevin who I adore for their broad narratives and beautiful language.

What other works, your own or by others, would you recommend for people interested in supporting diversity in the field of speculative fiction?
I think short stories are excellent if you want to read new writers. I would of course recommend the annual *Fox Spirit Books of Monsters* that I edit. We have so far presented European, African and Asian monsters, told by authors in the different regions. I now work with the Pacific area and will continue to the rest of the world after that. I would also recommend the anthologies *AfroSF* volume one and two, edited by Ivor Hartmann, and *We See a Different Frontier* from The Future Fire. There are so many more wonderful authors from all over the world. If I should point in direction of a few of them, seek out the work by Tade Thompson, Wole Talabi, Nnedi Okarofor, Ken Liu, Isabel Yap, Fabio Fernandes, Nick Wood, Joan de la Haye, Nerine Dorman, Yukimi Ogawa, Johann Thorsson, Karin Tidbeck, Jacob Drud, Nina Niskanen, Tina Makereti and Chris Nguyen Galvin.

The District of Wonders is creating this anthology because we wanted to do something constructive at what many are seeing as an alarming time in world history. Is there a message that you would like to send to the readers of *Everyone: Worlds without Walls?*
Listen to all the voices in the world, not just one. Most important: Stay awake! This is not a time to sleep.

LUIS G. ABBADIE

You were invited to be interviewed as part of this anthology to celebrate diverse writers and stories. Do you consider yourself to be bringing an important or unique perspective in your work?
I've never thought about my work being "important;" at any rate, the one thing I strive for that I find quite rare in the field, is to write "pagan-friendly" fiction, in contrast to so many authors that seem to work with the monotheistic, heaven/hell paradigm as a given, no matter how liberally. Other than that, I spend a lot of time blurring lines.

When I started out, like many young Mexican genre writers, I fell in the trap of thinking that writing stories around Pre-Hispanic cultures and-or around Colonial history was the way to do "different" stories – now, I still find stories by aspiring young people that do exactly that, and the subtly-forced tone is so similar that they even read like my own early efforts: "Bradbury-with-Mayans," "Lovecraft-with-Aztecs," "Dick-with-Conquistadores."

I started to gain solid ground when I began to liberally abuse the pseudo-factual form, toying with pseudonymous characters, with mixing in real people –contemporary and historical- in my fiction in every possible way. I started to play the same game started by H.P. Lovecraft and continued by such extremely different authors as Colin Wilson and Jorge Luis Borges. And there was a reason for it. Among the then-scarce genre readers and writers (I'm speaking of the 1990s), there was a strong bias. Most were used to reading about SF and horror in foreign settings; they could be thrilled by Dracula either in Transylvania or in old London, or by a XXXth-Century Paris; they could believe that Pennywise terrorized a Maine village, or that aliens invaded the USA; but aliens and weird creatures and mad science in Mexico City, in Guadalajara –in actual, mundane places they actually knew and were used to? That, they said, was ridiculous, laughable, unbelievable. If a SF or weird story, misquoting Lovecraft, should be crafted like an elaborate hoax in order to create suspension of disbelief, most Mexican readers demanded twice as much effort. Places like London, Paris and New York were both homes and background for SF and Fantasy for so many, but to Mexicans, they were distant from their own reality, as much as Arkham or Gotham City –exotic places where the unreal could safely happen, without intruding into their own daily life.

So I had to devise ways to break through into their safety. Others have found their own keys; mine was to blur the limits between fiction and fact, to mix autobiographical tidbits, writing of found manuscripts or objects; ironically, this gimmick was old when Mary Shelley "found" the manuscript of *The Last Man.* Yet it somehow worked! But that was merely the pointer, I didn't want to be a one-trick pony. If Lovecraft, Wilson and Borges taught me to weave in fictionalized reality, Robert Anton Wilson and Grant Morrison showed me ways to go several steps further, to cause fiction to stop being safe; to have it take hold and insinuate itself into the reader's own secure reality, much like the unnamed presences in Julio Cortazar's "La Casa Tomada."

I was already writing when I was immersed in the roots of the Mexican Neo-Pagan movement. I first tried to keep this well apart from my literary life, but then, inspired by Wilson and Morrison, I started to mix the pot, writing fiction to develop Neo-Pagan concepts, and drawing inspiration and resources from spirituality and the occult not merely as subject matter but to develop my writing. If you've read Grant Morrison writing about his graphic novel *The Invisibles* as an hyper-sigil, and/or Soror Nema about art and magick, you've got the gist of it. I once met a young man in my teacher Flaviano Castañeda's literary workshop who was toying with writing poetry by applying the structure of music composition; I have similarly applied the structures and methods of ritual, of a Shamanistic journey, and other methods drawn from Scottish Cunning Craft, to crafting fiction. I have been striving to break down all dividing lines between my spiritual Craft and my crafting of written fiction, with each drawing from the other. The written word is powerful, after all; its power to provoke change is rarely appreciated in full –and if the powers-that-be ever do, then we might be in for a *Farenheit 451* scenario. I also believe that a growing number of writers are aware of this potential, and willing to make use of it. It's, if I may say so, a new form of magick being developed for a future marked, some say, by the manifold symbol of a Feather –in ancient Egyptian symbolism, both the quill of the scribe and the symbol of the Goddess Ma'at who weighs the soul. By allowing our voices to be heard, and setting our fears and hopes and intent down in writing, we are setting down the manifold future, that's no small aim. But I aim only to do my best within my small patch of Land.

Why do you think that diverse voices are important in speculative fiction?
I may seem to stray from the subject, but it's difficult to give you an answer without going quite a bit over the context and background of Mexican genre fiction.

When I began to explore the literary community, most other writers, both professional and beginners (due both to ignorance and Hollywood), saw horror, SF and fantasy as something intrinsically North American and reeking of commercialism, so I was constantly asked, "why don't you write something serious?" Even academic studies in those days spanned Mexican and Latin American authors, those from Spain and France and Germany, but would hardly touch anything in English language (that's all changed for the better). That was one of many abstract walls a genre writer had to face (keep counting, there were several walls, and we did pay for them ourselves in those days). These genres had always been present in our country, but they were sparse, early genre writers were rare enough that one cannot draw lines of influence between them the way it's usually done in other instances. Even our pulp magazines –which were around in the 1950s and 1960s- went mostly unnoticed and both they and their authors are now mostly forgotten. In the 1970s and later, people started to meet, research, network and –most importantly- write. SF writers were the first, a few groups took shape, and privately circulated SF magazines appeared, expanding their fields to mystery and horror, mostly because mystery often proves a cheating code to be grudgingly acknowledged by academia thanks to Jorge Luis Borges' open appreciation of the genre, but horror –my main love- came as an afterthought, SF and fantasy authors and researchers cradled it like the ugly cousin they kept in the attic; the few prominent authors were first and foremost SF authors, and they wrote the occasional fantasy and horror piece; awards were ccreated for SF and fantasy, and sometimes cradled horror. Back then, when we learned of these groups, magazines and awards, a few of us continued to feel just a bit out of place… while most authors enthusiastically shared their SF, and produced the occasional horror story, we shared our occasional SF story and kept most of our weird fiction stored away. Nobody told us to go up to the attic where the ugly cousin crouched, but we found the murky stairway very easily. What happens after all when four Tolkien fans board a bus and they find themselves surrounded by a busful of trekkies? Some of us started to write more stuff that might be palatable for the "gang" while our most personal materials gathered dust on a shelf; others preferred to keep some distance, or to find our own way. As readers and as writers both, we were again and again coerced by circumstances to "line up," even within genre fiction –even when those majorities would never have coaxed us consciously; for the growing SF community would never have tried to impose anything; in fact, we forced ourselves, built our own walls.

How often do we read books from authors with wholly different outlooks on life? We love reading about the vast diversity of cultures and philosophies of, say, Jack Vance's carefully crafted alien worlds, but there are so many true worlds being lived and experienced by our fellow humans, and writers who dwell in those worlds will themselves often craft worlds so vastly different from anything we've seen elsewhere –and we may even realize at some point that we are watching ourselves through somebody else's eyes.

I can safely say that it's only in the last decade that horror has gained strength of its own, and stopped being a rarity. Genres finally stand together and we may explore them or stray off without feeling like we crashed the party. But when I started, we were the "wetbacks" in the Mexican literary field, SF and horror writers (and readers) were looked down upon by respectable, "legitimate" authors and readers, who saw us and felt the need to raise a higher literary wall that kept illegals like me from prowling around. We were told again and again to either obtain legitimate papers (write "serious" literature) or I might be cast off beyond the border into the wastelands of best-sellers and newsstand drivel. Or, if we managed to get in, we could get the shady paperwork that would gain us a back seat in the meeting hall of the SF neighborhood (which was still avoided by most respectable citizens and whose locals were discouraged to stray from) and a comfy couch in that serviceable attic.

See what I was aiming at?

Looking back, it's very ironic that my first breakthrough, and the one most people still identify me with, is a short story written from the perspective of a North American come to Mexico, as a lens through which to look at both countries. Diversity is not a matter of nationality, it never was; it's a matter of acknowledgement against rejection, and it can and does happen in every country and culture, we all have our walls to be broken through –or broken down.

I've always argued that for readers, a writer's works are what should matter, and not the author's life, personality or circumstances. Of course it's historically important, and fascinating, to learn about the lives of authors, but when you get down with a book in your hands, and read, if the writer does his job, you will –like Arthur Conan Doyle once promised, and delivered- forget all about the author and the story will be all there is. The value of diversity in the field lies not in the reader's appreciation –that is, an "I'm now reading a so-and-so writer" attitude-, but in the very source of stories, the soil in which they were grown; for the life and experience of the writer will infuse unique aspects, views and angles to their stories just like the soil of a variety of fields will yield fruits with surprising flavors, textures and scents. Even when entire worlds and universes are being crafted in a novel, the immediate reality the author lives in –the way they see themselves, their beliefs, their feelings and reasoning and loves and fears- informs them, and the reader may obtain glimpses of the unexpected ways they see those worlds, and share and contrast those views with their own even as they explore new universes together. I've often found myself thinking, "I completely disagree with this writer," and yet at the same time understanding the hows and whys of those views I disagree with in a way I never would have in a mere straightforward debate with said writer. What better way to understand each other than to look through each other's eyes?

How do your own works reflect those values?

I personally love debate, and this got mixed in my work with the famous quote by Forrest J Ackerman about how, if you are an actor and Jewish, at some point in your career you must take on the role of Hitler. I often experiment by assuming, when writing, the views and postures of characters with whom I completely disagree. This gets complicated for some readers who usually assume that one always expresses their own views in fiction, but I find it a good way to try to gain an understanding of other people, as well as putting my own opinions and beliefs in perspective. There are some standpoints that I strongly disagree with, such as, for example, New Age thought; instead of writing against it or simply expressing my views, I find it better to create characters who fully embrace New Age or whatever other view I dislike; then I get other characters who hold opposing views which I also disagree with, add some character who does share my point of view, and have them all explore their reality and contrast each other's interpretations of their experiences; this forces me to sustain arguments from other's stances, to see my own from diverging angles, and the challenge lies in not fashioning an argument by having the other side fulfill my own prejudices; to make it strong enough that while I may often strengthen my own views, I am at times forced to think twice –outdone by my imagined characters' arguments!

Who were some of the early influences on your writing, inside or outside of the field? Who do you see as some of your heroes, or guiding lights?

H.P. Lovecraft, Ray Bradbury and Stephen King have always been, and still are, there to point the way for me. Robert Anton Wilson came later, but his books are probably the ones I've re-read the most. H.G. Wells, Emile Salgari, M.R. James, Rod Serling, Paul van Herck, Forrest J Ackerman and Robert Bloch. Poppy Z. Brite has proven to me that absolutely any subject, no matter how droll, grotesque or unpalatable, can be turned into a thing of beauty when language is mastered. Robert Aickman, Ramsey Campbell, Paco Ignacio Taibo II, Robert E. Howard, Jack Kirby and Steve Ditko. Sergio-Jesús Rodríguez, longtime sparring partner in debates, is probably the one author I've known personally for years who has made a lasting influence, in spite that we disagree about mostly everything – or perhaps because of that! And while it may seem trite, there is one poet, SF author, sometimes plastic artist and cultural promoter I have to include: Elsa Abbadié, my mother, who instilled my love for reading and certainly influenced me even more than all the rest.

What other works, your own or by others, would you recommend for people interested in supporting diversity in the field of speculative fiction?
Thinking of works that might be less likely to be known already, two authors/works come to mind: the works of Arturo César Rojas, whose short story "El Que Llegó Hasta el Metro Pino Suárez" (1986), often considered groundbreaking, was ostensibly denied the Puebla Award due to his sexual orientation, and Sofía Guadarrama, formerly Antonio Guadarrama, who authored the SF novel, *Piso 931.*

The District of Wonders is creating this anthology because we wanted to do something constructive at what many are seeing as an alarming time in world history. Is there a message that you would like to send to the readers of *Everyone: Worlds without Walls?*
We are fortunate to be living in these times; yes, this is an alarming moment, but it is also groundbreaking. The egg is cracking; many wonder if what will come afterwards will be a span of wings to marvel at, or, well, a boiled egg. Let's not harbor any doubts; the world will grow – and outgrow – far beyond this apparent entropy. It's up to us to place the markers that will point the particular direction of that growth. The continuing battle for freedom and equality has reached a turning point, and while resistance was expected and is now met –the status quo never surrenders meekly, nor should it- we are also facing the stumbling missteps which translate in censorship in the name of freedom of speech, in discrimination in the name of equality (yes, I'm talking about shameful things such as the World Fantasy Award thing, so there; as a mestizo with occult leanings who would no doubt have horrified HPL, I still did daydream way back when of someday having one of those Gahan Wilson busts on my shelf). Let's write our future; and let's listen to each other, because we are speaking out in so many different ways, and they are all foreshadowing the shape of things to come –what we may hope for, and what we must dread.

TAIYO FUJII

You were invited to be interviewed as part of this anthology to celebrate diverse writers and stories. Do you consider yourself to be bringing an important or unique perspective in your work?
I don't write dystopian. It's unique, I think. My contributed work "Violation of the TrueNet Security Act" is not so positive, but it exemplifies diversity including network and machine intelligence.

Why do you think that diverse voices are important in speculative fiction?
Speculative fiction reminds us of the sense of wonder. Diversity is one of the base designs of SF.

How do your own works reflect those values?
I hope my work lets readers see that science or technology could be diverse perspectives. Not only in terms of the sorcerer's apprentice, or doubt, or fear. For example, "wanna hack this" could become something else.

Who were some of the early influences on your writing, inside or outside of the field? Who do you see as some of your heroes, or guiding lights?
Richard Dawkins opened my eyes. *The Selfish Gene* is my favourite speculative fiction... opus - that is, essay."

What other works, your own or by others, would you recommend for people interested in supporting diversity in the field of speculative fiction?
To give your readers a little nudge, my second novel *Orbital Cloud*.

The District of Wonders is creating this anthology because we wanted to do something constructive at what many are seeing as an alarming time in world history. Is there a message that you would like to send to the readers of *Everyone: Worlds without Walls?*
Thanks for inviting me to take part in this. I used to write novels with hopes for the United States to exemplify freedom, fairness and hospitality. I hope you will remind them that many people outside the US hope they will keep those values.

CHIKODILI EMELUMADU

When the folks from *StarShip Sofa* got in touch with me to contribute to this anthology, it seemed a bit like a wasted opportunity to me, in this talk of diversity, not to include future leaders in the African speculative fiction field. To this end, I asked the authors Chinelo Onwualu, Tendai Huchu, Wole Talabi and Tade Thompson what their views on diversity are. Not only are they inmersed in the genre, but they are - or have at one point been - beyond the borders of what would be considered their 'home countries'. Here are their responses below.

You were invited to be interviewed as part of this anthology to celebrate diverse writers and stories. Do you consider yourself to be bringing an important or unique perspective in your work?
To be honest, I don't think my voice is unique but I do think my perspective is important. The genre of African speculative fiction is so dominated by a certain male point of view that I think it's important that alternate points of view are presented.

A good example of this can be seen in the number of men on the shortlist for the African Speculative Fiction Society's recent Nommo Awards. More women need to write - and write well. So I think that by adding my own work, which comes from an African feminist perspective, to the genre I'm expanding the range of what is available. - Chinelo Onwualu, co-founder and editor 'Omenana' magazine. Currently living in Nigeria after years in the states.

Why do you think that diverse voices are important in speculative fiction?
Why would anyone in this world so full of variety, choose to remain stuck in a monochrome existence? One which only reflects one view out of the thousands - nay, millions - of views out there? It doesn't make sense to me. Growing up, we were used to this type of storytelling and so when we wrote, we tried to hack off bits of ourselves to suit popular trends. However, this helps no one. Luckily, editors have begun to realise the richness that having works from around the globe can bring. Or should I say, they have started to treat it as normal, not exotic. This attracts more of us. New ideas. New techniques. It only betters the genre. And if it becomes the case of life imitating art, then science (scientific innovation) will be all the better for it. - Chikodili
How do your own works reflect those values?
I'd like to think this is self-evident. I write as I have lived and I have lived on three continents. This perhaps makes for something altogether new, a certain harmony of cultural influences, I hope. I try not to shy away or overexplain things, if there is the danger of it losing its significance or 'colour' (I hate this connotation by the way. 'Local colour'.) - Chikodili

Who were some of the early influences on your writing, inside or outside of the field? Who do you see as some of your heroes, or guiding lights?

When I was much younger, I read everything. Literally. I read Encyclopaedias and classic English literature. I read Enid Blyton and Ikebe Super. I read the Sandman Graphic novels and Frederick Forsyth's political thrillers. I read Homer's epics and lots of pulp science fiction. I read a lot as a kid. I started early as an eclectic reader. And that influenced my writing. I think the early influences that have persisted are definitely Neil Gaiman, Eric Van Lustbader, Cyprian Ekwensi, Stephen King and Isaac Asimov. Recently I find myself more and more influenced by Ursula K. LeGuin, Amos Tutuola, Ray Bradbury and Phillip K. Dick, as I continuously discover more of their work.

I don't know if I have any heroes or guiding lights, I've never been fond of the concept of mentors or of looking up to anyone but I am a fan of people who produce things I enjoy. The writers whose work I enjoy a lot include: Nnedi Okorafor, Cory Doctorow, Charles Stross, Nick Wood, Nancy Kress, Neil Gaiman, P Djeli Clark, China Mieville, Ken Liu... There's a lot more.

But basically, I enjoy audacious ideas. All the writers I like write vastly different things but all have written something somewhere that captured my imagination with the boldness of its idea, and the elegance with which that idea was woven into a story. Because that's primarily what I aim to do when I write, create stories with bold, interesting ideas. - Wole Talabi, author of *Parse. Error. Reset,* amongst many others, he lives in Malaysia. wtaabi.wordpress.com

What other works, your own or by others, would you recommend for people interested in supporting diversity in the field of speculative fiction?

There's just too much great spec-fic out there, recommending would just turn into a name dropping exercise. If anyone wants a quick crash-course in contemporary African SF then they'd do well to try the anthologies *AfroSF, Imagine Africa 500,* or *African Monsters;* better still, read the free online magazine *Omenana*. - Tendai Huchu, Caine nominated author of *The Maestro, the Magistrate and the Mathematician.*

The District of Wonders is creating this anthology because we wanted to do something constructive at what many are seeing as an alarming time in world history. Is there a message that you would like to send to the readers of *Everyone: Worlds without Walls?*

Always keep in mind that attaching a prefix to any kind of writing comes with hazards. Saying "African speculative fiction" instead of just plain "speculative fiction" on the one hand, can help people looking to see themselves in narratives find books. On the other hand, there is a risk of the prefix becoming a signifier for inferiority. I'm not saying the prefix signifies superiority, I'm saying fiction by Africans just is. It can be fantastic, it can be mediocre, it can be shit. That is true equality." - Tade Thompson, author of *Making Wolf*,(Kitschie Award winner) and *Rosewater.*

YASSER BAHJATT

You were invited to be interviewed as part of this anthology to celebrate diverse writers and stories. Do you consider yourself to be bringing an important or unique perspective in your work?

My work from the start has been about helping jump start the Arabian SciFi culture, for that my work is bringing a new perspective on seeing the world from an Arabian point of view.

Why do you think that diverse voices are important in speculative fiction?
I have an analogy I use to explain this. Imagine that the universe was a huge dark desert, and imagine humanity as a group of people lost in that desert (each person representing a culture). At first we would most probably not move much around as we cannot see a thing, and those who do will stumble and fall.

When the first of us discovers how to create a flashlight and turns it on, now there is light. Where do you think we would all walk? Even if the path he lights is not the best path, it will be the only path we walk on as every other path is dark. The more of us turning on our flashlights and pointing them towards new paths, the more possibiities humanity has.

That is how I see diversity in speculative fiction.

How do your own works reflect those values?
My work in speculative fiction is not limited to writing, I have started a publishing house with the objective to jump start Arabian SciFi, and with every new work we start we always debate how that work reflects our culture and brings something new to the table that is unique to our way of seeing things. From our first published novel *HWJN* that became an instant best seller across Arabia, and throughout its trilogy (*Somewhere* & *Binyamee*).

My own novel *Yaqteenya: The Old World*, was the first every Arabian alternate history, where I explore how our history affects the entire planet, and chose the fall of Granada as the pivot point, because of how it is still affecting the psyche of the Arabian masses.

Who were some of the early influences on your writing, inside or outside of the field? Who do you see as some of your heroes, or guiding lights?
Dr. Nabil Farooq is by far the most important contemporary Arabian SciFi author, his impact on me and my partner is unmeasurable. I'm also a futurist and technologist, and I am highly influenced by people like Ray Kurzweil & Peter Diamandis.

What other works, your own or by others, would you recommend for people interested in supporting diversity in the field of speculative fiction?
All of the work published by *Yatakhayaloon* (translated: *They Are Imagining*), we have four novels so far: *HWJN*, *Somewhere*, *Binyameen* & *Yaqteenay: The Old World*. Originally written in Arabic, and translated to English (with the exception of *Binyameen* that is still in translation), and *HWJN* was also translated to Spanish.

The District of Wonders is creating this anthology because we wanted to do something constructive at what many are seeing as an alarming time in world history. Is there a message that you would like to send to the readers of *Everyone: Worlds without Walls?*
Diversity is what makes life interesting, and there is no better way to show that than in stories and speculative fiction. We as humans enjoy new things much more than the same old thing, and there is no better source to explore new ways of thinking and living than to have a rich diverse cultural mix that you can always explore.

ACKNOWLEDGMENTS

Michael Adams
John Aiello
Dave Alcock
Thomas Ally
Kenny Alperstein
Karen (K.G) Anderson
Rodolfo Arredondo
Juha Autero
Bruce B.
Stanley Bailey
Sean Bamforth
Jenny Barber
Adell L. Barnes
Steven Barnett
Bruce Baskett
Sean Beukes
Steve Bickle
Tim Blindauer
Greg Bossert
Tony Bourne
Russell Bowman
Edmund Boys
A.J. Bradbrook
Robyn Bradshaw
Christian Brunschen
Seth Burgess
Adam Bursey
Evan C.
Andre Canivet
Anthony R.Cardno
Marc Carpenter
Juli Carter
Mark Carter
Jeremy Carter
Eliza Chan
Zach Chapman
Jane Charlesworth
Natasha Chisdes
Brian Collier
Drsuzanne Conboy-Hill
Jen Cook
Donald Crossman
Paul Davison
Graham Davison
K.M. Degroot
Anthony Desimone
Vickie Disanto
Vincent Docherty
Brian Doob
Gary Dowell
Joe Drake
Ron Ducros
Leland Eaves
Nick Eden
Jon Ediger
Neil Eisenhauer
Leah F.
T. F.
Shayna Fagan
Iago Faustus
Michael Feir
Jenora Feuer
Phillip Fey
P.G. Finnie
Paul Fischer
Arne Fischmann
Joseph Flynn
Maurice Forrester
D Franklin
Fran Friel
Eurotrash Games
Gary Geling
Rodney Gentry
Marian Goldeen
Jon Goodbun
John Gorringe
Stephen Graham
Scott Grigsby
Guillaume Gronoff
Eben M. Haber
Terence Haddock
Trace Hagemann
Mikael Haglund
Jeanne E. Hand-Boniakowski
Anne C. Hanna
Ian Harris
Erin Hartshorn
Andrew Hatchell
Richard Hawkins
Eric Hendrickson
Yozen Hernandez
Simon Hildebrandt
Nina Hoffman
Georg Holderied
Lars Honore Hoffmann
Nancy Horne
Terrina Horton
Michael Horwitz
Melinda Howard
Dave Hurn
M. Huw Evans
Fatima Iqbal
Maureen Jacobs
Natalie Jaran
Ben Jarrell
Jon Jenkins
Tony Jennings
Bart A. Jereb
Duncan Johannessen
Douglas Johannessen
Wright Johnson
Rich Johnstun
Ari J. Joki
Andrew Jones
Cheri Kannarr
Jeff Kapustka
Jonathan Kay
Lee Keasal
Dan Kenneth Lee
Sean Keogh
John VinceKeogh
Robert Killheffer
Mike King
Raena King
Harvey King
Ashley Knight
Agnes Kormendi
Mark L.
Andrei Labin
Manuel JesLaiño
Jason Lapier
Alexander Lee Calhoun
Colin Leslie
Charlie Lior
Tessa Lloyd
Louise Löwenspets
Steven Luke
Alexander Lyle
Linda Mack
Angus Maclean
Kona Macphee
James Maenpaa
Gary Main
Mark Malcolm
Kim Maloy
Michael S.Manley
Derek Mantle
Ken Marable
Julio Marchini
Jon Marcus
Tim Maroney
Jeanette Marsh
Nick Matthews
Laura Mccarthy
John Mccord
Martin Mcgrath
Chris Mclaren
Alex Meadows
Skyboat Media, Inc.
Marla J. Mercer
Galen W. Miller
Mario Miniaci
Andrew Monk
Tim Moore
Philippa Moore
David Mortman
Void Munashii
Alister Mundy
Rich Ness
Glenn Nevill
Amanda Nixon
Emma Nuclearteeth
Padraig O'hiceadha
James Orenstein
Robert Paisley
Kenny Park
Christos Pathiakis
David Perlmutter
Nate Pink
Jason Pitre
Mateusz Pozar
Wolfgang Preiß
Nigel Price
Patrick Purdy
arko Radulovi
Andrew Rakowski
Brian Ramsay
Michael Rand
Will Rees
Zoran Regvart
Graham Reynolds
Andrew Robinson
Andy Roeper
Josh Roseman
Maria PilaSan Roman
Matthew Sanborn Smith
Pradeep Sanders
Gordon Sanfacon
Shawn Scarber
Carsten Schmitt
Pamela Seaman
Anne Semenuik
Amanda Serra
Diane Severson Mori
Ian Sewell
Travis Shamp
Robin Shantz
Matthew Sharpe
Julia Shaw
Robin Sheat
Jeff Shenk
Steven Sick
Daniel Simon
Mike Smith
Robert Smith
Jozef Sovcik
R.E. Stearns
Jim Steel
Ken Stewart
Grant Stone
Glenn Strong
Amy H. Sturgis
Nikolai Tatarnic
Peter Taylor
Nik E. Thistle
Josh Thomson
Gretchen Tiger
Steve Trower
Tasha Turner Lennhoff
Peter Venus
Alexandra Von Gries
Rich Walker
Phil Wall
Logan Waterman
Duane Watson
Craig Webster
Moritz Weglage
Matthew West
John Wetmore
Dave Willcocks
Neil Williamson
Alison Wilson
Cliff Winnig
Ralph Woodcock
David
Marlene
Jacqueline
Gormsby
Peb
Tomasz
Spookyfm
Vikki
Penwing
Trevor
Roy
Dergullen
Victoria
Mark
Jasonr
Mordanti
Tom
Fearlessleader
Ivan
David
Jimbo
Winterdragon
Firanai
Gavran
Silvia_c
M–
Anne
Josh

Lightning Source UK Ltd.
Milton Keynes UK
UKOW01f1612111017
310820UK00005B/171/P

9 781527 214675